TACTICAL DOG

The Scent of Duty

By Elias Rodriguez

* * * * *

PUBLISHED BY:

Elias Rodriguez

Tactical Dog – The Scent of Duty

Thank you for buying this book.

* * * * *

This book is inspired on real events. The characters are a work of fiction; any resemblance to persons living or dead is purely coincidental.

Thanks to all the people who contributed in the review and edition of this story.

This book is a tribute to soldiers, police, and civilians -two and four-legged- engaged in a courageous fight against drug traffic.

Table of Contents

Chapter 1: You're Dead, Congratulations!

Toluca Airport, Mexico, 2:05 pm.

The Boeing 787 rested on an isolated tarmac while a crowd watched from the airport terminals.

In a nearby hangar, Miguel and his team finished their equipment preparations and ran to get in formation.

"Ready?" Sergeant Cruz asked.

"Yes, Sir," Miguel and the other four agents replied in unison.

Sergeant Cruz performed a visual inspection. "Pedro, put on your glasses . . . Miguel, tighten that chinstrap." David, Carlos, and Salvador received no further instruction.

Miguel and his team were part of a special operations unit of the Policía Federal, a task force responsible for fighting organized crime. Dressed in their tactical garb, helmets, and protective vests, each man carried an Austrian Glock handgun, radio, and safety glasses. The sub-machine guns were a risk in a crowded plane; they were left behind.

"Questions?" Cruz asked.

"Sir, isn't the team too small for this kind of operation?" Miguel asked as he adjusted his helmet.

"Yes, but we have to proceed with whatever resources we have available," Cruz said.

The sound of a catering truck backing into the hangar made everybody turn their heads. The other two team members were inside. Co-pilot Pablo Aguilar drove while the pilot, Captain Juan Alvarez, sat beside. Both dressed in orange maintenance overalls.

Smiling, Captain Alvarez thrust head and arm out the window and gave a thumbs-up to the team.

"Let's go," Cruz ordered.

The team picked up three extension ladders and loaded them into the cargo bay of the catering truck. The men jumped in, leaving the rear door open.

"Ready!" Cruz radioed.

Pablo put the truck in gear and drove out of the hangar.

Miguel's worries stopped for a moment. The way the team traveled in the back of the truck, cramped and immovable between food carts, almost made him laugh. *Being tall and athletic, doesn't help in these conditions.*

"Last intelligence report mentions three hijackers with handguns, one each in the front, in the midsection, and the rear of the plane," Cruz said. "Counting passengers and crew, there are one hundred and eighty souls in that plane."

The catering truck approached the 787.

"Get ready, Falcon!" a voice on the ear buds of their radios warned.

"You know what to do," Cruz said. "Good luck."

Pablo made a sudden turn to align the truck with the rear of the plane, the blind spot.

"Deploy, Falcon. Deploy!" The voice on their radios yelled.

"Go, boys. Go!" Cruz commanded.

All six members of the team jumped from the moving truck in groups of two, each pair carrying a ladder.

Pablo performed another sudden turn and circled one of the wings of the plane.

The team took positions under the fuselage. Sergeant Cruz and Salvador ran to the front. Miguel and Pedro moved to the middle section, under the wings. David and Carlos stayed at the rear.

"Get ready," Cruz ordered through the radio as he visually confirmed everyone was in place.

The catering truck stopped next to the front service door of the plane.

Alvarez took his time exiting the vehicle. The only one in the team not in top physical condition. With gestures resembling the ones of a mime, he guided Pablo to park the truck in the desired position beneath the plane, and then jumped into the cargo bay.

Pablo started the scissor lift and the cargo bay went up.

"Raise the ladders," Cruz ordered on the radio.

Looking up, Pablo controlled the lift and deliberately made the ramp bump against the fuselage.

The team placed the ladders against the plane at the same time to conceal any noise.

Alvarez exited by the front of the cargo bay to the ramp and knocked on the plane's service door.

"Climb," Cruz ordered.

Miguel and Pedro climbed to the wing. They crawled across as close as possible to the fuselage to avoid being seen from the inside.

A flight attendant opened the service door. A hijacker behind her pointed his handgun at Alvarez.

"Anybody ordered pizzas?" Alvarez said, raising his hands, waiting for instructions.

"Come here, clown!" the hijacker ordered and dragged the attendant from the door.

Alvarez entered the cabin.

The hijacker searched his clothes for weapons.

"Hey! Only my ex-wife was allowed to tickle me."

"I hate funny people," the hijacker shoved Alvarez back into the cargo bay. "Bring the food!"

"My ex-wife said the same thing about funny people and about food." Alvarez pushed a food cart toward the plane, close to the edge, and deliberately stuck it between the ramp and the fuselage. "Damn!" he cursed, making sure he had the hijacker's attention. "Couldn't I get a decent cart for an event like this?" He pulled the cart and pushed again, smacking the edge of the plane.

"Open passenger doors," Cruz ordered at the same moment.

Salvador at the plane's front and David at the rear, pushed latches on the doors to release the emergency handles.

Alvarez pulled the cart and pushed for the third time. When the wheels got stuck, he pushed harder.

The cart overturned and smashed the floor. Soda cans, plates, and silverware spread on the floor.

"Open over-wing door," Cruz ordered as the front and rear doors sprang open.

Miguel rose on top of the wing and pulled a handle above the emergency exit window. Pedro pushed the door into the cabin. Miguel drew his handgun and, with Pedro on his heels, crouched low and went into the plane.

"Don't move!" "Drop your weapons!" the six team members shouted as they took defensive positions.

Shots, screams, and the clatter of falling objects followed. The hijacker in the front galley dropped. Another one fell over a row of passengers. The last lay near the rear lavatories.

As the commotion faded, Pedro noticed a red stain on his shirt. His knees hit the floor, then his body.

Miguel looked at Pedro, but the sound of a struggle made him turn. A fourth hijacker, wearing dark glasses, held a flight attendant as a shield and aimed a handgun at her head.

Miguel tried to aim but couldn't get a clear line of fire. "Drop your weapon!" he yelled.

The hijacker dragged the flight attendant backwards, between two rows of seats.

She gave Miguel a pleading look behind her glasses.

"Front is clear," Salvador yelled. "Back is clear," David called out.

"Your friends are dead!" Miguel shouted. "Surrender, or end up just like them."

The hijacker didn't move.

Seconds passed.

Miguel inched forward and to one side. "Drop your weapon, now!"

The hijacker hesitated.

Miguel opened his stance and took aim.

"Don't shoot! I surrender," the hijacker raised his hands.

"Discard your weapon!"

The hijacker tossed his handgun toward the aisle.

Miguel kept his eye on the weapon as it landed at his feet. A second later, another object was tossed. It landed next to the gun. *A hand grenade!*

The boom and the smoke were the ones of a firecracker.

"You're dead!" a passenger shouted. "Congratulations! It took you less time to be killed in this trail than in the previous one." He held out a stopwatch as he rose from his seat.

"We're done here," another passenger said into his radio.

"The drill is over," said a voice over the intercom. "Thanks for your cooperation."

Pedro rose, trying to clean the red paint from his uniform.

The three fallen hijackers rose and bowed. The passengers started to applaud.

Still surprised, Miguel turned to the flight attendant he was supposed to save.

She shook her head and rolled her eyes.

* * * * *

Toluca Airport hangar, Mexico, 11:00 pm.

Miguel looked at the pair of deuces among the mismatched cards in his hand. "I'm out," he said feeling more relief than defeat.

On the other side of the table, David made a gun with his fingers, shot Miguel, and blew the imaginary smoke from his fingertip.

"Unlucky at cards, lucky in love," Carlos said. "That's how the saying goes." He sat on Miguel's left, plucking his guitar between deals.

"Haven't verified the love part," Salvador added, seated at the right.

Everybody laughed.

Miguel left the table and Pedro, the newest team member, took his place.

"Finally!" Pedro said with a smile.

"Well, good luck at winning nothing," Miguel said.

"Results are in!" the command post operator said as he approached waving a sheet of paper. "Who wants them?"

David snatched the report form the operator's hands and started reading: "Pilot Captain Juan Alvarez, pass. Objective achieved. Copilot Pablo Aguilar, same. Sergeant Cruz, Carlos, Salvador, and me, pass." David paused to be sure everybody was listening. "Agent Pedro Guerrero, fail. Reason: shot and killed by hijacker. Agent Miguel Cordova, fail. Reason: failure to neutralize an enemy combatant, failure to maintain attention on target, failure to protect a team member, failure to protect a civilian, and killed by exploding grenade. Overall Mission outcome: fail. Reason: unable to neutralize all enemy combatants,

10

detonation of an explosive device over the wing section of the plane containing fuel tanks. An estimate of 75 passengers killed, 60 injured. Total loss of aircraft."

"Wow! That's ugly," Carlos said.

"A blown-up mission, literally," Salvador added.

"Who wants to take this rotten report to the Sergeant?" David asked.

A long silence ensued.

"I'll do it," Miguel offered as he was the only one standing. He took the paper and left.

* * * * *

Miguel walked across the hangar to the "quiet side," as the team called it. This was where they slept on fold-out beds lined up in a row with a tiny metal table beside each bed. *Not so encouraging for a team whose code name is Falcon,* Miguel thought as he looked at the furniture. It was late and several of his team members had already hit their bunks. The closest one was illuminated by a small lamp on the nightstand.

"What are you reading, Sergeant?" Miguel asked.

"Hey, Miguel," Sergeant Cruz said. "Tough Plants for Every Climate."

"Boring, isn't it?"

"On the contrary! It's gripping, especially the section related to cacti."

"Cacti? I can't believe it."

"Yes, all those colors and forms blooming in the middle of the desert. Whoever believes things happen by chance in this world is blind and deaf—"

"Excuse me, Sergeant," Miguel interrupted the imminent theological speech. "I have the results." Lips pressed in a tense line, he handed the paper to Cruz.

Cruz read the report and frowned.

"The intelligence report mentioned three hijackers with handguns," Miguel explained. "It wasn't accurate."

"Reports are never accurate or complete in real life, Miguel. Sometimes you don't even have a report. You have to expect the unexpected. That's why we do drills, so you can practice handling the unexpected. You should know that by now."

"I wonder when we'll have some real action," Miguel said, steering the conversation.

"We cannot choose when, but we can choose to be prepared. Besides, if today had been real action, you'd be dead. Are you in a hurry for that?"

"I guess you're right, Sergeant." Miguel sighed and walked away.

A few beds down, Captain Alvarez was sleeping. He was the team comedian, but often Miguel laughed more at the way Alvarez told jokes rather than the jokes themselves. Snores substituted for the jokes at that moment.

Pablo was in the next bed. He rolled to his stomach and covered his head with a pillow. On his bedside table was a picture of his wife and their twin daughters. Pablo flipped to his back, tossed off his blanket and got out of bed. He gave Alvarez an unfriendly glance and looked at Miguel.

"I can't believe it," Pablo said, dragging his bed away. "I have to listen to his jokes all day, and at night, this symphony. When I get my commercial pilot license, all this is going to end." He arranged the covers and lay down again.

Captain Alvarez and Pablo always went to bed early. They wanted to be fully rested in case of an emergency call, although Alvarez seemed to be the only one achieving the goal.

Miguel stopped at his own bed. The red digits of his alarm clock showed 11:25 pm. He wasn't sleepy and had no interest in reading, so he chose to go outside.

On his way out, he passed the operations post on the other side of the hangar.

The operator on duty was the same man who had delivered the results of the drill. Another man was seated beside him; both concentrated on the screens and controls of a mobile command station. They specialized in radio transmissions and radar operation.

"Any intruders?" Miguel asked.

"Only the Americans," one operator said. "The first flight arrived a while ago."

"I hope we get something soon," Miguel said as he continued towards the exit.

"Careful what you wish for," the operator said without taking his eyes off the screens.

* * * * *

Miguel reached the door and went outside. The chill winter air made him shiver. The cold moonless night was dressed in a sky full of stars. Nights were cool at that altitude, no matter the time of the year. Altitude and location were the main reasons Miguel and his team had come to Toluca. Air traffic was easier to track and, if necessary, to intercept for the southern and central regions of the country.

Better to watch the stars and be cold than to stare at the hangar walls and be warm. Miguel looked to the sky and rubbed his shoulders.

He turned toward the dark blue Dassault Falcon 20 business jet. The two lamps on the sides of the hangar made it look like a new car in a showroom.

Falcon, the team's code name for the assignment came from the plane's model. The aircraft always had to be ready to fly and transport the team for a mission. It had big white letters on the sides: "POLICIA", the agency shield, and "FEDERAL." The team had flown two missions on it. Each time, the Americans had detected an unauthorized plane entering Mexican airspace and requested the team's intervention. They followed the heading provided by the Americans, but the intruders had disappeared from radar screens and the missions were scrubbed.

Miguel's team was an elite group that conducted specialized operations: reconnaissance, surveillance, direct action, and drugs interdiction. Most of them had been together for over a year and had participated in several missions, and lots of training. They were on their first airborne assignment and had been with the pilots for just over a month. The radio and radar operators joined them from a support unit.

Miguel decided to walk to the next hangar, the one used by the Americans. He wondered if they still had decaffeinated coffee, an option not available in the Mexican hangar.

"Hi there!," he waved to a maintenance crew refueling the American plane, a surveillance Grumman E2C Hawkeye turboprop with an AWAC[1] dish mounted on top.

The Americans were members of the U.S. Navy, working under the DEA-FAST[2] program. They agreed to use the code name Hawkeye, Eye for short, when they carried out joint operations. The U.S. Navy and the DEA would help the Policía Federal intercept intruder planes inbound from Central and South America. After landing at an airport or a clandestine airstrip, the traffickers often unloaded the cargo and continued to the United States by other means.

The American hangar had more activity at that time of the night, as flights and crews changed shift. The first reconnaissance flight departed around 3:00 pm. and returned by 11:00 pm. The second flight left around midnight and returned by 8:00 am. The planes refueled mid-mission at Acapulco, Oaxaca, or any other airport, depending on the flight plan.

The second crew was already gathered and preparing their equipment. Miguel approached to greet them.

"Hey, Miguel," Sam, the radar operator, said. "What are you doing up?"

"I'm bored," Miguel said. "Lots of training, but we have no real action." He shook hands with Sam, the pilots, the Information Officer, and the Air Control Officer.

"Don't get desperate, *amigo*[3]." Sam said. "All in good time. The first two weeks, we got nothing flying south. The next two, we detected

14

planes inbound from Guatemala. Lost 'em in the mountains because we were too far west. This week, we're flying more to the east."

"I guess you're right, Sam. One of these days we'll make some arrests and make the national news."

"The bird is ready, gentlemen. Please proceed," a voice in the hangar's intercom commanded as Miguel finished preparing his coffee.

 "We'll be waiting for your call," Miguel said to the crew as they left the hangar. "Good luck."

Miguel walked back to the Mexican hangar. Despite the cold, he stopped and watched the Americans board the Hawkeye.

A moment later, the turboprops spun and hummed. The plane taxied to the end of runway 28 and stopped. The pilot gunned the engines, and the already loud noise increased exponentially. The Hawkeye raced along the runway into the darkness, marker lights winking as it passed and blocked them from Miguel's view. An instant later, the plane's lights rose upward, separating from the runway lights. The noise of the engines was soon swallowed by the night as the plane gained altitude.

Miguel watched until the strobes on the plane disappeared among the stars. He finished his coffee in a gulp, and then yawned.

* * * * *

San Diego, California, three hours later.

"Daddy, Daddy!" Annie, a blond five-year-old wearing pink pajamas and blue rabbit slippers, shouted while running toward her parents' bedroom.

She and her parents, George and Karen Hunter, lived in north San Diego. The family used to move often because of George's work as a helicopter pilot, but decided to settle permanently when Annie started school and George landed a position in the Coast Guard.

15

"Daddy, it's time!" Annie shouted as she jumped on her parents' bed.

"Ugh!" George reacted when Annie's knee hit him.

Karen awoke with the noise.

"Wake up, wake up! It's time," Annie urged.

"OK, OK! Calm down," George said with a momentary high-pithed tone of voice. The clock showed only three hours had passed since they went to bed.

"Hurry, Daddy!" Annie shouted as she ran out of the bedroom.

George walked in a zombie-like-trance, trying to avoid the furniture until he reached the laundry room.

Pretzel, the family's German Shepherd was lying on top of some blankets. She panted fast and seemed nervous.

"Don't worry, Pretzel," George said. "Everything will be OK."

"Is it going to be coffee or back to bed?" Karen asked.

"It's coffee," George said. "I'm calling the vet."

"Puppies are coming! Puppies are coming!" Annie started to dance.

Chapter 2: Do You Copy?

Toluca Airport, Mexico, 5:35 am.

A piercing alarm went off inside the hangar.

"The Americans detected something!" One of the radio operators shouted. "Get ready!"

Everybody sprang out of bed, except Pedro. His bed overturned and he landed on the floor.

Everybody laughed as they started dressing in their tactical uniforms.

"I hope we get something real this time," Miguel said.

"At least we're learning fire fighter procedures with these kinds of calls," Salvador said with a smile.

Everyone took their equipment, including the Heckler & Koch MP5 sub-machine guns. The pilots only had handguns for their own protection.

Captain Alvarez and Pablo ran to the plane to ready it for takeoff. The others gathered around the operations post.

A radio operator deactivated the alarm, allowing the team to listen to the transmissions.

"Target continues in Mexican airspace after entering from Guatemala," the Hawkeye's Air Control Officer said on the radio. "We sent coordinates to Tuxtla airport. They'll require the pilot to transmit identification . . ."

The team listened to transmissions from air traffic controllers in different Mexican airports.

David waved at Miguel and yanked at his own chinstrap, reminding Miguel to check his. He had forgotten to tighten it again.

"Controllers ordered the aircraft to redirect to Tuxtla and land there," the Hawkeye informed. "No response or change in trajectory was made. The plane is headed north at this moment."

"Start engines and standby, *Compadre*,"[4] one of the radio operators transmitted to Captain Alvarez on the Falcon.

Segments of conversations from air traffic controllers mixed with transmission noise. The Falcon's turbines started outside the hangar.

"I have a date with a flight attendant," Carlos whispered to Miguel. "She accepted only if I find someone for her friend and we double. Are you interested?

"Huh?" Miguel asked with a frown. "How does the friend look like?"

"Come on, she's a flight attendant—."

 "We repeated the procedure with Villahermosa airport and got the same results," a Hawkeye transmission interrupted Carlos. "The low altitude and flight path through the mountains indicate the plane is trying to avoid the radar. We're declaring code *Trueno*[5]. I repeat, code *Trueno*."

"Sending updated coordinates," Sam, monitoring the intruder from the Hawkeye' rear cabin, joined the transmission as he watched the rogue plane on radar. It appeared as a green spot to the southeast.

"Code Trueno. Code Trueno!" Sergeant Cruz shouted.

The team rushed into action when they heard Cruz's confirmation.

"Go, boys, go!"

"Good luck!" the radio operators yelled as the team members ran by and exchanged low-fives. "Give'em Hell".

"Toluca tower, this is P-F-P⁶ Falcon," Captain Alvarez said into the radio. "Code Trueno. I repeat, code Trueno, requesting emergency permission for takeoff. Hold all your traffic!"

The team ran to the plane. The strong wind scattered their steamy exhales. The temperature had dropped since Miguel's midnight walk.

"Permission granted, Falcon," the tower operator replied. "You're cleared to move to runway 28 and take off. Good luck."

The six team members climbed the stairs of the Falcon in a predefined order. The plane was already moving by the time Sergeant Cruz pulled the stairs to close the door.

"Please, be seated and fasten your seat belts, gentlemen." Captain Alvarez's voice came through the intercom.

The Falcon taxied fast and moved towards the end of runway 28. Without stopping, it turned to align with the runway as Alvarez gave full thrust. The plane galloped along the runway, turbines screaming and, seconds later, bolted into the sky.

As the Falcon climbed, they received updated intercept coordinates from Sam. They would fly east while the intruder flew northwest. "About one hour for contact!" Pablo shouted.

Miguel studied his teammates. Captain Alvarez and Pablo talked on the radio and checked the instruments. All the others were quiet. He knew, like him, they were thinking about the mission's possible outcomes. *If the Americans lose the intruder plane, we'll return to Toluca empty-handed. . . . If the Falcon makes contact, we'll force the intruder to land, arrest the smugglers, and secure the cargo. We'll make the national news.* A plane loaded with drugs could be transporting more than a ton of high-quality product. That meant a victory for the team and for the Policía Federal. *Which airport will we land in?* Miguel wondered. *Anywhere but Toluca means good news.*

A glimmer of sunrise illuminated the high-altitude clouds. Daybreak approached.

* * * * *

San Diego, California, same time.

"Everything looks fine," Dr. Ruben Padilla, said after checking Pretzel. "We're expecting at least six puppies. It's a matter of time. We'll let Mother Nature do her thing and be prepared if there's any complication." He sat at the kitchen table and sipped his coffee.

George observed Annie's excitement.

"We have to find six names, Daddy," Annie said. "Which ones are nice?"

"Wait, Annie, not yet," George said.

"Why?" Annie asked, extending her arms.

"We still don't know if they're going to be boys or girls—."

"Doesn't matter, Annie," Karen frowned at George. "Bring a paper and a pen. We'll make a list of names and decide later which ones to use."

Moments later, Dr. Padilla went back to the laundry room. Annie followed.

Soon, a soft cry was heard. Dr. Padilla peeked around the door corner and smiled. "Number one is a boy," he said and disappeared.

Annie appeared in the doorway with a smile. She raised one finger, and then gave a thumbs-up to her parents.

Later, another tiny cry was heard. Dr. Padilla appeared again. "Number two is a girl."

Annie followed raising two fingers, and then a thumbs-up. Her smile was wider.

The sequence repeated another four times.

"There's one more coming," Dr. Padilla said. "Can I have another coffee?" he asked Karen.

She reset the coffee maker, and Dr. Padilla returned to the laundry.

Annie returned to the kitchen. "Dad, do puppies sleep when they're inside their mommies?"

"Of course they do, sweetie. They're growing and that takes a lot of energy."

Not knowing what else to do, Annie, Karen, and George made faces at each other.

"Coffee is ready, doctor," Karen said after a while.

Dr. Padilla washed his hands, and then sat at the table. He took his time to drink his coffee. Later, he returned to the laundry room.

Dr. Padilla kept checking Pretzel's progress.

Annie followed him back and forth.

Time went by. Sweat appeared on Padilla's forehead.

Karen also started following the doctor. George rose from his chair.

Tired, Annie sat at the table without noticing the worried faces of the others.

"What's wrong?" Karen finally asked.

"We have to wait some more," Dr. Padilla said.

"I'll call the Station," George said as he picked up the phone. "I'm going to be late."

"Everything is all right," Dr. Padilla said. "It seems the puppy just doesn't want to get out."

The concern in Dr. Padilla, Karen, and George's faces slowly changed to exhaustion. Annie fell asleep on her chair.

Minutes later, a sharp cry urged them all into the laundry room.

* * * * *

Veracruz State, Mexico, 6:48 am.

The plane made a slight turn to the southeast.

The sun came through a window on the opposite side of the plane, looking large and red-orange at that time of the morning. Through the window next to him, Miguel saw Pico de Orizaba, Mexico's tallest mountain, a dormant volcano with permanent snow and glaciers around its peak. The sky was pale blue with a few white clouds. Below, the ground looked like a giant green carpet next to the mountains.

The team, now silent, inspected their weapons, looked through the windows, or chewed gum. Miguel had learned many things from them.

Sergeant Cruz specialized in procedures and intelligence. He had a special way of seeing things and was easily fascinated by the minutest details. He wasn't religious, but spiritual.

David, the most experienced of the agents, specialized in weapons and was an expert sniper. He held several national awards in target shooting.

Carlos knew about tactics and operations. He also played guitar.

Salvador specialized in crime scene investigation; he was methodical and focused on details. He loved to cook. When they were assigned to the airport, he asked for permission to access the kitchen and prepare his own meals. Soon, the team ate whatever he prepared.

Pedro was the newest member of the team, but he wasn't a rookie. To join a special operations team, an agent needed to have an excellent record in the Policía Federal.

Captain Alvarez, a man in his late fifties, didn't talk a lot about himself. He had been a Mexican Air Force pilot and a commercial pilot before joining the Policía Federal. When he wasn't telling jokes, or snoring, he talked about planes and faraway places.

Pablo, unlike Captain Alvarez, was morose, strict and organized. He seemed to complain about everything. Once he knew somebody, he became nicer and explained why he preferred doing things with discipline. He trained to become licensed as a commercial pilot. "A way to stay home at least a few nights per week," he used to say. "To be with my wife and girls is far better than sleeping in a hangar with a bunch of misfits."

"The intruder is approaching you, Falcon," a Hawkeye communication interrupted Miguel thoughts. "You should have a visual to the southeast at any moment."

"We already have intermittent signals on our radar," Alvarez said. "They're flying lower than the mountain peaks."

"Intruder is one thousand feet below at ten o'clock,"[7] Pablo confirmed the contact.

Everybody moved to the left-side windows anxious for a visual. A small jet came into view and then disappeared again beneath the Falcon.

"Gentlemen, please fasten your seatbelts." Alvarez said, and banked the plane into a turn.

The Falcon slowly approached the other aircraft. "It's a white Cessna Citation with twin engines, registration November, niner, four, seven, sierra, alpha.[8]" Pablo reported to Veracruz Air Traffic Control.

"We list no owner or no flight plan for that plane," Veracruz Air Traffic Control replied moments later. "The registration indicates it's an American aircraft."

"Contact them, Pablo," Captain Alvarez ordered maneuvering the Falcon beside the Cessna.

"November, niner, four, seven, sierra, alpha, this is the Policía Federal, please respond." Pablo called twice and waited. "No response on the ATC frequency, Captain," he said and switched the frequency. "November, niner, four, seven, sierra, alpha, this is the Policía Federal, please respond . . ." he insisted. "No response on the emergency frequency, Captain." Pablo switched the frequency and tried again. ". . . No response in the Air to Air . . ." He tried the private frequency, the military frequency, and some others. "No response, Captain. Either they have a broken radio or don't want to answer."

The pilot and a blond passenger in the Cessna could be seen turning their heads to look at the Falcon. Behind them, stacks of boxes filled the cabin.

"November, niner, four, seven, sierra, alpha, turn east toward Veracruz City airport and follow the tower's landing instructions," Pablo commanded.

There was no response or change in course from the Cessna.

"Driver of the clear white[9] Cessna, pull over to the side,"[10] Captain Alvarez said.

Everybody in the back laughed. Pablo shook his head but smiled.

Alvarez maneuvered the Falcon above and forward of the Cessna. He wagged the Falcon's wings to get the other pilot's attention.

Pablo kept trying to communicate but there was no response.

"They don't want to talk," Alvarez said. "Let's see if we can get some kind of response now." He maneuvered the Falcon lower, directly in front of the Cessna.

The Cessna shook in the Falcon's engine wash. The boxes bounced around the cabin.

Inside, the passenger gave some orders, "Just make it to the airstrip, we're near."

"As you wish, Mr. Weedman," the pilot said.

"We're almost there, but we have unwanted company," Weedman said through the radio, but not to the Falcon, nor any official airport.

The Cessna took a sudden dive, closer to the ground and mountainside.

"The intruder lowered its altitude and changed direction fifteen degrees east," the Hawkeye reported.

"They're trying to evade us, Captain!" Pablo said.

Alvarez pulled back the throttle to increase the speed, turned the wheel and sent the plane into a barrel roll.[11] The maneuver allowed the Falcon to maintain its original direction while quickly lowering the altitude.

In the back of the cabin, the team held their equipment to prevent it from falling to the ceiling while flying inverted, but soon discovered the g-force generated by the maneuver kept everything in place.

"I like this job," Alvarez said as the plane rolled over.

Alvarez positioned the Falcon above and behind the Cessna. "We'll follow them. Even with extra gas tanks they should be low on fuel by now."

It wasn't long before the team discovered the Cessna wasn't the only plane with fuel issues.

"We have to leave, Falcon," the Hawkeye radio operator said. "We're low on fuel and have to land in the nearest airport. You're on your own now. Good luck."

"Thanks for everything, Eye," Pablo said. "We'll see you later."

The Falcon followed the intruder's wild maneuvers among the canyons and peaks until the smaller plane leveled its flight path and reduced speed. Captain Alvarez knew what that meant. "Keep your eyes open and look for an airstrip!"

Everyone on board scanned the ground, searching.

The Cessna made a hard turn to the east, near a vertical rock formation.

The Falcon followed into the rising sun.

"Where did they go?" Alvarez asked.

Pablo checked the instruments, "Down, way down, Captain."

"There! There it is!" Alvarez shouted. He wasn't talking about the Cessna, he pointed to a small airstrip on an isolated plateau among the mountains. He gave full thrust to the turbines and descended.

"What are you doing?" Pablo asked.

"We're flying too high and too fast."

"Then . . . why are you increasing the speed?"

"We're going to make a low-level pass and check out that strip."

The men in the Cessna saw the Falcon pass above them. "I told you, they won't land. Their plane is too big." Weedman said. "They'll do a pass over and report the situation to a Land Command."

"Land Command?" The Cessna pilot lowered the landing gear.

The two men looked at each other and laughed.

The Falcon performed the low pass at full speed, slicing the air at less than ten feet above the ground.

Alvarez and Pablo gathered all possible information about the conditions of the airfield.

"A small bulldozer," Alvarez said. "Good for clearing vegetation and rocks when you're building a clandestine airstrip."

"Fifty-five gallon fuel drums to refuel and return to wherever the hell they came from," Pablo said looking to his side of the strip.

"Roger," Alvarez confirmed. "And the welcome party," he added when he located a white pickup.

The two people standing next to the pickup ran and threw themselves to the ground as the Falcon passed close to them.

"Everybody, hold on!" Captain Alvarez shouted. He maneuvered to gain altitude and banked into a hard left turn.

Everybody on the left side of the cabin was pressed against the fuselage, those on the right hung from their seatbelts.

"You can't do these maneuvers with commercial planes, Pablo." Alvarez said.

Pablo didn't respond. Instead, he concentrated on the instruments and on the Cessna.

The Cessna approached the airstrip.

"Look! There's a column of vehicles approaching," Miguel said.

Everybody turned in the direction Miguel pointed.

"It's the Army!" Sergeant Cruz said, recognizing the type of vehicles.

"Yes!" The team cheered when they realized help approached.

"Call them, Pablo," Alvarez ordered. "Explain the situation and tell them about the white pickup."

"Land Command, this is P-F-P Falcon. Please respond," Pablo called through the radio.

The Cessna landed at the time the Falcon flew over the west end of the airstrip.

Pablo tried military and emergency frequencies. "There's no response, Captain."

"Prepare for landing. This is going to be rough!" Alvarez shouted. He initiated another hard turn to the left to land in the same direction as the Cessna. "We're going to corner those bastards. They won't be able to take off. If they escape in the pickup, we'll at least seize the cargo and the plane."

"Are you sure you can land in that space?" Pablo asked.

"I sure can . . . but don't know in how many pieces."

The Falcon completed the second turn at a frightening low altitude and Alvarez released the landing gear.

The hard touchdown came immediately. Miguel, bouncing wildly in his seat, grabbed the armrests as he felt the bumps and shakes.

Alvarez reversed the engine power to slow the Falcon as quickly as possible.

Miguel felt the pull to the front and ducked his head just in time for his helmet to absorb the impact against the front seat.

27

On the other side of the airstrip, the traffickers exited the Cessna and ran towards the pickup when they saw the Falcon landing with a huge trail of dust behind.

"Stop! Stop! Come on, stop!" Pablo shouted as he and Alvarez held the plane's controls so tight they felt molded to them. The Falcon still rolled too fast.

In the back of the plane, the hard landing became a secondary issue. Gripping a seat, Sergeant Cruz stood to get a look at the traffickers and give instructions. "Get ready, boys! David, Carlos, and Salvador, you're going north after the traffickers. Miguel, Pedro, and I are going to secure the plane and the cargo."

Captain Alvarez and Pablo breathed a sigh of relief when the Falcon slowed down.

With the plane still moving, David opened the door, and jumped from the stairs. Carlos and Salvador followed. They hit the ground using the tuck-and-roll technique to avoid injury. Leaping to their feet, they gave chase after the traffickers.

Sergeant Cruz, Miguel, and Pedro stayed on the plane as it advanced toward the idle Cessna.

* * * * *

Several Army Humvees[12] reached the south side of the airstrip. "Fire!" a bald general in the front vehicle shouted.

The rattle of an M2 Browning machine gun burst from the turret of one of the Humvees.

David, Carlos, and Salvador were struck in the back and collapsed. Up ahead, the Cessna occupants continued running towards the pickup.

"Cease fire! Cease fire!" Lieutenant Rafael Gomez shouted. "They're Policía Federal—"

"Keep shooting!" the General interrupted. "Federals are a bunch of thieves and assassins. The plane and the cargo are ours!"

* * * * *

Captain Alvarez and Pablo were able to stop the Falcon just a few feet from the Cessna.

Sergeant Cruz jumped from the stairs of the Falcon and faced the approaching Army vehicles. "Policía Federal, don't shoot!" he yelled, hoping to be heard above the noise of the Falcon's turbines. He pointed at the agency's logo on his vest and lifted his rifle above his head.

Miguel and Pedro leapt from the plane and flanked the Sergeant.

"What the hell?" Miguel asked himself. He was worried about his teammates but had to follow Cruz' orders, all shooting had to be stopped first.

The Browning machine gun rattled again. Sergeant Cruz fell in a dust cloud as bullets hit the ground around him.

Miguel and Pedro turned at each other, realizing the situation wasn't an accident. They opened fire with their machine guns.

The bullets struck the soldier on the turret of the Humvee and he collapsed into the vehicle.

"Take them down!" the General shouted to the other soldiers and a heavy shooting exchange started.

Three more soldiers fell when Miguel and Pedro sent another volley into their ranks.

A burst of bullets found Pedro at the same time the Falcon's engines were shut down. He collapsed near the tail.

Miguel reloaded and fired again while walking backwards, seeking cover behind the plane.

Another two soldiers fell on the other side of the airstrip.

Miguel felt the impact of several shots, the force sent him backwards causing him to bounce against the fuselage of the Falcon and spin toward the front.

"Sounds like all hell broke loose." Alvarez said to Pablo in the cockpit.

A heavy silence followed.

"Sergeant Cruz, do you copy?" Alvarez asked through the radio. "Sergeant Cruz, anybody from Falcon, do you copy?"

There was no response.

Alvarez left his seat and withdrew his handgun. "Something's wrong, Pablo. Follow me."

Alvarez hurried when he noticed the scattered bodies through one of the lateral windows. When he stepped onto the top stairs a burst of bullets hit him.

The falling body of Alvarez pushed Pablo back inside the plane.

Pablo dragged the Captain into the cabin while the bullets impacted the fuselage around them. He tried to stop the bleeding from the Captain's neck, but Alvarez had stopped breathing.

The shots continued, now penetrating the cabin.

Pablo moved to the back looking for protection. Desperate, he hid behind the rear seats.

* * * * *

Everything and everybody went quiet.

The general gave some hand commands.

Two soldiers with machine guns climbed the stairs of the Falcon and slowly entered the cabin. Two gunshots broke the silence. One soldier fell inside the cabin. The other rolled down the stairs.

"This is crazy. Stop this!" Lieutenant Gomez shouted.

"Do as you're ordered, Lieutenant, or face court martial!" the General argued. "You should learn to obey higher ranks." He made a signal to another soldier.

The soldier approached the plane, extended his machine gun into the cabin, and fired until the cartridge was empty. Then, he coldly walked away.

"Check the inside!" the General shouted. "Verify nobody's alive."

The soldier, pretending not to hear the commands, moved away.

"Damn!" The General pulled the trigger of his weapon. The bullet hit the airstrip in front of the soldier's feet. "I told you to check the inside!" he repeated.

The soldier looked to the sky for a moment and sighed. He returned to the plane, climbed the stairs, and stopped on the top.

"Move, idiot! We don't have all day," the General urged.

The soldier crouched and walked into the cabin.

A single shot was heard. The soldier fell.

"Damn!" the General snorted.

A moment later, another soldier ran under the fuselage, threw something inside, and ran off.

The explosion blew out all the rear windows of the plane.

Chapter 3: Flying IV Bottle

Veracruz, Mexico, clandestine airstrip.

"What's your problem, Gomez?" General Mota shouted. "If you don't know how to follow orders, then why are you in the military? You're close to a court martial." He paused dramatically as Lieutenant Gomez stood in front of him. "Dispose of the bodies of those worms, now. Make them disappear! Is that understood?"

Gomez understood the General's orders, but he hesitated. "Some of the agents are still alive and need immediate medical attention," he dared to say.

"Damn!" the General almost exploded. He touched his handgun in its holster. "I said, dispose of those bodies and clean up this mess!"

Gomez didn't move. Pushing the situation to the limit, he risked ending up as the federal agents.

"Hurry with those boxes!" The general ended the conversation by turning to supervise the unloading of the Cessna. A group of soldiers were transferring the cargo to a M913 truck.

Gomez left the airstrip and walked to where the bodies of the agents had been laid out in a row. Their equipment had been removed. The Army medic had been instructed by the General not to waste any time or supplies on them. "Load all of them! dead or alive," he ordered to some of his men as he pointed to another military transport.

Gomez went to where the medic attended to the four soldiers wounded in the shooting. He stopped for a moment and observed the bags containing the bodies of five dead soldiers. Two of them were from his platoon, the other three from General Mota's squad. He knew his two men had died doing their job. Following the general's orders.

The day before, Gomez received orders to take his platoon into the mountains and carry out search and rescue drills. When they were in transit, late at night, a group of five Humvees commanded by General Mota joined his unit. New orders indicated the general would observe the performance of his unit. Before dawn, the orders changed again. They had to investigate suspicious activities in the area and General Mota took control of the platoon.

Gomez lowered a knee to the ground between the bodies of his two men and prayed for a moment. When nobody was watching, he grabbed a box of medical supplies and walked towards the transport truck.

The bodies of the agents were being thrown into the back of the truck like sandbags.

Gomez considered reprimanding the soldiers, but decided to remain silent to avoid any suspicion. After all, the soldiers considered the agents as enemies who murdered their teammates.

When the tailgate of the truck was raised and secured, Gomez jumped into the driver's seat and started the engine.

"Are you leaving without an escort, Lieutenant?" one of his men asked.

"I don't need it for what I'm going to do," he said. Gomez pressed the accelerator and drove off; checking his mirrors to be sure no one followed him. General Mota's attention was focused on the cargo transfer. Another group of soldiers were pushing the Falcon off of the airstrip.

When the truck was out of sight, Lieutenant Gomez stopped and climbed into the back. He checked the bodies one by one. Three agents were still alive.

One agent had serious injuries on the back. The vest helped, but couldn't do much against a .50 caliber machine gun. Gomez stopped the bleeding with the medical supplies.

Another agent showed a big wound on one of his shoulders. His vest had stopped two smaller caliber bullets.

The third agent had taken a hit in a leg; his vest had also taken several hits. He awoke when Gomez bandaged his leg.

"Who else is alive?" the agent asked as he looked around to see the bodies of his teammates.

"Sorry, man. Only two," Gomez said as he pointed to the bodies. "What's your name?"

"Pedro Guerrero. . . . Why are you helping us?"

Lieutenant Gomez thought about it for the first time. "If any of my men were in a similar situation, we would like to get some help. . . . Look after your two friends while I drive. I hope they make it to the hospital."

Gomez drove as fast as possible, but the condition of the road and the rough terrain didn't allow much. While driving, he thought about what happened. The traffickers fled in a white pickup during the shooting. When he volunteered to go after them with some of his men, General Mota refused and ordered him to secure the area and wait. *Two teams of good men end up killing each other because of a general with a personal agenda.*

Now, his own life had changed. From rising in the ranks for years, he became a rebel to help a group of strangers. Disobedience, no matter the nature, didn't sit well with high-ranking Army officials. *How many of them have a hidden agenda?*

He continued driving and checked the mirrors constantly.

* * * * *

San Diego, California, later that day.

A convoy of minivans arrived at the Hunter's house. Annie and Karen exited the lead vehicle. Annie's friends and their mothers spilled out of the others. The platoon of little people stormed the front porch.

"Hurry, Mommy!" Annie urged.

The moms reached the porch a moment later. The kids ran and screamed as soon as Karen opened the door.

"Shh!" Annie commanded the group as soon as they reached the kitchen.

The kids, eyes big and round, approached the door of the laundry room and peeked at the puppies nestled beside their mother. Pretzel was nursing them.

The puppies were black, except for the tan on their lower bodies and paws. Their eyes were still closed.

"Pretzel had seven puppies," Annie said. "Number one is Bashful," she pointed to one of them and continued. "Two is Dopey, three is Doc, four is Grumpy, five is Happy, six is Sleepy, seven is—" Annie stopped and looked around. "Where's Sneezy?"

The kids immediately began a search, first the laundry room, and then the kitchen. After a while, they spread out and searched the whole house.

"Mommy! A puppy is lost," Annie said crying.

"Don't worry, honey," Karen said. "The puppy should be around, somewhere." She joined the search.

Kids and moms concentrated on finding the puppy. Corners, underneath the furniture, and the fireplace were searched as time went by.

"I found him!" Karen shouted. "He's OK."

The seventh puppy had crawled under a pile of dirty clothes.

"How did you get there?" Karen said as she raised the puppy. "Why aren't you with your siblings? Look kids! This puppy has a spot on his chest."

When the truck arrived to Xalapa, the capital of the state of Veracruz, Lieutenant Gomez drove to a *Seguro Social*[13] hospital. Those large-scale facilities provided emergency services, general, and specialized medicine. He stopped in front of the emergency entrance.

Civilians and nurses turned to the windows. It wasn't common to see a military truck on the emergency ramp.

Gomez left the vehicle and ran to the door. "I have men with bullet wounds that need immediate attention! Please hurry!"

As doctors and nurses ran to the truck, Gomez dashed into the hospital through the emergency area, and then deeper into the building. He knew there were always policemen and reporters in the emergency area. That kind of hospital received violence and accident victims. Police demanded explanations, and reporters had a good source of news. He could easily be identified in his uniform. His days would be numbered if detained. The higher ranks of the Army wouldn't like the kind of media exposure he was creating. When he reached the maintenance rooms, he checked the closets until he found a doctor gown. He put it on over his uniform, and then left the hospital through the main entrance.

As Gomez walked away, he turned to watch the crowd gathered around the truck. *I hope the other two are still alive.*

* * * * *

San Diego, California, one week later.

The puppies began to stretch their legs. For some reason, they arched their backs when Annie held them. Dr. Padilla said that happened to all German Shepherds of that age. As a matter of fact, he suggested Annie and her parents to handle them frequently and for short periods of time to stimulate them, improve weight gain, hair growth, muscle development, and social skills. Annie thought it was funny that the puppies peed when she held them. "It's a common and beneficial reaction to stimuli," Dr. Padilla said when Karen asked about it on the phone. In time, the puppies' eyes opened; they seemed to be blue at that age.

Cleaning and maintenance of the laundry room became an issue. Annie, Karen, and George divided activities to keep everything in good shape.

Tiny whines and howls filled the house. At night, they could be heard all the way to the bedrooms. Lack of sleep made Annie and her parents quite tired; all had dark circles under their eyes.

* * * * *

Xalapa, Veracruz.

Miguel moved again trying to find a better position in his hospital bed. Bandages covered his chest and left shoulder. His left arm was immobilized and hurt like crazy.

The heat and inflammation below the bandages kept him from resting, but the itching was even worse. He moved to scratch himself and pain shot down his shoulder to his hand. He tried again. He stretched and reached his left shoulder with his right hand. "Oh! Ah!" he yelled and kicked the bed. He felt as if a hundred bees stung him at the same time.

The last days, the newspapers, radio, and television channels had been flooded with news and speculation about the incident. News of the clash between Federal agents and the Army started one day after Miguel and his teammates arrived at the hospital. Each channel had its own version: bribery of the Army, fighting for the drug cargo, agency rivalry, simple confusion, and more.

High-ranking officials from the Policía Federal started an investigation, as did members of the military, and reporters. Even hospital personnel asked Miguel questions. Always, and to all of them, he told the same story: how they tried to communicate with the Army since they were in the air, the surprising attack from the soldiers, how Sergeant Cruz tried to stop the shooting, and how they returned fire.

High-ranking officials from the Policía Federal praised Miguel's actions. Army officials threatened him; they said he would face charges for attacking the soldiers.

The only enjoyable event was the visit of his family. His mother Maria, his sister Susana, and his brother Luis came from Guadalajara to visit him.

That morning, Pedro was able to walk for the first time using crutches and visited Miguel from his room on the other side of the building.

"Any news about David?" Miguel asked.

"He's still in critical condition," Pedro said. "Doctors can't explain how he made it to the hospital with those kinds of wounds. It's been a long fight for him."

Miguel's initial confusion turned into remorse and sadness as days went by. *The team was annihilated in a matter of seconds by the people who were supposed to help us. How could Captain Alvarez and Pablo also be killed? The traffickers, the plane, and the cargo vanished.* Miguel wondered about all those issues while he flicked through channels on the TV, looking for information. Pedro told him about a press conference scheduled for 6:00 pm. The Public Safety Secretary, head of the Policía Federal, and the Defense Secretary would be the speakers.

The conference started on time. A government speaker gave an introduction and a general list of events. Safety Secretary and the Defense Secretary were interviewed and took turns giving explanations. "Detailed investigations concluded that the Army platoon opened fire because armed personnel, they thought were traffickers, refused to stop and identify themselves," the Defense Secretary said. "The federal agents returned fire to protect themselves," the Safety Secretary said. "The incident was a tragic confusion."

"What?" Upset by the comments, Miguel felt bile rise in his throat and he gagged.

The speaker continued with the report. "After the shooting, the Army platoon chased the traffickers who escaped in a pickup truck. Somehow, the traffickers or unidentified accomplices managed to return to their plane and took off with the drug cargo. No arrests were made. The drugs and the plane vanished."

A flying IV bottle crashed on the TV.

* * * * *

Miguel was crazy with rage. Doctors and nurses held him down and gave him an injection. He had nightmares. When he awoke in the middle of the night, he had restrainers around his wrists. He couldn't do anything -except drift back into the nightmares-.

When he awoke the next day, he noticed Sam next to the bed. He felt ashamed for an instant because of the restraints, but found out he didn't have them anymore. He didn't want to give the impression he couldn't control himself.

"Hey, Sam," Miguel said. "I'm sorry. The operation didn't work as expected."

Sam stood up and approached. "You're the last person who should apologize, Miguel. Don't worry about that right now, just worry about getting well. We'll catch those traffickers later."

"Yes, we'll nail those traffickers, those assassin soldiers, and those corrupt government officials."

"What do you mean? Do you think what happened wasn't an accident?" Sam asked.

"Policía Federal was written on each side of the fuselage of the Falcon, Sam. Do you know the size of each one of those letters?"

"Two feet?" Sam asked.

At that moment, Pedro entered the room. His face was pale and he walked slowly, using the crutches for support.

How strange, Miguel thought. *Pedro looked great yesterday.*

Pedro looked at Sam, then at Miguel before talking: "David died a while ago."

* * * * *

San Diego, California, one month later.

The puppies started walking. Tail wagging and fighting became their favorite pastimes. They became more independent from Pretzel and began exploring the house.

Annie realized that the puppy with the spot on the chest became harder to find every day. He always sniffed around in the kitchen, the bedrooms, the garage, or the farthest corners of the garden.

"Daddy, this puppy doesn't know how to behave," she complained. "He doesn't play with the other puppies. When I call him, he ignores me."

"It's not that he misbehaves, Annie," George said. "He's just different. He's more interested in exploring than in playing. Maybe he doesn't respond to you because he doesn't like Sneezy as his name."

George observed the puppy and wondered if something was wrong with him. He had seen the puppy play with his siblings for a while, but he seemed to get bored quickly and leave. When looking for some socks that morning, he found the puppy sleeping in a drawer under the bed. *The puppy didn't sleep with his mother and siblings. And how did he get there?*

"Why don't you call him Badger, instead of Sneezy," George said. "I always find him in the backyard digging holes, so the name seems more appropriate."

"You're right, Daddy," Annie accepted the recommendation. "I haven't heard him sneeze."

41

Another thing that caught George's attention was that, the day before when it started to rain, all the other puppies ran to the laundry room to hide under Pretzel when the first thunder rumbled. Badger went in the opposite direction and over to the glass patio door in the living room. He sat, jumped with the lightning, and then barked with the thunder. Sat again, and waited for the next.

* * * * *

Xalapa, Veracruz, same time.

Miguel was still in the hospital, but finally preparing to leave. He would go to Guadalajara, his hometown, and start a rehabilitation program at a hospital that specialized in therapy. He didn't know the details yet, but the rehabilitation had to be taken in daily sessions for several months. He no longer had pain in his shoulder when he touched it, but lifting or quick movements still gave him extreme pain.

Pedro left the hospital the previous week. He returned to Durango City, his hometown, also to start a rehabilitation program. Pedro told Miguel about his plans to resign from the Policía Federal and join a cousin in his auto repair shop.

Miguel did a lot of thinking of his own. *What's next?* He asked himself. He didn't know, but what he knew for sure, was that he would also leave the Policía Federal. *What's the point of dying doing your duty if only lies are going to be said?*

A knock on the door interrupted Miguel's thoughts. "How are you doing today, amigo?" Sam asked as he came in.

"I'm alive," Miguel said. "That's something, I guess."

Sam noted the irony and frustration in Miguel's response and changed the subject. "The drug detection program was modified," he said. "The Hawkeye teams only monitor suspicious flights now, nobody chases them anymore. If the plane lands in an airport with personnel from the

Policía Federal, a search is performed. Flights going to smaller airports or clandestine airstrips are recorded for future action."

"How many arrests have been made?" Miguel asked.

"None," Sam responded.

"How many shipments have been seized?"

"One."

"Really? How many tons of drugs?"

"It wasn't drugs," Sam said. "It was DVDs with illegal copies of music and movies." Sam started to feel frustrated himself. "The interdiction program was wiped out with the loss of the team. Plans to create similar teams and procedures were scrapped. The Mexican government hasn't decided what to do and the American government doesn't want to provide more resources without a plan."

"Somehow, I'm not surprised by that," Miguel said.

"Do you know where you'll be assigned after your rehabilitation ends?" Sam asked.

"Nowhere, I'm out." Miguel said. "The team was annihilated, and I'd be out of place in any other assignment. Besides, doing the job is impossible in a sea of corruption."

"You sound really upset," Sam said.

"No wonder. The major setback was the announcement that no memorial ceremony was going to be held for the team," Miguel said. "The bodies were returned to the families for discreet burials. Top government officials ordered the Policía Federal not to perform any ceremonies. They didn't want the public to think that the Army protected the traffickers. They also ordered the Army not to perform any ceremonies for the fallen soldiers. It could be interpreted as if the Policía Federal tried to steal the drug shipment. Carrying out ceremonies on both sides could generate mixed signals."

"I guess you're not the only one upset," Sam said.

"Everybody is upset. What a great political solution, not to honor the fallen heroes. Besides that, there's no intention to investigate what really happened."

"I'm sorry to hear that," Sam said. "Now I understand your decision to quit."

Chapter 4: Reflected Reflection

San Diego, California, two months later.

The puppies grew bigger and were ready for adoption. They were still black and tan, but the tan had become more prominent, extending up their legs to their sides and heads. Their eyes turned to brown, but their ears were still floppy.

George placed an ad in the newspaper and posted flyers in the neighborhood, hoping to sell the puppies. He felt that people who paid had more commitment to a pet than people who got one for free. There were exceptions on both sides, but his plan helped them search for good adoptive families. The money he received for the puppies would go to a fund to cover Pretzel's veterinary expenses. George was willing to give away the puppies for a token fee if the adopting people lived nearby so his family could "stay in touch" with the puppy.

Different families visited the house to see the puppies and had a chance to play with them for a while. They came in exited and left thrilled.

George tried to gather as much information from the families as possible. He included a questionnaire about their experience with dogs. "What would you do if your puppy got lost? What would you do if the puppy got sick or ate something it wasn't supposed to? What kind of food do you recommend?" In this way, he got to know the families who wanted to adopt the puppies.

"You're too fussy." Karen said when she realized he'd interviewed many families.

After that comment, George didn't tell Karen he kept an additional file to grade the families as they interacted with the dogs.

When the families came to see the dogs, everybody played, except Badger. When somebody went into the backyard, Badger sniffed that person and sat. The other dogs jumped and played, they liked to be pampered and rolled onto their backs to be scratched. When somebody pampered Badger, he sat and stayed steady. He wasn't rude or standoffish, but didn't play.

Karen also noticed the puppy's behavior. "That dog has issues," she said.

George worried that something might be wrong with the dog, but hoped for the best.

The weekend went by. George analyzed all the requests and organized them in descending order of the scores he'd given. *Great news!* Every puppy had more than three interested families. He called the frontrunners. When he reached Badger's possible families, he decided to skip him. When he finished the calls and Badger's turn came again, he decided to wait. *What am I offering? I don't want a family to make a commitment for a puppy that doesn't fit. Maybe, with some more time, I could find something more appropriate.*

All the interested families returned the following day and the event turned into a party when Karen offered cake and drinks. Happily, every family left with an embraced puppy, as if they carried a baby. Only Badger and Pretzel remained.

"What happened with this guy? Nobody wanted him?" Karen asked.

"Several people showed interest, but that's not the problem," George said. "The puppy was the one that didn't show any interest."

"What? So now is the puppy the one who decides?"

* * * * *

Early the next day, Karen had to cover her mouth to prevent a scream from going out. The backyard was full of holes and piles of excavated dirt. Her flower plants were flat.

Upset, she went to George. "What's going on?" she asked. "Is the puppy looking for his siblings or what? It was your decision to keep that dog. What are you going to do about my garden?"

George didn't want Karen and Annie to notice his own disappointment. *Now what?* He still had the contact information of the people interested in the puppy, but he couldn't decide. If one of those families still wanted to adopt, he had to tell them what happened in the backyard. *That's the right thing to do.*

* * * * *

Guadalajara, Mexico, same time.

Miguel returned to his hometown and stayed at the family's home. He used to rent an apartment in Mexico City, but after constantly moving around the country for different assignments, he decided to move all his stuff back. Now, he had to find his own place, but before that, find a job and quit the Policía Federal. He had already applied for different positions: sales, accounting, and private security. "Whatever, as long as it's not related to police, army, or government," he said to his mother. "As soon as the rehabilitation finishes, I'll present my resignation letter".

While he received therapy in the Guadalajara branch of Seguro Social, Miguel considered his options. He lifted weights and worked hard to improve over the previous day's achievements. He felt pain, but a different kind. This was a good and productive pain as his muscles strengthened. *That's a positive sign.* He felt motivated.

* * * * *

When Miguel returned from therapy, his mother was waiting for him.

"I prepared tamales,"[14] she said.

His mother loved to cook, and he loved her cooking. *If I keep eating like this, even with the rehabilitation and exercise, I won't fit through the door in a few months.* Nevertheless, tamales was one his favorite meals. "Great! Just what I felt like eating today, Mom," he said with a smile.

"Then get ready for lunch," she said.

Miguel hurried into his room and prepared to take a shower.

"Miguel, I almost forgot," his mother shouted from the kitchen. "You had two calls. One for a job, they want to set up an interview. The other call was an American, his name was Sam."

* * * * *

"How are you doing, Miguel?" Sam asked on the phone.

"Perfect, I'm about to finish my rehabilitation."

"How is Guadalajara?"

"Beautiful as always. Where are you now, Sam?"

"I'm in San Diego. I have a temporary assignment in the DEA's field office."

"I'll bet they're keeping you busy. What's up?"

"DEA is extending a program related to K9 operations. They're also trying to include it under the Cooperation Agreement against Drug Trafficking with the Policía Federal."

"Well, at least the Cooperation Agreement isn't dead yet."

"Fortunately not, and that's the reason I'm calling you. The K9 training director, Stevens, is trying to find a candidate from the Policía Federal. What do you think?" Sam asked.

"What? . . . Sounds nice, but you know my plans to quit."

"I do, but at least get in contact with this guy, hear the details, and then make a decision," Sam said. "He told me about a trip to Guadalajara to give several conferences and I wondered if you two could talk."

"OK, I guess I can make some time if he's coming to Guadalajara." Miguel agreed as a courtesy to Sam, not for any motivation to stay with the Policía Federal.

* * * * *

That night, Miguel went to bed thinking. Since he received the call from Sam, he wondered about the current arrangement between the Policía Federal and DEA. All he knew was that K9 related to dogs.

He had called the company that wanted to schedule an interview. It was related to sales. They were interest in him. The base salary wasn't great, but commissions could be. Miguel had scheduled an appointment with the company's director for the following week.

After an hour in bed, he reached a conclusion. *There's no sense in continuing with the Policía Federal. A lot has happened; my friends are all gone. Things change, and it's time for something new.* As he reached a decision, he felt more relaxed and fell asleep.

* * * * *

"The best people! That's the best description I can give of my team." Sergeant Cruz said at the ceremony where the team graduated in Tactics and Operations, in WHINSEC[15], in Fort Benning, Georgia. Government officials from both the U.S. and Mexico were in attendance. "Being the best is not a privilege, it's a responsibility," he continued. "We'll perform our duty to the best of our ability, with enthusiasm, and inspiration—" Machine gun shots rattled, and Cruz fell.

Suddenly, Miguel was back in that remote airstrip in Veracruz looking at his teammates, lying on the ground. He shot back but didn't know

49

where to aim. A complete darkness surrounded him. More shots hit the fuselage of the Falcon, and then he felt the impacts on his chest and shoulder. His back hit the plane.

Miguel jumped, gasping for air. He sat on the bed and slowly calmed down. A bright reflection danced on the wall in front of him. It stayed there for a while, drifted sideways, and then disappeared. Everything was dark again. "The reflected headlights of a car?" he asked himself before going back to sleep.

* * * * *

"Twenty-six, twenty-seven, twenty-eight … two more," Miguel lifted the weights with his left arm. He hardly heard his cell phone in the noise of the rehabilitation unit.

"Miguel Cordova?" the voice asked.

"Yes."

"This is Arthur Stevens from the Southern California K9 Academy. I wonder if we can meet."

"Just name the place and time. When are you going to be in Guadalajara?"

"I'm already here. I'm giving a series of conferences related to service and therapy dogs in several hospitals."

"Is Clinic 46 from Seguro Social included in your schedule?" Miguel asked.

"Yes, I'm having a conference there at four pm. today. Can we meet at six?"

Miguel smiled, *as expected, not a coincidence considering it's one of the biggest hospitals in Guadalajara.* "OK, I'll see you then," Miguel said.

Miguel went home and researched service and therapy dogs on the Internet. *Interesting subject,* he thought. Guide dogs assisted the blind. Signal dogs assisted the deaf. Dogs could be used for mobility assistance, medical alert, and psychiatric service. Therapy dogs are the ones trained to provide affection and comfort to people in retirement homes, hospitals, schools, and many other places. *What do these kinds of dogs do in an Agency like DEA?* Miguel wondered. *Where would I fit?*

* * * * *

Miguel returned to the hospital and searched for the conference room. When he arrived, the conference was still in progress. A person talking in English performed a presentation in front of the room. A Golden Retriever was at his side. Another person translated into Spanish. Judging by their uniforms, the attendants were doctors and nurses.

"A dog can be trained to alert their diabetic owners of dangerous changes in their blood sugar level. They can also be trained to bring medications, retrieve a telephone, and other tasks," the man said.

When the conference ended, Miguel approached.

"Are you Miguel?" Arthur asked.

"Yes, Miguel Cordova, nice to meet you."

"Sam Mueller recommended you. He's a good friend of mine." Arthur said. "I represent the Southern California K9 Academy. We have programs for police, service, therapy, mold detection, termite detection, among others."

"Mold and termite detection?" Miguel asked. "I didn't know a dog could do that."

"They can do that and much more. The DEA project is to train dogs and handlers for arrest, patrol, and detection of different types of drugs—".

"That seems really ambitious."

"Ambitious, necessary, and I haven't finished. An explosive and ammunition detection course will be held at a later date.

"Ammunition?"

"Yes, and besides that, the handlers are required to take simultaneous courses in CSI[16] training."

"Wow! I didn't know the program could be as extensive as that."

"It's even more extensive because tactics and operations training is required," Arthur said. "Miguel, you're our only option on the Mexican side. You already have that training from Fort Benning. Any other candidate requires additional preparation to start our program."

Miguel listened closely to everything Arthur told him. *I'd be working with dogs, but also tactical operations, drugs and explosives detection.* "Interesting. What do I have to do if I want to join the program?" he asked.

"Finish your rehabilitation as soon as possible," Arthur said. "DEA and I will recommend you. If the Policía Federal accepts, we'll begin in a few weeks."

* * * * *

Miguel returned home that evening reconsidering his decision to quit. *What to do? Pursue the sales position? Continue with the Policía Federal, with or without the mentioned CSI and K9 programs?*

He looked around at the framed photos of him with his father, now dead many years. His father often traveled to Mexico City when he worked for the *Procuraduría General de la República*.[17] The day his father died Miguel was eight years old, his sister six, and his brother only a toddler. Miguel played in his room while all the family waited for the taxi that would take his father to the airport. When the taxi arrived, everybody said goodbye except him. He stayed in his room. His father and his mother called him several times until his father had to leave. Later, in the middle of the night, some friends arrived at the house. After exchanging a few words with his mother, she began to cry. His mother explained that the plane had crashed and his father wouldn't be coming back. Their lives changed from that moment forward. No more private schools or karate classes. The house had to be sold. They moved to a much smaller one, away from all his neighborhood friends.

Susana, Luis, and he couldn't spend the same amount of time with their mother because she had to work. They stayed at Aunt Rosa's house when they weren't at school. His mother never gave more details. Years later, he learned more about the accident when he looked into it on his own. At that time, controversy filled the newspapers. Some stories reported the private plane suffered a mechanical failure, others suggested sabotage because of the high-profile cases his father worked on at that time.

Months ago, Miguel came close to a similar fate—and unexplained end. *What would have happened to my family if I had died in Veracruz?*

"Policía Federal. In or out?" Miguel said as he took one of the photos. "What do you think Dad?"

* * * * *

San Diego, California, two weeks later.

The puppy assigned himself the task of searching the bedrooms. He found out that, if he bit and pulled the handle on the front of a drawer, it opened and also helped to strengthen his teeth. He jumped inside and dug through the clothes. The digging was easy and felt soft. As soon as he reached the bottom of a drawer, he opened the one above, climbed inside, and dug again. The backyard only had digging. The bedrooms had digging and climbing, twice the excitement! George dug in his toolbox. Annie dug in her toy box. Karen dug in the washing machine. Dogs and humans are very much alike.

"George!" Karen yelled when she walked into the bedroom.

George came running into the bedroom. His eyes opened widely.

Karen directed a melting look at George but said nothing.

George took the puppy to the backyard.

The puppy searched for something else to do. *What's that?* Small white paws and grey legs could be seen beneath the fence. The alley cat! Yes, there he was again, walking down the alley and spreading that horrible feline odor. He did it on purpose. Badger growled softly. If he crept through the flowerbed, he would be able to advance without being detected, and when he reached the corner of the backyard, he could spring out and scare away the cat.

"He's cute, but you have to get rid of that dog," Karen argued with George inside the house. "We had some problems with the other puppies, but nothing compares with this. He's caused more trouble than all the others together!"

Barking came from the backyard.

"Now what?" Karen asked and stamped her foot. "He's barking like crazy. It won't take long for the neighbors to start complaining."

* * * * *

Guadalajara, Mexico.

Miguel received the call from Arthur to say they were almost ready to bring him into the program. The recommendation had been made. Miguel also had interviewed for the sales position and expected a decision at any moment.

"I'm going to need a release letter as soon as possible," Miguel said to the doctor the following day.

"You need two more weeks of rehabilitation," the doctor said.

"You always say I'm doing better than expected," Miguel replied trying not to be rude. The doctor had been a great help during his rehabilitation.

"But you have to—"

"I'll continue coming, but could I have the letter now? It's important."

It worked. Miguel received the letter and faxed it to the Policía Federal command and to the Human Resources department. He wanted his record to be ready before high-ranking officials reviewed it.

He didn't have to wait long, days later, the call came ordering him to report to the Policía Federal office in Guadalajara.

* * * * *

"Agent Cordova," Captain Guillermo Ortiz said when Miguel entered the office. "How is your rehabilitation going?"

"I just finished, Captain. I'm ready to return to active duty."

"First of all, on behalf of the whole Guadalajara office, I want to tell you how sorry we feel for the loss of your team."

"Thanks, Captain," Miguel said. *At least somebody still remembers them.*

"There's a new program with the Americans and you're being recommended."

"I'm ready, sir."

"I think this opportunity in the CSI and K9 programs could be great for your career. I was told you'll also receive field training. When you come back, you'll have to train others. With good results, you could be the leader of a new specialized unit."

"I also consider it a great opportunity, sir." Miguel liked what the Captain said. That was the first time in months anyone had talked with such optimism for the future.

"You'll have to give me a status report once a week."

"Yes, sir. I understand."

"You'll also have to document everything you learn."

"I will, sir."

The Captain and Miguel reviewed details about the assignment for a while.

"OK, it's done," the Captain said when they finished signing the papers.

"Thank you, sir."

"OK, Miguel. You're good to go." The Captain stood and shook Miguel's hand.

"Thanks again, sir."

Carrying the papers, Miguel smiled and walked to the door.

"Miguel," Captain Ortiz said when Miguel opened the door.

"Yes, sir?"

"This program is very important for your career. Remember, when you're out there you'll be representing the Policía Federal."

"I know, sir. I'll do my best.

"Remember that when you meet those California girls, too."

"What?"

The Captain laughed.

Miguel finally smiled.

"Good luck, Miguel," Captain Ortiz said.

* * * * *

San Diego, California, the next weekend.

Badger enjoyed the weekends. Many activities took place at home. Just moments ago, Karen arrived from the store with bags filled with plenty of different things to smell.

The puppy tore into the bags, inspecting them.

"No!" Karen screamed when she found the items scattered on the floor.

Was Karen scared of something inside the bags? There was no time to find out; Badger had a higher priority. He saw something moving in the backyard, and had to run to investigate.

George finished watering the plants Karen purchased to replace the ones destroyed during operation 'Alley Cat'.

The puppy arrived in the backyard just in time. Something was slithering. George almost stepped on it. It was a green snake! A huge one with its tail coiled around a water pipe. The puppy moved stealthily and approached. The confrontation would require all his strength, lots of courage too. Now! Badger jumped and bit the snake. He jumped back and charged again biting in another place. The puppy repeated the coordinated attacks, biting and shaking. Every time he pulled, the snake twisted, trying to get him. The fight continued until the snake bled from multiple wounds and went limp. How strange, it had transparent blood. Maybe it was the venom. The snake could be one of those really dangerous species.

George brought a can of white paint from the garage. He had to paint the fence to cover the scratches the puppy made with his paws and teeth. He opened the can and stirred the paint with a stick. "I need something to cover the plants," he said after thinking for a moment, "maybe some newspaper." He went back to the garage.

The puppy approached to inspect the can. It had a strong and different odor. He realized the stick in the can was the one Annie used to play with him the previous day. He grabbed it planning to go in search of Annie. He bit the top end of the stick and pulled. The stick hit the edge of the can and made it overturn. The paint spilled all over the ground among the new plants.

Badger noticed George dropped the newspaper and was running towards him. Maybe he wanted to play too.

After a quick chase, George quit the game. He had to do some cleaning.

The puppy decided to go back inside to check what happened with the suspicious items from the store. Nothing! Karen had cleaned everything. Whatever the suspicious items were, they weren't there anymore. After a thorough check of the kitchen, he went to the bedrooms. He didn't notice the kitchen floor's new white paw-print decoration.

The puppy was supervising the house cleaning activities when Karen opened the closet next to the front door. No! The monster! It's getting out! The beast started roaring. Here it comes. Attack! The puppy bit it and the monster retreated. Here it comes again. Attack! It retreated again. Biting and barking seemed to contain it. The battle continued and Karen provided support. When the animal charged, the puppy barked, and bit its big nose. At the same time, Karen pulled it from the tail. Their synchronized actions made the monster retreat. Careful, here it comes again! Badger and Karen continued fighting against the monster in different rooms of the house.

After an epic battle, the beast stopped roaring and moving. Success! Finally! The puppy jumped with joy. He and Karen defeated the monster. Karen tied it with a cord, pushed it into the closet, and slammed the door. Mission accomplished! Karen was brave too. She even pretended it wasn't a big deal.

George couldn't clean up the paint in the dirt. He had to remove the new plants and a layer of soil.

"George, the puppy bit off a piece of the vacuum cleaner," Karen shouted from the living room.

"Daddy!" Annie yelled from the other side of the backyard when she saw multiple jets of water escape from the water hose.

* * * * *

Karen and George had a serious talk that night. The puppy had to go. They didn't want to spend money on obedience classes because they didn't intend to keep him.

George would post ads again. Any behavioral issues would be a problem for the new owner. He didn't like that part. He feared an unhappy new owner would dump Badger at a shelter. But wasn't that what they were doing? Getting rid of a problem, and expecting somebody else to deal with it?

George still considered the puppy a good dog, but with a personality that didn't fit a suburban family. "That's it! That's the answer!" he shouted making Keren jump. "Dog training academies accept donated dogs. Those dogs, with the proper training, become service dogs or police dogs. The German Shepherd breed is always in demand."

"What are you talking about?" Karen asked.

George didn't even hear her, he was talking to himself. "The Coast Guard performs joint operations with the DEA and somebody from there commented about those academies. I'll call on Monday and ask for details."

* * * * *

Miguel took a flight to San Diego. His family members, though they were sad to see him leave, wished him good luck in his new assignment. He'd received an acceptance letter for the sales position the day before but declined. His mind and career were already focused on his new assignment. CSI, K9, and field training became his priorities for the next months.

Action again, Miguel thought during the flight. He had a place to go and a plan. How different his attitude was compared to how he felt about the Policía Federal a few days ago. He realized things were business as usual in the Policía Federal and DEA. He was the one that had changed. *This time, I have to excel and make a good impression in the training on my own. There's no team to back me up.*

Miguel did not realize how wrong he was. He would be working with a team, but with a different kind of partner.

Chapter 5: Dual Purpose

San Diego, California, next Tuesday.

Miguel arrived at the DEA building where he immediately began a series of meetings with various personnel and filled out a large amount of paperwork.

As he went through all the documents, he realized why he was recommended for the assignment. He already had a working visa, an American driver license, and training at Fort Benning to prepare him for his new role.

"How long can this paperwork be?" Miguel asked himself, looking at the remaining pile of papers. "I need to find an apartment as soon as possible."

* * * * *

After several calls, George contacted the Southern California K9 Academy. "I want to donate a German Shepherd puppy," he said. "I was told you offer police dog training and are always seeking potential dogs."

"Sorry, we're not interested," said the terse woman who answered the phone.

"I don't want to charge anything for him, and he's current in all vaccinations."

"No, thanks. We've just closed a new training group. We made an extensive selection of dogs, and handlers have already been paired with them."

"But I was told you constantly require dogs for your programs."

"Yes, sir. We often look for eligible animals, but we don't currently need any."

"Do you know of any other place that might be interested in a German Shepherd puppy?"

"No, but we can keep your contact information for the next training."

"That's perfect! Thanks." George calmed down. He gave the lady his contact information. "One last question, when's your next training?"

"Six months, maybe more. Bye now."

"Six months!" George said as he hung up the phone. "The house will fall apart in a matter of days."

Just that morning, when he woke up, he found the door of the pantry open. Ripped boxes, cereal, and flour covered the living room furniture.

* * * * *

Thursday.

Miguel drove to the K9 Academy to register. The training required only four hours in the afternoons for the first three months, the acclimatization period. Then, a more rigorous training would start on a full-time basis. The CSI training would be held at the DEA building in the mornings. Everybody warned him that this was a tough program. Subjects included evidence handling, fingerprints, shoe and tire track analysis, DNA, photography, evidence preservation and packaging.

"Acclimatization?" *Gives the impression we have to prepare to climb Mt. Everest. I guess the real deal begins after that. At least the CSI studies and the tough part of K9 training won't happen at the same time.*

Miguel entered through the academy's main door and walked towards a lady at the front desk.

"Good morning," he said. "I'm Miguel Cordova, here to register for the training."

"You're late, sir," the lady replied with an annoyed tone in her voice. "Registration closed last week."

"What?" Miguel was shocked to learn he might be too late and, most of all, by the lady's tone. Nevertheless, he kept his cool, "I'm in the DEA group." Not sure of it, he added, "the request and the authorizations should be in your file."

The grumpy lady took the papers Miguel handed her and apathetically went to another office.

"We're glad to have you here, Mr. Cordova," she said upon her return. "Please take a seat in the next room and complete this paperwork."

Thank God, Miguel relaxed. *Somebody from DEA sent the request before I arrived.*

"More paperwork," Miguel said to himself as he carried the packet to the table. "Is this ever going to end?"

He filled out the forms, authorizations, waivers, declarations, and more.

After an hour of writing and signing, everything had been filled out, except for one document. It required the name of the dog, breed, and age. For the first time, Miguel wondered how the dog issue worked. *Is a dog going to be provided to me? Will I work with a single dog, or different dogs?*

Miguel returned to the front desk and dealt with the lady again. "Here are all the documents. DEA has paid all my fees. But I can't provide information on the dog because I don't have one. Isn't one provided to me?"

The lady laughed in a way that sent shivers down Miguel's spine. "You're supposed to bring your own dog for evaluation, sir. We had some previously screened dogs for sale last week, but you missed them just like you missed the registration."

"But, do you still have any?"

"No, we assigned all of them."

"Do you know where can I get one?"

"No, and that's not my problem."

Both the woman's attitude and his lack of a dog concerned Miguel, but he was determined to show his resourcefulness in a difficult situation. "Don't worry, I'll have one by the time the training starts next week," he said politely.

The lady looked around and indicated Miguel should lean across the desk. "Take the form, get the dog, complete the form, bring it to me on Monday, and don't tell anyone."

Her rapid-fire burst of instructions threw Miguel for a moment, but he took the paper. He hadn't received such a stream of orders ever, not even when he was a rookie in the Policia Federal academy. "Thank you," he said and walked to the door.

"Wait!" the lady shouted and disappeared into an inner office.

Another order! Miguel returned to the front desk.

The lady came back with another paper and gave it to Miguel. "Dogs were selected and sold to police departments that required them last week. This list contains candidate dogs for future training. It could help you."

"Thank you!" Miguel said with a smile. *At least I have something to start with. Being polite, even when she was rude, paid off.*

Miguel almost reached the exit for the second time when the lady spoke again.

"Wait!" she ordered.

What's wrong with this lady? Miguel turned and forced a smile.

"Be sure to bring a German Shepherd, Dutch Shepherd, or Belgian Malinois. Those are the recommended breeds for Dual Purpose training."

"Dual Purpose?"

"Don't you know what your training's about?" the lady asked in a mocking way. "Dual Purpose means the dog will be trained for Police Patrol and Narcotics Detection."

"Oh! I understand. Thanks." Miguel turned and finally reached the door.

"Wait," the lady commanded, "I haven't finished."

"I knew it!" Miguel said and turned.

"You knew what?"

"I mean . . . anything new to add to it?"

"Be here on time on Monday," she warned. "There's an important briefing at the start of the first session."

Miguel looked to the ceiling, as if asking God for mercy. "Perfect, thanks for all your help."

Miguel left the building. He walked as fast as possible to the rental car, anxious to get away before she stopped him again. "Time to look for a used car and some furniture."

* * * * *

Saturday.

Sam attended several meetings at DEA's field office that week to coordinate operations with the Navy in the southwest. The Hawkeye team was scheduled to perform surveillance flights to detect drug loaded ships entering American waters. He had some free time that weekend and offered to help Miguel in his search for a dog.

"Here's the list," Miguel said to Sam. "After narrowing it to the breeds recommended for Dual Purpose training, it leaves only twelve. You call the first six and I'll call the other six."

"I have a map," Sam said. "We can plan the best route to check the dogs out when we finish calling."

"I should've known a radar operator would come prepared with a map."

The improvised call center started working.

Miguel found five of the owners had already given away their dogs for adoption. "It seems the list is really old. I only have one option. How did it go, Sam?"

"Only one."

"From a promising list, it has turned into a desperate attempt. Let's roll before those two options vanish. It would be embarrassing to show up for K9 training without a dog."

They proceeded to the first location.

* * * * *

Miguel and Sam arrived at the address. A smiling, polite man received them.

"Are you here for the dogs?" the man asked.

"Dogs?" Miguel said with surprise. "How many do you have?"

"I still have three for adoption."

"Perfect" Miguel smiled. "Maybe my luck is changing and I'll find a dog."

The man whistled and five beautiful dogs came running. "The three smaller ones are for adoption, the others are the parents."

"The dogs look great," Miguel said, "but—"

"Those are Dachshunds!" Sam laughed.

"Halt!" the owner commanded.

The Dachshunds stopped and sat in perfect alignment.

"The list mentioned you had a German Shepherd," Miguel said.

The man laughed. "German dogs, but not German Shepherds," he said. "It seems somebody made a mistake at the Academy."

Miguel couldn't contain his disappointment. He frowned, feeling defeated. "Those are fine dogs and seem to already have some training, but patrol and drug detection require a different personality".

"And size," Sam added.

"Dachshunds are used as guide and signal dogs for the blind and the deaf," the man said. "But they're a bit small for police dog training."

"I guess we check the last option," Miguel said.

* * * * *

"Somebody's coming!" George said after he finished talking in the phone. "The call to the Academy worked!"

"Let's hope that person likes the puppy," Karen said, "so we can get back to a normal life."

Badger barked in the backyard. Those tiny white paws and grey legs were prowling the alley again. He growled.

The cat flopped down and licked his paws.

The puppy continued barking as he stuck the nose under the fence. How dare that cat lie down in *his* alley? The cat odor was stinking up everything, and besides, taking the sun in the alley was prohibited. Badger had volunteered to patrol that area and decided to take appropriate action to enforce the rules. Trying to get out, he scratched and bit the fence sending wood chips flying. After a while, the fence continued there. Plan B had to be called on. He dug beneath the fence, soil flying out behind him and covering Karen's precious flowers.

* * * * *

Miguel and Sam arrived at the Hunters' house.

"Hey, are you here for the dog?" George welcomed them and invited them in.

"I know you," Sam said. "Do you work for the DEA?"

"No, the Coast Guard, but I've participated in several joint operations," George said. "I'm a helicopter pilot. Some friends in the DEA suggested I call the academy about having a puppy for adoption. Do you want the dog for an Agency program?"

"For dual-purpose training," Miguel said and explained about the K9 instruction and the bi-national program against drug trafficking.

"Great!" George said. "The puppy will have the same kind of job we all have. He'll be a colleague!"

Karen and Annie came into the living room at that moment.

George introduced them and repeated everything about the training and the bi-national program.

A moment later, everybody headed to the backyard.

"That's an impressive and beautiful dog!" Miguel said.

"Yes, but that's not him," George said. "That's Pretzel, the mother."

George turned around, trying to locate the puppy. He checked the corners of the yard and peered behind the bushes. He went into the laundry room and out again. "Please, help me," he said looking to Karen and Annie.

"Puppy!"

"Badger!"

"Sneezy!"

The three of them called and looked in the backyard and inside the house.

"No way!" George said when he saw a hole had been dug beneath the fence. "It's too small."

After a while, Miguel and Sam joined the search.

"Where are you?" Annie checked the closets. She knew the puppy liked new places to explore, but there was no trace of him.

The search continued under the beds, in the garage, even inside the cars, but there was no sign of Badger.

When they'd searched everywhere at least twice, both the Hunters and Miguel expressed disappointment.

"I guess we have to go," Miguel said, not knowing what else to do.

"I'm sorry. I don't know what happened," George said. "We'll call you when we find him."

At the same time, a nose poked beneath the fence. The snout followed, and then disappeared. The floppy ears appeared in a second attempt. The puppy was trying to get back in; he squeezed, dragged himself, and squeezed again. Finally, he squirmed through. Mission accomplished! A long time would pass before that cat tried to trespass again. Badger looked at George talking with two men near the back door. He didn't know the men and went over to get a good sniff and check them out. If they came to help with the alley cat, they're late.

He approached the group from behind and sensed something— something he only sensed when he was close to George. What was that scent? He tilted his head. Was that respect, confidence, security, or a combination of all three? He didn't know why, but he felt comfortable around those men. The three were alike. He drew close and sat down to listen to their conversation.

The three men kept talking and didn't notice him.

He wanted to join the conversation and decided to introduce himself. Just once, not too loud, not too soft, seated and unmoving, "Woof!" he barked.

George almost jumped. "Where were you? We've been looking for you." He knelt and patted the puppy. "Well, this is him," George said to Miguel and Sam while he tried to dust away the dirt covering Badger. "What have you been doing?" George asked. "Where did all this dirt come from?" George smiled and continued brushing away the dirt. "What's this?" He removed grey hair from paws and snout."

"He's smaller than I expected, but looks great," Miguel said. Smiling, he knelt to pat the puppy.

The puppy didn't jump or lick. He stayed still and seated.

Miguel stood and moved away to look from another angle.

The puppy stood and followed Miguel with a steady walk, not playing, and not barking.

George noticed it was the first time the puppy followed something other than cats and lizards. "Well, what do you think?" he asked.

"I like him," Miguel said. "How much are you asking for him?"

"What?" George didn't expect the question. They'd been paid for all the other puppies, but this one he wouldn't sell. *It's a different kind of dog for a different purpose.* "Nothing at all—" he said. "No! Let me correct myself. I'm asking a lot for him: a sincere promise that you'll take care of him."

Complete silence reigned for a moment.

"I promise to take care of him," Miguel said in a formal tone after recognizing the true meaning of the request. "But there has to be some kind of transaction to formalize the exchange."

"If I charge you any amount of money, I run the risk of being sued for damages," George said looking at the holes in the backyard.

Confused, Miguel and Sam turned to see each other.

"I'm kidding," George laughed.

"What's his name?" Miguel asked as he knelt next to the puppy.

"We haven't given him a formal name," George said. "We've called him Sneezy, then Badger, sometimes just Puppy, only on a temporary basis. The new owner is free to name him as he wants."

"Sneezy, Badger, or Puppy?" Miguel asked Badger. "Which one do you like?"

The puppy replied lifting his two front legs, placing them over one of Miguel's knees.

"What's that?" Miguel asked. He lifted the pup's front legs to check. "Look at that! It has a clear spot on his chest. What do you think if, instead of calling you Badger, we call you Badge?"

"Woof!" the puppy replied.

"So, how do we do it, Mr. Hunter?" Miguel asked.

George thought for a moment, "I know what to do. It's something that doesn't require any payment, but is still formal. I'll prepare some papers you'll have to sign. You'll declare you're responsible for the puppy's care and training. You'll have custody until you declare you want to transfer it back to us, or you're unable to care for him."

"Obviously, we also have to agree to take him back," Karen added.

Miguel consulted with Sam. He wanted to make sure everything was done correctly, and according to American laws and rules.

"Perfect, let's do it like that," Miguel said when Sam assured him this sort of arrangement was acceptable.

The group went back into the house. George wrote out what they'd discussed. Annie and Karen packed the puppy's leash, the box with

71

towels used as a bed, and his favorite toy, a rubber stretch chicken. A folder with the shot record and Dr. Padilla's contact information completed the package.

Annie, Karen, and George each said goodbye, patting and hugging the puppy. Pretzel licked one of his ears.

The puppy, now named Badge, walked with Miguel and Sam to the car. He wasn't being dragged or carried, he walked with them.

Miguel opened the car door and Badge jumped in. At the last moment, when the car was already moving, Badge poked his head through the window. "Woof!" he barked once to say goodbye.

The Hunters stood at the sidewalk and watched the car drive away.

After a while, Pretzel whined.

"I'm going to miss him," Annie said crying.

"I got my house back, but I'll miss him too," Karen said wiping her tears.

"He's in good hands," George sighed.

Chapter 6: Heap of Bodies

After six months of inactivity Miguel wanted to be in the game again. He spent the weekend getting to know Badge and settling into a new apartment.

They spent Sunday walking and running in the parks, starting in Mission Beach Park and going north along the shore. Then, after turning to Mission Bay Park, they returned through the marinas.

A beautiful place to enjoy the sights and stay in shape. Miguel wanted Badge to exercise as much as possible. An apartment was a small place for what would soon be a large German Shepherd. A daily walk or other exercise would be necessary to keep Badge in top condition.

Badge enjoyed the walk and the exercise as much as the ride. He loved to poke his head through the car's window to feel the breeze.

* * * * *

On Monday, Miguel had the first CSI class in the DEA building while Badge stayed in the apartment. At noon, he picked up Badge in such a hurry he didn't notice Badge's landscaping skills. The bedroom was covered in a snowy layer of pillow stuffing.

They arrived fifteen minutes late to the K9 Academy and ran to the entrance.

"Not a good first impression," Miguel said as he entered the building. "This is the worst day to be late."

After going through several halls, they found all the classrooms were empty. "How can this be?"

Indifferent, Badge took any opportunity to smell each of those new places.

A few minutes later, Miguel discovered everyone had gathered in a huge outdoor yard. The yard had plenty of space for running and structures that reminded him of a playground: tunnels, ramps, poles, flags, and timbers.

The classes hadn't started yet. Miguel relaxed. He and Badge walked around to meet other students, human and canine.

The lady from the front desk spotted them, frowned, and immediately approached.

"Is that your dog?" she asked.

"Of course," a proud Miguel said with a smile, expecting a compliment.

"How old is he?"

"Six months."

"He's too young, we cannot accept him."

The comment shocked Miguel. He prepared to have another verbal confrontation with the lady. "You recommended him! He's one of the dogs on the list." Miguel took the list from his shirt pocket, and showed it to the lady. "Look!"

"Let me see," the lady snatched the list from Miguel's hand and reviewed it.

Miguel waited for an apology . . . it never came.

"Wait a moment," the lady said and walked away to a place where a group of trainers gathered. A discussion began.

A moment later, a trainer from the group approached Miguel. "Your dog is too young," he said. "We don't accept dogs younger than one year."

"Why?" Miguel asked.

"It's not that they can't learn. It's the way they behave."

"How is that? How can you judge the personality of a dog if you don't know him?"

"Your dog is what's considered a young teen in dog age. Dogs of that age are easily distracted."

"The form asked for the age, but didn't mention any restriction."

The trainer paused. "I don't remember reviewing your form."

Miguel's worries increased.

"We'll fix that form for future students," the trainer said. "It's too late to make a change, but be aware of the issue. If your dog is able to perform as expected, he'll receive his certificate the same as any of the other dogs."

"Thanks." Miguel felt lucky he wasn't required to look for another dog. He had spent two days with Badge and a strong bond had formed. He didn't want to exchange Badge for any other dog.

* * * * *

Miguel found out that the Academy offered dog-sitting services. He could drop Badge off early in the mornings and go directly from his CSI class to the Academy at noon. *Besides saving time, Badge won't be alone in the apartment ripping pillows or trying to find other forms of mischief.*

Miguel's classmates were police officers and agents of different government agencies, making a total of twenty, each with a dog. They came from all over the United States and most worked closely with the DEA.

Miguel confirmed that Badge was the youngest and smallest of the dogs, but he was determined that they both excel in the program. The first classes focused on theory. The instructors talked of general interactions between dogs and handlers, personalities, and communication.

The following week, they started with voice commands. They followed a sequence: command, guiding the dogs to the desired position while holding a food treat, making them perform, and rewarding them with the treat.

With repetition, the dogs learned the commands without being guided. Consistency and patience always worked. Sit, stay, down, come, and stand, were the commands for the second week.

Miguel and Badge practiced the routines in the evening and in the morning. "You know what the trainer said, Badge. You have to perform like the older dogs— or better."

Miguel noticed he had to repeat the commands more times to Badge than the other handlers did with their dogs. On the other hand, once Badge learned the commands, he recalled them easier than the others. "As Sergeant Cruz used to say: Each weakness has an intrinsic strength and vice-versa."

As they advanced with commands training, the canine treats were used less and less until they weren't needed at all. Praise and a firm pat on the head proved to be enough. The dogs executed as commanded with no distractions. Sometimes, even a look was enough reward.

"Performing the routines is fun for Badge," Miguel wrote in his report. "Getting a treat or praise is an extra bonus. The classes and daily practice wear him out. He is no longer being destructive."

Miguel also arranged to attend target practice to become familiar with the firearms used by the American agencies. Badge always stayed with him, getting used to those sounds.

Advanced commands were taught the following weeks. "Heel" required the dog to stay with his handler, either standing still, walking, or running. "Fetch," was taught to bring different objects. "Jump," made under different conditions, heights, and positions. Out, inside, and ahead, came later. At the end of the performance, a "good" was given for praise or a "no" for correction. Some of the commands were accompanied by hand or arm signals.

Well into the second month, more sophisticated commands were taught: "track," to follow somebody, and "search" for objects.

Agent Robert West, from the DEA, joined the trainers. He and his dog, Sarge, a Dutch Shepherd short coat, carried out the commands in front of the class and taught by example.

"If there's an ultimate example of an athletic dog, it has to be Sarge," Miguel wrote in his report. "He's black in the front with white spots on the chest. His rear legs look kind of grey because white hairs are mixed with the black. He's smart, strong, and anxious to work."

Sarge's performance in the obstacle run impressed all the students so much that admiration expressions and applauses were common as they watched.

"All dogs should be able to perform like Sarge in the future," Robert said. "Keep working."

Badge continued growing and learning. The tan spread until it dominated the black. His ears weren't floppy anymore.

Besides the large outdoor area, training moved into the classrooms of the Academy and out into the parking lot. More commands were taught: "bite" and "release" using wood logs or plastic objects; "guard" to stay alert and guard an object or person; and "bark,"[18] which the dogs did while holding position in front of a person or an object.

"Hide," and "stealth," were especially enjoyable. Badge and Miguel had fun when executing them.

Miguel kept practicing with Badge in the apartment and in parks. He added some commands of his own, like: left, right, open door, stairs up, stairs down, lights on, and lights off.

Badge learned "open-fridge" without any training or command.

* * * * *

The first three months went by, and the CSI training ended. Miguel took a long written test and a hands-on test the next day. He had to detect, collect, and preserve evidence in the correct way from different types of crime scenes.

What Salvador taught me became really helpful, handling of evidence is critical in drug related cases.

Later that week, Miguel received his certification. By that time the basic training for Badge, and for him as a handler, ended.

"I never imagined the number of commands a dog could learn," he said to Badge after finishing writing his report.

The class had a midterm get-together in the Academy. All classmates shared experiences, talked about themselves, and their plans. Miguel borrowed a guitar and tried to play in public for the first time. Songs, cake, and jokes were shared. The dogs ran free in the huge backyard and collapsed in the grass, exhausted.

* * * * *

That Wednesday night, Miguel called Captain Ortiz with the intention to tell him about his achievements with the CSI certification and the conclusion of the first phase of K9 training.

"Did you see the news?" the Captain asked Miguel, without as much as a "hello".

"Sorry. I haven't seen the TV lately," Miguel said. He had no idea what the Captain referred to.

"There's total chaos as conflicting versions of the incident are circulating in the Guadalajara office," the Captain said.

"Please, Captain, tell me what happened." *Judging by the Captain's tone of voice it has to be something important.*

"Twelve of our agents were slain. The team of eleven men and one woman fell in an ambush. They were off-duty and unarmed, afterward they were tortured and shot. That was only one of at least ten different attacks in the State of Michoacan. Traffickers attacked in retaliation

78

after the capture of one of their leaders." The Captain didn't ask for a progress report.

Miguel's certificate and the K9 training didn't seem so important now that he knew twelve agents had been murdered. That night, he found the event in the international news. Details of the massacre were also reported on the San Diego TV channels. The news showed blurred images of a heap of bodies, beside them, a banner. "They refused a deal and refused to leave."

Miguel continued his search for details of the attacks on the Internet. He found out he knew two of the victims. They were members of his graduating class when he became an agent. Another team, sent to investigate the attack, was also ambushed, and another agent died. The last thing Miguel found made him get goose bumps. A popular website had a video, uploaded by the traffickers, of the torture and execution of the twelve agents.

"How is everyone over there, Mom?" Miguel called home at midnight. "I saw the news." He was worried because Michoacán is south of the state of Jalisco, where Guadalajara and his family were located.

"Everyone in the family is OK," Maria said, "but shootings are an everyday event."

"Be careful when you go outside. Those shootings can happen anywhere and at any time. No one is safe."

"Not only that. Kidnappings are becoming common in Guadalajara. Rich people are kidnapped for huge ransoms. Middle class people suffer express kidnappings, where the families must pay their life savings in a short period of time if they want to recover their loved ones. Poor people are also kidnapped and forced to work as slaves in drug plantations. Nobody's safe. Police and soldiers are ambushed and killed daily."

* * * * *

"I'm celebrating my achievements while Policía Federal agents are being slaughtered," Miguel said to himself as he prepared to go to bed. "How important the certification seemed to be this afternoon, and how insignificant it seems now."

Badge tilted his head, trying to understand.

Miguel felt ashamed, as if he'd run away from his duty as an agent and abandoned his friends in the Policía Federal.

"Is all this training worth something?" he asked Badge. "Can we use the skills we are learning in the kinds of situations happening in Mexico?"

Badge raised his paw on top of Miguel's knee.

Miguel went to bed. The video images of the massacre crept into his dreams. Twelve bodies left in a heap, like a pile of trash.

* * * * *

Miguel was with his team. They were kneeling on the floor, tied, beaten, and bleeding. Steps echoed. A dark figure stood behind one of them. A shot thundered and one body slumped to the floor. Steps echoed again, another thunder, and another slump. Echoes, thunder, and slump repeated for each one of his teammates. No matter how hard Miguel tried, he couldn't move. He couldn't do anything for his friends— or for himself, only wait his turn.

Nightmares had returned.

Chapter 7: The Four-Legged Officer

The second phase of K9 training came with a full-time schedule. Robert West and Sarge became the lead instructors. More than commands, the teams were expected to execute coordinated actions.

"Bite-and-hold" was the most anticipated class, everybody wanted to learn the command. Dogs were taught to bite a trainer's arm. A thick sleeve, reinforced with a wire shield, was used for protection. For speed and ease of learning, the command was divided in two. In one part, the dogs used a muzzle and had to attempt to bite a person who didn't need to use protection. There was no bite, just the jump and the contact. In the other part of the command, the dogs bit the arm with the protection and held it until given a "release" command. The class was divided into teams; some students took the role of criminal while others worked with their dogs.

When both parts were learned, the complete exercise was attempted, although with more caution. The people playing the criminals, called decoys, used a "bite suit" to completely protect their bodies. A football helmet protected the head. If still learning, the dogs could bite anywhere.

A trainer selected Badge and Miguel to try the command first.

"Bite and hold, Badge. Bite and hold," Miguel commanded and gave Badge a push toward the fleeing decoy.

Badge ran in the direction of the target.

Miguel, proud of his dog, watched him reach top speed. "No doubt Badge is the perfect crime-fighting machine," he told to his fellow students. Badge covered the distance to the man with ease. "Training and discipline always work."

Badge reached the decoy. Instead of a final jump, he stopped. He bowed and barked. Then, he started running around the decoy with the clear intention to play.

"Way to go!" somebody said. "He's distracting the criminal until the police arrive."

Everybody laughed, except Miguel.

Later, Miguel laughed while the other dogs made similar errors. Nobody made it on the first attempt. Most dogs ran and stopped in front of the decoy without knowing what to do next. More attempts, and the run towards the decoy ended with the dogs leaping up and pushing off with their front legs. Later, they bumped the arm with their snouts.

The decoy tried to entice the dogs to bite. Like fishing, he tried to hook a dog with his protected arm.

Sooner for some, later for others, they all made it. They bit the arm and didn't let it go. The dogs weren't fighting or attacking. They just caught the arm and secured it. Some even ran away with the arm protection to play with it. The "release" command still needed some work.

"There are variations of the bite-and-hold command," Robert said. "Some people instruct their dogs to bite multiple times, others to bite with their fangs. Training to attack is against the policy of the Agency and the Academy. To minimize wounds to suspects, the accepted practice is to teach the dogs to bite with the middle of the mouth."

A variation of the "guard" command was taught to secure a suspect, not a place or an object. The dog remained still and watched the suspect. If the suspect made a slight movement, the dog barked. If the suspect moved his feet or made a sudden movement, the dog automatically performed a bite-and-hold restraint.

* * * * *

Two months went by. Badge became one year old and was nearly full-grown. He was still considered a teen dog, but about to become an adult.

His colors already had the pattern they would have for the rest of his life, a pattern called a "saddle," because of the solid black across his back. His head, shoulders, and legs were tan. The pale tan mark on his chest could still be seen when he raised his front legs.

The training took a new direction with the introduction of firearms. All dogs, except Badge, ran away in fear when a trainer fired a gun loaded with blanks.

"I can't believe it!" Miguel laughed. "Badge is the youngest dog and is already prepared for this."

Guns with blanks were distributed to the handlers to execute shooting simulations.

"A review of all the commands is going to be performed with noise," a trainer said.

When music that blared through huge speakers was set, Badge ran away while the other dogs stayed with their trainers.

"I guess he doesn't like Heavy Metal," a trainer said while Miguel tried to make Badge return.

The dogs had to perform the commands without hesitation or fear. Heel, stay, down, and bite-and-hold were practiced again and again.

Captain Fred Holder, SWAT[19] team leader, and several SWAT officers joined to help in the training sessions. "In most police departments, SWAT officers are deployed like regular police officers," he said. "When an emergency arises, the SWAT teams come together."

"What are the requirements to become a SWAT officer?" a student asked.

"The candidates have to fulfill extensive training and pass physical agility, oral, and written tests," Holder said. "Psychological tests are also performed to find out if the candidates are suited for tactical operations. Besides physical training, the officers train extensively in areas such as firearms, explosives handling, sniper skills, negotiation skills, rappelling and roping, first-aid, or handling K9s."

Miguel listened carefully. When he joined the Policía Federal Special Operations Group, he'd received some of that type of training.

"There will be situations where we're going to work together," Captain Holder said. "Also, as a regular K9 officer, you can apply to become a SWAT member."

For several days, the SWAT team simulated situations where they worked with the handlers and the dogs: hostage rescue, barricaded suspects, building and house assault.

"In a shooting situation, be careful to select the place where you command your dog to 'stay', or 'heel'," Robert said. "The dog is going to obey you. If you don't pay attention, he could be left in a place where he's vulnerable. If bullets are flying around, command your dog to stay behind a wall, a vehicle, or behind you. Those considering using a dog as a shield can walk out the door right now. Your dogs will be officers as you are. They trust you, and you have to learn to trust them. Believe me, there will be life threatening situations where you'll rely solely on your dog."

"Is the dog an effective defense against a criminal with a knife?" a student asked.

"Absolutely not," Robert said. "Cases have happened where officers having a handgun consider they have an unfair advantage and send the dog instead. What a lack of judgment! If the officer throws away his handgun and approaches the criminal, trying to bite him, it would be the same kind of stupidity. Your dog will be trained to defend you, even without a direct command from you. Please return the favor. The dog is not an appliance or a weapon– he's your partner!"

* * * * *

Training continued without major incidents until the dogs completed the patrolling part of the course. "Badge follows commands and handles situations without any problems and has the advantage of being the youngest dog to have this level of instruction." Miguel wrote in his report.

When the drug detection training began, Miguel became worried about something he hadn't considered before. "Is it ethical to make dogs become addicted in order to motivate them to look for the substances?" he asked to one of the instructors.

"It's a fact that dogs have no interest in eating or smelling drugs," the instructor explained to the whole group. "What they're looking for is their favorite toy. Our training will lead them to associate that toy with the smell of drugs."

"The best drug training for dogs has been a matter of discussion between different groups," another trainer said. "Japanese scientists carried out studies trying to define the best breed for narcotics detection. Some people studied the combined personalities of the handler and the dog. Others tried working with altered dogs as a way to reduce distractions."

"We don't spay or neuter the dogs," the first trainer said. "We've found that the more the dog wants to play, the better the results and they seem more active if left intact."

Miguel and other handlers sighed with relief. The dogs didn't know how lucky they were.

All the trainees were advised not to wear any new cologne or deodorant, nor increase the amount they normally used. They were not to clean their cars or take them to a detailer that might use an air or carpet freshener. At home, they were to avoid using new detergents or deodorants.

"Do not alter the everyday baseline of odors the dog is used to for the weeks ahead," an instructor said. "You don't want to distract the dogs with new odors when they're learning which ones to detect on command."

The trainees were encouraged to use a small towel as a toy because dogs love to play a vigorous game of tug-of-war. At the beginning, Miguel played with Badge and the towel. The towel had to be carefully washed, so it had no scent of its own. Later, a bag of marijuana was rolled up in the towel. After playing for a while, Badge recognized the smell of marijuana as the smell of his toy.

Miguel hid the towel with drugs in various places, and Badge sniffed for the odor. Soon, he learned that if he sniffed the drug, he would be rewarded with a tug-of-war game.

Miguel used "find dope," as the command associated with the activity. Badge was trained to extend his neck and point toward the concealed drug with his nose, much like a hunting dog points at birds.

As training progressed, different drugs were placed on the towel until Badge could sniff an array of illegal substances. He was also trained to sniff out currency.

The teams trained in the classrooms, offices, cars, or in the open field. Searches extended to places with people, like warehouses, hospitals, and schools.

* * * * *

A graduation event was held for the handlers and dogs when the drug training ended. All of the officers were dressed in gala uniforms from their own agencies.

Miguel invited the Hunters to the ceremony. He considered them Badge's family. He liked it that way. Badge had his roots somewhere. If something happened, Badge would always have a place to go, as anybody with a family.

Dr. Padilla also accepted the invitation. He continued to be in charge of Badge's health and had become a good friend of Miguel.

High-ranking officials from different police agencies joined the ceremony to give the officer's oath to the dogs who would be assigned to their departments. The Chief Officer from the DEA San Diego field office, sponsor of the event, would give the oath to Badge.

Miguel prepared Badge for the occasion. When the moment came, Badge would make the promise as any other officer, human or canine.

When called, each student walked to the front to receive his certificate. Miguel received his while his classmates and trainers cheered. The CSI certificate and the K9 handler certificate would help him in his career. Most of all, he had the knowledge to teach fellow agents in Mexico.

Later, the oath ceremony for the dogs began. One by one, they took the oath.

The DEA Chief Officer rose on Badge's turn.

Badge and Miguel left the line of officers and dogs and walked to the front. "Sit, Badge. Sit. Attention," Miguel commanded.

"Please, repeat after me," the Chief Officer said.

Miguel repeated the words as Badge's representative:

On my honor, I will never betray my badge,
my integrity, my character,
or the public trust.

I will always have the courage to hold
myself and others accountable for our actions.

I will always uphold the
Constitution, my community, and the Agency I serve.

"Accept, Badge, accept," Miguel commanded.

Badge straightened his body, raised his head, and "Woof!" barked once.

The Chief Officer crouched to get closer to Badge and placed a small metal shield with the legend "DEA K9" on his collar. He rose, stepped backwards, and saluted.

"Attention Badge, Officer Salute," Miguel commanded.

Badge straightened his body, raised his head, and "Woof!" he barked again.

The new officer and Miguel returned to the line.

At the end of the ceremony, a man in an unfamiliar and very formal uniform approached Miguel and saluted.

Miguel returned the salute. He had seen the man in the DEA building before.

Badge sat, straightened his body, and raised his head. "Woof!" he barked without being asked.

"Agent Cordova," the man said. "Congratulations to you and Badge for your new credentials. I'm Captain John Williams from DEA."

The Captain and Miguel shook hands.

"It's nice to meet you, sir. I have seen your name on a lot of the paperwork I've had to complete."

Williams laughed. "Yes, we have a lot of that sort of formality here. You two are going to be assigned to my unit. The field training phase you're about to begin conducts formal activities as agents working for the DEA under the FAST program."

"We'll continue our training in actual investigations?" Miguel asked. "When do we start?"

"Yes, real-life training," The Captain said. "You'll start in one week, Miguel."

"We're ready, sir."

"Nice to hear that, Miguel," Williams said. "First, you'll practice search and patrol. Find drugs and execute arrests. You'll be issued a DEA tactical uniform, equipment, handgun, and badge."

"Woof," Badge barked.

"What's going on?" Williams asked, looking down at Badge.

"You said Badge, sir."

"What's special with the badge? — Oh! You mean it should be 'two' badges."

The men laughed; Badge moved between them, tongue lolling happily.

"Second, keep learning. You'll be introduced to police procedures for K9 units in the field. The usual scenarios are border crossings, airports, mobile checkpoints, buildings— things like that."

"We're willing to learn all that, sir."

"Third, do your paperwork. All cases or incidents have to be documented in detail. That information is used for prosecution and to gather intelligence."

"Nobody likes that part of the job, but I guess it's necessary, sir."

Williams laughed again. "Fourth, do more paperwork. Document all tactical and operational procedures you learn so you can share that knowledge with your peers in Mexico."

"That's the big value of all this, Captain."

"I'm glad you see it that way," the Captain said. "Keep in mind that all reports you write related to ongoing cases will be reviewed and forwarded to the Policía Federal by the Agency. Some information may be considered classified and censored to avoid compromising Agency operations."

"I understand."

"You'll be in a team with Robert and Sarge. That's the best option I can find to train you."

"Wow! That's great, sir. Thanks." Miguel couldn't believe his luck. He and Badge would learn from the best.

"We're glad you're here, Miguel. These kinds of programs will make a difference in the fight against drug traffickers. They work on both sides of the border, and we have to respond with coordinated actions."

"Thank you, sir. We won't disappoint you."

Chapter 8: Was That Meatloaf?

Miguel flew to Guadalajara to report to the Policía Federal and take a few days off. Badge also traveled on the plane, but in a crate in the cargo deck.

Badge hasn't been in such a small enclosure in his whole life, Miguel worried. *I hope the baggage handlers take good care of him and don't toss his crate around like they do to the luggage. At least it's a nonstop flight; the crate won't be transferred from one plane to another.*

Fortunately, the flight was smooth. After landing in Guadalajara, Miguel picked up Badge at the airline office.

"Mom!" Miguel ran the last steps to embrace his mother.

"You are too *flaco*,[20] *mijo*,"[21] she said.

"How's everybody at home?"

"Everybody's fine—waiting for you. Is that the friend you mentioned?"

"Mom, this is Badge. Badge, this is my mom Maria."

"Woof!"

Maria smiled and Badge wagged his tail.

"I have prepared some special food for you Miguel. I hope you like it."

"Thanks, Mom." Miguel thought about her delicious cooking. "I have a long list of the dishes I miss."

"Rosa is also waiting for you. She prepared some of her specialties. And maybe we can make a treat for Badge, too."

"Woof!" Badge responded. He seemed to understand the meaning of those words.

* * * * *

Captain Ortiz and a group of agents gathered in the conference room of the Policía Federal building in Guadalajara. Besides giving a written report, Miguel and Badge were scheduled to carry out a demonstration of their new skills.

"Just wait a moment before we start, Miguel," Captain Ortiz said. He made a phone call.

A few moments later, the Guadalajara Branch Office Chief and the Regional Director of the Policía Federal walked into the room followed by other people.

A little nervous, Miguel started the demonstration.

Those in attendance gasped and murmured approval as they watched Badge execute the different commands.

When Miguel mentioned the bite-and-hold command, everyone crowded closer to get a better view.

"I'm sorry," Miguel said. "I can only explain the command. I can't demonstrate because it requires special equipment for the person playing the criminal."

After some discussion, one of the agents improvised a protective gear by wrapping his arm in a leather coat. Miguel inspected it and recommended a second coat to be wrapped over the first.

"Everyone move back, please," Miguel said. Most of the audience returned to their seats but craned their necks to get a good view.

When everything was ready, the agent playing the criminal moved into a far corner of the room, and then charged at Badge and Miguel.

"Bite and hold, Badge, bite and hold," Miguel commanded.

Badge ran and jumped at the agent, biting into the wrapped arm.

The force of Badge's action made the agent stumble backwards, knocking a whiteboard from the wall as he fell.

People sprang from their seats fearing their fallen colleague had been injured.

"Release, Badge. Release," Miguel ordered.

The frightened agent was helped back on his feet. When everyone saw he was unharmed, they laughed and applauded.

The drug detection demonstration followed. Everybody wanted to see Badge perform. It turned out that the setting was the appropriate one. They could proceed without preparation or need for planted drugs.

"Perform an inspection and locate any drugs in the building," Ortiz requested.

"Find dope, Badge. Find dope," Miguel commanded. He and Badge walked, and the complete group followed. They went through different offices and halls in the building. In one of the evidence storage rooms, Badge stretched his neck and pointed his nose at some boxes.

Miguel opened the boxes, took out two cellophane-wrapped bricks, and handed them to the Captain.

The Captain unwrapped the bricks and displayed the contents to the group. "Pure cocaine, from last week's operation."

Everybody applauded while Miguel awarded Badge with a tug-of-war game.

"Let's go back to the conference room," the Captain said. "There's one last thing that has to be done."

When they returned, Miguel noticed a small box on the table at the front of the room.

The Regional Director came forward. "Be seated, please," he said.

When everyone was settled and quiet, he continued. "We'd like to take a moment to recognize one of our agents."

Miguel froze in his seat.

"An agent who has demonstrated courage, honor, determination, and effort," the Director said. "Courage, when he fought at that lone airstrip in Veracruz over a year ago. Honor, when he defended his badge and the seal of the Agency. Determination, when he endured multiple surgeries and a long rehabilitation. Effort, when he participated in a new program that will lead to a more effective fight against drug traffickers. Agent Miguel Cordova, please rise and come to the front."

Miguel didn't know want to do, except following the order.

The Director opened the box and picked up a golden object, a five-pointed star with an eagle on top. The proud bird's wings were extended.

The Merit Medal!

The director pinned the medal on Miguel's shirt and saluted him.

"This is an honor I didn't expect," Miguel improvised. "I can't believe over a year has passed since the events in Veracruz. Hundreds of years ago, in these lands, the hearts of people were cut out of their chests to be offered to the gods. Now, agents and soldiers willingly offer their own hearts for their country. Maybe it's a matter of necessity. Their hearts are so big that they can't fit in their chests." A lump formed in Miguel's throat, but he continued. "Please, keep my team in your prayers. I promise you, and them, I will dedicate myself and serve with honor in my future assignments."

"We wish you all the luck in the mission you're about to begin," the Director said. "You represent our Agency and our country." He nodded to an employee near the door. When the door was opened, a *Mariachi*[22] band entered playing a fiesta tune. A team of waiters followed, pushing carts with food. Office assistants followed with balloons and decorations.

Badge popped balloons, made new friends, and ate food he had never tried before.

* * * * *

It was time to go back to California. Miguel secured Badge in the travel crate provided by the airline.

By the look on his face, Badge seemed to be as uncomfortable as the previous flight.

Two employees raised the crate and put it on the conveyor belt at the check-in desk. The crate moved away and disappeared through a square hole in the wall. Nobody noticed Badge's whine.

Miguel planned to carry his backpack and new guitar onto the plane.

"Well, this is it, Mom," Miguel said, turning to his mother. He gave her a hug and a kiss.

"Have a nice trip, Miguel," she said and took a crucifix on a leather cord from her purse. "May God bless you and keep you."

Miguel lowered his head so his mother could slip the necklace on him.

"Don't forget to wear it, always," his mother said.

"I won't forget, Mom," Miguel bent again and his mother kissed his forehead. "Don't worry, God's angels will take care of us," he said.

Miguel walked towards the security gate while his mother waited in the main area of the terminal.

When he cleared the security check, he turned and waved to his mother one last time.

She waved and wiped away tears. "You're the angel, Miguel," she said to herself. "A flesh and blood angel. And Badge is another one."

* * * * *

Miguel took a window seat. He watched a baggage cart approach the plane, and then a crew transferring the suitcases. He noted how they handled Badge's crate and was relieved to see Badge had been loaded onto the correct plane.

After the baggage cart had left, Miguel saw another one approach. It carried a single yellow suitcase. *A last minute passenger, no doubt, but who'd choose such an ugly suitcase? Maybe the owner likes it because it's easy to identify.*

The plane took off, and Miguel studied his hometown from the sky. He wondered when he would return. It had been a great trip, from receiving the Medal of Merit to seeing his family and making new friends.

Miguel recalled something the Regional Director said. "Determination during surgery and rehabilitation." He felt ashamed. At that time, he had the determination to quit the Policía Federal. The old team, the Policía Federal, the DEA, doctors, his family, and many others maintained confidence in him and gave him their support. The best way to thank them would be to do the very best in his assignments. He had to pay forward the help he'd received.

Meanwhile, down below with the luggage, Badge started to get excited. A scent floated in the air, something like gasoline combined with medicine. Playtime! Somebody left a packet for the tug-of-war game.

He began to kick and bit the door of the crate. He had seen those locks on the fence outside the apartment building. He had to kick the door to make the lock jump and then pull with his nails before it fell again. He tried several times and from different angles. It took a long while but he finally pulled at the exact moment the lock jumped. The door popped open.

He squeezed out and immediately started the search, sniffing around.

It seemed the odor came from a pile of suitcases held together with a net. He walked around the pile, sniffing it.

A simple net wouldn't stop him. He bit and pulled the cords and hooks that secured it. One hook slid free and the pile of suitcases trembled. He jumped backwards, but the pile didn't fall. He attacked another hook, and jumped away as the suitcases slid and fell, thumping and bumping as they hit the floor and each other.

"Wow!" the man seated next to Miguel said, clearly startled.

The passengers turned to look at each other.

"Turbulence?" another passenger asked.

"I heard a noise but didn't feel any shaking," Miguel said while looking around.

Some passengers pushed their call buttons.

"I think the noise came from the cargo deck," one flight attendant said to another.

A male flight attendant took the intercom and called the cockpit: "Captain, I need your permission to check the luggage holds. The passengers are reporting strange noises."

The captain gave his permission.

The attendant pulled up a rug on the floor of the front galley, uncovering a hatch. He turned a handle and opened it. "Yes, it's the suitcases," he said while peering into the opening. He turned and began descending into the hold via a metal ladder.

"Be careful!" a female flight attendant warned.

As soon as the male flight attendant reached the lower deck, he discovered Badge in the middle of the scattered suitcases.

Badge was frantically sniffing and scratching the yellow suitcase.

"Hey! How did you get out of the crate?" The flight attendant yelled.

Badge looked at the flight attendant, stretched his neck and pointed to the yellow suitcase with his nose.

"Go back to your crate!" the flight attendant yelled again, far from understanding Badge's signal. "Look at all the mess you've made." He attempted to catch Badge, but tripped on the suitcases covering the floor.

What a strange man, better go look for Miguel. Badge jumped over the suitcases, avoiding the man, and reached the stairs.

"Stop right there!" The flight attendant tried to return to the stairs swimming through the suitcases.

Badge climbed.

"Everything's OK," the female flight attendant said to the passengers via the intercom. "The noises you hear are suitcases being put back in place."

"Hey, you! Come back here, you four-legged suitcase. You belong in here." the male attendant yelled again.

Badge reached the top of the stairs.

"A giant rat!" the female attendant screamed when she saw the back of Badge's head emerge through the hatch. Her scream carried over the intercom.

Passengers began screaming too. They raised their feet from the floor and peeked under the seats.

"Giant rats loose in the plane?" the man seated next to Miguel asked. "Once I saw a movie about loose snakes on a plane."

Badge jumped up through the hatch and ran down the aisle. He had to find Miguel. His nose told him Miguel was there, somewhere.

"It's a dog," someone yelled.

Flight attendants and passengers screamed. Some tried to catch Badge.

Badge bolted between the seats and away from all those crazy people.

The door of one lavatory opened and a large woman emerged blocking his way. He was cornered. He leapt onto a seat and walked across laps and trays, spilling food and beverages. Then he jumped from one row to another, and another.

People yelled and more hands reached for him.

Badge jumped over more trays and plates to reach the aisle again, and then ran straight down. Suddenly, he stopped and turned back to sniff something that fell. Was that meatloaf?

People yelling and trying to grab his collar approached.

Dinner had to wait for a better time. Badge turned again and ran away down the aisle.

Miguel and the passengers next to him tried to look around seats and standing passengers to get a better view. People were yelling, dashing around, and tripping. "Is it rats, a hijacker, or a medical emergency?" Miguel asked.

"Terrorists!" a passenger a few rows ahead yelled.

"We're all going to die!" a woman screamed.

The commotion continued. It reached the middle of the plane and increased.

Miguel noticed a pair of ears pass down the aisle, "Badge!"

Badge stopped and turned.

This time it was Miguel jumping over people and overturning food trays in his haste to reach the aisle. He immediately grabbed Badge by the collar, "Sit, Badge. Sit," he commanded.

Flight attendants and some passengers reached the row where Miguel and Badge were located. They stopped when they saw Badge completely still.

"Everything is under control," Miguel said.

Passengers and flight attendants turned to stare at each other, mouths gaping, and unsure of what to do next.

After a while, the passengers returned to their seats and the flight attendants started to clean up the mess.

"We have to secure that animal," the male flight attendant said. "All this is against regulations."

"Sure, I wonder who let Badge come into the passenger deck," Miguel said.

Miguel walked to the front of the plane holding Badge by the collar. As he moved forward, Badge pulled harder. They reached the front galley and Miguel went down the ladder carrying Badge.

Halfway down the stairs Badge jumped. He ran through the suitcases and pointed to the yellow one.

Miguel realized the cause of the commotion. He used the cargo net to reward Badge with a tug-of war game.

"Now what?" the male flight attendant asked when he reached them.

"I'm going to need a lock, or something to secure the crate's door." Miguel said. *The suitcase doesn't show any tags. Maybe it's an operation between ground crews. They load and unload baggage without registering it.*

The flight attendant found a power cord and handed it to Miguel.

In, Badge. In," Miguel commanded.

Badge walked into the crate, and Miguel tied the door.

"Problem fixed," the flight attendant said with a smile to the other members of the crew when he and Miguel returned to the passenger deck.

"I think we have another problem," Miguel said showing his shield.

* * * * *

The captain turned on the fasten seat belts light and announced they were on their final approach to San Diego-Lindbergh airport.

We're about to arrive, and there have been no further instructions. After the "giant rat incident," Miguel called airport security in San Diego from the cockpit and explained the situation. He was told to wait.

100

If there's going to be any action regarding the suitcase, it'll need to happen as soon as we land.

A moment later, a flight attendant approached. "Mr. Cordova, you have a radio call in the cockpit."

"This is Cordova," Miguel said when he put on the headset inside the cockpit.

"A DEA agent is going to meet you at the gate," the person from airport security said. "Your instructions are to watch the suitcase from the plane's passenger deck and inform us of any person coming in contact with it."

"Captain, I request your permission to bring my dog back into the passenger deck." Miguel asked as soon as the radio communication ended. "Better to be ready in case something happens."

"If the food and the carts have already been taken away, I see no problem," the captain said.

* * * * *

The plane landed as scheduled and proceeded to the gate.

"Miguel Cordova?" a man in maintenance overalls asked as soon as the door opened. Away from the passengers, he identified himself as James Kelly and showed his DEA badge and identification. He had a radio and gave another to Miguel.

While the passengers left the plane, Miguel, James, and Badge took positions, each at a different window.

The ground crew approached and parked the baggage trailer and a cart with a conveyor belt near the plane. The cargo door opened, and a baggage handler began unloading suitcases.

Badge gasped and jumped on his seat when the yellow suitcase came out of the plane.

"That's it," Miguel said.

The driver of the trailer skipped several suitcases and picked up the yellow one. After looking around, he put the suitcase on top of the cart and covered it with a canvas.

James, Miguel, and Badge turned to each other. "We have a suspect," James said through the radio and gave a detailed description of the driver.

"OK. Wait in the plane until the cart leaves," a voice in the radio said.

When the ground crew finished unloading the baggage, the driver jumped into the cart and drove away.

"Baggage's on its way to the terminal," James said on the radio.

"OK. We're tracking it".

James, Miguel, and Badge left the plane and ran down the gangway stairs. They completed their part of the operation, but wanted to follow the action in case they were needed.

The baggage trailer parked next to the terminal. The crew unloaded the baggage onto the conveyor belt that took it to the claim area.

Time went by. "No yellow suitcase on the claim carousel," an agent inside the terminal said on the radio after all the baggage was unloaded.

The baggage trailer moved to a maintenance building and stopped among other carts. The driver got off carrying a package, put it on the back of a pickup truck, and drove away. He had no idea more than ten agents observed his movements.

"This is it guys," the leader said through the radio. "We don't see any other suspect, proceed with the arrest."

The pickup reached one of the airport's service exits, but the gate stayed closed. Suddenly, three black cars flashing red and blue lights appeared and skidded to the sides and back of the pickup, cornering it.

"Step out of the vehicle! Hands in the air!" several agents yelled aiming their handguns at the driver.

The driver turned around and obeyed without any resistance.

"Down on the ground!" an agent ordered.

The agents handcuffed and searched the driver.

"Suspect in custody," an agent radioed.

James, Miguel, and Badge were too far away to see the action, but Miguel was relieved when he learned the arrest had been made.

The agents searched the pickup. "There's no suitcase or any suspect cargo in here, only tools," an agent informed.

James, Miguel, and Badge looked at each other. "It should still be in the cart!" James said. The three of them ran to the maintenance building

James reached the cart and lifted the canvas. "Nothing! The suspect hid it somewhere else, or somebody took it while everybody followed the pickup."

"Find dope, Badge. Find dope," Miguel said and led him on a search pattern of the area.

Badge sniffed carts, maintenance trucks, and the different areas of the maintenance building.

An hour went by and nobody found the suitcase in the maintenance area or anywhere else at the airport.

The suspect didn't say a word.

"All units end the search." the operation leader said through the radio. "I repeat. The search is over."

In silence, James, Miguel, and Badge walked to the terminal.

"We identified the suitcase in the airplane, followed it, and now it's gone." Miguel started to feel tired and disappointed.

"That kind of contraband does that all the time," James said.

At that moment, Badge tugged on the leash leading Miguel to a trash container.

Miguel followed Badge and gestured for James to come too.

The closer they moved to the container, the more excited Badge became. He stood on his back legs, front paws against the container and, sniffed.

Miguel lifted the plastic cover and moved things around. "Finally!" he said with a big smile. "The suitcase!" He took it out and handed it to James.

"We found it!" James said through the radio. "Let's see what's in it." He placed the suitcase on the floor and opened it with a pick set. A dozen perfectly aligned cellophane-wrapped bricks filled the interior. "Way to go!" he smiled. . . . "What are you doing?" he asked with surprise when he turned to see Miguel.

"I'm giving Badge his reward," Miguel said playing a tug-of-war with Badge and using a discarded piece of plastic.

"Well, it seems somebody lost his baggage," James laughed. "Let's take this suitcase to the lost and found department—the special one at airport security."

Miguel laughed too but his smile quickly disappeared. "Oh, no! My backpack! My guitar!"

Chapter 9: Jumping Over Hoods and Tops

San Ysidro Point of Entry, Mexican-American Border.

K9-56 was the code assigned to Miguel and Badge when they picked up their equipment at the DEA office. After some additional paperwork, they were ordered to report for duty the next day at the border crossing into Mexico.

The border crossing from Tijuana, Mexico, to San Ysidro, California, lies less than twenty miles south of San Diego, where Interstate 5 begins. Two streets heading north from Tijuana converge at the international crossing. Then, they expand to twenty-three lanes for cars and one for buses. Another six lanes return to Mexico. Because of the heavy traffic, a large number of people cross on foot to get through faster. This is the busiest border crossing in the world; more than fifty million people and seventeen million vehicles cross it every year.

Miguel and Badge's shift started at 7 am. They met with K9-29, Robert and his partner, Sarge, the Dutch Shepherd.

"Where do we start the inspections?" Miguel asked.

"I admire your enthusiasm," Robert said, "but some preliminary work has to be done. You two have to familiarize yourselves with the facility and meet Customs and Border Protection officers."

After the introductions, Miguel and Badge toured the offices, traffic departments, immigration offices, checkpoints, inspection and detention areas. This preliminary training took Miguel and Badge two working days.

The third day, they were assigned to the vehicle lines. Robert and Sarge demonstrated the inspection routines on cars and pickups at a checkpoint. While an officer reviewed the documents, Robert and Sarge walked around each vehicle. Sarge sniffed, and Robert performed a visual inspection. Robert also used a small mirror on a telescoping pole to check each vehicle's undercarriage. If necessary, he and Sarge inspected under the hood and in the trunk. If Robert wanted Sarge to inspect some things more closely, such as tires, truck beds, or fenders, he tapped the location and Sarge gave it special attention.

Later, Miguel and Badge executed the routine under Robert's supervision. When they became comfortable with the process, they were assigned to the next lane to do their own inspections.

"Call me on the radio if you find anything suspicious," Robert said. "If Sarge and I find anything, we'll notify you."

They moved to different lanes every hour and always stayed in contiguous ones.

The morning went by without incidents. When they stopped for lunch, Robert continued giving Miguel information about different situations and warning signs.

"K9-56," Robert called on the radio during the afternoon inspections. "K9 flagged a vehicle. Come over here, but remain calm. Engage only in case of emergency."

As Miguel and Badge approached, they observed how Sarge stretched his neck and pointed to one of the front tires of a car. Robert moved around, commanding Sarge to check the other tires.

"Please, step out of the car," Robert asked the occupants. "Come to the front."

The men slowly exited the car.

"Stay here and don't move," Robert commanded. "Guard, Sarge. Guard."

Sarge approached and stood a few inches from the men.

"Your turn," Robert said to Miguel.

Miguel and Badge moved around the vehicle with the same results. Badge pointed to the same tire.

The suspects shuffled nervously. Sarge growled. The two men stood still, now looking more frightened than nervous.

"Take them away," Robert commanded two customs officers to move the suspects to a detention area and the vehicle to an inspection garage.

When the technicians removed the tire, they found marijuana in several plastic bags held to the rim with a wire.

Robert and Miguel awarded the dogs with a tug-of-war game.

The drug was sealed and put it in a box that included documents with all the information about the case. Tags were printed and attached. All the operation, from the checkpoint to the tagging was recorded by CCTV[23] cameras.

* * * * *

The next day, Miguel and Badge started in one of the vehicle lines on their own. Robert and Sarge worked on the one beside them.

That afternoon, Miguel got an indication. Badge jumped and pointed with his nose indicating the car's trunk.

"K9-29," Miguel called Robert. "I think we got something."

Miguel approached the door. "Please, step out of the car and open the trunk," he told the driver.

107

"Come on! There's nothing in there," the driver argued as he left the car.

As soon as the man opened the trunk, Badge raised his two front legs over the fender and frantically pointed inside. Miguel restrained Badge with one hand and moved papers and bags with the other. When he lifted the rug covering the spare tire, he found several cellophane-wrapped bricks.

The driver shoved Miguel down and took off into the vehicle lines.

Badge kept pulling indicating drugs in the trunk.

"Bite and hold, Sarge. Bite and hold. Go," Robert commanded and sent Sarge after the suspect.

Miguel got back on his feet, and he and Badge joined the pursuit.

Sarge ran among the lines of cars, jumping over hoods and tops, and when close enough, leapt onto the driver. The man slammed to the ground with a dog attached to his arm.

Moments later, Robert, Miguel, and Badge reached them.

"Release, Sarge. Release." Robert commanded and scratched Sarge's neck as a reward while Miguel handcuffed the driver.

The group returned to the checkpoint among the vehicle lines. Astonished faces stared at them from closed car windows.

"That was an error," Robert said. "The number one priority is security, no matter what. Always keep an eye on the driver and the vehicle occupants. The search and the drugs can wait until backup arrives. You can make the suspects move their own things. That way, you'll always be watching them and have your hands free."

Miguel's face burned, he was embarrassed, but even more he was angry with himself. He was excited that Badge found something and compromised their own safety. As he processed the evidence, he realized the intention of the "hands on" training. "We're just a pair of

108

rookies," he said to Badge. "We have a lot of work to do to be on the level of an experienced team."

Badge whined.

* * * * *

Miguel and Badge grew more confident with the inspection process as days passed. They moved quicker performing inspections of several vehicles in one line before moving to the next. If Badge or Sarge made an indication, the vehicle was directed to the inspection garage for a thorough search.

In one case, when they were walking near a big red Hummer,[24] Badge jumped and pointed to the roof. They unloaded all the suitcases from atop it but Badge and Sarge still jumped and pointed to the roof. Careful inspection of the roof rack revealed the metal bars were hollow pipes stuffed with drugs.

They also found money. Sarge warned another vehicle and, when the technicians removed the ceiling fabric, they found $30,000 in currency. It isn't a crime to transport money, but transporting amounts greater than $10,000 without declaring them is forbidden. Hidden currency often indicates illegal activities.

Drugs and cash were found in door hollows, motor parts, dashboards, false batteries, inside seats, grocery bags, gas tanks, patches attached to people's skin, and more. But, no matter how cleverly concealed, Sarge and Badge found the contraband.

Miguel and Badge detected four or five illegal shipments per week. Sarge and Robert had similar numbers.

* * * * *

Days later, the team was assigned to inspect the bus lane. Passengers had to leave each bus, take their baggage from the luggage compartments, and form a line to pass through a checkpoint on foot. After that, they took their baggage across the border and returned to the bus. By then, the bus had been inspected and cleared to proceed.

When the dogs were there, the inspections were quick and effective. Searches of both passengers and buses were more thorough than random selections.

Robert and Sarge inspected the passengers and baggage while Miguel and Badge inspected the buses. After lunch, they switched positions.

Near the end of the shift, while inspecting the inside of an empty bus, Sarge scratched the floor and pointed with his nose.

"K9-56, we got something." Robert called. "We require support."

Miguel and Badge went to the buses area and climbed into the one Robert indicated. Badge pulled and pointed at a specific spot; the same one Sarge signaled earlier.

The team executed a detailed search but couldn't find any drugs.

"What do we do now?" Miguel asked.

"Call the technicians," Robert said.

The technicians executed a thorough inspection of the engine and the undercarriage, but found nothing.

"Are you sure of this?" one technician asked. "Maybe drugs were transported on a previous trip and left a scent."

Robert and Miguel worked the dogs through the bus again, both dogs made the same indication in the same spot. Everybody was puzzled.

"This is taking a lot of time, but we're not finding anything. Do we end the inspection?" an officer asked.

"No. If the dogs are sure, I'm sure," Robert said. "Bring the torches!"

The technicians removed several rows of seats and cut the floor with acetylene-cutting torches. In time, they removed a square section of the metal floor and uncovered a hidden compartment. The hollow was packed with cardboard boxes full of cellophane-wrapped bricks.

"Nice bit of work. This cache is bigger than the previous ones," Miguel said while playing tug-of-war with Badge.

"It's bigger than all the other ones combined," Robert replied and took Sarge's reward towel. The elated dog jumped for his prize.

It wasn't clear if the bus driver participated in the smuggling, but he was taken into custody. The entire bus was seized. The operation caused chaos in the customs area. Since the dogs detected something suspicious, all personnel in the bus lane started different procedures. The lines of buses and people lengthened. People traveling in the seized bus were stranded.

The dogs had hit on a hundred-pound stash of cocaine. The thwarted smuggling operation made the evening news.

* * * * *

The next day in the lines, Badge signaled a green car.

"K9-29, we require backup," Miguel radioed Robert. "I have a suspicious vehicle."

When the vehicle reached the checkpoint, Miguel's inspection with the mirror revealed several cellophane-wrapped packets stuck to the chassis.

Robert and Sarge carried out their own inspection and confirmed the result.

Miguel walked toward the driver to perform the arrest.

Robert moved into Miguel's path and stopped him at the last moment. He signaled Miguel should move away from the car.

"We're letting this one go," Robert said.

"What!" Miguel said with surprise.

"This one is too obvious," Robert said. "The driver is a woman and has two small kids. The profile doesn't fit. We're going to let her pass if she isn't flagged in the system."

"I don't understand. How can this be allowed?"

"We'll follow her."

The checkpoint officer verified the records in the computer. The passengers and the vehicle had clean records.

Robert instructed the officer to pretend he hadn't finished the verification to give the team extra time to get to Robert's car and request backup.

"You can let them go," Robert said on the radio to the checkpoint officer when everybody were in the car. The team followed the green car when it left the checkpoint. Another unit joined them to switch off leading the surveillance and avoid being discovered.

"The location of the drugs was so evident," Robert said, "probably placed there by somebody without access to the inside of the car. That somebody wants a free ride without the driver knowing and could also be following the car at this moment."

"A blind mule!"

"Exactly."

The green car drove to a residential area of San Diego and parked in front of a house. The woman and the children left the vehicle with grocery bags and went inside the house.

Robert drove past and parked the car half a block away. The backup unit parked a block away.

112

After a few moments, a black car with darkened windows approached slowly. It moved past the house, but didn't stop.

"Down, Badge. Down," Miguel said. He, Robert, and the dogs crouched down to hide.

The black car continued down the street and left.

Badge moved around in the back seat after a while. Sarge stayed seated.

"How long do we wait?" Miguel asked.

"Probably until dark," Robert said.

"You heard that, Badge. Calm down."

"Central, we require night vision equipment," Robert requested through the radio.

The team prepared for a long wait.

Just after dark, an agent, dressed all in black, approached their vehicle on foot. "Evening. You gentlemen enjoying the view?"

"Yes, beautiful night," Robert said. "Mark, this is Miguel. Miguel, this is Mark. He's in operations support."

"Nice meeting you," Miguel said.

"Hey, I was told you needed some goodies." Mark passed a duffle bag full of equipment through the window to Miguel. With a grin and a nod, Mark walked into the darkening shadows as if he'd never been there.

Miguel and Robert put on their helmets and the provided gear. They stepped out of the car with the dogs to take positions. Robert and Sarge went across the street from the house. Miguel and Badge went down the block and found a position to observe, a few houses beyond where the car was parked but on the same side of the street.

Time passed and the lights in the house were turned off.

Miguel scanned the area. He had a good view with the night vision goggles.

Noises and traffic diminished. One by one the lights in the area were extinguished. The entire neighborhood went to sleep.

Badge was quiet and steady, but alert, listening to the crickets.

The black car turned at the corner and moved slowly down the street. It parked near the house, and two people stepped out.

The men moved stealthily toward the green car. One went to the ground, next to the vehicle and the other kept watch, looking nervously from the street to the nearest houses.

"K9-56, get ready," Robert warned through the radio with a soft voice.

Miguel withdrew his Colt 1911.

As soon as the man on the ground retrieved one packet from the car, Robert turned on his flashlight, "DEA, stop right there! Hands up!"

The two men ran in different directions.

"Bite and hold, Sarge. Bite and hold." Robert directed Sarge toward the suspect running back to the vehicle.

The other man ran down the street without knowing Miguel and Badge were ready to ambush him.

"Bite and hold, Badge. Bite and hold," Miguel commanded, turning on his flashlight.

Badge only ran a few yards and jumped to catch the suspect by the arm. The pull made the man slip and fall to the ground. Seconds later, Miguel handcuffed the man and searched him for weapons.

On the other side of the street, Robert did the same.

Miguel stayed on top of the suspect pressing a knee into the man's back. "Good work, boy. Good work," he scratched Badge's neck, but kept looking around. He didn't want to be caught off guard again.

Police cars arrived at the scene, and the officers took the men into custody.

Up and down the block, lights snapped on and people came out of their houses.

Miguel and Badge returned to the apartment after midnight. "Long day, Badge," Miguel said. "Robert's fast thinking allowed us to catch the real smugglers. How did you feel with your first on-duty bite-and-hold?"

"Woof," Badge responded.

Miguel couldn't sleep. "How can we differentiate the bad guys from innocent?" he asked Badge in their dark bedroom. "It would have been so easy to arrest that woman and close the case, Badge" he said after a while. "What about the bus driver? Was he the real smuggler?" Miguel talked in the direction Badge was located. "Criminals use innocent people for their own advantage all the time. We have to be careful," Miguel didn't notice Badge had been asleep for a while. "Obviously, they could use not-so-innocent government officials and law-enforcement elements as well," he continued.

Chapter 10: Polleros!

Otay-Mesa Point of Entry. Mexican-American Border.

Miguel and Badge's next assignment sent them to the Otay-Mesa border crossing to continue with the training.

Miguel noted the crossing was only six miles east of the San Ysidro crossing. Thirteen-million people come into the U.S. every year through Otay-Mesa but it has half as many vehicle lanes as San Ysidro, including a commercial area used by trucks. Three-thousand trucks cross daily to the north. Each year, 1.4 million truck crossings move $31 billion in products.

"I know, I know," Miguel said to Robert. "Tour the facility and meet people before we get to work."

"You learn fast," Robert said. He showed Miguel the vehicle crossings, inspection and detention areas, and the commercial area for trucks.

"All cargo trucks, northbound and southbound, are inspected," the Inspections Manager said. "Cargo, driver, truck, and all documentation have to be in order to move from one country to the other. After an initial inspection in Mexico, the northbound cargo traffic goes to the checkpoints on the American side. That area handles seven truck lanes. Sixteen percent of the traffic is redirected to a secondary inspection where the cargo is verified by open inspection at the docking bay or with X-rays. The rest proceeds to the exit booths and are randomly stopped for canine inspections."

"Only a small number of trucks are inspected thoroughly?" Miguel asked.

"Yes, more inspections or more detail means longer waiting times," the Manager said. "The overall time to cross is two hours. If a secondary inspection is performed, the average time increases to five hours. If a secondary inspection is also carried out on the Mexican side, add another three hours, and you get eight. The lines already extend for miles."

"Wow, that's a whole business day," Miguel said.

"That's when all the paperwork is correct and ready," the Manager added. "If not, the trucks have to go to waiting areas where they can be stuck for days. Perishable products can become rotten and parts for manufactured goods could cause production delays in American factories."

Miguel and Robert continued their tour in the secondary inspection area. They observed the screens of the giant X-ray machines. Instead of looking at the inside of suitcases, these scanned 18-wheel tractor trailers from nose to tail.

"This is a great facility with the latest technology, but it's a random process," Miguel said. "Catching the criminals is a matter of chance."

"You're right," Robert said. "The importance of the dogs increases exponentially. Seizures can be in the range of tons."

* * * * *

Miguel, Robert, and the dogs started in the northbound truck lanes. They were assigned to carry out random inspections of the vehicles clearing the first checkpoint and heading to the exit booth.

While they moved around each truck, the dogs sniffed underneath the trailer and tractor. The process took time because of the size of the vehicles. If they performed an inspection in one line, they tried to do the next one in another line to distribute the waiting times. Everybody worked in a hurry. Truck drivers moved as soon as a spot cleared in front of them. Customs officers worked against the clock.

If Miguel and Robert wanted to cover a segment of a line of trucks, they had to run with the dogs. That was a strenuous pace to maintain, dangerous because of the sudden starts and stops of the trucks, and unhealthy because of the exhaust fumes. Doing detailed inspections, where they got to walk around a vehicle, was considered a time to rest.

The dogs liked the running part, but after a while, even they became tired.

* * * * *

After a couple of days at this rigorous pace, all the bones and muscles in Miguel's body hurt. He knew Badge felt the same. When they returned to the apartment, Badge ate and immediately went to sleep on his mat. He lay down on his back with his legs in the air.

Miguel tried not to laugh and disturb Badge.

Minutes later, Miguel reversed position on his bed and propped his legs on the headboard. "I guess that's a good idea, Badge," he said.

Miguel thought the work they were doing was important, but he still worried. "The more trucks we check, the less detailed the inspections," he said to the sleeping dog. "The more detailed the inspections, the fewer trucks we can check. . . . What's the middle ground, Badge? How can we be fast and efficient, yet more thorough?"

* * * * *

The next day, Miguel and Badge had to run again. They were in the lane reserved for empty trucks. Robert and Sarge ran in the next lane.

The intent of the reserved lane was to make empty trucks move faster. Miguel initially thought it would be easier because of the absence of cargo. Soon, he discovered it wasn't the case. He and Badge had to move faster. Even in an empty truck, drugs could be hidden in plenty of places. On top of that, the day turned extremely hot.

Near the middle of the afternoon, when Miguel and Badge made a pass along the line, Badge jumped and pulled the leash. "What is it, Badge?" Miguel asked. "Do you smell something?"

They returned and moved around the truck. Miguel tapped the gas tanks, the spare tires, and different points underneath the truck to make Badge pay special attention.

Badge checked all those places without making any signal, but he whined.

"What's going on?" Miguel scratched his head.

"Can I go?" the driver asked.

"No. Turn off the engine and step outside," Miguel said. "I need you to open the trailer."

Badge whined again.

"K9-29, we need support," Miguel called Robert. "I'm not sure, but we might have something here."

"Get in," Miguel said, indicating the driver to climb inside the trailer.

"What do you think you're going to find?" the driver argued. "The trailer's empty. See?"

"Inside, please," Miguel repeated.

Still arguing, the driver obeyed.

"Jump, Badge, jump," Miguel commanded. "Guard."

Miguel climbed inside, covered by Badge.

"All yours," the driver said.

Using his flashlight, Miguel performed a first inspection following the driver inside the trailer. Nothing could be seen.

Badge whined and moved from one side to the other, pulling the leash.

Something's upsetting him. Miguel tried to find an explanation. "A cat, is that what you smell, Badge?"

Backup arrived. Sarge jumped in and Robert climbed into the trailer.

Two more officers approached. Robert ordered them to guard the outside.

"What do we have in here, or what don't we have in here?" Robert turned around, inside the empty trailer.

"I don't know, but something's going on," Miguel said. "Badge is really agitated about something."

Robert and Sarge swept through the trailer.

Sarge whined.

"What's going on, boy?" Robert asked.

"You and your crazy dogs," the driver argued again. "I had a shipment of dog food to Mexico just yesterday."

"A false alarm?" Miguel felt disappointed.

"We're going to check your shipping history to verify that," Robert said to the driver. He took him by the arm and directed him outside. "Take care of him," he ordered to the officers guarding the trailer.

Miguel knocked on the walls of the trailer with his flashlight. "I think I get a lower tone at the front, but I'm not sure."

"Woof!" Badge barked as Sarge scratched the front wall of the trailer.

"This is weird," Robert said.

"Maybe it's the mother of all drug loads." Miguel said. "Robert, can you knock from the outside?"

Robert went out.

"Quiet boys," Miguel said to the dogs.

"I'm at the front," Robert said on the radio. "Ready?"

"OK, knock." Miguel leaned into the corner between the front and side wall.

Robert's knocks seemed to come from far away.

"Keep knocking and move along the side."

The sound came closer and louder, as expected. Miguel felt the vibrations.

"Definitely, there's a hidden compartment in the front." Miguel said. He leaned and set his ear on the warm metal of the front wall. "I think I hear some squeaks."

Badge scratched the wall vigorously.

"Is it rats, Badge?"

Miguel and Robert continued with a detailed inspection. Horizontal beams supported the front wall, welded to the sides.

"Send some technicians with cutting torches," Robert radioed to the secondary inspection station.

By the time the technicians boarded the trailer, curious agents and employees had gathered outside.

The suspension of normal activities stalled traffic in the whole truck crossing area.

"Bring some pry bars," Robert requested.

The technicians cut the upper and lower beams on the right side. After that, they started cutting on the left side.

Robert and Miguel used the pry bars and pulled the wall from the cut beams on the right.

"Nothing, no movement," Robert said.

The technicians continued cutting on the left side and Robert and Miguel continued pulling on the right.

The beams on the left gave way. Robert and Miguel pulled again. The wall opened on the right side with a loud metallic screech.

Heavy sacks rolled out, landing on Miguel and Robert and making them fall. The dogs started to bark.

The sacks are moving! Miguel tried to push them off. *They have arms, and legs!*

"Aire, por favor!" "Aydenme!" "Saquenme de aqui!"[25] the sacks begged.

They are people!

After a moment of shock, Miguel, Robert, and the technicians reacted.

"Take them out. Hurry!" Robert commanded.

Miguel reached the rear of the trailer dragging the first person. "Call the ambulances!" he yelled and ran for another person.

Robert and the technicians each dragged a person from the hollow wall, and then returned for more.

At the trailer's door, officers and employees helped unload the people and put them on the ground.

The last five people didn't move. They were taken outside, but appeared dead.

Miguel jumped from the trailer and started giving CPR[26] to a young woman. Robert worked over a boy, trying to return life to the limp body. The technicians and employees cared for the other three.

Within a few moments, the situation turned to chaos. Officers, employees, and drivers yelled, giving orders, and ran back and forth bringing water, food, ice, and blankets. Soon, helicopters circled the crossing point, adding their drone to the noise and confusion. When Miguel looked up, he noticed TV station logos on them.

"Come on!" Miguel pumped the woman's chest and alternated with mouth-to-mouth resuscitation. Those working on the other lifeless migrants did the same.

Badge was seated behind Miguel, Sarge behind Robert.

Every one of the five groups continued doing their work as they waited for medical help.

The boy coughed.

Soft applause and murmurs of congratulations came from the onlookers near Robert.

"Vamos! Vamos!"[27] Miguel repeated and pumped.

Paramedics arrived and started to help.

One by one, the other three groups became quiet.

"Come on! Come on! I know you want to live," Miguel yelled and continued pumping.

A paramedic shook his head at Miguel.

Miguel stopped pumping and quietly sat back. Sweat dripped from his face.

Eighteen people were rushed to area hospitals with asphyxia and dehydration symptoms. Later, when the ambulances carried away the deceased, the scene turned calm and somber.

Miguel remained where he'd been, sitting, staring at the spot where the woman had been. His elbow was propped on his knee, and his hand covered his mouth.

The driver was taken into custody. The staff and technicians returned to their duties and the news teams left.

Robert approached. "Come on, Miguel. Let's get out of here."

Miguel staggered up. "Pinches Polleros!"[28] He couldn't remember a time in his life he had been as tired or as angry as that moment.

The team moved to a shaded place, and drank some water. No one talked or woofed.

"What about moving the line?" one of the drivers shouted.

"Yes, let's go," other drivers shouted and honked, anxious to cross the border and make their deliveries. A radio report mentioned the waiting line in the Mexican side extended more than six miles.

Some employees picked up objects left on the ground. Others moved the confiscated truck out of the lane.

The drivers turned on the engines and the trucks advanced to the empty positions.

"Let's call it a day," Robert said. "We'll do all the paperwork tomorrow."

"Yeah, let's go," Miguel finally said.

The four of them walked away, moving slowly from fatigue. Miguel poured water over his face and Badge's head.

Robert opened the door to the custom offices and the group felt the freshness of the air conditioning.

They walked through the door into a different climate and a different world.

The horn of one of the trucks honked.

Miguel turned and caught the door before it shut. He observed the lines of trucks starting to move.

"What's going on?" Robert asked.

"A hunch," Miguel said. "Heel, Badge! Heel!" He ran back to the trucks followed by Badge. "Hold the lines. Hold the lines!" he yelled and called the exit booth by radio. "Don't let anybody get out!"

"What's going on?" Robert asked when he and Sarge reached Miguel.

"I want to check the trucks behind the one carrying the people."

The drivers cursed and booed yet another delay. Miguel and Badge took one side of the line of empty trucks. Robert and Sarge took the other.

"Move, you're clear to go," Miguel shouted when they finished inspecting the first trailer. They repeated the operation for the second and third trucks.

When they reached the fourth trailer, Badge pointed with his nose. On the other side, Sarge did the same.

"Hey! Get out of there and open the rear door," Miguel ordered the driver while bumping at the door.

"We need back up again," Robert radioed.

The team went into the trailer as soon as the doors opened and started their inspection.

"We're going to need those cutting torches again," Miguel said when he located two horizontal beams on the front wall.

The operation was repeated, but this time nothing fell when the front panel was removed. Instead, bags and cellophane-wrapped bricks secured with elastic cords and tape lined the wall.

After unloading and weighing the load, the team learned they'd found 3,000 pounds of marijuana in fifty bags, a hundred half-pound bricks of cocaine, and 30 half-pound packets of crystal meth.

The driver was taken into custody and the trailer removed from the line.

"They used live human bait to distract us," Robert said. "That was vile. How did you know, Miguel?"

"I didn't know. But I was told to expect the unexpected from the traffickers."

Robert turned to see the long line of trucks starting to move for the second time. "Do we leave now or do you have another hunch?"

Chapter 11: The Pregnant Mule

Mexico, office of an important man.

"Jackasses! You have the mental illness I call 'excess of initiative'," a hefty man wearing a suit shouted to General Mota, in uniform, and to Weedman, also in a suit. "You're useless!"

The big man had an important position in the Mexican government. His office was large and luxurious with fine wood furniture and thick cushions on the chairs. The walls were covered with pictures of him with presidents and other important members of the Mexican government. Ancient Egyptian figurines decorated furniture and walls.

"Calm down, sir," Mota said. "The shipment wasn't too big for the size of our operations."

"I know, but it's the largest shipment we've ever lost. You two and your fabulous idea to create a distraction with one trailer and send the cargo in another one right next to it. And what happens? Both trailers were detected, and by a couple of pooches!"

"Don't worry," Weedman said. "Our project will start operations next month, and we'll forget about all these little inconveniences."

"Yes, but that doesn't erase your stupidity," the big man argued. "And it's not our project! It's my project! Mine! It's my big creation, my money, my dreams!"

"Yes, sir, it's your great creation," Mota said in a placating tone, trying to move the conversation on to something other than the failed shipment.

"Yes, a great idea," Weedman said. "A creation worthy of a pharaoh."

"It's my baby," the big man said. "With this project, we'll be able to escalate our shipments five-hundred percent. We'll be in the major leagues." He dropped into the chair behind the desk made of imported wood. "This is the business of the century, and we'll be major players in it. This is going to make us multimillionaires." A cellophane-wrapped packet lay on the desk. The man picked it up, tapped it on the desktop a few times. He wore a big gold ring with a huge emerald. "The almighty, the all-powerful free market says the demand is there. If we're able to supply that demand, we're in the right business. If the product is illegal, better! The profits will soar because of the risk. We'll make dozens of times the initial investment. If the stupid gringos[29] keep demanding the product and are willing to pay for it, the supply will reach them no matter what. Air, land, or sea; marijuana, meth, cocaine, heroin; natural or synthetic, whatever! We're the ultimate businessmen! World-class financiers who are not afraid of getting their hands dirty. If police and drug-enforcement agencies seize shipments, great! The supply lowers and the price goes up. . . . Of course, it has to be our competitors' shipments, not ours."

The big man continued with his monologue. General Mota and Weedman looked at each other, unsure if the big man was still talking to them or just ranting.

"The gringos aren't the only stupid ones in this world," the big man continued, staring up at the ceiling. "With the same infrastructure to move drugs north, we can move weapons to the supplier countries in the south. Planes and trucks will be loaded on their way back, another illegal business with amazing margins. If there are people willing to kill each other, we can supply them with the most sophisticated armament they can dream of, as long as they pay for it. Every time they kill each other, we benefit from the anarchy created and with another sale to the next guy down the line looking to settle a score."

The big man stopped talking. "Why are you still here? Get out and go to work if you want to be millionaires. Move!"

Weedman and Mota bumped into each other as each tried to be first out the door. After some confused attempts at courtesy and taking turns, they sorted it out and left.

"What a bunch of Neanderthals,"[30] the big man sighed when he was left alone. "It's like negotiating a free-trade-agreement with chimpanzees. They just don't have the brains to understand." He pushed a button in the intercom, "Juanita, precious."

"Yes, sir," the assistant replied.

"Bring me the report about prescription drugs margins in the U.S., Canada, and Mexico, and some coffee, please . . . hazelnut."

* * * * *

San Diego International Airport.

Weeks later, the team received their new assignments in the Customs and Border Protection area at San Diego International Airport. James Kelly, from Operations Support, became K9 Support. He would review activities, record information gathered in the field, and provide information from law enforcement databases.

"We'll carry out searches in the baggage claim areas and support the customs personnel in the checkpoints," Robert said. "If we detect something, it'll be the other way around; customs personnel will support us."

"Dogs aren't used in passenger areas of airports very often," James said. "Some people get scared, and the risk of an accident is higher. People trying to pet the dogs risk being bitten. Dogs may bite-and-hold the wrong person when trying to catch a suspect on the run in the middle of a crowd. The Agency wants to prevent lawsuits. Better have the dogs on the leash and keep a tight grip on them."

Miguel and Badge would alternate positions with Robert and Sarge. One position made searches in the baggage claim carousels whenever a flight arrived from an international location, especially Mexico and South America. It included searches in nearby areas, like storage rooms, restrooms, and service areas. The other position searched passengers and baggage upon request from customs personnel. It also "sniffed" in the lines of people waiting for baggage inspection or waiting to get their documents verified.

Miguel and Badge started in the carousels. The airport was a busy place but didn't compare with the hectic rhythm of Otay-Mesa. The international customs area was isolated from the general airport terminal where domestic flights arrived. It also had a semi-controlled environment; people arriving had previously been screened and searched in their countries of departure.

"Come on, boy." Miguel commanded Badge. "Let's check those suitcases."

Badge rose from the floor, stretched and walked with Miguel toward the baggage carousel that had just started to move.

Miguel reminded himself to be always alert. *Don't be confident at all; expect the unexpected from drug smugglers and criminals in general.*

* * * * *

The next day, Miguel and Badge walked along the lines of people waiting for baggage inspection when Badge made an indication with his nose. It was a young man with a small carry-on bag.

"Excuse me, sir. Please come with me." Miguel asked politely.

The man opened his mouth and pointed at his chest. "Me?"

"Yes, sir. You."

The man looked around, still trying to verify if Miguel meant him.

Miguel moved closer and pointed at him with his index finger.

The man sighed, left the line, and walked with Miguel to the checkpoint.

"Please, check the bag," Miguel asked the customs officer.

While the man waited, Miguel discretely used the radio. "This is K9-56, we require backup in the baggage checkpoint."

The officer at the checkpoint tugged on gloves and started a detailed search. He inspected each object in the man's baggage.

A moment later, two backup officers approached pretending to be there by chance.

The inspections officer finished without finding anything. He turned to Miguel and Badge, hands out, and shrugged.

Miguel was confident in Badge's warning. "Find dope, Badge. Find dope," he commanded and pointed to the items on the counter.

Badge rose on his rear legs and sniffed. He made no signal.

The young man's face changed from worried to cheerful.

If the objects from the suitcase are clear, then it's the bag, Miguel thought. "Find dope, Badge. Find dope," he commanded Badge pointing to the empty suitcase.

Badge approached and pointed with his nose.

"It's here," Miguel said to the inspections officer. "Just search for it."

After a few moments, the agent figured it out. He pulled some threads from the zipper and a strip of plastic containing a white powder appeared.

One of the officers handcuffed the young man and the other took the evidence.

"Is the man a user or was he going to sell it?" Miguel said to Badge. "What is sure is that a few ounces of the drug have changed his life."

Badge attention was on the tug-of-war.

131

* * * * *

Days went by, and Miguel and Badge made four more seizures. Smugglers carrying small amounts of drugs tried to conceal it in their baggage or in their clothes. People were often contacted by traffickers and convinced to carry the drugs. Some saw it as a way to make fast money. Some were addicts themselves and did it in exchange for a portion of the shipment.

Besides the paperwork and evidence required for each case, James found similarities with other cases in the United States. "The smugglers are young people who travel to South America as winners of vacation trips," he said. "There, they have parties and a good life. Traffickers approach them with an offer to make easy money, and the promise of more trips and more parties."

"Their dreams ended in a sniff at a customs checkpoint," Miguel added.

* * * * *

"I taught Badge to open doors, push, and tackle." Miguel said to Robert. "In some situations, as in the airport, a 'Push' command would be enough to make the suspect fall giving enough time for an arrest. 'Tackle' commands Badge to position himself between the legs of a fleeing suspect until he falls. If Badge pushes or tackles the wrong person, it won't be as critical as a bite-and-hold. The Agency won't have to worry about being sued so often."

"I have to see that," Robert said.

Miguel, Robert, and the dogs went to the park to try the commands. Robert played the suspect and both times, when Miguel commanded Badge to push or tackle, Robert ended up on the ground.

"Sometimes the student can teach a few tricks to the teacher," Robert said.

Robert invited Miguel and Badge to a gathering at his house to celebrate his wife's birthday. Diane was pleased to meet Miguel and Badge since Robert told her so much about them.

Diane and Robert's families were there. Miguel hadn't been invited to any parties or anything since he came to San Diego. He enjoyed meeting everyone and making new friends.

Everybody asked about the Mexican war on drugs and the kind of program Miguel was participating in.

Miguel enjoyed talking about Badge and, especially, talking with Robert's father, a decorated Vietnam veteran. *Now, I understand where Robert gets his passion for this kind of work.*

The party had an unexpected surprise. Robert and Diane announced they were expecting their first child. The party became a double celebration.

Miguel felt happy when he and Badge returned to the apartment that night. After several months in San Diego, he didn't feel like an outsider anymore.

* * * * *

Miguel and Badge observed people in line at the customs checkpoint. A plane from Mexico City had landed.

"It's time to sniff around, Badge."

The first ones in the line only had carry-on baggage. Profiling techniques identified them as a high-risk group.

"Traveling a long distance and not having big suitcases doesn't match, unless the travelers are businessmen in a quick business trip," Miguel said to Badge.

He liked that, with Badge, he could inspect everybody and most of the time they didn't even notice. People thought they had to open their suitcase and pass each object in front of the dog's nose, like the product scanner in a supermarket. Just walking along the line was enough for Badge.

When a good number of people stood in line, Miguel and Badge carried out their first pass. *As expected, most passengers without registered baggage are wearing suits, like businessmen.* Others didn't, but carried garment bags. *Their business appointments might be tomorrow.*

Miguel noticed a man without a suit and walked toward him. He walked slowly to give Badge time to sniff.

The man turned, and backed away when he saw Badge.

"Good morning," Miguel said to ease the situation. *Nothing, Badge didn't make any indication.*

The next person of interest was a pregnant woman. She carried a big handbag and no suitcases. She looked tired.

Why keep carrying the bag when she could put it on the floor to be able to rest? Miguel wondered. *Judging by her size, she's in her sixth or seventh month.*

Miguel and Badge approached.

She's beautiful, Miguel thought.

Badge knew what to do and didn't require any command.

"Good morning, do you need help with that bag?" Miguel asked.

"No, thanks," the woman said. "I can handle it."

Badge stretched his neck and signaled with his nose.

Pregnant or not, beautiful or not, we got you! Miguel thought. "Please, come with me," he said.

"What?" the woman asked.

"Please, step out of the line and come with me," Miguel repeated politely.

Badge pulled. He wanted Miguel to find the drug to have his tug-of-war reward. His movements made the woman nervous and caught the attention of other people.

"What do you want?" the pregnant woman asked loudly, expecting to be noticed by everybody in the line.

"Step out of the line and come with me," Miguel repeated in a more serious tone.

Everyone turned to see what was going on. "You should show more respect!" "You should be ashamed!" "I'll file a complaint!" The people in the line shouted as Miguel and the woman walked to the checkpoint.

When the woman reached the checkpoint, the officer asked her to hand him the bag.

The woman crossed her arms over her belly trying to melt Miguel with her eyes.

Miguel returned a false smile.

The customs officer inspected all the objects in the bag and found nothing. "Your turn, dynamic duo," he said when he gave up. He already knew what to do when he couldn't find anything.

"Find dope, Badge. Find dope," Miguel commanded placing the bag on the floor.

Badge poked his nose into the bag and sniffed, but made no indication.

The woman stood quite still, scowling at Miguel and Badge. She tapped one foot on the floor.

"Find dope, Badge. Find dope," Miguel commanded again pointing to the bag.

Badge sniffed again but gave no signal.

What's going on? Miguel wondered. *Drugs are present, but where?* "Find dope, Badge. Find dope," he insisted but didn't point at the bag. "Find dope, boy. Find dope."

Badge stretched his neck and pointed to the woman's abdomen.

Oh, no! You wouldn't dare. Not next to your unborn child? Miguel took his radio. "We're going to need a female officer in the inspection room right away."

"What? How dare you do this to me!" the woman shouted.

Miguel realized she wanted to be noticed by the people in the line to create a commotion and prevent a search. "Please, come with me and bring your bag," he commanded.

The woman snatched her bag from the floor. "This is unfair! You think you can do whatever you want because you have a uniform and a handgun."

"And a dog," Miguel added.

The woman turned to the line of people.

Miguel wanted to applaud her theatrics, but didn't.

Boos erupted from the line as they approached the inspection room.

A female officer already waited for them at the door.

"You can't do this to me," the pregnant woman said, making one last attempt.

Miguel noticed the change in the tone of her voice. *Now she's begging. When will she stop acting?*

Just a few feet from the inspection room the woman threw her bag at Miguel and ran.

"Wow! She stopped acting. Call for backup!" Miguel shouted to the female officer and he and Badge ran after the woman.

Badge tried to run faster, but Miguel restrained him with the leash.

Miguel couldn't command Badge to bite-and-hold, or even push, or tackle. Not to a pregnant woman. He decided to trail her at a jog until she decided to give up.

The woman ran from one side of the terminal to the other. She jumped over the baggage carousel, then over some seats to avoid being cornered.

She's so agile for being pregnant, Miguel thought.

The woman ran toward the exit door, but turned when two officers blocked her way.

More running, more jumps, and several flat plastic packets fell to the floor from between the woman's legs.

"The load is coming loose, Badge," Miguel said.

"Woof!" Badge pulled.

The woman continued running. More flat packets fell.

No wonder she's so fast. She's not pregnant at all. He could attempt an arrest without risking injury to an unborn baby. He and Badge ran to catch up.

The woman noticed Miguel and Badge getting closer and ran into the women's restroom.

Miguel stopped at the entrance and turned. No female officers were nearby. He decided to enter. "Excuse me. Excuse me, officers on deck."

Screams started.

"The sound really echoes in here," Miguel said, his ears throbbing.

Some ladies screamed and hit Miguel with their purses. Another screamed twice, once when she saw Miguel, again when she saw Badge.

"Somebody call the police!" an old woman yelled.

"We're already here," Miguel said. "Don't you see?"

A direct hit to the head with a bag was the response.

"What are you carrying in there lady, hardcover books?"

Badge started to bark.

Miguel searched for the woman while rubbing Badge's neck to keep him calm.

Most women ran out of the restroom. One didn't care and took her time in front of the mirror to apply lipstick before leaving.

Miguel checked every toilet. A quiet sob behind a closed door caught his attention. He waited for a moment, and then knocked on the door. "Ma'am, please come out."

The sob became louder.

Miguel knocked again.

The response was an even louder sob.

Miguel felt sorry for the woman. *What do I do now?*

At that moment, a female officer came into the restroom.

Miguel pointed to the door where the lady was located.

The female officer knocked at the door as if wanting to demolish it. "Open the door, or I'll open it for you!" she shouted.

The lock made a click and the door started to open. Big tears slipped down the woman's face.

As soon as the door opened enough, the female officer pulled the woman out and handcuffed her.

Miguel and Badge escorted the officer and the woman out of the restroom and back to the inspection room. When they were about to enter, Miguel stopped. *Poor woman, she earned a nonstop ticket to jail.* He realized it was the first time he was sad for the person being arrested. *I'll do the paperwork later.*

The lady gave Miguel a last look of helplessness.

Other officers picked up the drug packets and normal activities resumed at the checkpoints. Miguel and Badge walked back to the passenger lines.

As they approached the line they were inspecting before, the passengers began to applaud.

Miguel's mood changed quickly. He rewarded Badge with a tug-of-war.

* * * * *

The team gathered in their office in the airport.

"The supposedly-pregnant woman had sixteen pounds of pure heroin, Robert said. "That's a lot!"

"What? Sixteen pounds a big deal?" Miguel asked.

"If it's pure, it is," James said. "I estimate a street value close to a million dollars if it's mixed with other ingredients and sold in small amounts. Before it's sold, this stuff is cut so many times that the final product may contain less than ten percent of the substance."

"Wow! A million dollars," Miguel said. "Now I understand why somebody risks everything to smuggle drugs."

"Well, that's the value on the street," James said, "what the big traffickers get. They might have paid only a small fraction to the producers. The 'mule' may get another small fraction. Not a large amount compared with the final value, but enough to take the risk."

Lying on the floor, Sarge and Badge followed the discussion with their eyes.

Miguel finished writing his report. "It's the same old story," he said, ready to go home. "Somebody else makes the big bucks. Those are the kind of crooks I'd like to send to jail, not mules, tourists, or bus drivers, but the masterminds."

Chapter 12: Tired Nose

One week later.

Miguel carefully watered the miniature cacti he had around the apartment while he hummed a song.

Badge followed, sniffing each one of the plants.

"Be careful with the thorns."

After that, Miguel flipped on the TV and went to the kitchen to prepare dinner.

Badge watched closely as Miguel prepared *quesadillas*.[31]

The telephone rang.

"Yes?" Miguel asked.

"Hey, Miguel," James said. "Meet Captain Williams tomorrow at 8:00 am. The agenda is to review activities and plans for the next several weeks."

"OK, I'll be there at 8:00 am. Anything else?"

"That's it. See you."

Miguel hung up the phone and noticed the expression on Badge's face. "Don't look at me like that," he said. "I'm eating human food, fortunately Mexican. You're eating dog food because you're a dog." He took out dishes and silverware. "Hey! That could be a great business idea!"

Badge tilted his head.

"If we invent Mexican dog food, we could get rich! What about Italian dog food?" He set Badge's food bowl on one side of the table and a plate for himself on the opposite side.

Badge jumped onto his chair.

Miguel served Badge a generous amount of dog food. After that, he served himself the quesadillas. "As Salvador made them, perfect!" He said and sat on his chair. He was about to bite the first of his quesadillas, but Badge's look made him stop. "Look, I'm sorry. This is the way it has to be."

Badge continued staring without touching his food.

Miguel picked up the dog food bag and showed it to Badge. "Look, total nutrition, lamb and rice formula," he said. "Lamb is the number one ingredient . . . highly digestible for optimal nutrient absorption . . . Omega fatty acids and vitamin E nourishes skin and coat . . . contains natural sources of glucosamine for strong, flexible joints."

Badge kept his eyes fixed on Miguel's plate.

"Don't you want strong, flexible joints?" Miguel asked.

Badge replied with a whine.

"Sorry, Badge. I kind of understand you, but I can't help."

"Big hit to drug traffickers . . ." the TV news anchor said.

Miguel turned his attention to the TV and ignored his stubborn dinner companion. The report was related to the Mexican Drug War.

"Important seizure operation in Mexico City," the anchor continued. "Traffickers were arrested and drugs seized. A large amount of money was also secured by the Policía Federal."

"Yesss!" Miguel jumped from his chair and went to the living room to get the remote and turn up the volume. "Go, Policía Federal! Well done!" he said pumping his fist.

The report continued, "More than twenty-five thousand people have been slain in drug-related violence in Mexico in the last two years. Although most have been traffickers, police, and military, the number includes numerous civilians . . ." Miguel's excitement faded. He sat on the edge of the couch and continued listening to the statistics. "Four-hundred women, one-hundred and fifty minors, forty government officials, and a dozen journalists have died since the beginning of the year . . . Last month's shooting of a drug lord, in an operation that also took the life of a Mexican marine, was followed within days by the slaying of the marine's grieving mother, sister, brother, and aunt."

Miguel's face turned pale. He turned off the TV and leaned back on the couch. "Mother, sister, brother, and aunt," he repeated several times.

Moments later, he returned to the kitchen table and picked up the dishes. He didn't remember he hadn't eaten, nor did he notice his plate was empty. He threw the dishes in the sink and went to the bedroom.

Puzzled, Badge stared at Miguel. He expected a reprimand. What happened?

* * * * *

Noises made Badge jump from his bed in the middle of the night. Miguel, sound asleep, moaned and thrashed about in his bed. Worried, Badge lowered his head and watched his partner.

"Miguel, help me!" somebody called.

Miguel heard several people crying out. He tried to find where the cries came from. He ran and opened several doors, but only found darkness. He continued searching and running until he reached a big iron door and pushed with all his strength until it swung open. When he looked inside, he could see a tunnel and a soft light far away. He ran toward it while the cries continued. When he reached the light, he could see several people kneeling on the floor, their hands tied behind their backs. At that moment, he realized who they were.

"Miguel, help me!" his mother begged.

The others are Susana, Luis, and Aunt Rosa! All of them were bleeding, had scratches and bruises.

Miguel tried to move closer, but as he did they seemed to slide farther away.

"Help!" cried his mother.

"This way Miguel!" Luis said.

"Please," begged Susana.

Over their cries boomed a menacing laugh. It echoed off the metal walls.

Miguel jumped, startled when a shadow slithered behind his family.

"You can't help them," the shadow said. "Don't you know why? You're so dumb." It laughed again.

Miguel reached for his handgun, but it wasn't in its holster. He tried his radio, but it wasn't working.

"Miguel, Michael, which language do I need to use to make you understand?" the shadow said.

"Mom, Luis!" Miguel ran, waved his arms, and yelled to his family, but again, he couldn't close the distance.

"Can't you see?" the shadow laughed. "You can't help them."

"That's what you think," Miguel said as he tried to approach from different directions. "I'll find a way."

The shadow laughed even louder. "You can't help them for one simple reason."

"Really? Why?"

The laugh continued, ". . . because you're already dead!" The voice ended in a thunder.

Miguel felt a stream of icy water on his back. He sprung out of the bed, looking around, fists raised, prepared to fight.

Seconds later, he realized he was in his bedroom, he lowered his guard. He was feeling an icy chill. "It's too cold," he said, walked to the hall and turned off the air conditioner.

When he turned back toward the bed, he found Badge standing, staring at him. "Go back to bed, Badge. It's nothing. . . . I'm just going crazy." Miguel jumped into bed and pulled up the blankets. He felt warmer, but the lingering nightmare images kept him awake.

* * * * *

Miguel and Badge arrived at the DEA building and went directly to Captain Williams's office.

"Come in," Williams said when Miguel knocked at the door.

"Good morning, Captain. You wanted to see me—us."

"Miguel, how are you?—Badge?" Captain Williams stood and shook Miguel's hand. "Please sit down."

"I was told you have instructions for me, sir."

"Instructions? Oh, yes, but the most important thing is to congratulate you—the two of you."

"Congratulate us? Why, Captain?"

"For the great work, Miguel. The heroin seized the other day. It sounds small compared with the trailer in Otay-Mesa, but we're talking about thousands of doses retired from the streets. Besides the dollar value, there's a high saved human cost. Don't know how to measure it, but it's big."

"Thanks, sir," Miguel said.

Badge woofed.

"The woman you arrested in the airport gave us valuable information about the organization who hired her. We offered her a reduced prison sentence if she cooperated. With that information, yesterday, the Policía Federal performed a seize operation in Mexico City."

"Really?"

Captain Williams took a paper from his desk to read the details. "Fifteen traffickers arrested; seven-hundred pounds of heroin, four-hundred-fifty pounds of cocaine, two-hundred pounds of meth, three-hundred pounds of marijuana, and fifteen million dollars in cash seized!"

"I saw something on the news yesterday."

"Yes, Miguel! It made the international news. It was a really big hit! A great operation and it all started with your arrest!" A broad smile spread over his face.

"Thanks, Captain."

"That's the kind of operation this program is all about," Williams said. "Connect the dots on both sides of the border, and fight the traffickers with that information." The Captain couldn't understand why Miguel seemed sad despite the great news.

"Did you hear about the case of the slain family of a Mexican marine?" Miguel asked.

"The family of a marine?" the Captain responded. "Violence is getting worse in Mexico as we speak. The marine must be devastated."

"No, the marine died in a shooting a few days earlier."

"Sorry, Miguel, I don't follow you."

"The family was killed in retaliation for the killing of a drug lord. The marine died during the confrontation against the drug lord."

"Wow! That's dirty—and sad," the Captain said. "A dirty war going on right next to us, and every day it spills more violence across the border."

"Yes, sir."

Resigned, Captain Williams changed the subject. After listening to what Miguel said, he didn't feel cheerful anymore. "Let's plan the schedule for the next few weeks."

* * * * *

The team's new assignment was to inspect passenger planes. Drugs were found in planes inbound from Mexico and South America, and although less often, drugs could also be found on flights from Asia.

The team maintained coordination with other airports. Sometimes San Diego was the final destination for a plane that came from another city in the United States, but originated outside of the country. Because of the schedules, planes couldn't be inspected until they reached San Diego, where they had to stop for maintenance.

Baggage crews, flight crews, maintenance crews, or cleaning crews could be traffickers' accomplices. Plenty of places on a plane could be used to conceal drugs. There were also plenty of things that shouldn't be touched because of safety issues, but they could be smelled: electronics, cables, safety equipment, pressurized doors, pneumatic lines, and more.

Inspections were carried out in the passenger and cargo decks. When the planes reached the gate, the team inspected the baggage as the ground crews unloaded it.

"Cockpit, galleys, restrooms, seat rows, overhead compartments . . ." Robert explained the procedure and Sarge showed by example how to go through the inside of the planes.

"Find dope, Badge. Find dope," Miguel commanded and Badge followed the routine executed by Sarge.

The dogs climbed on the seats to sniff the overhead compartments where the flight crew stored equipment. Standard compartments used by passengers were visually inspected by Robert and Miguel.

The cargo deck and other sections like avionics, tail, and landing gear were thoroughly inspected. Any compartment that could contain drugs had to be sniffed, but not necessarily opened. If the dogs made a signal, different teams of technicians were called, depending on the location, to open or dismantle compartments and equipment.

Soon Miguel and Badge became familiar with MD-80s and 737s. The 757s and 767s were more work, but practice boosted their confidence.

They had to start early. They were running again, this time along the tarmac between terminals, and between rows of seats inside the planes.

The team used sound-deadening earmuffs to protect their hearing from turbine noise when working on the tarmac. Miguel and Robert's muffs had an integrated radio. Badge and Sarge's muffs were specially designed for dogs but without radios.

* * * * *

Badge suddenly tugged on the leash as they searched an MD-80 airplane.

"What is it, Badge?" Miguel asked.

"Woof!" Badge jumped on the first seat of economy class. He pointed to the overhead baggage compartment with his nose.

"Tell me, where is it?" Miguel asked with the intention to play and motivate Badge.

"Woof!" Badge jumped and wagged his tail as fast as a fan. He wanted Miguel to find the drugs as fast as possible to get his tug-of-war reward.

"The plane came from Houston," James said on the radio, "but originated in Cancun."

When Miguel opened the compartment, he found a bag with an inflatable life raft.

Two agents, two technicians, and an airline representative were called to remove it.

"You nailed it, guys," an agent said when the raft was opened. They discovered that only the plastic floor was present and was used as an envelope for 150 pounds of marijuana.

"There's no sense in waiting for a smuggler to show up," Robert said. "If the smuggler saw us remove it, he would walk away or pretend to be as surprised as anyone else."

When Miguel was doing the paperwork, he learned more details.

"It's clear the drugs were placed there by technicians," James said. "They knew the dimensions of the compartment, how to pack the raft, and had the time to do it. Because of the weight of the package, including fifty pounds of life raft, at least two people were involved. We can generate some leads with that information and send them to the Mexican authorities."

"Interesting," Miguel said when he realized the amount of information that was gathered.

"On this side, it's difficult to uncover who intended to unload the drug," James continued. "It could be anybody with access to that plane in this airport or any other airport in the plane's future schedule."

"At least they lost the shipment," Robert said.

"Anything you want to add to the report, Miguel?" James asked.

"No. I'm just angry they used a safety device to transport their drugs. What would've happened to the fifty passengers relying on that raft if they'd crashed in the sea?"

* * * * *

Miguel and Badge finished the inspection in a Boeing 737's cargo deck. Robert and Sarge were about to finish the passenger deck. Miguel wished he had more time to observe the planes' touch downs and take offs. The sound of turbines at full thrust made him recall the Falcon, Captain Alvarez, and Pablo. "My friend Pablo would be flying commercial planes by now," he said to Badge. "Maybe arriving at San Diego airport once in a while." . . . *his wife, the twins* . . . Miguel never knew them in person, but wondered what happened to them.

Robert and Sarge came down the gangway.

"K9 Support," Miguel called James through the radio, "any other birds to inspect?"

"Hold on, K9-56. Let me check," James said.

Robert and Sarge approached. "Anything else?" Robert asked.

"James is checking."

"Kilo-Niner, proceed to gate thirty-one for the next inspection," James called back.

"Ten-four."[32]

Robert, Sarge, Miguel, and Badge ran. The terminal wasn't too far. All terminals related to international flights were together to share the same customs checkpoints.

"It's good to run and exercise the dogs," Robert said as they ran. "The distraction prevents the dogs from getting nose tired."

"Nose tired?" Miguel asked. "What's that?"

"If dogs are commanded to search for drugs for long periods of time, their effectiveness reduces. It isn't a physical condition. They just get bored and lose interest in the game."

The team reached the gate, but there was no plane.

"K9 Support, the nest is empty," Robert radioed.

"Let me verify, over," James said.

"Well, we can rest for a moment," Miguel said as he pampered Badge.

"The bird has just scored a touchdown," James called back. "Korean Airlines, flight 11-21. You'll receive the ball at any moment."

Robert and Miguel observed several planes taxiing in line on the tarmac immersed in a sea of turbine noise. Then, one of them turned to approach the terminal.

"*Orale!*"[33] Miguel said when he observed the first Airbus A380[34] he and Badge had to inspect.

"Welcome to America, Korean Airlines 11-21," Robert said.

"This is going to be fun, Badge," Miguel smiled. "I hope your nose is fully rested."

Chapter 13: Eighty Five-Pound Dog Hanging

Miguel and Robert had their lunch in the cafeteria. Badge and Sarge had two bowls each, dog food in one, water in the other.

Miguel didn't usually put Badge's bowl on the floor, but he wanted to prevent Badge from staring at Robert's food.

Fortunately, Badge was concentrating on his own food without staring at anybody.

Miguel didn't realize it, but he was the one staring—at how Badge ate on the floor.

"Maybe I'm spoiling Badge unnecessarily," Miguel said. "I let him eat at the table at home. If not, I feel sad for him. Of course, when he eats at the table, he stares at my food and, in the end I still feel sad."

"What are you having for lunch today?" Robert asked, paying more attention to Miguel's lunch than to his words.

"I made a Cuban *Torta*."

"And what exactly is that?"

"It's a Mexican sandwich. . . . The mother of all sandwiches. The bread is a French roll, soft inside, crusty outside. It's stuffed with ham, Swiss cheese, *milanesa*[35], and chipotle. Add mayo and mustard. Vegetables are optional. . . . Oh! Almost forgot, you can also add scrambled eggs."

"Wow! Would you trade it for my Chinese food?"

"Nope, no way, Jose! If you want, I'll bring lunch for both of us tomorrow, but I wouldn't trade mine for anything."

"So, if it bothers you that Badge stares at your food, doesn't it bother you when I stare at your food?" Robert laughed.

"How strange, actually, no."

"K9-29, K9-56," James called on the radio when Miguel bit into his torta. "There's been a report of a shooting at a bank a few blocks away from the airport. Immediate back up is required. I'll pick you up at the arrivals entrance."

"Come on, Badge. Let's go." Miguel left his torta on the table and took the leash.

Already moving, Badge swept past the table and stole the torta without so much as a tug on the leash. Only Sarge noticed the move.

The team ran across the terminal.

"Why is the torta a Mexican dish?" Robert asked as they ran.

"What?" Miguel asked.

"The torta—it has Swiss cheese, French bread, and it's called Cuban. Nevertheless, you say it's a Mexican dish."

"I don't know, man. I guess you can call it the United Nations Torta if you want."

They ran through the door. A black Suburban with red and blue lights flashing behind its windows waited for them. Inside, James waved for them to hurry.

The team jumped into the vehicle.

James turned on the siren, and the Suburban squealed off.

"This is a nice car," Miguel said as he checked the interior from the back seat. The vehicle was plush and had about every gadget he could imagine in a car. "I didn't know DEA had such fancy vehicles."

James and Robert looked at each other and smiled.

"Am I missing something?" Miguel asked.

"It's a scized vehicle," James said. "When a vehicle is used to transport drugs, the Agency can seize it. It goes to auction or can be used by the Agency."

"That's nice. I like the idea."

The Suburban approached the bank. Three squad cars from the San Diego City Police could be seen, one at the front of the bank and two more forming a barricade in the parking lot.

James parked far behind the squad cars. He didn't want to take unnecessary risks.

They all jumped out at the same time.

"Get your gear on," James said. He opened the rear door and handed out the vests and helmets. Badge was going to use his vest for the first time.

"Sorry! No helmets for dogs," Miguel said. "They haven't been invented yet."

James tapped his chinstrap twice to remind Miguel to fasten his.

The team double-checked their equipment.

"Follow me!" James said when everybody was ready.

The team approached a group of officers crouched behind the squad cars.

"What's the status?" James asked.

"We received a silent alarm from the bank," an officer said. "When the first car arrived, an automatic weapon fired from inside and blew out the glass doors. The cruiser looks like Swiss cheese. Fortunately, the officer in the unit escaped."

"Any demands . . . hostages?" James asked.

"No idea," the officer said.

"How many suspects?"

"As far as we've been able to tell, just one."

More police units arrived at the scene.

Miguel, Robert, and the dogs helped evacuate stores and restaurants nearby. If the situation escalated, bystanders could be hit by stray bullets.

A SWAT team arrived in a BEAR[36] armored vehicle. Two snipers ran to get in position on rooftops facing the bank. The other four members took cover behind the squad cars and the BEAR.

By the time Miguel and Robert finished the evacuation; two TV-station helicopters were already circling the scene.

The SWAT team leader, Captain Fred Holder, called the bank to contact the robbers. He intended to start negotiations, but got no response.

"Get ready," James said to the team. "Captain Holder is in command. He mentioned the dogs can be an option in case the snipers are unable to act—". A burst of bullets from an automatic weapon interrupted James's words. The glass windows in the front of the bank fell into pieces and the interior became totally exposed. Miguel saw people lying on the floor; some were screaming and crying.

One of the SWAT snipers on the rooftop radioed Captain Holder. "There seems to be a group standing in the middle . . . there are three —no!—four of them. It appears to be one man surrounded by women."

"Hell!" Holder shouted through the radio, "The hostages are going to be used as human shields. Amber five and Amber six, each of you get a K9 team and take positions."

A SWAT officer slipped a bullet-proof shield over one arm and waved for Miguel to start moving.

Miguel couldn't see the officer's face. A black balaclava covered everything, except the eyes. Miguel ducked his head, held Badge firmly by the leash, and closely followed the officer.

The officer moved to the east, always with the shield toward the bank, covering them.

Robert and Sarge did the same with another SWAT officer on the other side of the parking lot.

Miguel's group moved among parked cars and empty spaces. Captain Holder directed them to the desired positions via radio.

The officer gave hand commands. Miguel and Badge had to stay low and move faster.

A rain of bullets impacted the shield. The officer fell backwards, toppling Miguel who fell over Badge.

"Darn!" the officer growled and stood up, holding the shield firmly in position.

Miguel got up and checked Badge. *Something's going on, but what is it?* He sensed something strange, but couldn't identify what it was in the middle of the commotion.

"Are you all right Amber five?" the Captain asked in the radio.

"Fine, Amber one."

"The K9 unit?"

"Are you two OK?" the SWAT officer turned and asked.

"We're fine," Miguel said. At that moment, he realized what was strange about their situation. *The SWAT officer is a woman!*

They continued moving until they reached a position lateral to the bank on the east side. They took cover behind the concrete column of a fancy store front.

Robert, Sarge, and the other SWAT officer hid behind a car in direct line with the bank entrance.

"They're coming out," one of the SWAT snipers yelled through the radio.

"Do you have a clear shot, Amber two?" the Captain asked.

"Negative. The suspect is surrounded by hostages."

"What about you, Amber three?

"Negative, Amber one. Wait! Three female hostages are walking with the suspect, two in the front, and one in the back. They're tied with straps. There are objects hanging from the robber's chest, appear to be grenades."

Another burst of bullets impacted the police vehicles where the Captain, James, and others were located. Everybody threw themselves to the ground. Glass and ricocheting bullets flew everywhere.

"Is everybody all right over there, Amber one and four?" the officer next to Miguel asked in the radio.

"Everybody is OK," the Captain responded while he shook pieces of glass from his tactical uniform. "It seems this guy wants to make himself a way out—"

"Grenade, take cover!" one of the SWAT snipers shouted on the radio.

Miguel could only see an arm emerge above the women's heads. An object flew from the hand toward the closest police cruiser.

Everybody dove to the pavement again, covering their heads. The explosion made the disabled squad car in front of the bank fly into the air. It landed on its side and rolled over on its top.

The bank robber took advantage of the confusion and advanced with the three women toward several parked vehicles. Each woman was carrying a heavy bag; Miguel assumed they were stuffed with cash.

"Any clear shot, Amber two or three?" The Captain asked again on the radio.

"Negative, one," the first sniper said.

"Negative, Amber one," the second sniper said. "Even with a clear shot, we could hit a grenade and blow up the hostages."

The Captain and the others were just getting up when another spray of bullets hit the squad cars. Everybody hit the ground again.

"He's reloading," one of the snipers said in the radio.

After a few seconds, another burst impacted the police cruisers. Everybody was already on the pavement.

"They're opening the door of one of the cars," the sniper said. "He's untying one woman . . . she's taking the back seat—"

Another burst of bullets interrupted the sniper.

"Tell me when you see him reload," the Captain said. "Amber five and six, tell the handlers to be ready to release the dogs on my command. You and the handlers are going advance on a second command."

Miguel heard the instructions in the radio. He detached Badge's leash and held him by the collar.

"Are you ready?" the SWAT officer asked, turning to Miguel.

Miguel was kissing the crucifix his mother gave him.

The SWAT officer looked at the crucifix and turned away again, watching the robber and hostages. "Do you think that thing is going to help you?"

"I'd bet my life on it," Miguel said.

She turned again and looked Miguel in the eyes for a moment, and then, with a quick turn of her head, her blue eyes were again on the robber and hostages.

The bank robber untied the second woman and pushed her into the back seat. After that, he fired another burst.

"Reloading," one of the snipers shouted through the radio.

"Not yet. He still has one woman tied to him," the Captain said to James. "First, I hope to have a chance to act. Second, I hope this works."

"He's untying the third woman . . . she's getting into the driver's seat," a sniper said.

Another machine gun burst impacted cars in the parking lot, shattering windows and blowing tires.

"Now or never," the Captain said. He rose with his rifle and fired a burst at the overturned police car as a distraction. "Amber 5 release your dog!"

"Bite and hold, Badge. Bite and hold. Go," Miguel commanded and pushed Badge in the direction of the bank robber.

The Captain ducked for cover just before another burst of bullets impacted the vehicle he and James were using for cover.

"Reloading," a sniper said in the radio when he observed the bank robber raise his AK-47.

"Amber 6 release your dog," the Captain shouted.

"Bite and hold, Sarge. Bite and hold. Go," Robert commanded.

Sarge started to run. The bank robber detached the empty cartridge and threw it away.

The bank robber shifted his attention from the car where the shots came from and watched Sarge who appeared from behind another car at a run. The robber shoved a new cartridge into the receiver of the AK-47.

Sarge accelerated.

The bank robber pulled the charger handle of the AK-47 as he watched Sarge charging. He leveled the weapon and closed one eye to aim. Wham! At that moment he felt something slamming into him. His right hand lost its grip on the weapon when a fierce pull yanked his arm down hard. He discovered an eighty five-pound dog hanging on his arm, shaking and snarling.

Sarge jumped to the car's roof like a guided missile seeking its target.

The robber juggled the AK-47 with his left hand and tried to fight Badge when Sarge slammed into his chest and grabbed the other arm. The three of them fell.

"Amber 5 and 6, go. K9 handlers, go." the Captain shouted in the radio.

The SWAT officers ran toward the robber still holding up their shields. Miguel and Robert ran after each of them.

The bank robber lay on the ground, yelling in pain. Each dog was clamped down tight on an arm and pulled in opposite directions.

"Don't let the dogs release him yet," the female officer yelled. "We have to secure the grenades and weapons."

The two SWAT officers removed the grenades, a handgun, and a knife from the robber. Miguel picked up the AK-47.

Captain Holder, James, and others arrived and helped the crying women out of the car.

Other police officers ran to the bank to check for other suspects and the condition of the people inside.

"Release, Badge. Release," Miguel commanded after the robber was searched. Robert gave the same command to Sarge.

A SWAT officer handcuffed and helped the robber up, then escorted him to a squad car.

Some people in the bank and several officers were treated for minor cuts and bruises.

Police officers, SWAT members, and the K9 team smiled and shook hands. Badge and Sarge received praise and were scratched and patted.

As she approached Miguel, the female officer removed her helmet and balaclava, revealing her blond hair. "Great job! We make a good team," she said.

Miguel replied with a nod and shook her hand. He was so amazed by her, he couldn't think of a thing to say. *Wow! Why isn't she a movie star?*

The teams came together and congratulated each other. Miguel stared after the SWAT team as they gathered to debrief. "Did you notice the girl on the SWAT team?" he asked while he took off Badge's vest.

Robert and James turned to each other and smiled as they removed their own vests.

"Yes, she's hard to miss," Robert said. "Officer Rosenberg. I don't remember her first name."

"Abira Rosenberg.," James added. "At the police station, they call her Icy Abira."

Everybody put the vests and the helmets in the rear of the Suburban.

"Icy? Why is that?" Miguel asked, trying to get as much information as possible.

"Don't know firsthand," James said as he jumped into the Suburban. "Everybody says she's cold and unfriendly. You have to find out for yourself."

"I'm married," Robert said while he and Sarge jumped into the vehicle. "I don't mess with those kinds of investigations anymore."

Miguel listened as he waved Badge to jump inside.

"I'm happily engaged," James said as he started the car. "I'm out of those games, too."

"Well, thanks for the detailed intel," Miguel said and jumped into the Suburban.

Next to the BEAR, a pair of blue eyes followed the Suburban as it drove off.

Chapter 14: A.K.A[37] Chiva.

The team reviewed flight schedules in their office at the airport the following week.

"Charlie Whiskey to Kilo Niner San Diego International, please respond," Captain Williams said on the radio.

"Kilo Niner here," James responded.

"I need all of you in the office for new instructions," the Captain said. "Make it fast. Over and out."

"Wow! Sounds like he's in a rush about something," James said.

"Hasta la vista[38], big birds." Miguel gathered his paperwork.

"We haven't inspected cargo planes yet," Robert said. "I wonder what's going on."

"I guess we're about to find out," James said.

Before leaving, the team packed up their papers and dog bowls, and discarded the flight plans for that day.

* * * * *

"Hey guys, remember the red Hummer?" Miguel asked when they climbed into the Suburban. "The one carrying drugs in the roof rack? Would the Agency use a car like that? ... A fancy red one?"

"It was confiscated," James said. "I don't know if it was sold at the seizure auction, or if it'll be used by the Agency. I don't think they would keep a red one. Nevertheless, it would look great with big black letters on the side."

"The Seattle office has a seized Hummer," Robert said. "Painted dark blue with white letters, smashing!"

163

"Imagine an Airbus A380 seized in a drug operation," Miguel said. "They could paint that with DEA letters and colors. It'd be cool!"

Everybody laughed.

"Private planes can be confiscated, from light aircraft to large jets," James said. "I know of DC9s that have been seized. An aircraft like that can accommodate more than 120 passengers. The ones I mention were not transporting any people. They were stuffed with drugs. Imagine the amount!"

* * * * *

The team arrived at the DEA building and went directly to Captain Williams's office.

"Please come in and take a seat. I want to congratulate you on your excellent performance at the bank the other day. Both the city's highest-ranking officials and Captain Holder praised your role in the operation. In the future, we'll certainly be working with SWAT more often."

"Is more training going to be needed?" James asked.

"Yes and no," Williams said. "Joint operations can start right now. When it comes to K9 tactics, we're the ones that can teach them. As for explosives, negotiation skills, and assault tactics, we're going to schedule more training in the future. Robert and Sarge already have training in explosive detection. Miguel and Badge will have to catch up."

"We're anxious to begin that training," Miguel said. "What do you think, Badge?"

"Woof!" he agreed.

"We'll schedule that later," Williams said. "Right now, we have to score more brownie points. We have a good record of arrests and seizes, but we haven't executed operations. A successful operation was launched by the Policía Federal with the information we provided, but we have to conduct our own investigations with K9 teams in order to catch traffickers doing big drug shipments. Hitting them here in the U.S. hurts them the most. Besides losing the product, they'll have to duplicate all the work, expenses, and bribes."

"Do you have an operation for us, Captain?" Robert asked, seeming anxious.

"Unfortunately, no," he replied. "But we might have one if we're able to gather more intel."

"So we won't be in the airport anymore?" James asked.

"No," Williams said. "The bank robber from the other day, Margarito Flores, also known as The Bull, gave us some information in exchange for reduced jail time. He received a deal because no one was seriously injured. He was completely coked out during the robbery attempt. He said he took drugs to get the courage to carry out the robbery."

Miguel smiled and covered his mouth with one hand, trying to avoid being noticed by the others.

"Anything to add, Miguel?" Williams asked.

"Sorry, sir. It's the name. Loosely translated into English, Margarito, means Daisy, and Flores is flowers. So, Daisy Flowers got the courage to rob the bank."

Everybody laughed.

"Well, your psychoanalysis may explain why he was frustrated," Williams said.

"At the end, the coward had to take drugs to perform the crime," Miguel said.

"And used women as shields," Robert added.

"Now the facts," Williams said. "Drugs and weapons were present. In the confession, Flores gave us an alias, *El Pollo*.[39] That's the supplier who provided him drugs on a regular basis, and later, the weapons—a handgun, an AK-47, cartridges, and five fragmentation grenades, all for five hundred dollars."

"Five hundred dollars?" Miguel argued.

"That's ridiculous!" James said.

"Are you sure that's the amount?" Robert asked.

"Believe it or not, that's it," Williams said. "A small amount of money and one person can compromise the security of a whole city. I think this so called El Pollo doesn't know what he's doing. He gets the drugs and weapons from somewhere and has his own operation on the side. He may lack the connections to make good sales and makes them on an irregular basis. By the way, what does El Pollo mean, Miguel?"

"El Pollo means The Chicken, sir."

"Well, we can't say they lack imagination for choosing aliases and names. . . . Getting back to the point, we have to find El Pollo and set up surveillance. I guess a good code name for him would be "Crunchy" in our future transmissions. Our number one priority is to find the wholesaler who supplies drugs and weapons to this chicken fellow."

The team and the Captain discussed details of detection and surveillance activities. Badge scratched his side with a rear paw but he and Sarge listened as closely as their human partners.

* * * * *

 Two days after, The Bull, James, Miguel, and Badge waited inside the Suburban in the parking lot of Tecolote Canyon Park. Robert and Sarge waited in a car nearby.

Handcuffed, The Bull shared the rear seat with Badge. He was warned not to attempt any sudden movement. Badge's snout, next to his ear, reinforced the message. "This is the place I purchased the drugs," he said. "Pollo should be here soon."

They waited. Bull's face stuck to the window as he tried to move away from Badge's breath. Moments later, a red Mercedes entered the parking lot.

"That's the car," The Bull said.

"K9-29, that's the car," James said on the radio, warning Robert. "It seems business is good."

The red Mercedes parked, and a slim blond male stepped out. He wore jeans, a t-shirt, and lots of showy gold jewelry.

"Well, Crunchy looks typical for a low-level trafficker," Robert said through the radio. "The only thing he has good taste in is cars."

"He sells the drugs in the park," The Bull said. "When I bought the weapons we made the exchange here, in the parking lot. That's all I know."

"Isn't that nice?" James said. "Mention a location, identify a man, and you've already sliced several years from your sentence. Lucky you, Bull."

El Pollo walked into the park.

"Well, it's our turn," Miguel said and gave a last check to his concealed radio and handgun. He opened the door, and stepped out with Badge. He was wearing tennis shoes, blue shorts, and a jersey. The jersey had white and red vertical stripes, and the logo of his favorite soccer team in Mexico. The jersey's neck hid a small microphone. He received communications through a tiny bud in his ear. He pretended to be listening to the cell phone strapped to his arm. He also carried a Frisbee like any guy out playing with his dog.

Miguel walked near the Mercedes and radioed the plate number. "How original, the plate is Papa, Oscar, Lima, Lima, Oscar, Niner, Niner."[40]

Miguel followed El Pollo, but not too close; he didn't want to create any suspicion. He kept in radio contact as he moved. "I'm behind him. . . . He's walking beside the baseball fields."

El Pollo greeted several people as he walked but didn't stop for any of them.

Some people seated on the benches stood and followed El Pollo. Others left the bleachers by the baseball field and did the same.

Miguel and Badge followed as El Pollo took a trail that went deeper into the park.

El Pollo slowed down; looking around cautiously, he left the path and leaned on a tree.

Two people approached him at a time while others kept walking up the path. After the ones near El Pollo left, another small group approached.

Miguel walked on an angle toward a small grassy area. "Crunchy has lots of customers," he said through the radio and threw the Frisbee. "There's no line, but people approach in intervals."

Doing his part of the undercover work, Badge dashed out and caught the Frisbee.

Several people walking down the trail greeted Miguel and some shouted: "Go, *Chivas*![41] Go, Guadalajara!"

No! Miguel realized he had made a mistake. His jersey caught too much attention. He didn't expect his hometown's team to be known by so many people in San Diego. He threw the Frisbee farther and he and Badge moved away.

An hour later, it started to get dark. El Pollo moved closer to the baseball fields where the lights were on and continued selling his merchandise.

"I'm moving out. Send the replacement," Miguel said. He followed the procedure to avoid any suspicion.

On the way out, Miguel walked closer to El Pollo to observe the transactions. He could see buyers giving money and getting a small yellow envelope in return.

"Hey, you!" El Pollo shouted to Miguel.

Miguel almost jumped. He'd been discovered!

"Go, Guadalajara! Go, Chivas!" El Pollo shouted.

"You bet," Miguel called out and walked faster, trying to leave.

"Hey, Chiva!"

"What?"

"Wanna buy some good stuff? Only twenty bucks," El Pollo said holding out a yellow envelope to Miguel.

"I didn't bring any money," Miguel said, walking away. He didn't want to be recognized by El Pollo or any of his customers if they had been in the airport lately.

"Don't worry. Pay me later if you like it," El Pollo said. He approached Miguel, offering the envelope. "It's good quality. If you bring your friends, you'll get a discount."

"OK." Miguel took the envelope with one hand and tried to hold Badge by the leash with the other.

Badge pulled and stretched his neck pointing to El Pollo with his nose, indicating the presence of drugs.

"I think he likes me," El Pollo said.

"He wants to play," Miguel said and held Badge by the collar to stop the pointing signal. He turned and walked away.

"Hey, Chiva!" El Pollo shouted again.

"Yes?" Miguel turned back.

"Nice dog."

"Thanks, man." Miguel walked away tugging Badge who pulled in the opposite direction.

"We're in position," Robert said through the radio by the time Miguel and Badge reached the parking lot.

Miguel sighed, relieved to be back at the Suburban.

"Miguel Cordova, A.K.A. Chiva," James laughed.

Miguel didn't mention it, but he liked it. After all, it was his favorite team. He rewarded Badge with a tug-of-war.

"By the way, the plate is registered to a Gavin Pollock," James said.

"What's that, Scottish? And he's using a Spanish alias?" Miguel asked. "That's original."

Another unmarked unit approached. In a dark corner of the parking lot, Bull was transferred from the Suburban to the other vehicle while Badge growled in close proximity.

"See you in a few years, Bull," Miguel said before the door of the other unit closed.

El Pollo continued his sales for another hour. He ran out of product and went back to his car. Several customers approached him as he walked, but they left empty-handed.

"Wow! He really has a nice little business," James said.

The Mercedes left the parking lot.

James turned the ignition key and followed the Mercedes. "Is everything all right, K9-29?"

"Just getting back into my car," Robert said on the radio. "We'll follow you."

The team followed the Mercedes. After a short drive, they arrived at an apartment complex.

El Pollo went into an apartment on the second floor. Using night vision goggles, the team observed all his movements. "That Pollo looks green to me," Miguel said.

An hour went by and the lights of the apartment were turned off.

James called for a backup unit. No movement was expected, but somebody had to maintain surveillance until El Pollo's supplier was identified.

James and Miguel still had to go to the DEA. Miguel took the yellow envelope to the supervisor in charge of the night watch. The drug in it would be used as evidence and a laboratory analysis had to be performed immediately.

* * * * *

As Miguel drove home, he talked to Badge. "A park is supposed to be used for recreation and sports, not as a drug distribution center with families and kids around."

Badge growled.

"The most curious, was the way the addicts followed El Pollo and gathered around him. . . . Like people at church gathering around the priest. . . . How sad. . . . They want to enjoy a quick hit for fun and will end up in an uncontrollable addiction?"

Badge whined.

"Wanting to quit, but after suffering through detoxification, going back to the drugs. They'll need more and more to reach the same euphoria and they'll suffer more each time they try to quit. . . . Repeat the cycle, again and again. Their physical condition deteriorates, the families disintegrate, and all their money drains away. . . . Robbery and prostitution are only ways to get some cash to continue buying drugs."

Badge gasped and rubbed his face with one leg.

"That's the best description of hell I can find."

Badge whimpered.

Chapter 15: The Dog from Hell!

Early the next day, the team took positions in two cars to watch El Pollo's apartment.

"Crunchy's on the move," James said through the radio when their suspect left the apartment at 8:00 am.

The team followed him to a local golf course. There, he played a round with other people, but the team couldn't determine if he knew them or they were a random foursome. The team followed El Pollo's movements but couldn't hear his conversations.

"Kilo Niner, what's your status?" Captain Williams called near mid-morning.

"We're following Crunchy," James said, "and trying to gather information."

"We received the lab results for the sample," the Captain said. "It's high-grade cocaine, seventy-percent pure. Crunchy could cut it twice and get four times the amount of money he's making. Either he doesn't know or just doesn't have the means to do it. Because of the high grade, we think he's close to the supply chain wholesaler."

"Let's hope so," Miguel said. "Finally! A big fat fish to catch."

"K9-56 and K9-Support, I need you to search Crunchy's apartment. The warrant is ready."

"Is Crunchy going to be informed of the search?" James asked.

"No, and he shouldn't be," Williams said. "The USA Patriot Act[42] entitles us to a sneak and peak[43] without notification. Because weapons and explosives are involved, the warrant was issued without complications."

"We're on our way," James said.

"K9-29, stay with Crunchy," Williams said. "Watch for any exchange of merchandise or money."

"Roger that," Robert confirmed from the other car.

"Another unit will provide you with the surveillance equipment and the documentation, over and out."

The Suburban returned to the apartment complex. Another black SUV was already waiting for them.

An agent approached their vehicle.

"Mark, how are you?" Miguel said.

"Hey, Miguel," Mark said. "Here's the requested equipment."

Mark passed a duffel bag through the window. Miguel checked the content.

"Do you know how to install and activate it?" Mark asked.

"Yep, no problem," Miguel said.

"We're establishing a phone tap right now," Mark said. "I'll call you when it's ready for a test, good luck." He walked away.

James and Miguel tested the surveillance devices for the apartment while Badge tilted his head, looking at the gadgets.

When everything was checked and double-checked, Miguel and Badge went into the apartment complex. On the second floor they approached El Pollo's apartment.

At that time, just before noon, most of the tenants were out at work.

Miguel knocked on the door and waited. He looked up and down the hall and when he was certain no one was around, he took out a small cylinder and put it on top of the peephole.

Badge turned his back to Miguel, providing cover so no one could sneak up from behind.

"All clear," Miguel told James after checking the inside with the peephole reverser. He took out a pick set and used it on the door lock.

Seconds later, the lock clicked and Miguel opened the door. He and Badge slid in and eased it shut.

Miguel didn't waste any time. He placed a tiny wireless microphone behind the headboard and quickly left the bedroom. "First one in place," he said on the radio as he went into the kitchen; he opened a drawer and placed a second microphone. "Second one, in place." He looked around and decided to place the third one on the underside of the living room table. "Third one is in place."

"Roger that," James said.

"Now, we'll sniff around," Miguel said. "Find dope, Badge. Find dope," he commanded. Badge sniffed, methodically searching the apartment.

Miguel tapped closets and pieces of furniture for Badge to sniff. They went through the kitchen and the living room. In the bedroom, Badge tugged on the leash and pointed with his nose.

"There's something below the bed," Miguel said on the radio. He pulled a small brown box and opened it. It held dozens of small yellow envelopes. "That was easy," he said. He opened one envelope. "Empty!" He opened others. "All empty! I guess this wasn't that easy after all."

Badge panted; waiting for his reward.

Miguel continued searching below the bed. *Badge made the signal; something has to be in here.* He found a wrapped brick inside the box spring, "I got another *something*," he said through the radio. He opened it. "Found it! A half pound of cocaine more or less. Crunchy must get these wrapped bricks from his supplier, and then divides it into the small envelopes."

"Crunchy is fried," James said.

Miguel took photos with his cell phone, and then put a sample of the substance in a plastic bag for lab tests, and as evidence.

Badge grunted and wiggled.

Miguel wrapped the packet and put everything back as it was. He took out the little towel and rewarded Badge with a tug-of-war. "Well done, boy, well done."

The telephone rang.

"It's our guys, Miguel," James said.

"Narcotic Pizza, may I take your order," Miguel answered.

"I want three two-gram pizzas, uncut, please," Mark said on the other side of the line.

"Would you like the Methamphetamine extra topping with your combo?"

"Sure. How much is it going to be?"

"Your health, your savings, and ninety-nine cents. It's a limited time offer!"

"I have a coupon, can I use it?"

"Sure, it's good for the ninety-nine cents."

"Considering I have no health and no savings, it's a nice deal."

"We appreciate your business. Remember, our pizzas are a-ddic-tive." Miguel hung up the phone.

"The test was good," James said, laughing on the radio. "I hope you have a permit to sell pizzas."

Miguel and Badge searched other areas of the apartment but found nothing.

"I think that's it," Miguel said on the radio. "We're coming out."

"Wait! Somebody's outside about to pass the door," James said.

Miguel commanded Badge to stay quiet by pressing an index finger to his lips. They could hear heavy footsteps approaching. Miguel held his breath, listening closely and holding his hand, palm open, near Badge's face, encouraging him to stay quiet.

The footsteps stopped outside the door.

"Be careful, Miguel!" James warned.

Miguel froze, but his brain churned. He had to do something.

A metallic click came from the door.

No! That's the key. Miguel ran to the bathroom. "Sit, Badge. Don't move," he said softly and with a hand signal. Badge sit outside the bathroom door, facing the apartment door. Miguel closed the door, leaving it ajar so he could watch Badge and Badge could see him.

The apartment door opened. A rotund maid entered carrying a bucket, mop, and other cleaning items. She walked in and closed the door. "Aaaah!" she screamed, dropping the bucket, "a giant dog!"

Badge looked at the maid, then at Miguel through the gap.

From the bathtub, Miguel ordered Badge to remain still with precise hand signals.

Badge continued to sit with his tongue hanging out.

"Where did you come from?" the maid asked. "Mr. Pollock should know that pets are not allowed in the apartments without management's approval. Let's hope you haven't left any stinky mess around or Mr. Pollock will have to pay extra for my services."

The maid cleaned the kitchen. "You know, I'm thinking it would be good if you made a mess, so I can charge extra to Mr. Pollock."

The maid moved to the living room. "As a matter of fact, you may not have left any mess at all, but I can still tell Mr. Pollock you did." She smiled. "He's going to believe me because I can talk. Yes, sir. I sure can talk. It's a gift God gave me. Nobody is going to believe you. You don't even talk." She laughed.

Badge stayed seated in front of the bathroom door. Miguel repeated the sit and stay hand signals from his position in the bathroom.

After a while, the maid stood in front of Badge with an authoritarian expression. She held the mop like a lance and hoisted the bucket like a shield. "OK, Mister Big Ears. Move! I'm doing the bathroom."

Badge looked at her, and then turned to Miguel for instructions. The commands were the same.

"Hey! I'm talking to you, dog face!" the maid shouted. "Don't stare at me and hide that tongue. Come on, move!"

Badge turned again to check Miguel. No change.

The maid backed up a step and nudged Badge with the mop.

Miguel looked to the ceiling, as if asking for help. *I can't believe this! Since when, is somebody so eager to clean somebody else's bathroom?* He made a tight fist and jerked it in Badge's direction.

Badge growled.

"Aaaah!" The maid withdrew the mop.

The maid looked at Badge up and down for a while. "You don't look so tough." She nudged him again.

Miguel repeated the command and Badge growled again.

The back-and-forth continued for a few moments, with the maid pushing harder each time, her face grew angrier and redder. Badge sat stock-still and growled each time he was nudged.

Enough! Miguel thought. He changed the command and opened and closed his hand several times.

"Woof, woof!" Badge barked.

The maid stepped back suddenly, staring at him, mouth agape and eyes popping.

Now or never! Miguel thought. He set his hand horizontally and raised it. Then, he continued opening and closing his hand at a faster pace.

"Woof, woof!" Badge stood, stretched out his neck as he barked louder and faster, lips curling back to expose his teeth between barks.

"Crazy dog!" the maid screamed. "You got rabies or somethin'?"

"Woof, woof!" Badge continued.

Nervous, the maid gathered her supplies and backed toward the door. She opened it a few inches but stopped. "No! No pooch is going to tell me what to do," she said and turned to face Badge with a defiant glare in her eyes.

Miguel watched her through the gap. He set his hand in a vertical position and quickly moved it forward to command Badge to push.

Badge walked toward the maid.

"Aaaah!" she screamed and turned, trying to pull the door open and hold onto her bucket of sponges and bottles, plus the mop.

Badge jumped and gave her a push on the buttocks with his front paws.

The force sent her stumbling through the door. The bucket flew from her hand and the mop shot out across the hall.

Miguel needed to tell Badge to close the door, but they hadn't devised a hand signal. It had to be a spoken command.

Badge didn't even stop to see if Miguel had a command for him. He remembered what Karen did with the roaring monster. When the maid was past the door jam, he reared up and slammed the door with a mighty shove.

Miguel bolted from the bathroom and ran toward the door as fast as a rabbit.

The maid was scared but angry. She straightened her clothes, pushed up her curls and turned to the door. When she was about to touch the doorknob, the lock clicked.

"Aaaah! The dog from hell!" She screamed and took off down the hall. At the top of the stairs, she stopped and looked back. Her bucket and mop lay where they'd landed in the hall. For a woman of her build, she was quick and agile. She dashed down the hall, snatched up the bucket and mop in a move worthy of Indiana Jones, and bolted toward the stairs again.

Still holding the lock, Miguel sighed when he heard the heavy thumps of her fleeing footsteps.

The maid ran downstairs while James observed from the Suburban. "Are you OK, Miguel?" he asked through the radio. "What's happening?"

"We're OK. Where's the maid?"

"She ran downstairs like an Olympic athlete . . . right now she's crossing the parking lot like a gazelle."

The maid stopped behind a car, opened the trunk, and threw the bucket and mop inside. She paused to fan her face with her hands, jumped into the driver's seat, and drove away.

"She's gone. You're clear," James said.

"Finally!" Miguel said as he looked around the apartment.

Several minutes passed.

"What's going on?" James asked. "You are clear to exit, any problem?"

"We're OK," Miguel said as he hung clean towels in the bathroom. "Could you bring me some bleach, Windex, and paper towels?"

"What?"

"Call 29, where's Crunchy?"

"K9-29, please give me a status," James called through the radio.

"Everything's fine," Robert said. "We're waiting for Crunchy to get out of the spa."

"Woof!" Sarge confirmed.

"56, Crunchy is still far from here," James informed.

"OK, we still have time," Miguel said.

Minutes later, James arrived at the apartment with the cleaning items and knocked at the door.

Miguel opened the door and snatched the cleaners and the paper towel before James could close the door, "Please finish doing the bed and take the trash out."

"What's going on?"

"Hurry! I'll explain later."

When they finished, Miguel inspected the apartment. He sprayed some air freshener and picked up the cleaning items.

"What was all that about?" James asked when they returned to the Suburban. "I'd say we should leave the apartment as we found it, not as if the prince of Persia is going to use it."

"The maid saw Badge," Miguel said. "If she tells Pollo about it, the whole operation could be compromised. If we clean the apartment, especially the bathroom, her story won't make any sense. I hope it works."

* * * * *

The team was gathered in the Suburban when El Pollo returned to his apartment that evening. For the first time, they had a chance to hear what their suspect was saying.

El Pollo received several calls on his cell phone. He was organizing a golf game.

Later, he received a different kind of call.

The team heard half of the conversation.

"I have the product, but it'll take a few days . . . twenty thousand . . . that's it, take it or leave it . . . yes, cash . . . in the park . . . three days . . . I'll call you."

"It seems he has an important customer," Robert said when the call finished.

"But first he has to contact his supplier. For that, he needs extra time," Miguel said.

El Pollo made a call on his cell phone after that. "I'll need an extra pound this week," he said. "Four thousand more . . . no . . . five thousand more . . . OK."

"Either we're lucky, or he has a larger operation than we thought," James said. "He may do this kind of business frequently."

Minutes went by. Only soft noises came through the radio.

"Do you think he's filling the envelopes with the drugs?" Miguel asked.

"Probably," Robert said.

The telephone in the apartment rang. James switched the frequency to hear both sides of the tapped line.

"Mr. Pollock? This is Linda, the maid. That dog's gonna get you in a heap of trouble. He attacked me. Thank God, I was able to escape because I'm so agile—"

"What are you talking about?" El Pollo said. "I don't have a dog."

"Yes, you do. And you're in big trouble, sir. You shouldn't have a dog in the apartment without management approval. I hope they fine you. He's a nasty one."

"What? I don't understand."

"He attacked me before I could clean the entire apartment, but I expect to be paid in full. I was there on time with all my equipment ready to do the job. And an extra tip for all my trouble wouldn't—"

"Listen, Linda, the apartment's spotless," El Pollo said as he looked around. "Actually, you did a better job today."

"What do you mean the apartment's spotless? I couldn't even get near the bathroom, and then that beast pushed me out the door before I was done."

"You're crazy. The apartment's clean including the bathroom, and there's no dog. Got it? You're talking to the wrong person."

"But, Mr. Pollock, are you sure?"

El Pollo hung up the phone.

"Yes! We're still in the game. Gimme paw!" Miguel said to Badge.

Badge raised his right paw and Miguel slid his hand under it. The team did high fives all around. Sarge didn't know what happened, but Robert roughed him up and patted his head.

"Clear heads in a crisis. We're awesome!" James said.

"The best team!" Robert cheered.

"And the best maids!" Miguel added.

Chapter 16: Canis Lupus Familiaris

El Pollo went to the park that evening and sold more little envelopes. The team followed him and observed who he met and how much he sold.

"I don't expect him to take delivery of his next shipment in the same place he sells it," Miguel said.

"Neither do I, but you never know. Better keep our eyes open," James said.

"Nothing!" Robert said through the radio when El Pollo finished doing business, hours later.

Upon returning to the apartment complex, Robert hid a tiny microphone in El Pollo's car. The team wanted to be sure they knew his every move and whenever he made contact with customers or his supplier.

"Support is here," Miguel said when the relief team approached to take the nightshift. "Let's get out of here."

* * * * *

The routine repeated the following day until El Pollo went to the bank with a small duffel bag. The team's mood changed instantly.

"Normal withdrawal or robbery withdrawal? What do you think guys?" Miguel asked.

"I think it's a normal withdrawal," James said. "I haven't seen him bothering with a weapon, but better to be prepared. . . . It's my turn.

185

I've been the least visible." He stepped out of the Suburban and went into the bank.

Inside, the target talked to an employee and followed her to the safe deposit box vault.

After a while, he returned, carrying the duffel. Judging by the strain on the straps, he'd made a withdrawal and not a deposit.

"He's loaded and ready for the transaction," James radioed.

El Pollo climbed into the Mercedes and left. James, Miguel, and Badge followed in the Suburban, Robert and Sarge in the other car.

The Mercedes went to a downtown shopping mall and entered the underground parking lot. The mall was nearly deserted at midmorning.

James and Robert parked on opposite sides of the main lot but kept El Pollo's vehicle in sight.

"Your turn, Miguel," James said. "By now, all of us have been around the target. Be careful, don't let him see you."

"Stay, Badge. Stay," Miguel commanded. Taking a dog into the mall would attract too much attention. Miguel left the vehicle and entered the mall the same way El Pollo did.

El Pollo walked fast with the duffel bag, didn't glance to any window, or stop at any shop.

That's a good sign. That means business.

When El Pollo reached the food court he greeted a man at one of the tables and sat down opposite him. There was a small box in the center of the table.

"Crunchy has made contact," Miguel radioed. "The guy is Hispanic, hefty, possibly short, and wearing blue overalls. He may work in a repair shop or warehouse. He's seated at a table."

El Pollo and the man chatted for a while.

After about ten minutes, the man in the overalls took the duffel bag, El Pollo picked up the box. And whey walked away in opposite directions.

186

"The exchange has been made!" Miguel said in his concealed microphone. "I'll follow the new target."

When Miguel looked up, he saw El Pollo coming toward him. The other man was moving off, fast. *Now what?* Miguel darted into the closest store at the last moment and hid behind the mannequins.

Two female clerks looked at Miguel with their mouths wide open.

"I told you," a customer said to another lady beside her as she pointed at Miguel. "You can find anything a girl wants in here."

Miguel didn't notice them and watched down the hall as El Pollo walked away. When the way was clear, he moved toward the door.

"Can I help you find something?" one of the clerks asked while the customers smiled at Miguel.

Miguel noticed the four women staring at him. "Ah, no, thanks. Maybe later." Almost running, he left the Victoria's Secret store and hurried through the mall in the direction taken by the man in overalls.

"Should we wait?" the second lady asked the first, staring after Miguel.

Miguel found the man in the overalls. "We're moving to the south now. Yes, he's short and even chubbier than I thought."

The transaction could send both parties to jail for years. If the team made arrests now, they could keep those drugs off the streets, but they wanted something else. Clearly, short and chubby wasn't the mastermind, but they were one step closer to the wholesaler, the organization moving hundreds or even thousands of pounds of product on a regular basis. Capturing its members, would disable dozens of small dealers, like El Pollo.

"He's coming down the stairs to the south section of the parking lot," Miguel said.

As Robert and James received the information, they moved to the south section of the parking lot to be ready to follow the new suspect.

The man wearing the blue overalls reached an old pickup, threw the duffel bag inside, and jumped in.

"Our guy is driving a brown pickup," Miguel said. "California plates Alpha, Nilo, Four, Five, Eight, Niner, Tree, Zulu."

"Central, I need information about a vehicle," James requested by radio.

"Support, I'll follow the pickup while you pick up 56," Robert told James.

Miguel jumped into the Suburban, and the vehicle started moving.

"Taking G Street to the east," Robert said. "Now we're turning onto Fourth, southbound."

"The vehicle is registered to Mauricio Farias," Central called back. "He's Hispanic, age thirty-five, five-foot-one. He has an arrest for robbery three years ago. Served a year and got probation. His address is five-three-nine-zero Rosco Street. Farias's only known alias is *Chango*."[44]

"Thanks, Central. Over and out," James said.

"The Pollo-to-Chango Connection," Miguel said.

"One step closer."

"That Chango might be a climber."

"Well, he's not going home," Robert said through the radio. "That address is to the north and we're going south."

The team followed the pickup for half an hour and changed positions on the lead several times. They approached the Mexican border, but far from any crossing.

The pickup turned into the parking lot of a warehouse a couple of blocks from the border. "Atlantic Trading Company," James said as he read a sign. "Nothing out of the ordinary, that's a logistics company like dozens in this area."

James parked the Suburban across the street. Robert parked on a side street.

Chango found a parking space, exited the pickup, and walked to the gate. "Target is moving," James said. "He's not carrying the bag."

A road ran beside the parking lot to the entrance, which had a sliding gate and a guardhouse beside it. A ten-foot-high wire fence surrounded the warehouse and the area where the trucks were parked. Inside, several trucks waited near the dock with their rear doors open. Several forklifts moved in and out loading and unloading cargo.

Chango presented an identification to the guard who allowed him to enter the property through a smaller gate beside the guard house.

The team observed Chango and the warehouse using their binoculars. They took down plate numbers of all the cars and trucks going in and out of the facility. They calculated the totals for loaded and unloaded cargo, counting pallets and boxes per pallet. Special attention was given to the trucks leaving the warehouse; Chango could be in one of them.

After several hours, the team decided to send Robert for food. Everyone got cheeseburgers—even the dogs.

"Sorry, pal, not a healthy meal for you today," Miguel told Badge.

Badge ate the cheeseburger in a few bites.

After watching Badge eat, Miguel corrected himself, "I withdraw the apology, and you should thank me, *amigo*." He was about to bite his cheeseburger, but stopped. He was very hungry, but he couldn't stand Badge's begging face so close to him inside the Suburban. "I guess I'll have the fries," he said as he gave the cheeseburger to Badge.

Night fell, and Chango didn't appear. His pickup was one of a few vehicles still in the parking lot. Most employees had left and the trucks near the dock were locked up.

The team took out their night vision goggles.

"Do we wait?" Miguel asked when the dash clock showed 10 pm.

"We have to," James said. "We can't leave our target. Either he comes out today or in a week, but we have to stay here. He's the next link to the drugs and possibly the weapons."

"The money is still in the pickup. He has to come back." Robert said on the radio.

Robert was right. Around 11 pm., Chango came out.

"Target is leaving the building," Robert alerted.

"He's carrying a box," Miguel said. "Like the one he gave Crunchy."

"Seems he's already resupplying what he gave to Crunchy," James said.

Chango reached the guardhouse and talked to a different guard. After some arguing, he left without the box and walked to his pickup.

"What? Is he leaving?" Miguel asked. "The guard didn't let him take the box."

"We're about to find out," Robert said on the radio.

Chango opened the pickup's door but didn't get in.

"He opened the duffel bag," James said. "He's taking out a wad of money!"

Chango hid the duffel bag again and returned to the guardhouse.

"He's giving the money to the guard," Miguel said.

The guard counted the money and smiled. He waved Chango on. The little man picked up the box and left.

"It seems he has to slip the guard a bonus if he wants to leave with the product," James said.

"If the boss finds out, those two will end up hanging from a bridge," Miguel said.

Chango took the box to the pickup, tucked it behind the seat, and drove away.

"We stay with the target," James said turning on the engine.

"But the drug comes from the warehouse," Miguel said.

"You're probably right," James said. "But that warehouse isn't going anywhere, and we can't do anything else without more evidence, or a warrant. We'll follow Chango and the box."

The Suburban and Robert's car both followed the pickup. They drove for half an hour until they arrived at Chango's house.

Chango parked the pickup out front and took the box and duffel bag in with him.

Just before midnight, another unit arrived for the nightshift. The team still had to deliver their information to the supervisor at the DEA building. Chango was assigned the code name "Junkie Kong," to be used in radio transmissions.

Exhausted, Miguel and Badge went home. It was nearly 1:00 am.

"How would it be to be married and have a family with this kind of work?" Miguel asked Badge.

Badge didn't pay attention and went straight to his mat.

"At least the operation is advancing. We're getting some good leads."

* * * * *

Early the next morning, the team gathered near Chango's house. Robert and Sarge were assigned to follow him. James, Miguel, and Badge would do surveillance on the house and wait for a warrant.

"Hey, team," Captain Williams called them on the radio. "Nice progress in the surveillance. Starting today, activities are escalating and resources have been multiplied. Your main focus is to get evidence that confirms Junkie Kong is Crunchy's source for drugs and weapons. You're team number one and have the lead. All other teams will move according to the information you provide. Team number two will continue to track Crunchy in case he has different sources. Team three will gather additional information about the warehouse, installations, shipments, and traffic. If a seize operation is launched, we'll need that information to prepare. The fourth team is already working here in the office, gathering intel about Atlantic Trading's owners, tax history, customers, whatever."

"Nice to know all this work is paying off," James said.

"The judge just issued the search warrant for Junkie Kong's house. Keep in mind that so far we have confirmed the exchange of a box for a duffel bag. We need hard evidence if we want to advance against the warehouse. Call as soon as you're able to sneak and peek and verify if drugs are present. It's 6:00 am and all teams are deployed. Good luck."

"If drugs are there, we'll find them," Miguel said.

"Woof!" Badge confirmed.

"Oh! One last thing," Williams said. "It's your operation, you name it. Agree on a code name and inform me on your next communication, over and out."

Everybody in the team smiled, feeling energized.

"Wow! This is getting interesting," Miguel said.

"Yup! We have to double our efforts and be extremely alert," Robert said on the radio.

"What do you think about a name for this little operation?" James asked.

"What about, Sarge," Robert proposed.

"Hmm, like the name, but don't think the name of a team member is valid," James said. "It could be confusing. . . . What about Hummingbird?"

"Hummingbird?" Miguel asked. "Come on, we need something with more personality. What about Godzilla?"

Nobody answered. James shook his head and wrinkled his nose.

"I'm kidding! What about Lobo?" Miguel said.

"Lobo, Spanish for wolf?" James asked.

"Yes." Miguel said. "Dogs are a domesticated form of wolves, and we're the K9 team."

"How do you spell it, L-O-B-O?" Robert asked.

"Yes, plain and simple," Miguel said.

"Isn't that just a theory," James asked, "that dogs are descended from wolves?"

"Not anymore," Miguel said. "Dogs were classified as Canis familiaris centuries ago, a species belonging to the Canis family, like wolves, foxes, jackals—"

"And that changed," Robert said.

"Yes," Miguel confirmed. "A few years ago, scientists corrected the classification and the dog was classified as Canis Lupus familiaris. Not a species, but a sub-species of Canis Lupus, which refers to wolves."

"Wow! All that Latin makes my head hurt," James said. "Let's stick to English, if you don't mind."

"The grey wolf is the common ancestor of all dogs," Miguel said.

"All dogs?" James asked, "German Shepherd and Dutch Shepherd look a little like wolves, but Beagles and Dachshunds?"

"All dogs, from Yorkshire Terriers to English Mastiffs are the result of selective breeding done for thousands of years," Robert added.

"Wow! I didn't know all that," James said.

"Well, let me tell you that a recent study mentions that Chihuahuas may come from foxes and not from wolves, but it is not yet—"

"OK-OK-OK!" James interrupted. "I like Lobo. Count me as a yes vote."

"Lobo, count two more votes from Sarge and me," Robert said through the radio.

"Add another two from Badge and me," Miguel smiled. "Everybody likes—"

"Woof!" Badge interrupted and pressed an empty food bag with his right paw.

"What? You want cheeseburger as the codename?" Miguel asked.

"Woof!" Badge responded.

"Sorry, Badge," James said. "Operation Lobo has four votes, Operation Cheeseburger only one."

Badge whimpered.

"Don't you want to know the story about the Chihuahuas?" Miguel asked after a while.

Chapter 17: Dinodog

The garage door opened. A blue car driven by a woman backed out.

"Any sign of Chango?" Robert asked through the radio from the other car.

"Nope, keep looking," James said.

Hours passed and the team continued waiting.

Badge huffed.

"No, sir," Miguel said. "You're not getting burgers again. A fat police dog doesn't run fast and doesn't look good."

The house's front door opened. Chango came out, wearing blue overalls again.

"Finally! I hope he's going to work," Miguel said.

Robert and Sarge followed the pickup when it left. Miguel, James, and Badge waited.

"Do you know where is he going, 29?" James asked Robert a few minutes later.

"Seems he's going directly to the warehouse," Robert said. "We're halfway to it."

"OK, time to go to work, Badge." Miguel hooked the leash to Badge's collar and they stepped out of the Suburban.

"Voice check. Can you hear me?" James said to test the radio communication.

"Loud and clear," Miguel said as he and Badge crossed the street walking toward the house.

"Great! Now, stay alert for maids."

Miguel smiled. He went to the door and rang the bell. He waited. He knocked on the door. After a few moments, he knocked on the window. He wanted to be sure everybody had left before attempting the sneak and peek.

Badge started sniffing some bushes while Miguel scanned the neighboring houses. No lizards and no people were detected. Miguel took out his pick set and inserted two wire-like tools into the key hole. After some flicks and turns, he heard a click. He opened the door and knocked at the same time.

"Is anybody here?" he shouted as he and Badge entered. "There's a gas leak and the area has to be evacuated!"

"That was original," James said on the radio.

Miguel kept his attention on the doors and hallways. He and Badge needed to thoroughly search the house, but before they could, they had to be sure Chango didn't have any more friends or relatives around. "Kitchen is clear . . . living room, clear . . . laundry, clear . . . main bedroom, clear." Miguel stopped cold when he turned.

A hefty dog stood in the bedroom doorway, looking at them.

Miguel didn't move, but his heart was about to jump out of his body. "Is it an oversized pit bull, or is it a new species?" Miguel asked Badge.

The dog didn't move; but he watched the pair closely.

Miguel and Badge moved slowly toward the door. "Easy, easy, humongous puppy. We're all friends in here."

The pit bull growled.

Badge also growled.

"Houston, we have a problem," Miguel said on the radio.

"What's going on?" James asked.

"We discovered a new species; a mix of pit bull and dinosaur . . . Dinodog!" Miguel unhooked the leash from Badge's collar so he could move freely in case of a fight.

"Are you OK?" James asked.

"We're OK, but may not be for long," Miguel said with a quiet voice. "We're about to become breakfast."

The pit bull growled louder.

Badge responded the same way.

Miguel touched the grip of his handgun for a moment, but thought that idea better. He didn't want to use it. The pit bull was defending his home and didn't understand about search warrants or the Patriot Act.

Miguel kept moving towards the door. *If something's going to happen, better sooner than later.*

The dogs jumped at each other. Just when they were about to make contact, they stopped. Badge stretched out his front legs and bowed. The pit bull hesitated for a moment, and then did the same. Badge wagged his tail. He ran in a small circle, stopped, and bowed again, as if waiting. The pit bull mirrored Badge's movements.

Does Badge want to play or does he has a plan to distract the pit bull? Miguel wondered.

Badge ran from the bedroom followed by the other dog.

Moments later, the pit bull came back running, followed by Badge. When Badge took off, the other dog followed him.

The chase and follow game continued for several minutes, tromping over furniture, knocking down knick-knacks, and creating general havoc through the house.

"I guess I have to do my part," Miguel started looking for the drugs.

Minutes went by. The dogs continued playing, and Miguel couldn't find anything.

"Badge, come here! Come," Miguel called.

Badge approached followed by the pit bull.

"Find dope, Badge. Find dope. Go!" Miguel tapped the bed, the closet, and some furniture to make Badge search in those places.

Badge sniffed.

The pit bull growled again.

"Come, Badge! Come here," Miguel commanded. "Run, Badge! Run," he said and the chasing game with the pit bull resumed.

Miguel moved to another room. "Come, Badge! Find dope." Miguel pointed to different places to search and the sequence repeated.

The pit bull didn't like to be left alone and growled again.

"Come, Badge! Come. . . . Run!"

The house and its contents were in serious disarray with all sorts of fallen objects. Bed sheets, pillows, books, and clothes covered the floor.

This is frustrating. How can Badge find any drugs if he's not focused on the task? Miguel continued searching. He approached the chimney in the living room and felt around inside between the fire box and the flue. "Got something!" he said on the radio. "It's not a box, maybe just a metal bar." He pulled, it was loose. He pushed, then pulled and finally the object came free.

Another vase crashed on the floor, behind the dogs.

"What's this? Is it metal? *Andale!*"[45] Miguel realized what it was and tried to handle it as carefully as possible.

"What is it?" James asked.

"It's a folded Kriss."

"A folded what?"

"A Kriss. A Super Vector caliber 45," Miguel unfolded the stock, leaned the butt plate on his shoulder, and pulled the charger handle.

"Are you talking about a weapon?" James asked.

"Yes, a really nice piece. This isn't metal, it's a special polymer. Sub-machine gun, no recoil, ten to fifteen hundred rounds per minute. I have to get myself one like this."

"Well, the weapons link seems to be there," James said.

Miguel flipped the weapon over and checked the selector. "Semi, two-round, and full-auto modes. It's the military version!"

"Well, he didn't get that at the mini mart," James said.

With some sadness, Miguel folded the gun and tucked it back inside the chimney "Makes me wonder what happened to my MP5 that day in Veracruz."

"Can't reminisce now, Miguel, gotta keep moving," James said. "Who knows what else you may find."

Miguel called Badge again. "Come, Badge! Come here. . . . Dope. Find dope."

The pit bull wanted Badge's full attention and growled again.

Miguel didn't want to interrupt Badge again. Instead, he approached the pit bull. Each step he took the growling became stronger. He raised his right hand slowly, hoping it wasn't the last time he'd get to see it. "Easy, easy, doggie. I know you're a friend."

The pit bull's muzzle came up lightning quick, aiming for Miguel's hand.

Miguel didn't have time to retire his hand. Only to close his eyes.

The dog mouthed the hand softly and licked Miguel's fingers.

Badge sniffed and searched around the sofa in the living room.

Miguel tried to find something to clean the slobber from his hand and decided to go for the carpet. He petted the pit bull. More confident, Miguel moved to the kitchen and pointed to different places for Badge to search. The other dog followed them.

"We're starting to move faster now," Miguel said on the radio.

They advanced to the pantry.

The pit bull walked away and entered the laundry. "Woof, woof!" he barked.

"What's going on?" Miguel asked as he and Badge followed to see what he was barking about.

Badge pointed with his nose to several detergent boxes in front of the pit bull.

Miguel searched the boxes. At the bottom, he found one containing two cellophane-wrapped bricks.

"Is this what you wanted to show us?" Miguel asked the pit bull as he held up the bricks.

"Woof!" the dog replied.

Miguel opened the bricks to verify the content. As expected, both contained a white powder.

"Nice job, Badge." Miguel rewarded Badge with a tug-of-war game.

The pit bull growled.

"Do you want to play tug-of-war too?" Miguel asked.

Badge tilted his head as he watched Miguel being dragged by the pit bull during the tug-of-war play.

Miguel had to focus on the evidence, but the pit bull wouldn't release the towel. "What do I do now? . . . Badge!"

Miguel took photos and a sample of the substance, then wrapped the bricks and put everything back as he found it. Meanwhile, the pit bull dragged Badge, each dog pulling the towel in opposite directions.

"I think we're done in here," Miguel said through the radio.

"Well done, 56, now get out," James said.

A couple of minutes went by.

James worried, "What's happening? Are you cleaning that house too?" he asked.

"No, this time we found it clean and it'll be a mess as we go out, Miguel laughed as he turned around. "We're just saying goodbye to an old friend." He scratched the pit bull's belly.

"Well, hurry up!" James ended the communication.

"Sit together boys, I'll take you some pictures," Miguel said.

* * * * *

Miguel and Badge jumped into the Suburban, "A dog is going to be grounded today."

"Because of the mess?" James asked.

"Yes, he had a party and didn't ask for permission."

"Are you there, 29?" James called Robert.

"We're outside the warehouse," Robert said. "Still waiting for some action."

"You may get some soon. A search of Junkie Kong's house indicates he's loaded."

"As expected, but now confirmed. Does the Captain know?"

"I'm calling him right now. Stand by for instructions."

"Any news, team?" Captain Williams asked when Central transferred the call.

"Confirmed. Drugs and weapons are present in Junkie Kong's house," James said.

"Perfect! That's what we needed to proceed to the warehouse. Come to the office to document all the details. I'll instruct the other units to do the same."

"Ten-four."

"What's the name?"

"Who's name?" James asked.

"The operation."

"Lobo!" James, Robert, and Miguel responded at the same time.

"Lobo. Lima-Oscar-Bravo-Oscar? Wolf?"

"Yes, that's it," Miguel said.

"Short and clear, good work. Over and out."

* * * * *

The team gathered to have lunch. They took the burgers to a park to let the dogs eat and play afterward.

Badge already knew the routine. He ate his own burger, and later Miguel's.

Miguel also knew the routine. "I'll eat the fries," he said to Badge. "And don't think I'll buy another burger. You'll end up eating all of them, and that's too much".

After lunch, the team went to the DEA building and entered the details of the search of Chango's house into the database, including the location, estimated amount of drugs, the hidden weapon, and schedules of the occupants. "Friendly Pit Bull on premises," Miguel said as he typed in the comments section.

When they finished, Miguel and Badge used their spare time in target practice. Miguel wanted to be in the best shape possible. *Missing a target by a fraction of an inch during a raid, means that the target has an extra chance to shoot back.*

* * * * *

Back in the apartment, Miguel was too anxious to fall asleep. "The Captain said we have all the information to proceed against the warehouse," he said to Badge in his mat. "The operation can be launched at any moment." He picked up his guitar and started to play.

Badge lifted his head and watched Miguel.

"Walker, your footprints are the road, and nothing else," Miguel sang. *"Walker, there's no road. The road is made by walking—"*[46]

Badge howled.

"No, no! OK, no singing," Miguel said and continued only with the guitar.

Badge dropped his head, setting his chin on top of his rubber chicken. He closed his eyes.

Miguel thought he'd try singing again: *"Walking the road is made. And upon turning to look behind, the path that will never be used again is seen. Walker, there's no road, but wakes upon the sea—".*

Badge raised his head and howled again.

"All right, you win," Miguel said. He knew if he didn't stop singing, the neighbors would probably complain about the howling.

Badge's head went back to the mat.

The lone sound of the guitar continued.

Chapter 18: Riding the BEAR

The phone rang shocking Miguel awake. He sprang up from the bed, bumping and thumping his guitar, striking random chords as he grabbed and laid it on the bed. Miguel reached for the phone. His alarm clock showed 5:30 am. Badge gave him an interested look, stretched and yawned.

"This is Miguel."

"Lobo is in effect," James said.

"Awesome! Are we going in?"

"Don't know the details, but bring your tactical uniform. Be in the office at six-thirty." James hung up.

"Time to go to work, Badge," Miguel said when Badge was closing his eyes again.

* * * * *

Miguel and Badge arrived at the DEA building at 6:30 as instructed. The office was bustling with employees and agents preparing for operations. Uniformed officers gathered in groups, speaking in quiet tones. James waved Miguel over to where he, Robert, and Sarge were waiting.

"What's going on?" Miguel asked.

"We need to go to the conference room," Robert said. "The briefing is about to start."

"Anything I need to know before that?"

"No. It's been kept confidential so far," James said. "I expect this briefing will give us details on the warehouse raid and anything else they derived from our evidence."

According to procedure, everyone dropped his cell phone into a box before entering the conference room. Inside, some employees setup the projector while others placed folders on each of the chairs.

Captain Holder and the SWAT team arrived; ten members of the team were present. Miguel smiled when he saw Abira among them.

At least forty uniformed officers and twenty in plain clothes attended the briefing.

"Good morning," Captain Williams said as he walked to the front. "Operation Lobo is in effect. We're going to secure a warehouse located near the border. The evidence indicates they receive drugs and ship them to different cities in the country. Weapons may also be present. You'll see the address and blueprints in the documents provided. Lieutenant Thompson will now proceed with more details."

Thompson presented an aerial video of the warehouse and described the normal operation of Atlantic Trading, including the number of employees, truck movements, and operating hours.

"Most Mexican customers are *maquiladora* companies," Thompson said. "Most American customers are manufacturing companies. Auto parts and machine parts are expected in a normal operation. The trucks with shipments to American destinations leave in the morning. Receiving, from trucks crossing the border, happens all day long. The main purpose of the business is logistical shipping, consolidating products from different sources into single shipments to common destinations." He paused. "The operation will be conducted early this morning in order to capture any trucks before they depart for their deliveries on this side of the border."

Exterior photos of the 50,000-square-foot warehouse, shipping areas, main entrance, rear access, and emergency exits were presented and explained in detail.

"Now the strategy," Williams said. "The operation consists of taking the premises by surprise. The SWAT team in the BEAR will lead the convoy and take up a station at the main entrance. Two units behind the BEAR will take side roads, continue all the way to the rear of the building and cover those exits. The three following units will go left, cover the shipment area and secure any truck preparing to leave. The next unit will go right and cover the emergency exit on that side of the facility. The last two units will establish a blockade at the entrance. They'll prevent anybody from leaving and detain anyone attempting to enter."

Williams reviewed some documents. "Once the perimeter is established and the operation has begun, two transport buses and an ambulance will arrive. The buses will stop at the parking lot entrance preventing any vehicle movement in the area. Their primary purpose will be to transport suspects taken into custody during the operation."

Captain Williams received an additional folder and paused to read it. He smiled. "There will also be simultaneous raids on El Pollo's apartment and Chango's house."

A complete envelope operation, Miguel smiled, proud that their reconnaissance and evidence-gathering had been useful.

"Be alert for weapons and treat all employees with both caution and respect," Captain Williams said. "We don't know if all employees are involved in illegal activities. Good luck and stand by for group assignments."

Thompson read out the team assignments. Robert, Miguel, and the dogs would be attached to the SWAT team in the BEAR. James would drive the Suburban. Captain Williams and other agents would ride with him. "Everybody has to be in their assigned transport in twenty minutes,"

Thompson said. "Let's make the Lobo bite the tentacles of the Octopus." The conference ended at 7:30 am.

The teams started to gather in groups to review strategies and positions.

Miguel and Badge stood at the same time, prepared to join Robert and Sarge. As Miguel collected the documents he'd received about the operation he felt a tug on his shirt sleeve.

"Hey!" Abira greeted him.

"Hey, how are you?" Miguel said, pleasantly surprised. "Are you ready?" he asked, far more relaxed than he'd been outside the bank.

"Yes, ready and excited about the operation's intensity," Abira said. One hand went to her necklace. She fingered it nervously.

As her fingers flicked and rubbed the pendant, Miguel realized it was a Star of David. "Yes, we'll hit them hard this time," he said. "I've been waiting a long time for this."

"Really? You must have had interesting experiences with the Policía Federal. I guess you have a good story to tell."

"Maybe not be the happiest story, but it's still worth telling."

"I'd love to hear it," Abira said, tilting her head to the right. "But, right now, I have to go."

"Good luck, and watch yourself," Miguel said.

Abira turned away.

Miguel finished picking up his stuff. When he raised his head, he noticed Robert, James, and members of the SWAT team staring at him.

Miguel turned to the left, then to the right. "What?"

Some of the SWAT team members smiled and left, others avoided Miguel's question and returned to their activities.

"We just haven't seen that kind of behavior in Abira before," the SWAT member closest to Miguel said. "She's never interested in starting a casual conversation with a guy. This must be serious- Sorry! I should introduce myself before I give you a good ribbing. I'm Tim Carter, A6." He shook hands with Miguel, James, and Robert. "We met after the bank standoff."

"Yes, I remember," Miguel said. "Is it A6 or Amber 6?"

"The official code is A6. The call out for A is defined for each operation, taking care there's no conflict with other units. Well, I have to go. See you on the BEAR guys."

The team went to the armory, and each received an M4A1[47] assault rifle. Miguel packed multiple cartridges for the rifle and for his Colt handgun.

They proceeded to the Suburban to collect their helmets, radios, and vests, including Sarge and Badge's.

Robert tugged on his chinstrap and smiled at Miguel who had forgotten to tighten his properly.

* * * * *

Miguel and Badge climbed into the BEAR followed by Robert and Sarge. The SWAT team already occupied their seats, eight in the back and two in the front. Miguel took a seat on one side and Badge sat on the floor. Robert and Sarge did the same on the opposite side.

Miguel studied the BEAR. He had participated in several raids that required this kind of transport and protection when he was in the Special Operations Group of the Policía Federal. The BEAR looked like a bigger version of the armored trucks used to transport money and other valuables, but the BEAR's interior was different. Miguel noticed the roof hatch, designed so a SWAT sharpshooter could take careful aim and shoot while thoroughly protected. It also facilitated access to a building's second floor from the BEAR's roof, or a third floor with the use of a portable ladder carried on the vehicle.

"Group Two, go," a voice commanded on the radio. "Group Three, head out."

Two plain black SUVs formed Group Two. They left the parking lot and turned right. According to the briefing, they would go south taking State Highway 163 and then Interstate 5. An unmarked SUV and a car formed Group Three. They turned left to go south, taking Interstate 15 and then Interstate 805.

Miguel and Badge waited two long minutes.

"Group One, go." the voice in the radio ordered. The BEAR and two cars rolled out. They turned right to follow highway 163 until they could move onto Interstate 805 about halfway to their destination.

After the BEAR had moved several blocks away, "Group Four, go," was heard through the radio. James and Captain Williams were in that group. They would do the opposite; initially take Interstate 15, and later Interstate 5.

The multiple routes used by the assault teams made them and the pending operation less conspicuous to sinister groups or the media.

The BEAR and the other two vehicles in the group proceeded along their designated route, sirens off and flowing with other traffic. When they reached highway 163, they increased speed.

Miguel looked around at his team members. Some chewed gum, others checked their rifles, and some watched out the front windows no doubt anxious to stay focused on their progress toward the target—the BEAR's side windows were too high and narrow to be used while seated. Miguel kept focused and steadied his nerves by reviewing the team member identifications: A1 designated Captain Holder, seated at the front; A2, Gregg, one of the snipers; A3, Wu, the other sniper; A4, Rajeev, at the wheel; A5, Abira, and A6, Tim. The other four team members had been assigned the codes B1 to B4.

Miguel stole a peek at Abira. She sat on the other side, just behind the driver. *It was nice to talk to her after the briefing.* The Star of David she wore was now covered by the balaclava. *Seems she's a person of faith, different religion, same God. Why so many different religions for the same God?* Miguel wondered. *Only on planet Earth.*

What everybody had in common is that nobody talked. Even the dogs were still. Each team member was lost in his or her thoughts, getting mission-ready. The last time Miguel was in a similar situation was a year and a half earlier. For a moment, he found himself back in the Falcon with his old team. *They were quiet, chewing gum, contemplating the snow on top of the dormant volcanoes, and the majestic red-orange sun over Veracruz.*

"Units Ten and Eleven, go," the voice on the radio said. Miguel was drawn away from his old memories.

Ten is for you, Pollo. You won't be able to attend the golf course today, and for a long time. Eleven is for you, Chango. I hope you feed our friend the pit bull before you're taken away.

Group Three turned east into State Highway 905. Group Two reached them and moved to the front. Moments later, Group One, with the BEAR, joined and advanced to the front of the column. Group Four approached and continued in the rear. As established in the mission protocol, all units turned on their vehicle lights but not their sirens. If a civilian car obstructed the path, the BEAR's driver honked to get the driver's attention. At red traffic lights, they reduced speed, and then accelerated as soon as the cross traffic moved from the intersection. *Not the fastest way to go through, but a silent one.*

They took a street to the south when the convoy reached the area of warehouses near the border.

"Get ready," Captain Williams shouted in the radio.

Miguel kissed his crucifix.

The vehicles turned east to travel the final block to the warehouse. When they reached Atlantic Trading, one by one the units turned south into the property.

"Hold tight," the driver shouted. The BEAR didn't stop at the gate nor did it reduce speed. It crashed through the wire mesh and kept moving.

Chapter 19: Scratching the Metal

The man in the guardhouse stared at the assault convoy, seeming unsure of what to do.

The BEAR continued toward the building and stopped beside the front door. All the other units followed their designated routes and moved into position.

"Go, go, go!" Captain Holder shouted. Weapons drawn, everybody jumped out, quickly but with military-style order. They divided into two groups, proceeding single file, behind the leader who carried a shield. Robert and Sarge were assigned the rearmost position in one column, while Miguel and Badge were at the end of the other. Two agents opened the main entrance doors, and the columns advanced.

By the time the front desk receptionists stood up, ten officers and two dogs had already gone down the hall. One SWAT officer stayed by the front desk and another one went to check the offices nearby. The main group entered the warehouse through a second door.

The two SWAT groups divided into four and started a fast check of the 50,000-square-foot warehouse. Their guns zigzagged as they scanned the area. Their immediate objective was to find armed personnel.

The employees in the warehouse stopped their activities, staring at the advancing officers with wide, fearful eyes. "Are we under arrest?" one man asked. Some people raised their hands without even being told, still others shouted out questions.

The agents in the shipping area did a fast walk-through, checking the parked trucks. Some of the agents from the units behind the building forced a door open, and entered the warehouse.

213

The guard out by the gate was disarmed and taken inside where he could be monitored during the operation.

"We have a search warrant," Captain Williams said to the receptionists when he entered the building. He put the paper on top of the counter. "Who's in charge?"

Silence. Two surprised faces stared back at him.

Soon, the Captain's radio blared out status messages from the teams: "Group Three, clear;" "Group One, on the rear, clear;" "Group Two, clear." The SWAT team, that had the biggest area to cover, took more time to report: "Group One, inside, clear." Captain Williams sent his own message: "Group Four, clear. Gather everybody."

The agents directed the employees and drivers to an empty area in the middle of the warehouse. Around sixty people were put in line next to a wall guarded by ten agents. In the parking lot, another ten agents secured the warehouse perimeter.

Only one firearm was found in the general search, the one from the guard.

Twenty agents proceeded to conduct a thorough search of the facility.

"OK, let's go." Robert commanded half of them to search the inside of the building.

"Follow me," Miguel ordered the other half to search the trucks and building exterior.

Miguel made two teams. Each would perform an in depth search of six trucks, one at a time, for a total of twelve. "Come, Badge. Dope, find dope." He and Badge made a quick inspection around each of the trucks.

The agents inside the trailers opened each box and container they found. Besides drugs, they also looked for weapons.

* * * * *

Badge made no indication of drugs on the external inspection.

"Let's check the inside, Badge. Heel." Both jumped into one of the trucks to perform a detailed search. "Find dope, Badge. Find dope," Miguel tapped the places he wanted Badge to give special attention to.

Inside the warehouse, Robert and Sarge executed the same kind of operation. Ten agents formed a line, with twenty-foot gaps between them, and they advanced rear to front of the building. As they advanced, each agent checked boxes, containers, or equipment in their assigned area. Robert took Sarge around piles of boxes and equipment.

Time went by, Miguel and Badge continued with the detailed inspection inside the trailers.

"Nothing in the first six trucks," Miguel reported on the radio. "We're starting the other six."

Robert and Sarge scanned the warehouse. Sarge didn't detect anything suspicious. None of the agents found anything out of the ordinary, only auto parts, and appliances.

Two agents searched the offices, primarily for drugs and weapons; they also checked invoices, bills of lading, and any records that could contain valuable information. Some documents were also seized for a more thorough inspection at the DEA building.

Williams moved from the offices to the warehouse, and then to the shipping area to monitor the operation.

Employees and drivers sat on the floor and chatted, often staring suspiciously at the armed agents. One agent requested their identifications and recorded their names and information so they could be cross-checked for criminal records in the database.

Miguel, Badge, and their team continued searching without finding drugs or weapons.

Robert, Sarge, and their team got no results the first time. They searched again.

Williams walked around the three areas for a fourth time. Each time his face reflected more concern.

The teams checked and double-checked.

Miguel leaned against the front wall inside a trailer. "Knock now," he said into the radio to Mark, who was outside.

Mark knocked with a metal bar.

"Stop it, stop it!" Miguel said rubbing his ear. "Plain and simple metal."

Another twenty minutes went by.

Miguel and his group finished the search in the trucks, and around the building still finding nothing. "Let's go, Badge." He and Badge walked into the warehouse to give Captain Williams a pessimistic report.

The agents searching the offices reported the same results.

It still took several minutes for the final report from the team in the warehouse. Disappointed, Robert approached Captain Williams and shook his head.

"How did we get it all wrong?" James asked. "All the time we spent on this operation and the evidence at Chango's and El Pollo's but there's nothing here?"

Williams walked from one side to the other. He crossed his arms over his chest and covered his mouth with his left hand, thinking. "It's not that," he said. "We didn't get it wrong, but they were faster and smarter than us."

Miguel studied the employees; most of them looked bored. Some of them looked at each other and smiled. *Why are they smiling?* He wondered. *There seems to be a smaller clique within the big group, and they're the ones grinning. What's going on?*

"Everybody back to the vehicles," Williams shouted, completely upset.

Some agents cursed, others lowered their heads.

"Pa' su mecha!"[48] Miguel said and lowered his head at the same time. "The first big operation and the first big blunder."

"You are clear to go," James said to the employees. "Go back to your activities."

The agents walked back to their vehicles.

Robert, Miguel, and the dogs walked back to the front of the warehouse. They did it slowly, trying to use every second left to give the dogs' noses time to find something.

When Robert passed beside a pile of timbers, Sarge turned his head. Robert stopped to give Sarge more time. The agents had gone through that area several times. The other side of the pile was visible through the loosely stacked wood. The rough boards were scrap material from pallets and shipping crates.

James, Miguel, and Badge approached.

"Anything here?" Miguel asked.

"I don't know." Robert kicked a few of the boards from the pile.

Sarge scratched some of them.

"If he's doing that, there's a reason," Robert said.

"Could that material be part of a container previously used to transport drugs?" James asked, trying to find an explanation.

Sarge continued scratching.

"Something's there," Robert said. "I don't know what, but there's something."

Sarge tugged against the leash. He didn't point with his nose but became excited and started bouncing from one side to the other.

"Charlie-Whiskey, we may have something," James called Captain Williams.

Robert and Miguel moved more boards. On the floor beneath them, they found a square of sheet metal.

"What's that?" Williams asked when he arrived.

"No idea," Robert said.

"Everybody back to your previous positions," Williams ordered on the radio. "Gather all employees and drivers again."

Miguel, Robert, and other agents removed all the discarded wood from the area, leaving the metal plate fully exposed. It was square, about six-foot by six-foot.

Sarge and Badge forgot the timbers and began scratching the metal plate.

"It's the platform of a cargo scale!" Miguel said. "Common in warehouses".

What isn't common are two drug detection dogs scratching it," Robert said.

The large floor scale was a standard type used to weigh pallets and crates before loading on trucks.

Miguel checked out the surrounding area. "There should be a computer or control panel nearby." He knew there should be a place to monitor and record each item's weight. He spotted a panel on the closest wall and went to it.

"It doesn't work," one of the employees shouted. Miguel stopped and turned to see who had made the comment.

Miguel proceeded toward the panel and pushed several buttons. Nothing happened. *That was one of the smiling guys. If he says it doesn't work, then I'll bet he's lying.* Miguel located a breaker box in the same wall. He flipped open the cover. Each breaker switch had a label. He read them aloud while the team waited. "Lights one, lights two, overhead door one, overhead door two, ventilation, don't touch. . . . don't touch?" Miguel turned that switch on.

An electric motor started a hydraulic equipment. Everybody turned in different directions, trying to locate the source of the sounds.

Mark knelt down and put a hand on the scale. "The noise comes from the floor beneath the scale."

The agents around them stared at Miguel and Mark, looking confused.

Miguel smiled. "It's not a scale. It's a hydraulic lift!" He walked back to the panel. "Careful! Everybody get back." He tried the buttons again.

The lift bumped and thumped, and then the metallic plate began to sink.

"That's more original than a pregnant mule," Miguel said.

The agents pointed their rifles into the deepening hole. The platform moved down, out of sight in the dark, bumping to a stop when it hit bottom.

Robert flicked on his flashlight and shined it around the lower level. "There's a ladder," he said. "Miguel, the access should be about eight feet to your right."

Miguel followed the directions and reached a stack of timbers against the wall. He shoved it over, the wood smacking onto the concrete floor. "Here it is," he said when he found a hatch. He opened it and took out

219

his flashlight. "I'm going in." He went down the ladder. "Expect the unexpected," he said softly as he reached the floor below.

Above, everybody waited.

Miguel located another panel. "Anybody want a ride?" He pushed a button and the platform rose back to the main level.

Williams was the first one onto the platform when it reached the upper floor. Robert, the dogs, Mark, and another agent joined him.

"Ready!" Williams shouted.

Miguel pressed another button and the platform came down.

"This is a beefy piece of equipment," Williams said tapping the platform with one foot. "It could easily support a ton."

The platform went all the way down, and stopped level with the basement floor.

Miguel located a light switch and turned it on. Several rows of fluorescent fixtures flickered on. The basement appeared to be a room approximately twenty feet long on each wall. A couple of pallet movers occupied an area next to the lift, but of more interest to the men were the stacks of small wooden boxes lining one wall.

Sarge and Badge started pointing to the boxes with their noses.

"Somebody bring a crowbar," Williams shouted as other agents came down the ladder.

A couple of agents grabbed boxes and set them on the floor near the Captain.

"There are forty boxes, Captain," Robert said.

"Here's a crowbar," an agent said above. He let it fall to be caught by Miguel.

Miguel went directly to one of the boxes. He stuck the bar's end under the top edge and levered the lid up.

Mark grabbed the loose lid and removed it.

Rows of perfectly aligned cellophane-wrapped bricks filled the box. "They have the same size as the ones in El Pollo's apartment and in Chango's house," Miguel said.

After one of the boxes was emptied, Robert counted the bricks. "Twenty-five bricks per box, times forty boxes, equals a thousand bricks. . . . Times two pounds each, equals two thousand pounds," he said. "A ton of what appears to be pure cocaine."

Williams finally smiled. "It's official! Read those people their rights and start the arrests," he commanded.

"Bring the transport buses to the shipping area," James said on the radio and commanded the officers to separate the people in two groups.

Other agents continued opening boxes to confirm the content.

"Great job, boy. Great job," Miguel rewarded Badge with a tug-of-war game.

All the agents smiled, offered each other high-fives and a few even cheered. Sarge's sharp sense of smell had turned their mission from failure to success.

While playing with Badge, Miguel noticed a wood panel attached to one wall.

He left the towel hanging on Badge's mouth and walked toward the wall. The eight-by-four wood panel seemed peculiar surrounded by all the concrete. He stood in front of the wall, studying it and the floor.

"What's going on Miguel? Another hunch?" Robert asked, standing beside him.

Williams joined them.

"Look at the dirt on the floor and some of the boxes," Miguel said. "Where did it come from?"

"Well, not from the warehouse," Williams said. "The floor was clean."

"The dirt goes to the wood panel." Miguel pointed at the trail on the floor. He tugged one side of the panel.

Robert went to the other side and tugged. The panel was fixed to the wall.

Williams gave a hand command and the surrounding agents raised their weapons.

Miguel felt the panel moved when he pushed upwards, "Robert, it seems to slide up. I think we have to do it at the same time. . . . One, two, three!"

They pushed up, and the panel detached easily. Behind it, they found an empty black hole, about five feet tall and three feet wide.

Miguel switched on his flashlight and pointed it into the void. "It's a tunnel!"

The sides and the ceiling were rock and soil.

Miguel and Badge went inside to have a better look. They walked slowly. The flashlight revealed more and more of the same, rocks, soil, and more darkness. The sides and the ceiling were irregular. The floor was flat and clear of rocks and debris.

Miguel turned back. The entrance could be seen as a small opening in the distance. He estimated they had walked one hundred feet. "Let's go back, Badge," he said.

Badge emerged from the opening followed by Miguel.

"What did you find, Miguel?" the Captain asked. "Does it go to another hidden room?"

"Nope, I think this one goes all the way to Mexico."

Chapter 20: March into Hell

The hidden room became the new center of operations. Captain Williams, Captain Holder, the team, and others were there. Options were being discussed.

"Protocol suggests we should call the Mexican authorities and ask them to look for the other end of the tunnel," Williams said. "We do our part and wait for them to do theirs. What do you think?"

"It's the correct procedure, but it could take days or weeks for them to find the other end of the tunnel," James said. "It could go to a garage or a cantina. We can't even tell them where to start looking."

"I think we should go through the tunnel and find out what's on the other side," Miguel said.

"I agree. We use the tunnel, and when we get to the other side, we call the Mexican authorities from there," Robert said.

"Whatever we do has to be done now," Holder said. "We're losing the surprise factor as we speak.

Sarge and Badge turned their heads watching whoever was speaking as if they understood the options.

"Well, I agree," Williams said. "We have a consensus that we have to act now. Next, what do we do? Do we send a team? How many?"

"We could still cause an international incident if we send armed personnel into a foreign country," Holder said.

"Traffickers rely on just this sort of hesitation and the limitations put on us by government courtesies and protocols," James said.

"We're cleared to go," Miguel said, patting Badge's head.

"Woof," Badge agreed.

"Yes, Miguel, the dogs, and I can go," Robert explained. "We're cleared under the DEA-FAST program. We can execute operations on both sides of the border."

"You can operate on both sides of the border, but the Mexicans have to be informed," Williams said.

"Again, bureaucracy inhibits us from a surprise operation," Miguel said. "We should inform the Mexican authorities if we find out we're in Mexico when we surface. At that moment, it will be a proven fact."

"OK, I agree with that, but sending two agents is quite different from sending twenty," Williams said.

"Woof!" Sarge barked once.

Everyone looked at the dogs.

"Sorry! Two agents and two dogs," Williams corrected himself. "I can't order the two of you—sorry, the four of you—to do that, go into an unknown situation without support, especially when it's literally a dark hole."

"You don't have to, sir. We volunteer," Robert said taking a step forward.

Sarge also moved forward.

"Yes, we volunteer," Miguel said, also stepping forward.

Badge followed him.

"I didn't expect less from you," Williams said. "If that's your decision, then get ready." He turned to James and whispered, "Are those dogs trained to do that, or is it my imagination playing tricks on me?"

* * * * *

Robert and Miguel checked their Colt handguns, M4A1 rifles, and radios. Each one received an additional flashlight and extra ammunition.

"Give us the address as soon as you reach the other side so we can inform the Mexican police," Williams said. "Do not engage in any shooting if you don't get support from the Mexican police. Return immediately if you encounter hostile personnel."

"You'll lose radio contact when you get deeper into the tunnel and will get it back when you surface," Holder said.

"Be careful of booby traps," James warned. "The conditions of the tunnel could also be dangerous. Keep a sharp eye for crumbling walls or ceiling cracks and falling debris."

"Don't worry, we'll be OK," Robert said and went into the tunnel with Sarge on his heel.

"You remind me of my mother." Miguel said. "Now, I wonder why I volunteered." He laughed and went into the tunnel followed by Badge.

The group started walking in the darkness. They would keep radio contact as long as possible.

"Approximately one hundred feet, all clear," Miguel called when they got to the point he'd reached before.

"Ten-four," James said.

Some parts of the tunnel had wood supports along the walls and on the ceiling.

"One hundred and fifty feet."

"Ten-four."

The group advanced checking the floor ahead for a hole or a trap, but then the tunnel's condition could be more dangerous than a trap. Faulty construction or a collapse could kill all of them within seconds.

"Two hundred feet, I think."

James responded, but what he said was distorted and unintelligible.

"We've lost contact already?" Robert asked. "I guess the tunnel is deeper than we expected. It seems we're at the gates of hell."

"To be willing to march into hell for a heavenly cause,"[49] Miguel said, making reference to the song he always hummed.

"Don Miguel of La Mancha and his lean dog Badge Rocinante in their chivalrous quest."

"I guess that makes you Sancho Robert Panza and Sarge Rucio."

The laughs filled the cramped tunnel, echoing out into the darkness.

As they proceeded, the tunnel grew increasingly damp, until they reached a flooded section which slowed their pace.

Sarge and Badge growled and tugged on their leashes when the flashlights' glare sent a bunch of rats scurrying for cover. "Stop it!" "No!" Robert and Miguel ordered and silence returned.

"I wonder if those were American or Mexican rats." Miguel said.

"Does it matter?" Robert asked.

"If they're Mexican, could mean we're closer to the exit. If they're American, we still have a long way to go."

"Very funny," Robert said not sounding at all amused. "Why don't you ask them if they speak Spanish?"

They continued walking for a while. The floor had become slippery and constantly damp now, causing Robert and Miguel to keep a hand on one wall at all times to avoid falling. Having an extra pair of legs, the dogs were more sure-footed and seemed to have no trouble.

"I estimate we've walked over eight hundred feet," Robert said.

"The warehouse is two blocks away from the border," Miguel said. "That's nine hundred to one thousand feet. So, we're still in America. Those rats were American."

"Well, they could be Mexican rats looking for a new home in the north," Robert said.

"Maybe American on their way south, looking for better food," Miguel replied.

The men and their four-legged partners continued through the tunnel. The air was stagnant and wet, smelling of mud, decay, and something irritatingly pungent. The dogs panted. Robert and Miguel breathed like long distance runners.

"What's that?" Miguel asked. He pointed to a metal plate with a giant screw on the ceiling.

"I think those are called anchors," Robert said. "They're used in mines and underground construction to prevent a collapse."

"Thanks, to whoever did it."

They had been in the tunnel about twenty minutes; it felt like they had walked for hours.

They found several boxes full of drugs. "It seems somebody was in a hurry and had to leave them," Robert said.

"We should have crossed into Mexico by now," Miguel said after a while. "If we're halfway, then the worst case is that we have to walk out to Mexico as long as it took us to walk in." Miguel tried to cheer Robert up—and himself.

"I'm all for going forward instead of back, if that's the case," Robert said. "Wish we could be sure."

Dripping walls, slippery rocks, rats, and looming claustrophobia were all they encountered for several hundred feet more. The march continued while the dark tunnel, their way back to security, grew out longer and longer behind them.

Moments later, Miguel realized they were not panting as heavily as before. The quality of the air had improved. "We should be close to an exit."

At the entrance of the tunnel, Williams, Holder, and James became impatient.

"All the people are in the buses," a voice said on the radio.

Everybody anxiously awaited news from the tunnel, but transporting the suspects and seizing the drugs still had to be addressed.

"Take the suspects to the detention center for processing," Williams ordered. "Secure the warehouse and start gathering evidence."

In the tunnel, Miguel was growing impatient again. "I guess we've walked another eight hundred feet from the estimated border. Can this be that long?"

"Shh!" Robert interrupted. "I hear something."

A soft sound came from the darkness in front of them. It was continuous and uniform, but stopped after a while. It was different than the rats' squeaking.

After walking a few more feet, a tiny light shone out of the deep blackness. They walked slower trying their best to be silent. As they advanced, the light took the form of a ring.

"What's that?" Miguel asked about the light with a quiet voice.

"The entrance to hell, maybe." Robert said keeping his voice down.

Stronger and closer, the sound started again. Then it stopped. "That's an electric motor." Robert said.

In a short time, they reached the light, so faint that they thought it was farther down the tunnel. The light was less a circle now and more a square. The dark center wasn't empty. "Another wood panel," Miguel said. "We're at the opening."

The motor started again. The noise was even stronger, almost vibrating the ground beneath their feet.

"That's another hydraulic lift," Miguel said when the sound stopped.

They located two hooks in the wood panel and two eyes screwed into the sides of the tunnel.

"Same configuration as on the other side," Robert said.

"Now, what?" Miguel asked.

"Now, we go in."

"Any idea how we should prepare for this?"

"Get ready with your handgun," Robert said. "We don't have enough space to use the rifles. On the count of three, you lift the panel from the bottom, and I'll push."

"OK, I get it. But what happens after that?"

"We arrest whoever is out there and get the location. Be careful, we don't know how many people we're facing or if they're armed. Stay low and be ready to hide until we have a clear picture of what's going on."

"OK, I'm ready," Miguel said when his hands were under the panel.

Robert started to count. "One, two—"

"Wait, wait, wait!" Miguel interrupted trying not to raise his voice.

"What?"

"The light! We'll be blind until our eyes adjust. Use the flashlight and point it at your face to make your eyes get used to the light again."

They became momentarily blinded when they pointed their own flashlights at their faces. A moment later, their eyes had adjusted and they took their positions.

"Ready again," Miguel said.

"OK," Robert said, "One, two, and three."

* * * * *

Miguel pulled, and Robert pushed. The panel fell out and away from them. Agents and dogs stormed into a room.

A couple of men carrying boxes stopped mid step, mouths agape.

"*Alto ahi!*"[50] Miguel ordered as he pointed his gun at them.

"Don't move!" Robert extended his weapon, ready to shoot if one of the men attacked.

229

Miguel scanned the room. It was identical to the one at the other side. A hydraulic-scissor lift sat mid-room. At that moment the platform was raised, so the opening above them was closed off by the platform.

Sarge and Badge stood quite still, at the ready beside their handlers.

One of the men eased his left hand toward an AK-47 machine gun leaning against the wall.

"Don't even think about it," Miguel warned.

Robert handcuffed and searched the two men.

"You don't know who you're messing with," one man threatened.

"We'll ask about that later," Miguel said. "Where are we? What's the address?"

"*Vete al Diablo!*"[51] the man said.

The other man also responded with a curse in Spanish, a more personal one about Miguel's mother.

Robert aimed his gun at the man's head. "Watch your mouth." He took a roll of duct tape from the top of a nearby box and used it to cover their mouths, then used it to secure their feet. They forced the two men to sit against a wall where they could keep an eye on them while they looked around.

"Look," Miguel pointed to a huge fan on wheels.

"I see," Robert said. "That explains how they carry those boxes through a tunnel full of stale air."

Miguel and Robert inspected the boxes. Some were similar to the drug-packed ones on the other side, but the others were bigger.

"Find dope, Badge. Find dope," Miguel commanded while tapping the big boxes.

Robert and Sarge did the same.

Neither dog made the signal for drugs.

"Well, let's see what we have," Robert said.

Robert and Miguel pulled a big box from a stack and put it on the floor.

"It's light compared to the others," Miguel said as he took out his radio. "Support, this is Kilo Niner 56, do you copy?"

"Finally, we were about to send the Marines for you!" James said.

"We're in a room, same configuration. We have two bogies in custody."

"Do you have an address?" James asked.

"No, not yet. The bogies didn't want to cooperate but we found some boxes. We're about to open them to see what we're dealing with."

"OK, but make it fast."

Robert turned two small handles, pressed, and then raised the lid. "What's that?"

Inside the box was a tube, four feet long with a telescopic sight on top, a handle, and a trigger below.

"That's a MANPAD,"[52] Miguel said to Robert and through the radio. "A portable missile launcher."

"A missile launcher?" Robert asked.

"Yes, to fire surface to air Stinger missiles."

"Why would they want something like this?"

"To knock down a surveillance plane, a competitor, the plane of a politician that refuses to be bribed . . . resale is always an option."

"OK, OK, you made your point."

"What else do they have?" Williams joined the transmission.

"Well, there are several boxes like this one," Miguel said. "I guess more launchers."

Sarge sat and placed a paw on top of a box.

"Hold on, we'll open a different kind of box," Robert said. "Sarge made the signal for explosives."

Miguel opened the box. He let out a long slow whistle. "RPGs, rocket-propelled grenades. The launchers should be near."

"Wow! Fragmentation grenades," Robert said after opening a different box.

"Seems like Christmas for terrorists," Miguel said as he moved toward another pile of boxes.

A hydraulic noise interrupted their search. The scissor lift was retracting bringing down the platform.

The team hid behind the boxes. There was no time to hide the tied guys, they were in the open.

"Hurry up with those boxes!" a voice from above shouted.

Noise from above came down with the lift, the whine of forklifts, and yelling.

Badge raised his head above the boxes.

Miguel did the same as he aimed his M4A1 rifle up at the shaft. He couldn't detect any movement and decided to rise.

"We have to get out and find the address," Robert said. "Put some boxes on the lift, enough to have some cover. I guess it doesn't matter if we make noise moving the boxes. It's what the people above expect."

Miguel dragged boxes to the lift platform while Robert guarded, aiming his rifle to the shaft.

"Make sure to put boxes containing launchers or rifles, not the ones containing grenades or rockets," Robert warned in case of a shooting.

"Done, four stacked boxes on each side," Miguel said.

"Ready?" Robert asked as he stood next to the control panel with the buttons.

Miguel gave a thumbs-up, and he and Badge hid between the boxes.

Robert pressed the button that activated the lift and jumped onto the platform with Sarge. They also hid between the boxes as the lift went up.

Badge and Sarge showed their heads above the boxes, curious about what might be up there.

The lift stopped on the next floor. The team made a fast visual inspection. Nobody was nearby.

It appeared to be another warehouse, a smaller one. People moved back and forth on the other side. A couple of forklifts carried boxes to what appeared to be a ten-wheeled stake-bed truck parked in the shipping area.

The team moved in the opposite direction, trying to find a way out to get the location. They walked among stacked boxes of different sizes and checked the ones that differed from those they inspected down below. One large box contained long cylinders with a glass in the front.

"I guess these are the Stingers," Robert said.

"Yup!" Miguel said. "That's what you can buy when you sell a couple pounds of cocaine."

They reached a heavy metal door at the rear corner of the warehouse.

"It's welded to the frame," Miguel said after pulling it several times.

"These people should know about fire codes," Robert said.

"No way in for thieves, but no way out either."

They turned and looked for another exit.

Miguel moved between piles of boxes, dashing and taking cover behind the next pile as quickly as possible. He turned and gave hand commands to Badge.

Badge left the previous pile of boxes and joined Miguel.

Robert and Sarge did the same. In this fashion, they worked their way around the perimeter, avoiding workers who moved and packed stock in the middle of the facility.

"A different box, what's in here?" Miguel asked as he stopped to investigate.

"AK-47s," Robert said when they opened the box.

"Sort of expected in a standard weapons shipment," Miguel said. "It's like French fries, they're served with everything."

A little further back in the warehouse, they found yet another type of box. "The RPG launchers," Robert said. "These and the rocket grenades were designed to be used as antitank weapons."

"Now they're used for everything," Miguel said. "Even to hunt rabbits—"

A series of fast knocks made the box tremble. The launchers started to jump inside and splinters started to fly. A stream of quick pops from a machine gun came from the other side of the warehouse.

Chapter 21: Smoke Signal

Robert and Sarge dove behind a stack of boxes. Miguel and Badge ducked behind the adjacent stack.

The firing continued.

We've been discovered, under fire, and worst of all, cornered! Miguel turned around trying to find the place the shots came from. *The scissor lift is too far. If we ever get out, we have to make our way through enemy fire.* "Down, Badge. Stay," he commanded. Until then, the stack he and Badge used for cover hadn't been hit by any bullets. Robert had all the attention of the gunmen. The boxes he and Sarge used for cover were hit several times.

Miguel threw himself on the floor and rolled. He located a gunman, aimed his M4A1 and fired a round.

The man fell, knocking over several boxes.

Robert fired back, downing a second attacker, but others joined the fight. "Stay down, Sarge," he commanded.

"How many shooters do you see?" Miguel shouted.

"Two down and at least another two hidden among the boxes."

The agents and gunmen alternated shooting at each other. When Miguel and Robert fired, the gunmen took cover. When the gunmen fired, Miguel and Robert ducked to reload.

"We have to end this or we'll run out of ammo," Robert yelled. "I'll fire, and when I take cover you have to be ready to shoot."

When a pause came from the other side, Robert and Miguel rose above the boxes. Robert shot and Miguel prepared.

Robert emptied his cartridge and hid to reload.

A second later, a gunman rose to shoot.

Miguel aimed immediately and shot, taking him down.

More shots were exchanged, and Miguel ducked. He couldn't locate the other gunman.

Another burst of bullets hit the boxes where Robert and Sarge hid. Pieces of wood splintered into the air.

Among all the flying debris, Miguel saw Robert turn abruptly and fall on his back. "Are you OK?" he shouted.

Robert groaned in pain.

From his position, Miguel could see Robert's right sleeve starting to turn red.

Robert rolled to his side; his face screwed up in pain, and clutched at his right leg.

Sarge noticed Robert's groans, looked at his face, and rose.

"Down, Sarge, down!" Robert yelled.

Sarge wasn't there anymore. He had already jumped over the boxes and was running across the warehouse.

The man in Sarge's path had emptied his weapon with the last burst but didn't try to reload. Instead, he pulled the safety pin from a hand grenade.

Sarge jumped over the pile of boxes in front of the man.

The man put up his arm, but Sarge bowled him over.

The gunman, Sarge, and the grenade sprawled on the floor.

Miguel's attention was on Robert's wounds, while holding Badge's leash tightly.

As Robert writhed in pain, an explosion rocked the place.

A deep silence followed.

Miguel stood. "Stay, Badge. Stay with Robert," he commanded. He had to secure their position before checking Robert's condition. He scanned the warehouse for more gunmen, and raced toward the area of the explosion.

He reached a pile of fallen boxes and ducked. He slid to the side, and then rose, aiming his rifle.

He slowly lowered his weapon. Two bodies lay on the floor.

Saddened, Miguel ran back to Robert and knelt to check him.

"Where's Sarge?" Robert asked.

Miguel couldn't respond.

Badge whined.

Miguel tore open Robert's uniform to check the wounds. He found a large wound on Robert's forearm. The bullet ripped the skin from just above the wrist almost to the elbow but didn't penetrate deeply. The thigh wound looked worse. Seeing blood pour out profusely, Miguel tried to stop the flow. His hands were immediately covered in blood; the bullet seemed to have hit a main artery.

Miguel took Robert's belt and hastily applied a tourniquet to the leg several inches above the injury. He raised his head and turned around; knowing there had to be more gunmen.

"Sarge!" Robert called again and again, each time with a weaker voice.

"Eleven-ninty-nine, two officers down," Miguel yelled on the radio.

"What happened?" James asked.

"I need immediate help. 29 is badly injured . . . K9 is dead."

Robert lost consciousness.

"We're sending help," James said after a moment of shock. "What's 29's condition?"

"He's taken two bullets; the worst one is in his leg." Miguel tried to remain calm. He had to keep his head until help arrived. "He's losing too much blood. I think the bullet severed the femoral artery. Please, hurry!"

"Calm down, 56," Williams joined the conversation. "Do you have an address?"

"No!"

"Is there a place to land a helicopter?"

"I don't know!"

"What about the tunnel? Can we evacuate 29 through it?"

"I don't think he could survive the time or the conditions of the tunnel."

"We'll call a bird for Medevac.[53] We know the general area, but you have to give us additional information or provide some kind of signal."

"OK, I will. Just get down here," Miguel said.

"We need a helicopter for immediate Medevac of an injured officer," James requested on another frequency. "Extraction conditions are unknown."

"What's the status over there?" Williams asked Miguel. "Are you still under enemy fire?"

"Not now, but we've been fired on by several gunmen."

"Hold tight. We're sending Medevac and backup. Communicate your position as soon as possible."

"Ten-four," Miguel scanned the area again, looking for gunmen. He dragged over a box and put Robert's feet on it. Emergency procedures recommended lifting the legs of an injured person who had lost a large amount of blood. The brain, heart, and lungs would keep a blood supply for a longer time.

* * * * *

On the other side of the tunnel, Williams and Holder discussed the best way to provide help to Robert and Miguel.

"Shall we wait for Mexican law enforcement?" Captain Holder asked.

"Call them, but we can't wait for them," Williams said indicating James should make the call.

"My team is ready," Captain Holder said.

"I need a fast response," Williams said. "Snipers for cover and support personnel."

"Are we using the tunnel?"

"No. That will take too much time."

"Otay-Mesa?"

"No, too far. I know you have a folding ladder in the BEAR. Do you have ropes?"

"We sure do."

* * * * *

Miguel adjusted the tourniquet and made Robert comfortable.

"Stay, Badge. Take care of Robert. Stay." Miguel stood and ran toward the shipping area. Nobody moved inside the warehouse. People ran away when the shooting began; the gunmen who stayed were dead.

Miguel ran outside through one of the overhead doors.

Three ten-wheeler stake-bed trucks were parked there.

"Ay, Guey!"[54] Miguel skidded to a halt when he saw gunmen rushing people to load the trucks. *Despite the shooting, they continued loading the trucks!*

Several men stopped what they were doing when they saw Miguel; they turned to alert the gunmen.

By the time the gunmen turned to locate him, Miguel was already running for cover behind some stacked boxes.

The shooting started again. AK-47 bursts hit the boxes a fraction of a second after Miguel reached them.

"This is a game I like to play," Miguel said. He switched the mode of his M4A1 from fully automatic to semi-automatic. "Open spaces and longer distances. Now, it's a matter of training, not the number of bullets." He shifted slowly to have his rifle in a better position, shot twice, and hid again.

Both shots hit the intended target. A gunman on the other side of the shipping area fell.

Miguel kept his head low and moved behind a trash bin. He repeated the sequence, shifted, aimed, shot twice, and covered.

An armed man fell from the top of a truck.

Miguel lay down and crawled between some containers until he found an opening in the desired direction. He aimed and shot twice.

Another gunman fell, this one next to the building.

"*Corran! Corran!*"[55] a man shouted. Armed and unarmed personnel ran away through a large gate to the street.

Miguel changed position again. He crawled below one of the trucks and hid behind the rear tires. From there, he looked for hidden gunmen. He detected some movement behind three 55-gallon drums and waited. He didn't want to shoot unarmed people. A gun barrel poked up from behind one of the drums and moved along to another. In quick succession, Miguel shot each of the drums twice.

The gunman fell to one side.

Miguel searched for another hiding place. He kept moving to avoid being cornered but took care not to leave himself exposed.

The engine of one of the large trucks started up. It roared a couple of times as the driver pressed the gas pedal. The gearbox clunked several times and the truck started to move. The strained sound of the motor revealed the overloaded condition.

"No, no, no. You can't leave!" Miguel yelled. He shot several times with no effect on the truck. He ran out of his hiding place, and stopped next to a box to pick a cylindrical object.

The heavy truck crossed the main gate.

"Wait, this isn't over yet!" Miguel ran toward another box and opened it. "Damn! Not in here."

The truck turned right on the street.

Miguel turned around. He had an idea of the kind of box he needed. He ran to another box. "Yes! "

The diesel engine chugged and churned as the truck slowly gained speed.

"Wait for me!" Miguel yelled and ran to the street, loading a rocket-propelled grenade into the RPG-7 launcher.

By the time Miguel reached the middle of the street, the truck was half a block away. He put his right knee to the asphalt, using his left knee to support his left elbow, and aimed. "I need a smoke signal," he said and pressed the trigger.

The rocket zigzagged in the air leaving a smoke trail. Two seconds later, it impacted the rear of the truck and exploded, sending boxes and debris into the air. The truck drifted to the left with its cargo in flames. It knocked down a light pole, then hit another parked truck and stopped.

"I hope that helps," Miguel said while he ran back to the warehouse. When he was about to reach the gate, an explosion shook the complete area. A wave of hot air shattered windows of businesses and houses and sent him to the ground.

A huge mushroom cloud rose from the street, changing colors from bright yellow to red, and finally black. Only a pile of twisted metal was left of the truck. The secondary explosion was triggered by the load of missiles and grenades. Vehicles and buildings on both sides of the street were engulfed in flames.

"That will definitely help," Miguel spit some dirt from his lips as he rose. He ran back into the warehouse.

Badge raised his head from Robert's chest when Miguel approached.

"How is he doing, Badge?"

Badge whined.

Miguel knelt and checked Robert's pulse on the wrist, "Nothing!" Miguel's spine went cold. He started to panic. With his fingers pressed to Robert's neck. "Is it there?" Miguel checked several times to be sure. Yes, there was a faint pulse. "Don't scare me like that, pal," Miguel said and sighed.

"Stay, Badge. Stay," Miguel commanded. He rose and ran again.

* * * * *

The BEAR reached the border walls dividing the two countries. It stopped just a few inches from the sixteen-foot-tall north wall. The hatch on top of the vehicle opened and the officers climbed to the roof. A folding ladder was set on top.

Two officers climbed up the ladder and cut the barbed wire on top of the wall. When finished, they dropped ropes down the other side.

The other officers took turns climbing up the ladder and rappelling down the ropes on the other side.

"We're in the twilight zone," Gregg, the officer in the leading position radioed. "We're moving to the south. Bird Three and Bird Four will stay at the north wall."

The remaining six officers ran across the two-hundred-yard-wide strip of land and reached another wall, only eight feet tall. Some officers climbed the wall using the knees and shoulders of others as steps, and then jumped down on the other side. The last officer was lifted up by two officers who stayed on top of the wall.

"We're in Mexico. Repeat, we're in Mexico," Gregg radioed again. "Bird One and Bird Two are staying at the south wall." He made some signals to the others, and the group separated. Wu went east. Abira and

Tim went straight south. Gregg ran to the west. They would approach the warehouse from different directions and watch for enemy gunmen.

* * * * *

Miguel located a forklift and loaded a wood pallet on the fork. He pushed the forklift to its top speed and rushed back to Robert and Badge. "Look what I found, Badge," he said. He reduced speed and carefully maneuvered the pallet beside Robert.

Badge raised and tilted his head to the right, then to the left, trying to understand what Miguel intended to do.

Miguel jumped from the forklift and dragged Robert up to the pallet as gently as possible.

"Jump, Badge. Jump. I'll give you a ride."

Badge jumped onto the forklift, squeezing into the space behind the seat.

"Sit, Badge. Sit. I don't want you to fall."

Miguel jumped on, raised the pallet and drove slowly, maneuvering around boxes and containers. He crossed to the overhead doors, turned on the shipping docks, and took the ramp down to the ground level. He stopped between the parked trucks and the entrance gate, the biggest open area.

"Support, is there any news about the bird?" Miguel shouted through the radio while he knelt next to Robert. "We're located one hundred yards east of the smoke column."

"A bird is on its way," James said. "ETA[56] is ten minutes. The Mexican police should be near. The SWAT team is on its way."

"Calvary is coming, Badge." Miguel felt relieved.

Badge turned and made several short and soft barks.

"What's going on Badge?" Miguel asked.

A moment later, Miguel recognized the distant wail of sirens.

"Finally! Mexican police are coming."

An SUV approached down the street at full speed.

"They're here!" Miguel said with a smile.

The vehicle didn't stop. Somebody from the inside fired a machine gun toward the warehouse.

Miguel threw himself to the ground, holding Badge.

When the vehicle moved away, Miguel rose. "What was that? Are they afraid and don't want to engage in a shooting, or was it a distraction?" He turned around to check for possible gunmen on top of the roofs of the nearby buildings. All businesses and buildings appeared deserted. The shootings and the explosions scared people away. Nobody wanted to get caught in the middle of a confrontation.

"Maybe it's a bad idea to have Robert out in the open to wait for the helicopter," Miguel said to Badge. "Feeling safe is a dangerous mistake. This is far from over and could get even more complicated at any moment." He carefully dragged Robert away, making sure the forklift shielded them from any attack from the main gate. He knelt next to Robert to verify his pulse again.

Shots started again, but from far away. Miguel realized the wail of the sirens wasn't getting any closer. "Support, what is going on?"

"Wait, we're getting a report," James said on the radio.

"We're sitting ducks here, Badge." Miguel reached for the RPG launcher he left on the ground and double-checked the location of the box containing the rocket-propelled grenades.

"Mexican Police have been blocked!" James said. "The units approaching found hostile forces barricaded to the west and to the east of your position. They're engaged in multiple shootouts."

"What? Are they coming?"

"They'll be there when they can make their way through."

Three pickup trucks moved down the street heading west at maximum speed. Each truck carried multiple men with assault rifles.

Miguel felt isolated and uninformed. Mexican officers were fighting, trying to help them, and he couldn't do anything. "It seems the traffickers want to keep the police away from the warehouse," he said to James. "There's too much investment in weapons and drugs in here."

Badge made several short and soft barks again.

Miguel recognized the far sound of a helicopter. He turned and saw a small black shape in the sky, approaching from the northwest. "Help's coming! Hang on, Robert."

Two gunmen took positions on top of the roof of the building south of the warehouse. Both carried Barret LRSR rifles with telescopic sights.

A red dot appeared on Miguel's back, then another on the rear of his neck.

Two shots popped almost simultaneously. Miguel fell over Robert's body.

Chapter 22: Help From Above

Tongue lolling, Badge crawled closer to Miguel.

"Down, Badge, down. Don't move," Miguel commanded. He still covered Robert's body and didn't know where the shots came from.

"Nice shot, Angel Three," Gregg's voice came on the radio.

"Nice shot as well, Angel Two," Wu replied.

Two bodies and their rifles lay on top of the building south of the warehouse.

"56, we're covering you from the top of buildings at the east and at the west," Gregg transmitted. "More help will approach through the main gate at any moment, hold your fire."

"Ten-four," Miguel acknowledged.

The helicopter came closer. Besides the black nose, the orange and white colors of a Coast Guard HH-60J Jayhawk could be seen.

"Kilo Niner, this is Coast Guard Triton Two. Please confirm your position," the pilot requested.

Miguel rose and waved his arms. "This is Kilo Niner 56. We're at a warehouse, near the main entrance, one hundred yards east of the smoke column."

"We see you, Kilo Niner," the pilot confirmed. "Starting final approach."

"Hurry, please!"

"I think I know him," George said to the co-pilot as he maneuvered the helicopter closer.

The helicopter lowered its altitude to sixty feet and hovered. If there were other sounds or communications, Miguel couldn't hear them because of the noise. Clouds of dust rose and swirled around making vision difficult.

At that moment, Abira and Tim appeared at the front gate. They stopped at the edge of the gate for a moment and scanned the area, weapons at the ready. They separated and ran to the shipping area, holding positions to the east and west of Miguel's.

The helicopter couldn't land, buildings and electric cables made it impossible.

A Coast Guard paramedic and a stretcher were lowered on a cable. As soon as the man reached the ground, he sprang away from the stretcher and went to Robert, taking vital signs and beginning emergency treatment to stabilize him.

Miguel asked for Robert's condition, but he couldn't even hear his own voice. He turned to the forklift and leveled his weapon toward the street, providing cover for the paramedic and Robert.

A moment later, Miguel felt a tap on his shoulder. With hand signals, the paramedic asked for help to transfer Robert to the stretcher.

With Robert belted in, the man gave a thumbs-up to Miguel, and then raised his arm to give the same signal to the helicopter. A second rescuer started the hoist.

The rescuer and Robert went up and spinning. When they reached the helicopter, they were pulled inside. The second rescuer leaned out and waved to Miguel as the helicopter gained altitude and turned north.

"Triton Two, how is he?" Miguel asked through the radio as soon as the helicopter's noise allowed him to talk.

"Hold on, Kilo Niner," George said.

Miguel waited an eternity for a response.

"He's in critical condition. We're taking him to the nearest trauma facility."

"Please make it fast," Miguel begged.

"We will. We will. . . . Tango-Mike-Mike."

* * * * *

Miguel realized he now stood alone in the lot, partially exposed with only the forklift for cover. "Was that George?" he asked Badge.

"What do we do now, Support?" Miguel asked James through the radio.

"We're waiting for the Mexican police to arrive. Weapons and drugs have to be secured."

"Ten-four," Miguel confirmed.

When the noise of the helicopter faded, Miguel noticed the gunfire to the east and west had increased.

Thirty minutes went by, and the confrontation continued. The team maintained their positions.

"Hey, guys, what's to the north of our position?" Miguel asked.

"A big *maquiladora* company, beyond that, the border," Wu said.

"And more *maquiladoras* to the northwest and northeast," Gregg said.

"Were the people evacuated?" Miguel asked.

"I don't think so," Gregg said. "There are too many people. They may have locked down the buildings when they heard the explosion. Probably just waiting now."

"Support, any news?" Miguel asked again.

"No, the police are stuck," James said. "They're holding ground, awaiting reinforcements from different precincts in Tijuana City.

Mexican police and DEA have already requested help from the Mexican Army."

"And what happened?"

"We're still waiting for a response. . . . Stand by."

Time went by.

"Anybody think to bring lunch?" Gregg asked.

"No, but I know a great little place near here," Tim said.

There were some laughs, but not from Miguel; he was thinking something else. "I'm going in, guys."

Miguel and Badge went back into the warehouse, running from one stack of boxes to another for cover.

Inside, Miguel removed a canvas tarp covering a stack of 55-gallon drums. "No one gets left behind." He went over to Sarge. He and Badge approached without making any noise, as if they were afraid of disturbing Robert's partner. Miguel laid out the canvas on the floor and knelt beside the canine officer. He took a moment to firm his resolve, and then slid his arms under Sarge. He lifted him onto the canvas.

Badge whined.

"It's OK, Badge. He's resting now," Miguel said with a quiet voice. "You know, all dogs go to heaven—all of them, with no exceptions. Some people say dogs cannot go to heaven because you don't have souls. The same was said about women long ago. Sarge died saving Robert, you, and me, Badge."

Badge stayed seated, following all of Miguel's movements wrapping Sarge with the tarp.

"We should be proud of him, Badge, and thankful. But we shouldn't thank him with words or barks. We should thank him with actions. That's what really counts." Miguel's voice began to falter. "Now we have a responsibility to live and perform our duty as bravely as he did." Miguel cleared his throat, and picked up the body.

"All teams, this is the status," Captain Williams said on the radio when Miguel approached the overhead doors. "The Mexican army from the Second Military Zone won't be able to help. They're engaged in another operation a hundred miles south."

Miguel carefully put Sarge's body on top of a box and listened to the transmission.

"Mexican Police said it will take a while to reach your position," Williams continued. "Multiple gunmen are at the barricades and their fire power is too much for the equipment the police have. How do you see the situation over there?"

"We can hold our position for a while," Gregg said.

"We could help the Mexican police," Wu said. "Advance from here and attack the traffickers from behind."

"You're only five officers, Angel three," Captain Holder joined the conversation. "Too few for that kind of operation. Remember there are two fronts, you could be cornered by fire from the rear at any moment."

"You have to hold on guys," Williams said. "Those weapons and drugs have to be secured. Miguel, you're in home territory, what do you think?

"Sir, the police are not coming," Miguel said. "The product in the warehouse is too valuable to the traffickers. They won't leave it."

"But they have already left it!"

"Sorry, sir. I don't think so. The shootings to the east and west are diversions. Not for the ones fighting, but for the ones behind all this. The south route is open and accessible. I think an assault from the traffickers will come from that direction. They haven't done it because they're not ready yet. They don't have the firepower we have, considering we have the weapons in the warehouse at our disposal, rather than just our standard equipment. As soon as night falls, with night vision equipment and an assault plan, they'll have the advantage."

"Are you sure, Miguel?"

"That's what I think, sir."

The Captain became notably upset. He didn't expect that answer and didn't want to abort the operation. "OK. Let's give the Mexican Police some more time, and we'll decide later. Nightfall is still hours away."

Miguel and Badge returned to the open area in front of the warehouse. Miguel dragged the box containing the rocket-propelled grenades, and took cover behind the forklift.

Abira hid among some boxes on the east side. Tim lay below one of the trucks on the west side. Gregg and Wu still covered the area from the roofs of nearby buildings. Bird One and Bird Two still waited two blocks to the north, ready to cover them in case they reached the border wall under enemy fire.

* * * * *

Another hour went by.

The sun hammered down, hot and dry. The team held their positions.

Badge panted.

Miguel tried to adjust their position so Badge was covered by his shadow. "Hang on, boy. Hang on."

The gunfire exchange to the east and west continued.

"This is pathetic. Are they fighting World War One?" Abira asked. "The War of the trenches, where they got stuck in foxholes for months."

"Feels like it," Tim said. "Maybe we should plan to spend Christmas here."

"Get out of there!" Captain Williams shouted through the radio. "I'm calling this off. Return to the BEAR as soon as possible." Williams' agitation made it sound as if he'd been out in the sun too.

The team was unsure how to react, but their murmurs indicated relief to be evacuating.

"Be careful on the way back, guys," James said.

"Support, what happened?" Miguel asked. "Why the sudden change in plan—and in attitude?"

"You're not going to believe this," James said. "The Mexican government filed a complaint, that armed personnel crossing the border were unacceptable no matter the reason. The complaint went to the State Department who forwarded it to DEA headquarters."

"That's fast considering it had to bust through all that red tape on both sides of the border."

"I agree," James said. "I'll see you in a while."

Miguel stood still for a moment, thinking. "I have to go in," he said to the team through the radio. "There are a couple of guys tied inside." He picked up the RPG launcher from the ground and took a rocket-propelled grenade from the box.

He and Badge went back inside the warehouse to the scissor lift. He pushed a button and he and Badge jumped onto the sinking platform.

The two traffickers followed the lift with their eyes, the only part of their bodies they could move.

Miguel dragged each of them away of the tunnel's entrance. "Stay, Badge. Stay away," Miguel commanded. He stood in front of the tunnel, loaded the RPG and aimed, centering it so the rocket could penetrate the tunnel as deeply as possible.

"James, did anybody else use the tunnel after we came through?"

"No, only you, Robert, and the dogs. Why?"

Miguel pressed the trigger and the rocket disappeared into the darkness. He ran for cover behind the wall.

The explosion rocked the place and a dust cloud burst from the tunnel.

"What's going on?" James asked.

"Is everything OK?" Gregg also asked on the radio.

"The tunnel needs some maintenance," Miguel said. He took out a pocket knife and cut the duct tape from the legs of the traffickers. He helped them up and removed the duct tape covering their mouths.

"Where are we going?" one of them asked.

Miguel didn't answer. He pushed them to the lift, pressed the up button, and he and Badge jumped onto the platform.

When the platform reached the top Miguel pushed the men off the lift and directed them to the overhead doors. "*Para afuera, los dos.*" [57]

"What do you want?" one guy asked, worried because no police were anywhere in sight.

"I'm going to release you," Miguel said. "We cannot take you with us across the border, and can't leave you in here, either."

"I told you. You don't know who you're messing with."

"Precisely, and because of that, I'm letting you go," Miguel said.

"You never had the authority to arrest us, stupid gringo!" the man argued.

"Policía Federal, *cabrón!*" [58] Miguel said. "I have the authority, and I'm not a gringo. You're the ones who should be afraid. Being at the entrance of the tunnel and not preventing us from coming in. Your boss won't like it."

The group reached the overhead doors. "Coming through," Miguel said on the radio.

"Are you releasing them?" Tim asked when he saw them.

"We can't take them with us."

Miguel walked the men across the lot between the warehouse and the entrance gate. He stopped near the forklift and pointed to the gate. "Go! You're lucky, but watch your backs."

Still handcuffed, the two men walked through the main gate and ran when they reached the street.

"Let's go!" Gregg commanded.

Miguel jumped into the forklift. "Jump, Badge. Jump," he tapped the area behind the seat.

Badge jumped and sat behind Miguel.

Miguel drove to the warehouse, took the ramp, and stopped inside the building in an area for fuel storage. "Stay, Badge. Stay." He picked up several containers with gasoline and put them on top of the wood pallet on the forklift.

"Let's go, Kilo Niner," Gregg urged.

"I'm not finished yet," Miguel said. "You can leave. I'll catch up with you." He jumped on the forklift again and drove into the warehouse.

Gregg wondered about Miguel's plans, but he had to direct the SWAT team first. "Angel Five, you're going to exit the premises. Move west to the corner, turn north, and take a position to cover Angel Six."

"Ready," Abira said.

"Go!"

Abira ran, following the indicated path. She took cover behind a parked car on the street going north.

Gregg instructed Tim to follow the same path.

Meanwhile, Miguel lowered the scissor lift into the hidden basement again and poured the fuel of one container down into the pit. He walked around, and continued pouring gasoline on top of stacks of boxes nearby. He drove the forklift and kicked out opened containers in other areas of the warehouse as he approached the overhead doors.

"Kilo Niner, we're leaving!" Gregg shouted through the radio.

"Don't worry about me. I'm almost finished."

"When you're done, take the street to the west. Go two blocks, and you'll find the border wall. We'll be waiting there."

"Ten-four."

Gregg ordered Abira and Tim to start moving north. Wu and he did the same using different paths.

Miguel finished spilling gasoline in the rear of the two remaining trucks.

"We're almost done, Badge," Miguel said as they returned to the bundled tarp with Sarge inside. "Let's go home, Sarge." Miguel raised the covered body and placed it on top of the pallet on the forklift.

"Ready, Badge?" Miguel asked as he jumped into the forklift.

As they descended the ramp, Miguel observed the buildings nearby. "I wonder how many people are observing us". He stopped in the same place he'd parked the forklift earlier. Taking cover behind the forklift, he took a rocket-propelled grenade, and loaded the launcher. He aimed to the fuel storage area inside the building and pressed the trigger.

The rocket went through the overhead doors into the warehouse and exploded.

Miguel didn't wait to see the results. He jumped back into the forklift and drove across the lot turning west when they'd passed through the gate. When he turned north on the corner, gunfire struck the vehicle. "Stay down, Badge. They may be a little angry with us."

As Miguel drove north, several explosions rocked the area. He reached the south wall of the border at the same time as the SWAT team.

"What happened, Miguel?" Wu asked.

"I left some fireworks for them to celebrate our retreat."

The explosions in the warehouse increased in frequency and magnitude. The ground shook.

"Good job, Miguel," Gregg said.

Everybody smiled.

"What's that?" Tim asked.

Miguel's expression changed. "That's Sarge. I couldn't leave him there."

A heavy silence fell over the team.

$$* * * * *$$

Moments later, everybody was loaded inside the BEAR and on their way back to Atlantic Trading. The group was very quiet. The covered body on the floor made it difficult to talk.

"Support, do you hear me?" Miguel broke the silence.

"Loud and clear," James said.

"What do you know about 29?"

"I called a while ago. He's getting trauma care in emergency."

"Where is he?"

"University Medical Center."

"Do you know his condition?"

"Critical."

"Does his family know?"

"A local patrol car took them to the hospital."

The mood in the BEAR went from somber to tense.

The BEAR arrived at Atlantic Trading. Several squad cars were still there. Police officers guarded the place and tried to control a crowd of reporters and civilians gathered on the other side of the street.

Miguel noticed several people in the crowd pointing toward the south. When the rear door of the BEAR opened, he learned the reason; flames and a huge smoke column could be seen in the distance.

Nobody in the rear of the BEAR moved.

Miguel realized they were waiting, like an honor guard, for him to remove Sarge's body first.

Miguel and Badge jumped out. The SWAT team eased Sarge's covered body toward the door. Miguel lifted it and walked away looking for the

Suburban. When he didn't see it, he laid Sarge's body across the hood of a squad car and called James. "Support, where are you. Where's the Captain?" Miguel asked.

"I'm looking at you. Approaching now with the Suburban," James said. "The Captain left in another vehicle. He had an urgent appointment with the Divisional Director."

Miguel placed his hand over Sarge's wrapped body. "What would be the most appropriate for you, my friend?" he said quietly. "What would Robert want?" He had to go to University Medical Center as soon as possible.

Badge approached and put his front paws up on the cruiser's hood also touching the covered body. He whined.

"He'll be OK, Badge. We'll take care of him."

One by one, the SWAT team approached. Each placed a hand over Sarge's body. James arrived, and did the same. It wasn't necessary to speak to express respect.

The explosions, the flames, and the shootings continued on the south side of the border while the sun vanished in the west.

Chapter 23: Delicate Situation

"Doctor, Miguel Cordova is here to see you," the surprised assistant called Dr. Padilla's extension. "He has no appointment, but I think you should hurry." Two men and a dog stood near her reception desk. One of the men carried a canvas tarp.

"How are you, Miguel?" Dr. Padilla said with a smile when he walked into the waiting room. His smile faded as he looked from Miguel to James. "Is there something wrong?" he asked looking at Miguel's dirty, blood-stained uniform. His eyes settled on the bundle in Miguel's arms. "Oh, no. Badge!"

Badge appeared from behind the counter when the doctor mentioned his name. He whined a reserved greeting. He looked just like Miguel, dirty and a bit bloody. Even his face was drawn and sorrowful.

"What's going on?" Dr. Padilla asked.

"Doctor, we need your help," Miguel said. He paused for a moment trying to find the best words. "We lost Sarge in a confrontation with traffickers. Robert, his partner, is at the hospital in critical condition. And—"

"And you need the body cared for?" Dr. Padilla asked.

"Yes. Until we can talk with Robert or his family."

"Don't worry. You go to Robert, and I'll take care of Sarge." He asked his assistant to bring out a gurney. Miguel placed the bundle on the cold steel surface.

"We'll be back, Sarge." Miguel said running his hand over the canvas.

* * * * *

259

"It's been a long day," Miguel said to Badge as he drove to the hospital. "It'll be longer for Robert, his family, the injured police officers in Mexico, and their families."

Miguel and Badge arrived at the hospital and went directly to Emergency.

Diane and other members of Robert's family were in the waiting room. She stood and embraced Miguel.

"How is he?" Miguel asked.

"The doctors just finished stabilizing him. He needs surgery to repair the artery in his leg," Diane said, wiping tears from her face. "After that, he'll be in the intensive care unit. They said the next hours are critical."

"The leg . . . how is the leg?"

"The femoral artery was severed by the bullet. They bypassed it temporarily until the surgery's done. The doctor said the artery's collapse and your tourniquet kept him alive."

"When can I see him?"

"He's in a coma," Diane said. "Nobody knows how long he'll be like that—" Diane began to cry and Miguel drew her close, offering what little comfort he could.

"Please sit down, Diane." Robert's father led her to a seat next to her mother.

Miguel and Badge stayed in the middle of the waiting room. Miguel looked around for a nurse or someone who could provide more details, but the bustling staff members seemed intent to avoid eye contact, as if doing so might require them to share more bad news.

"Calm down, Miguel," Mr. West said quietly when Diane was settled. He gently directed Miguel away from the others; Badge followed. "We don't know what to expect, not even the doctors know at this time. They said we have to wait."

"But what's his condition? When is he going to wake up? The leg, will he walk again?"

"Miguel, listen to me. We don't know, yet. Nobody knows. Right now, the main issue is Robert's life. Saving his leg or being able to walk again is secondary at this moment."

"I'm sorry, Mr. West," Miguel said changing his tone. "I know how difficult this is for all of you. I'm the one that should be comforting you and your family. Please forgive me for being so impatient."

"Don't say that, Miguel. We want to thank you for what you did to help Robert. The Coast Guard rescuers told us your tourniquet kept him from bleeding to death."

Robert's father was so kind; Miguel felt ashamed for his inconsiderate outburst.

"Look!" Mr. West pointed to the waiting room TV. "You helped Robert get out of there."

The TV showed scenes of Tijuana where squad cars, ambulances, and fire trucks moved back and forth. The fire in the warehouse still blazed wildly. Mr. West patted Miguel on the back to show his appreciation.

"Gosh, look at you two," Mr. West said. "You're a real mess. You should get cleaned up and rest."

Miguel looked down at his uniform. Tunnel mud still clung to his clothes and boots. His shirt was stained with sweat, and soot. There were small cuts and scrapes on his hands. Badge was just as filthy, his fur encrusted with mud.

After midnight, Robert was settled in ICU after surgery. Miguel and Badge were allowed to peek in at him through the glass wall of his room.

Badge rose on his two rear legs and placed his front paws against the glass so he could see.

Later, Miguel and Badge returned to the waiting room and sat for a while. When Miguel noticed Mr. West had walked away from the rest of his family, he followed him. "Sir, I'm sorry, but I have to ask you something."

"Yes, Miguel?" Mr. West turned.

"I know this isn't the most appropriate time to ask you this, but what do we do with Sarge's body?"

Mr. West bowed his head. "Thanks for asking, Miguel. Where is he?"

"At a veterinary clinic. The doctor's a friend."

"Please give us some time, Miguel. I'll talk it over with Diane and her mother. We'll all have to help decide what to do."

"I'm sorry, sir. I know this is difficult. I couldn't leave him behind."

"We're grateful you looked after him. We were wondering what happened to him. It's difficult to deal with that issue right now, but it's also important to us. He's a member of the family too."

"Yes, sir, I'm sorry about Sarge. But, if it's any comfort, he died doing his duty, protecting Robert."

While Mr. West and Miguel walked the hallway and talked. Badge walked between them. Miguel told Mr. West about Sarge's work. Mr. West talked about Sarge living with his family since he was a puppy.

When they returned to the waiting room, they found James had arrived. He had changed out of his uniform into jeans and a t-shirt.

They shared what they knew of Robert's condition.

"It's nice to know my son and Sarge have such good friends," Mr. West said. "Miguel, you and Badge should go home now. You've earned a rest, and I think both of you need a bath."

* * * * *

Miguel and Badge returned to the apartment after 3:00 am. Miguel turned on the TV hoping for a news update on the warehouse operation. "Nothing, only infomercials." It was too late. Not even the repeats of previous news broadcasts were being shown anymore.

Badge collapsed on his mat. His head dropped onto his paws.

"Wait, Badge! You have to take a bath first," Miguel said. He took Badge's soap and towels from the laundry into the bathroom.

Miguel looked in the mirror. "Scorned and covered with scars. Now I know why Mr. West wanted me to take a bath." He turned on the faucet and washed his face.

"Oh, no! I'm a big stupid!" he said when he raised his arms and noticed his sleeves. "How could I do that?" Upset, he took off his shirt. "You're the dumbest person I know!" He said to the mirror. "Walking around in the hospital and in front of Diane and Robert's family showing this." He wadded up the shirt, put it in the sink and soaked it. The running water turned red from the blood—Robert's blood.

Downhearted, Miguel walked to the bedroom. Badge had already fallen asleep. He decided to leave Badge's bath for the next morning, just a few hours away. He sat on the bed and took his boots off, the last thing he did that night.

* * * * *

Miguel stirred to the sound of ringing. He rolled over and tried to silence the alarm clock, but no matter how many buttons he pressed he couldn't do it. When he got used to the light, he saw the time, 8:00 am. An adrenaline boost made him jump. "It's too late," he said loudly to wake up Badge. "Even for a Friday. We should be at the DEA by now."

The ringing continued.

"Why don't you shut up?" He asked to the alarm clock. "I didn't set you this late." Angry, he pulled the power cable. He sighed and turned to check Badge, who stretched on his mat with no intention to rise.

The rings started again making Miguel jump.

"What?" he said to himself picking up the alarm clock plug.

The next ring made him realize it was from the phone.

"Yes?"

"Miguel Cordova?"

"This is he."

"This is Sarah, Captain Williams's assistant."

"How can I help you?" Miguel asked. *Damn! They're already looking for me.*

"The Captain said you can take the day off in case you want to visit Agent West in the hospital."

"That would be great, thanks."

"Some other people are doing the same or at least taking half of the day off. We will require you in the office on Monday to complete reports of all Operation Lobo activities."

"Understood, thanks."

"One last thing. You're not to give any interviews to the media or discuss the operation with anyone outside the DEA. Captain Williams mentioned this is still a delicate situation. There's no need to complicate things more."

Miguel didn't respond. *What is she talking about? What's the problem?*

"Have a nice day, Agent Cordova."

"Thanks." Miguel put down the phone.

Badge still lay on his mat; he turned and closed his eyes.

"No, no, no, Badge! We have to take a bath, and you're going first. We got the day off, but we have many things to do."

An hour later, and smelling much better, Badge devoured two cans of dog food. It had been more than twenty-four hours since either of them had eaten. Miguel served himself double portions of cereal with milk.

Miguel searched for news on TV. American channels mentioned an operation where dozens of people were arrested, a tunnel to smuggle drugs discovered, and a ton of drugs confiscated. Other news contained accounts of shootings between police and traffickers in Tijuana and a fire. "It's not clear at this moment, but we theorize the events could be related," the reporter said.

Miguel changed the channel to get Mexican news. "A fire occurred in a warehouse used to store explosives. Several fatalities have been reported. In other news, several shootings occurred between the police and armed groups, possibly related to drug cartels. Fatalities and injuries are heavy on both sides," the anchorman said.

"They still don't get the big picture, Badge," Miguel said as he continued flipping channels. "Maybe in a couple of days."

Miguel called James. The telephone rang several times. He was about to hang up when he got a response.

"Hello?" James said softly.

"Oh! Sorry, James. Did I wake you up?"

"No problem, Miguel. What's going on?"

"Do you have any news about Robert?"

"I came home just a while ago. There's been no change since you left last night. I guess no news is good news."

"I hope so. Did you get the call from the office?"

"Yes, we'll regroup on Monday and discuss our next assignments."

"OK, James. I'm on my way to the hospital."

"Cool. Keep me informed."

Miguel and Badge prepared to leave for the hospital. Miguel took the remote to turn off the TV, but a report got his attention: "In more police related news, Gavin Pollock, also known by the alias El Pollo, is in custody. He's accused of cocaine possession and distribution."

"Looking good, Pollo" Miguel said when the mugshot appeared in the screen.

Badge woofed.

The news continued. "In a separate case, also drug-related, Mauricio Farias, also known as Chango, evaded police when units arrived at his house to arrest him." A video taken from the news helicopter showed police officers searching the area and the pit bull barking."

"Don't tell me he got away," Miguel said.

Badge whined.

"The barks of a dog alerted police and Chango was found up a tree in his backyard," the reported said.

Miguel laughed. "Nice work by our pit bull friend!"

"Woof!" Badge replied.

"I guess he belongs to the lady and not Chango, because he sure doesn't seem to like that monkey very much. Gimme paw, Badge!"

Paw and hand met.

* * * * *

Everything was quiet when Miguel and Badge arrived at the hospital. All visitors who stayed late had left to get some rest, like James. Only Robert's mother and brother were still in the waiting room.

"Is there any news on Robert's condition?" Miguel asked.

"No, the doctors told us to be patient," Robert's brother said.

"Wait and pray, Miguel. Wait and pray," Mrs. West added.

Miguel thought about his mother. She would have said the same thing. "Yes, Mrs. West, pray."

Miguel and Badge entered the intensive care unit to see Robert.

Badge reared up again so he could look in the window. He whined.

"He's resting, Badge. It's going to take time for him to heal."

Miguel and Badge stayed at the hospital for a while. At noon, Diane and Mr. West arrived. They looked better after having some time to rest.

"Miguel, can I talk with you for a moment?" Mr. West asked.

"Sure. What can I do?"

"Miguel, we need your help. Our family talked about Sarge and what to do with his body. Can you ask the veterinarian to have him cremated?"

"Yes, sir."

"We want to give Robert a chance to decide later what to do with the remains and give him some closure. He loved that dog. Sarge was a partner and a brother to him."

"I know exactly what you mean, sir."

"It's because of that, Miguel, that we ask you for this favor."

"It's an honor, sir."

* * * * *

Miguel decided that, rather than waiting around idly, he would walk in the gardens of the Medical Center. He had to think. "Will Robert be able to recover?" He asked Badge. "If he does, how are things going to be without Sarge?"

Badge huffed.

"Will training end? Will it be time to go back to Mexico?"

When Miguel and Badge returned to the hospital, they found James in the waiting room.

"Still no news," James said. "Robert hasn't recovered consciousness."

"How long can he be like that?" Miguel asked.

"The doctors said as long as he's stable, it's a good sign." James tried to be cheerful.

Miguel talked with different members of DEA and the SWAT team that arrived to check on Robert and lend support to Diane. Everybody was sorrowful. Even Karen and George came and stayed there for a while.

"Robert's family has been very strong," he said to Badge. "They had to deal with those TV reporters." When the reporters approached him, he just walked away. He couldn't think of anything appropriate to say.

Miguel and Badge went back to the intensive care hall and observed Robert through the window. "No media! I even forgot the warning." He remembered the words of the captain's assistant: *No interviews . . . still a delicate situation.*" He turned to Badge. "What's the delicate situation?"

"Hey!" the voice of a woman interrupted Miguel's thoughts.

Miguel was pleasantly surprised to see Abira, She was dressed in something other than her tactical uniform. *Wow! She looks good in casual attire. Does she look like this every day?* He pulled himself out of his surprised stupor. "Abira! How are you?"

Abira just nodded and smiled faintly. Maybe she didn't consider it appropriate to talk about herself under the circumstances. "How is Robert?" she asked.

"Stable," Miguel said, "but nobody knows how long he's going to be in intensive care."

"Is he going to be OK?"

"It's too soon to tell. Healing will take some time."

"Will there be a permanent effect? I mean, will he be able to return to his normal activities?"

Miguel sighed. "Nobody knows yet. According to the doctors, his chances are good. The first milestone will be regaining consciousness."

"How do you feel?"

"Fine, I guess. Trying to understand what happened and how this whole thing's gonna come out."

"How about you, Badge?" Abira steered the conversation away from the operation and Miguel's concerns. "How do you feel?" She rubbed Badge's neck.

"Woof!" Badge barked once as he wagged his tail.

"Shh! This is a hospital, Badge," Miguel said.

Kneeling, Abira gave Badge a hug.

Several people from the DEA approached to see Robert.

"Well, I have to go," Abira said as she stood.

She was nearly toe to toe with Miguel. She gave him a quick hug and a kiss on the cheek.

Miguel ran his hands down her forearms to her hands as she pulled back.

"I'm sure everything is going to be all right," Abira said before she turned away.

Miguel watched her until she rounded the corner and went through the ICU's doors. When he realized she was truly gone, he turned to Badge.

Badge's continued looking down the hall, as if searching for Abira.

"Hey, pal! You got a rub and a hug. I got a hug and a kiss. I win."

Badge responded with a short growl.

Miguel's cell phone buzzed. It was Dr. Padilla.

Chapter 24: Barking in Intensive Care

Miguel and Badge arrived at the clinic with pet cremation services. James was already there.

The group greeted Dr. Padilla and met Dr. Johnson, the clinic's owner.

"We're ready," Padilla said. "We hope you find everything acceptable. If not, let us know."

"Thanks, we're sure it is properly arranged," Miguel said. "What has to be done now?"

"What follows is a very private act," Johnson said. "Families and friends are given two options. One is to observe the cremation process through the window of the waiting room. Dr. Padilla and I execute the entire procedure. The other option is to have you in the cremation room, and you start the cremation sequence. We do everything else."

James and Miguel looked at each other. "We prefer the second option," Miguel said.

"We won't perform any special ceremony or make any speeches," James said. "We'll respect the right of Sarge's family to decide what kind of ceremony they want to perform when they're ready."

The men and dog went into the back room, all of them silent, out of respect for Sarge. Dr. Padilla excused himself, and Dr. Johnson set the oven ready while Miguel and James waited.

Dr. Padilla returned pushing a wheeled table with a cardboard cremation casket on it. He aligned the table with the front of the oven.

"You can open the casket if you want to see the body," Dr. Padilla said.

Slowly, Miguel approached and raised the lid. Sarge's body was posed as if he was sleeping. *The doctors did a great job cleaning him up.*

James also approached and paid his respects.

Badge reared up and put his front paws on the table, but the box was too high for him to see into it. He whined.

Miguel picked him up.

Badge observed for a moment. "Woof!" he barked moving his head upwards.

"No, Badge. You can't wake him up to play," Miguel said. "He's already in another place."

Miguel put Badge down. Nobody said anything for a while.

Miguel turned to Padilla. "We're ready."

Dr. Padilla slid the box into the oven and removed the wheeled table.

Dr. Johnson pointed to a button and stepped back.

Miguel turned to James unsure which of them should do it.

James moved aside and nodded at Miguel.

Badge sat and tilted his head, trying to understand what was going to happen.

Miguel drew a deep solemn breath and pressed the button.

The oven's door locked shut, and the hissing noise of gas passing through pipes followed. Behind the door, the gas ignited with a faint roar.

The four men were very quiet. Even Badge remained still and silent.

"It will take a while to complete the cycle," Dr. Johnson said.

Miguel nodded, and as he did, he felt a pleasant and warm wind for a moment. *Where is that coming from?* He wondered but said nothing.

James felt his hair move. He looked around but didn't react further.

Badge suddenly gasped and stood. He turned around, and then sat again.

"I'm going back to the hospital," James said after a while.

"I'll wait for the urn," Miguel said. "I'll see you tomorrow."

"Are you staying, Miguel?" Dr. Padilla asked after awhile. "This will take at least an hour, and then the ashes will need to cool."

"I'll stay, if it's ok with you?"

"We'll be here if you need anything."

"Thanks. Badge and I will be in the waiting room."

Time went by. "Sarge . . . Robert . . . delicate situation . . ." Miguel said to Badge, and to himself.

Badge laid down on the floor.

"What's next?" Miguel got lost in his thoughts.

Badge only moved his eyes.

"Why do people think they are the only ones with a soul?"

The dog didn't hear the question, he was asleep. It was already dark outside.

"It's done, Miguel," Dr. Padilla said as he came into the waiting room. "Sarge is here." He raised the urn, a simple rectangular pine box.

Miguel stood, and Badge woke up. "Thanks, Doctor Padilla." Miguel took the box.

"The remains are in a poly bag," Padilla said. "There's no risk of spilling them if the box is opened."

Dr. Johnson joined them to say goodbye and wish Miguel and Badge well.

Miguel held the box with his left arm and shook Padilla and Johnson's hands. "Thanks, you have helped me so much."

"Woof!" Badge also gave thanks.

"It's an honor to do this for Sarge and his family," Padilla said. "When I helped bring Badge into the world, I never imagined he'd be a police dog or that he'd have such a fine partner. And the two of you working against drug traffickers—working?—fighting this war! I should say."

"Keep doing what you're doing, Miguel," Dr. Johnson said. "Take those drugs off the streets. Lives of a lot of people depend on what you and Badge do. Most are not even aware of it."

"Thanks, again." Miguel turned to the door followed by Badge.

"Wait! I almost forgot," Dr. Padilla said when Miguel opened the door.

Miguel returned while Padilla ran inside the office. A moment later, he came back carrying a black plastic bag.

"What's that?" Miguel asked.

"I cleaned it the best I could," Dr. Padilla said. He opened the bag and removed what was inside. K9-29 could still be read on Sarge's shredded vest.

* * * * *

Miguel and Badge returned to University Hospital the next day. Miguel carried the urn. They walked into the waiting room and found it full of people visiting Robert. The weekend made the visits easier. The abundance of drawn faces and murmured conversations made Miguel uncomfortable.

"How is he?" Miguel asked.

"Still the same," Robert's brother said.

"Where are Diane and your parents?"

"They're with Robert. The doctors recommended that close family members talk to Robert to stimulate a reaction. They're not sure how, but it could help rouse him from the coma."

"I hope it makes a difference."

274

Miguel and Badge walked down to see Robert. Miguel found he could walk freely in the hospital with Badge. On his first visits, nurses approached but when they saw Badge's shield, they nodded, smiled and let them pass without question. Robert once advised Miguel to have Badge's shield on his collar when in a hospital. Miguel never imagined he'd use the suggestion so they could visit Robert.

Miguel and Badge saw Diane and Robert's parents through the observation window. They talked to Robert, but Robert didn't move. "Do you think the doctors' advice could help, Badge?"

Badge huffed.

A while later, Diane and Mr. and Mrs. West stood and came out. Diane's face was tired and sad.

Miguel greeted them.

Diane hugged Miguel for a moment. "He's not responding, Miguel," she said and started to cry.

Mrs. West put her arm around Diane and guided her to the waiting room.

"Has anything changed, Mr. West?" Miguel asked.

"Still the same. The doctors keep saying we have to wait. The more time that goes by the better the chances, but we still don't know if Robert will ever wake up or walk again." Mr. West lowered his head and turned toward the waiting room.

"Mr. West," Miguel said softly.

"Yes, Miguel." Mr. West turned.

"I'm sorry it's such a bad time for this, but I have Sarge's remains. I don't know if giving them to you would make your family feel better or worse at this moment. I'm very sorry." He held out the box.

Mr. West took it from Miguel and ran a hand over the top. He returned it to Miguel. "Miguel, do me a favor. Talk to Robert. Talk to him about work or anything you think he'd like. Leave the box in the room and tell him Sarge is there, with him."

"I will, Mr. West."

Officer and canine were left alone in the middle of the hall of the intensive care unit. Miguel sighed. Mr. West asked him for a favor; something he would do even if not asked to, but he didn't know how to proceed.

Miguel looked around the ICU. He was concerned about taking Badge into Robert's room. *What if a doctor or nurse didn't like it?* The nurses hadn't said anything about having a dog in the halls, but he was pushing things to the limit expecting to just walk a dog into an ICU room. Everyone in the unit seemed quite busy with charts, and monitors. Miguel laid a hand on the door.

"Get in, Badge, and don't make any noise," he said and ushered the dog into the room.

Miguel and Badge approached the bed.

"Robert, how are you?" Miguel asked.

Badge laid his front paws on the bed.

"No, Badge! Don't do that. Get down," Miguel said trying to use a soft voice. He turned back to Robert. "We came with a friend who wants to be with you." Miguel put the wood box on the table beside the bed. "Sarge is here, he wants you to wake up. Everybody wants you to wake up. . . . You've rested more than enough. You know, they're gonna take this out of your vacation days, don't you? You'll need those days when the baby comes. You can't leave Diane to take care of that baby by herself. . . . And your parents and brother, what will they think if you keep this up? They're here, waiting. . . . We're all waiting."

Miguel sat on a chair beside the bed and thought about what else he should say.

Badge sat beside the bed and rested his head over the mattress.

Miguel wanted to keep a cheerful tone, something that didn't sound worried or sad. "Lobo was a great success. It's all over the TV news. We destroyed lots of weapons and drugs. Now we have to be ready before the traffickers regroup."

Miguel talked to Robert for quite some time. He talked about everything and nothing, hoping just the sound of his voice might help no matter how silly the topic. "You know what? If you wake up, I'll bring you homemade Mexican food for lunch. . . . OK, OK, a different Mexican dish every day, for one week. . . . One week, no more," he added, as if they were negotiating.

Badge walked to the other side of the bed and sat again.

". . . and that's called hybridization. That's the theory behind the Chihuahuas being related to foxes." Over an hour had passed. Miguel had run out of conversation. He sighed. "OK, Robert, I'll see you later." He stood and signed for Badge to follow. "Come, Badge. Let's go. We'll come back later." He walked to the door trying not to make any noise. Just a moment before, he had wanted Robert to wake up. Maybe it was an unconscious sign of respect that he now wanted him to simply rest and improve. Miguel opened the door slowly.

"Woof, woof!" Badge barked.

Miguel jumped and slammed his foot with the door as he tried to close it before anyone heard Badge and kicked them out for good.

"Woof, woof!" Badge was next to Robert's bed. He raised his front paws and bounced them on the mattress.

"No, Badge. Don't do that!" Miguel ran over to pull Badge away.

"Woof, woof!" Badge barked again.

Miguel dragged Badge back with one hand and tried to hold the dog's mouth closed with the other, releasing it just for a second so he could open the door.

Outside the room, Miguel stood in front of Badge. "Badge! How could you? Don't ever do that again!" Miguel looked around, certain the hospital staff would descend on them at any second.

Badge tucked his tail between his legs. Miguel hadn't used that tone of voice since the day he emptied the fridge.

"It seems nobody noticed. You're lucky," Miguel said moments later.

Behind him, a nurse came running down the hall and into Robert's room.

Concerned, Miguel turned to the window. Had he or Badge dislodged a monitor or IV?

Badge raised on his two rear legs to be able to see.

A second nurse pushed Miguel aside and ran into the room.

The nurses moved fast, checking Robert and all the medical equipment connected to him.

"No! No, no, no," Miguel said. "Please, God, please." He didn't know what happened, but the nurses rushing around Robert convinced him it wasn't good.

One of the nurses ran back.

Anguished, Miguel stood in front of the door. When she left the room, he stopped her. "I'm sorry, but you have to tell me what's going on?" he asked holding her shoulders.

"He's awake!"

Chapter 25: Ghost Shipments

Mexico, office of an important man.

"Jackasses, idiots, Neanderthals!" the hefty man shouted to General Mota and Weedman. He paced to and fro, staring at the floor, hands clasped behind his back. "You're a bunch of big, lazy, retrograde chimpanzees." Cellophane-wrapped bricks and Egyptian figurines lay atop the nearby desk. "I think I said that before, but you seem to need somebody to remind you."

Abruptly, he ceased pacing, grabbed two cellophane-wrapped bricks, and threw them at the General and Weedman. He took two more and also threw them.

General Mota and Weedman dodged left and right like interpretive dancers but with limited success. One packet hit General Mota's bald head and bounced into a golden figurine on the desk. The figurine fell and the packet ripped open, releasing a cloud of white powder.

"The product, sir!" Weedman screamed.

The big man looked at the mess and finally became quiet and calm. He collapsed into his chair and exhaled. "My miraculous tunnel. My rainbow tunnel. It's gone."

"Miraculous?" the General asked.

"Rainbow?" Weedman asked.

"Schmucks!" The big man took another packet from his desk.

The General and Weedman ducked, but the big man didn't throw the packet. He handled it with extreme care, turning it over as he passed it from hand to hand.

"Whatever this little wonder's value is at the entrance of the tunnel, it emerges on the American side multiplied twentyfold. No cutting, no distribution, just move it from south of the border to north of the border."

"Don't worry, sir," the General said. "We'll recover, we always do."

"You dimwit!" the big man roared. "The clash against those illegal alien SWAT officers and the police is taking us backwards. It's a blow we cannot afford. Our competitors will overtake our market. The cost of the lost drugs and weapons equals six months of profits. Six months! That's an eternity in this line of business. We can replace the dead, injured, and arrested men in less than a week, but not the product. The product is everything."

The big man took a handkerchief from his jacket and dusted the powder from his desk. "We can ask the producers for shorter times to resupply the drugs, but we have to pay a premium. The weapons, besides the down payment, will take months to replace. That's a real problem."

"I can arrange to reroute some armament from the Army in the meantime, sir," the General said cautiously. "By the time they suspect something's missing, we'll be able to resupply it. I'll explain it was mistakenly taken to a different location."

"Finally! A good idea," the big man said. "What did those two guys say—the ones who escaped?" He shifted the conversation trying not to give too much credit to the general.

"They said two agents with dogs entered through the tunnel. They wore DEA uniforms," Weedman said. "When they were taken outside, they saw the SWAT officers."

"Is one of those DEA agents the one all the TV stations are talking about? The one injured?" the big man asked.

"Yes, sir."

"And only a dog killed! They killed twelve on our side! And add the ones killed in the shootings against police! We need to even the score or our reputation will be ruined. Everyone will think we're weak and ineffective unless we do something to retaliate."

"One more thing, sir." the General said.

"What?"

"The other agent said he was Mexican, Policía Federal."

"Policía Federal? . . . Interesting. One of those officers in one of those stupid exchange programs, no doubt." The big man swung his chair toward the wall, thinking. "First of all, I need you to get rid of those two guys from the warehouse. They say they escaped, and at the same time they say were taken out. They're lying and, therefore, unreliable. Do something original and gruesome as a warning for all the others."

"Yes, sir," the General said rubbing his hands.

"Regarding those agents and the SWAT officers, I need names, addresses, family members, hobbies, what kind of food they like . . . Everything you can find about them! And don't forget the pooch!"

* * * * *

On Saturday night, everybody felt cheerful in the hospital. Diane, her parents, and Robert's parents were able to talk with Robert for a while. They said Robert was able to talk, and had begun taking fluids.

The doctors said the leg continued to be a concern, but time would tell. *Same story, different circumstances,* Miguel thought. Previously, they said time would tell about Robert's general condition. Nobody liked what they said, but they assessed the situation correctly. With things looking better, everybody was willing to wait.

The hospital waiting room and hallway bustled with visitors for Robert. Family and friends were welcome to visit as long as they didn't overwhelm or tire him. Robert enjoyed the company, and the festive atmosphere seemed to help him heal. Eventually, he asked about the small pine box and grew quite sad when he was told about the content. Since then, he kept the box by his bedside.

When Miguel entered Robert's room, he left Badge outside to avoid any barking. Most of all, he was worried Badge might remind Robert too much of Sarge and become upset.

Miguel was wrong, as soon as he entered the room, Robert asked to see Badge.

* * * * *

On Monday, Miguel and Badge arrived at the DEA building.

"Are you ready for a long day?" James asked when Miguel approached the desk where he was working. He had already started the hated paperwork.

Badge whined. An active, eager dog, suddenly subjected to endless waiting. He suffered on paperwork days, often looking up at Miguel with sad, pleading eyes.

"The sooner we finish this, the better." Miguel said as he turned on the computer. He had to report everything he had done and seen from the operation briefing to the time they returned. "Fortunately, all the activities before the assault are already documented."

At noon Miguel took Badge to a park to ease the long waiting hours. He gave his burger a single bite, and then stopped. Badge had already devoured his and was staring at him. "Sorry! Not again. I'm eating my burger." He stared back at Badge for a moment.

Badge didn't move.

Miguel frowned.

"Do you know what, Badge? I promise not to tell you polite lies anymore. You don't need them. The truth is that I didn't forget the dog food. I just didn't think you'd feel like having more of the same today."

Badge seemed not to hear. He continued staring at the burger in Miguel's hand.

The gazing continued for a while.

"OK, you win!" Miguel gave Badge his burger. "I suppose I deserve this for not bringing the dog food."

Badge devoured the second burger.

"I think I'm starting to like the fries," Miguel said as he chewed, "as long as I use mayo, and not ketchup."

In the afternoon, Miguel continued typing while Badge lay under the desk.

"I'm finished, guys," James said after several hours. "I'll see you tomorrow." He stood and prepared to leave.

"Are you going to the hospital?" Miguel asked, still typing.

"I'll see you there," James said.

"We'll be there, but don't know the time. We have to finish all this."

"If I don't see you there, I'll see you tomorrow. Better finish today, so we can have a new assignment tomorrow."

James left and Miguel continued typing.

After a while, Miguel checked Badge. "How are you doing down there?"

Badge whimpered.

Concentrating on his report, Miguel continued to type.

Time passed.

"We're almost done, Badge. Hold on."

No response came from below the desk.

Miguel checked under the desk, but Badge was gone. Miguel turned around, *nothing!* "Badge, come here," he shouted.

Badge didn't come.

Miguel sprang from his chair, grabbing it from an armrest before it overturned. "Where did he go?" he asked himself and checked the offices nearby.

Badge wasn't around.

Miguel continued looking. "Have you seen Badge?" he asked several employees.

Everybody knew Badge, but nobody had seen him.

"Have you seen Badge?" Miguel asked the people he met in corridors and several offices.

"I saw him," a woman carrying documents said, "in the hall in front of the conference room."

"What? The one at the other side of the building?"

"That one."

Miguel ran to the other side of the building wondering what the problem was. When he approached the conference room, he saw Badge's silhouette lying on the floor.

"Badge, what are you doing here?"

Badge only moved his eyes, and then whined.

"What's going on Badge?" Miguel asked as he approached. "Did the burgers upset your stomach?"

Badge looked at the wall and whined again.

Miguel turned to see the wall. Photos of agents and employees receiving awards were there. One was a picture of Robert and Sarge.

* * * * *

Miguel and Badge visited Robert that evening. Robert had been taken out of intensive care, so they were able to enter Robert's room without any restrictions.

"Doctors anticipate a complete recovery," Robert said. "But after a rigorous rehabilitation plan."

"Tell me about it," Miguel said.

"Captain Williams came today. The Annual Agent Recognition Ceremony is on Wednesday, and a memorial ceremony for Sarge is going to be included."

"Are you going to the office?"

"No. Arrangements are being made to hold the ceremony in the hospital's gardens. The Captain suggested it"

"That sounds perfect. The Captain had a great idea."

"Yes, Miguel. I'm grateful they're doing it in the hospital because of me, but I'm nervous few people will attend or stay for Sarge's ceremony."

"Don't worry, Robert. Everything is going to be all right. A lot of people knew Sarge and his accomplishments."

"Miguel, will you prepare a few words to say at the ceremony."

"I would be honored."

* * * * *

Miguel and Badge returned to the DEA building the following day.

"Are you ready for a new assignment, dynamic duo?" James asked.

"Ready for the next big operation," Miguel said. "Badge is ready to sink his teeth into a drug lord's butt. Aren't you, Badge?"

"Woof!" Badge barked.

Everybody laughed.

Later, Sarah, Captain Williams's assistant, brought James and Miguel a big pile of folders and instructions to access data in the computer.

"What? More paperwork?" Miguel asked.

"Yes, sir," Sarah said. "Review all the intelligence information gathered from Operation Lobo. Verify if anything has to be corrected or requires further investigation."

"But when are we going to get a new assignment?"

"This is your new assignment," Sarah said politely.

"I'm talking about something real. I'm not asking for a whole new operation. What about the vehicle crossings, or the airport? Where's the Captain?"

"I don't see intelligence work as any less real or important than field work, Agent Cordova," she replied. "The Captain is busy with meetings. Some are to prepare the recognition ceremony. The others are to explain your incursion into a foreign country."

James made a cutting motion across his throat when Sarah was not looking at him.

Miguel accepted James's quiet recommendation and listened patiently as Sarah explained the folders and their content.

"Calm down, Miguel," James said when Sarah left. "Lobo may be over in the field, but the details have to be explained to Washington and to the Mexican government."

"What has to be explained?" Miguel argued. "Robert and I saw the opportunity and followed the tunnel before the traffickers vanished. We're authorized to work on both sides of the border as part of the DEA-FAST program. The SWAT team entered Mexican territory to provide cover for the rescue operation."

"All that is correct, Miguel, but the Mexicans say DEA-FAST is authorized to enter Mexican territory only in coordination with them."

"I'm a Mexican agent working for the Policía Federal."

"But you're assigned to DEA."

"If DEA contacts the Mexican authorities, it loses the surprise factor. They may be contacting the devil himself, somebody on the drug cartels' payroll."

"Don't assume traffickers only have undercover informants inside Mexican law enforcement. They may have them in the American side too—DEA, Washington, local police, or any other agency."

"Agreed, we have to expect the unexpected. But what drives me crazy is that we still don't know whether to consider Lobo a great success or a big failure."

"You know it was successful, Miguel. If the drugs and the weapons were destroyed, then they're not on the streets. And that's what really counts."

"I'm sorry." Miguel calmed down. "I'm just complicating things more than they already are."

"Let's just review all this stuff," James said. "Maybe we'll find names or locations for further investigation."

James and Miguel reviewed the information for hours, reading arrest reports, suspect lists, and criminal records.

"Did you find anything new, Miguel?" James asked.

"No, nothing that isn't already in our other reports," Miguel said. "There were no confessions. Those people seem to have found good lawyers and quickly."

Badge whined.

"Hold on, Badge. Hold on," Miguel said.

James and Miguel put aside the criminal files and proceeded to review the reports about Atlantic Trading Company, its owners, history, and tax records.

Hours went by.

"I've come up empty. You find anything?" James asked, stretching.

"No, there's nothing new here either. Sorry!" Miguel said and watched Badge next to the window. He dashed from one side to the other, trying to chase squirrels as they ran across the lawn.

The review of purchase orders, requisitions, suppliers, and received shipments took another few hours. Badge had settled at Miguel's feet again.

"Any luck, Miguel?"

"No. If they had something going prior to this, it's not showing up in this data. Maybe everything related to this tunnel is a new operation. I don't even see anything here to show us where the weapons might have originated."

Badge stood, stretched, and moved to a fresh spot to lie down again.

Reviewing invoices, sales orders, and customer files took two more hours.

Badge whined.

"We're about to finish, Badge. Hold on," Miguel said.

"I don't see anything new here either," James said as he closed a folder. "What about you?"

"No, everything as you'd expect. Well, except one small detail."

"What's that?" James asked as he pushed the piles of folders away and moved over to see what Miguel had found.

"I hope this is worth investigating. Does each shipment include the license plate of the truck transporting the cargo?"

"Yes."

"And do you remember the list of truck plates we made when we carried out the surveillance at the warehouse?"

"Yeah."

"That list was continued by Team Three the following day, wasn't it?"

"Please! What are you getting at?

"Well, the lists don't match. Some plates don't appear on the shipping orders."

"Yes, but those trucks could have left empty."

"No, that's the mismatch. We have it in writing. We and Team Three saw those trucks being loaded."

"You're right! Ghost shipments. Where are those lists?"

"They're in the folders marked as *other*, in the general information stack."

Night had fallen. Badge couldn't see through the window anymore. Bored, he rested his head on top of a chair to observe Miguel and James.

Miguel and James were too busy to notice.

"How could you find that information in this sea of paper?" James asked.

"Easy, just put the plate numbers from the shipping orders in a list in the computer and get them ordered. Do the same for the plates gathered during the surveillance. Then, I compared the lists."

"Where those trucks went is worth investigating. Let's e-mail those numbers to the Captain so he can request an investigation of those trucks."

"Perfect! There aren't as many numbers, only a couple dozen. We do that, and we're out of here." Miguel smiled for the first time.

Badge rolled onto his back and squirmed.

Miguel wrote the e-mail to Williams and James verified everything before sending it.

"Miguel, you have some duplicate numbers in here. Is it a mistake or is there a reason for that?"

"I didn't realize that. Let me check." Miguel reviewed his notes. "Those duplicates are correct," he said after a while. "They appear in our list and again in the list from Team Three the following day. What could that mean?"

"That means those trucks came back to reload the next day," James said.

"So, the other location is nearby, probably in the San Diego metropolitan area. . . . Does that make sense?"

"Hmm," James touched his chin. "Atlantic may be just one of multiple sources for that other location."

"Wow! That's big."

"Woof!" Badge reminded his partners. Dinner time was way overdue.

Chapter 26: Goodbye to a Friend

Early on Wednesday, Miguel and Badge went to the DEA building. Miguel looked forward to Sarge's Memorial, and to learning what plans would be made for locating the suspect trucks.

"Nothing?" Miguel said after reviewing his e-mail. He expected to find instructions about the next steps in the investigation. "The Captain might be busy preparing the Recognition Ceremony," Miguel said to Badge. He wondered if he and James had somehow mismanaged their time; they had stayed until midnight the day before, and they had no assignment that day. "Better do the analysis as soon as possible, while the case is still warm," he concluded. "The location of those trucks and their purpose will only be harder to track as more time passes. What you think Badge?"

"Woof!" Badge agreed.

"Let's go. We can still do something important." They went for target practice. Besides sharpening his shooting skills, range practice seemed to hone Miguel's thinking. "It's strange that, in the middle of the noise, I can concentrate on an idea or a problem," Miguel said to Badge as they walked. "Maybe it's like music and math. Music stimulates specific neurons in the brain and that seems to carry over to nearby neurons used for math."

Badge turned and howled.

"Sorry, Badge. I wasn't talking about that kind of music."

Badge replied with a short growl.

"In shooting, taking aim and focusing on a target could help focus on an idea." Miguel and Badge paused before entering the practice area. Badge turned to Miguel and tilted his head. "Maybe I'm just crazy, but as long as it works, it's nice to get two benefits."

Badge huffed.

"Hi, Tom," Miguel said to the training installation officer.

"Hey, Miguel. Did you come to practice again?" Tom verified Miguel's identification and called up his record from the database. "With this record, you don't need to practice."

"I practice, so I don't need to." Miguel grinned.

"Hmm," Tom frowned. "Strange reasoning, but it may be true." He gave Miguel a box of ammunition for the Colt handgun.

"You're trying to get rid of me or what?" Miguel asked as he shook the box of bullets.

"Sorry, Miguel, you only get one box this time. A cost-saving initiative, the agency's restricting all our supplies."

"Traffickers get better equipment each day and all the ammo they can shoot at us. The only things they don't have yet are surveillance drones."

"I know. I know. But that's the order. Sorry, Miguel."

"I'm the one who needs to apologize, Tom." Miguel said as he signed the receipt for the bullets. "I guess I just envy the traffickers."

Miguel and Badge walked to the station Tom had assigned.

"Next time we find weapons and ammunition, I won't destroy them, Badge," Miguel loaded his gun. "The agency can use them. Otherwise, we'll have to practice with a slingshot."

"Woof!" Badge replied.

"Sit, Badge. Sit," Miguel commanded.

Badge sat, head up, ears alert; it was also a practice for him.

As Miguel took aim for his first shot, he considered what he'd say at Sarge's memorial.

* * * * *

Miguel and Badge arrived at University Hospital just moments before the start of the Annual Agent Recognition Ceremony. Miguel was wearing his gala uniform from the Policía Federal. Badge wore his vest and his shield.

Many people had already gathered in one of the gardens. Most of the two hundred chairs were already filled. "That's a good sign for Sarge's Memorial. Don't you think, Badge?"

"Woof!" Badge replied.

"Miguel, Badge, we're waiting for you!" James waved them over. He was also wearing a gala uniform. "There's a reserved place for you in the front."

"I'm sorry; I didn't know." Miguel and Badge joined James, and the three of them walked to the other side of the garden.

"Holding the ceremony here in the garden required some improvisation," James said. "I hope it goes smoothly. The Captain only had a couple of days to pull it all together."

The Chief Officer tapped the microphone, and the team jogged to their chairs. Miguel saw Robert in his wheelchair on the other side of the first row. He was wearing his hospital gown with his uniform shirt draped over his shoulders. His right arm and leg were covered with bandages. He winced, clearly in pain, when he moved, but a smile returned when he greeted some fellow officers.

The ceremony started. The Chief Officer gave the keynote address, outlined plans for the agency's future, and gave seizure statistics from past operations. The presentation seemed to drag on. Information about new ways to exchange information with other field offices and agencies followed. After all this, the recognition ceremony began. Employees and agents were called forward based on their time in service: five years, ten years, and fifteen years or more. Highlights from personnel records were read, certificates awarded, and special service recognition noted. The audience applauded. As the ceremony proceeded, Miguel concentrated on Sarge's eulogy. Badge stayed seated next to him, enjoying the breeze.

"Today, we also recognize two fellow officers for their service to the Agency and to the community . . ." the Chief Officer said.

Finally! The moment Miguel waited for. He raised his head and turned around. *Wow!* There were so many people. Officers in uniform from other law enforcement agencies, a group with dogs, news crews, and several men with bagpipes stood behind the seated guests. Even the BEAR was in the parking lot. *Is she around?*

The Chief Officer read Robert's record and notable accomplishments for the Agency without disclosing his name. When he reached the end, he said, ". . . for being seriously wounded in the line of duty, suffering injuries which were a direct result of hostile action, the Drug Enforcement Administration Purple Heart Medal is conferred to Special Agent Robert West."

Robert's brother pushed his wheelchair toward the podium.

The Chief Officer placed the medal on Robert's shirt and both saluted.

Everyone applauded.

The Chief Officer talked with Robert for a moment, and then took the microphone again. "In a moment we'll hear some words from Special Agent West."

Robert nodded, and his family approached. They placed a tripod with a huge photograph of Sarge facing the crowd. Next to it, they placed a small table with the pine wood box and Sarge's shredded vest.

The Chief Officer continued. "The next officer I'd like to recognize is not with us anymore. He had a record of four hundred fifty-seven calls, two hundred fifty-four narcotics finds, fifty-seven criminal apprehensions, and ninety-one community demonstrations. He helped in the rescue of violence victims. He saved the lives of his human and canine partners. For dying in the line of duty, The Drug Enforcement Administration Purple Heart Award is posthumously conferred to K9 Officer Sarge."

The Chief Officer placed the medal on Sarge's vest and saluted, looking at the photograph.

Everyone applauded.

The Chief Officer made a signal to a sergeant on the other side of the garden.

"Load, aim, fire," the sergeant ordered a squad of officers. The sound of the blanks filled the air. The sequence repeated twice more. The crowd maintained a respectful silence. Then, another officer played "Taps" with his trumpet.

After that, Captain Williams walked to the podium. He cleared his throat and said. "Sarge had an enviable record. He trained to detect drugs and explosives. His keen sense of smell could detect certain items even if sealed in plastic or buried in materials intended to mask the scent. Sarge trained to perform criminal apprehension, using his canine speed to chase and catch fleeing or violent suspects. He was also trained in officer safety, protecting his handler and reacting if he sensed danger. This last commendable duty cost Sarge his life."

Williams continued after a pause. "Sarge had no salary and no benefits but performed like an exemplary officer. He helped train other canine officers and gave demonstrations at public events. He had no firearm to defend himself. He had his teeth and his speed. He had a loving family, the West family, and a multitude of human and canine friends."

"I know of cases where medals awarded to military dogs or police dogs have been revoked due to complaints that bestowing a medal on a dog demeans the men who received medals. What a ridiculous thing!" Williams struck the podium with his fist. "Whoever said that, didn't ask the human fellow officers for an opinion. Handlers and teammates understand the value and the merits of a canine partner. Sharing a medal with someone who knows about loyalty, courage, and hard work, only increases the medal's value. Learn from Officer Sarge and always remember him. Thank you." Williams bowed his head for a moment and then returned to his seat. The silence following his speech was almost palpable.

Next, James rose and walked to the podium. "Sarge—Officer Sarge— truly was an officer." James paused as if to gather his thoughts. "What I mean is that he was as much an officer as any human member of the team. He wasn't considered just a pet or an appliance, but a friend!"

James seemed to sense the heavy sadness in the crowd. "Sarge had an enviable record. I envied him because he attended his job naked. Sarge was exceptional at his job; few could compare to him. I haven't seen many officers eager to jump into conflict the way Sarge did. He was always ready and impatient for action, so much that he slobbered the window and the seat of the squad car with anticipation. Sarge had the courage of a lion. And, after hours of hard work, he smelled like one." James looked around at the smiling faces in the crowd. A few people even managed a laugh. "Godspeed on your new assignment, Sarge." James returned to his chair.

Short and effective. Miguel almost tripped when he stood up. After the long wait, he had to hurry to the podium. He didn't expect James to finish so fast. As he and Badge walked to the front, he became increasingly nervous. *The Captain and James said wonderful things already.*

Miguel began. "'Let there be light!' God said the first day of Creation. Light separated from darkness, and day and night were named. 'Let there be a firmament!' God said the second day of Creation. The waters above divided from the waters below and the sky was named. 'Let there be land!' God said the third day of Creation. The waters below gathered in one place, dry land appeared, and Earth and Sea were named. 'Bring forth grass, plants, and trees!' God commanded to Earth. 'Let there be lights in the firmament!' God said the fourth day of Creation. Two great lights and the stars appeared in the firmament to mark days, seasons, and years. 'Teem with living creatures!' God said on the fifth day. The sea produced fish; birds flew across the heavens. 'Bring forth living creatures upon the land!' God said on the sixth day. He made wild beasts, carnivores, herbivores, insects, and reptiles. Then, He created Man in his image and in his likeness. 'Very good,' God said on the seventh day. He observed the totality of his creation and rested."

Miguel looked at Sarge's photograph. "'Come here' God said on the eighth day to a creature whose wagging tail caught his attention. 'You shall protect Man and be his companion,' God commanded. 'To achieve your mission, I give you courage, faithfulness, and wisdom. You won't have the power of words. You won't need them because you'll have the power to speak through honest eyes. You'll be blind to the faults of Man, so you'll always be loyal to him. Be the silent friend of man, and guide him.' The creature listened carefully to what God said and happily wagged his tail for the task entrusted to him. 'I created Man in my image,' God said. 'You're a reflection of my love for Man. Thus, your name will be a reflection of my name. I'll turn my own name back to front and call you, Dog, my friend.'"

Miguel lowered his eyes for a moment, and then looked up at the crowd again. "The world will be a better place for what you did when you visited us, Sarge. May your heart be peaceful and calm." Miguel walked back to his seat with Badge at his side.

The crowd was held in absolute silence.

Looking down, Miguel sighed. No longer worried about his presentation, he focused on the memories of a lost friend.

The Chief Officer handed Robert the microphone.

From his wheelchair, Robert looked out at the silent crowd. "To work with a canine officer is to be in a special kind of brotherhood," he said. "It's a bond that only others like us could understand. When we trained and worked, Sarge always gave his best. His four paws never rested; He always did what I asked. Yet, he seemed to enjoy every task. Sarge searched for those who wished harm to others. He found fugitives, drugs, weapons, even bombs; nothing went undetected. He was always silent, always vigilant, always loyal, and always at my side. I considered him my right arm, nose, ears, and eyes.—He was my guide. Whether he was chasing criminals or going fishing, he considered my company his reward. He was protective and courageous up to the last breath. Thank you, loyal and faithful partner. Now, I'm proud I had the opportunity to be your friend and learn your silent message of wisdom."

Robert raised his face and his voice. "Until we meet again, my friend, may you always run fast, bite hard, and fear nothing."[59]

Robert nodded to the Chief Officer who signaled the bagpipers. They played "Amazing Grace".

Many people in the crowd dabbed at teary eyes or murmured quietly to companions, clearly moved by the ceremony and the music.

When the music ended, the Chief Officer took the microphone again. "All DEA agents get in formation and prepare for inspection. Officers from other agencies will engage in parade drills. When the inspection is over, the official ceremony will conclude. I want to thank everyone for joining us. You're invited to stay for refreshments which will be served in the back garden following the inspections and drills."

All DEA agents rushed into a line and stood at attention. Robert, in his wheelchair, was placed at the beginning. James, Miguel, and Badge took positions at the end. Miguel worried his different uniform might make the line look uneven.

"Sit, Badge. Sit. Attention," Miguel commanded. "Any activities after this?" he whispered to James.

"No, we're free to go for the day," James said, holding inspection posture. "Tomorrow is a normal day at the Agency. I hope we get a new assignment or at least know what to do with those truck plates."

The Chief Officer, Captain Williams, and several high-ranking officials started the inspection. They stopped for a while and talked with Robert and his family, who stood behind him. After that, the inspection moved much quicker.

"Who's the guy in the suit?" Miguel asked.

"Which one?" James asked.

"The tall one. He's the only one not wearing a uniform."

"I have no idea."

"Somebody mentioned he's a senior official of the Mexican government," Mark, standing next to them, said.

"Do you know his name?" Miguel asked.

"No. Maybe you'll be able to identify him when he walks in front of us," Mark whispered.

The group of high-ranking officials approached. From time to time, they stopped and talked with men in the line.

"This is Special Agent James Kelly, part of the canine team." Williams introduced James to the group.

"Nice to meet you," one man said. "Keep up with the good work," said another. "Way to go," said a third. As they passed along the line, the inspection group offered greetings and made polite comments.

"James Kelly? Nice to meet you," the man in the suit said, looking James up and down.

The group moved forward and stood in front of Miguel.

"This is Special Agent Miguel Cordova," Williams said. "He's the agent in the exchange program with the Policía Federal—a program that's already generated exceptional results. And this is K9 Officer Badge."

"Nice to have you with us," one commented. "Good work," said another. "Nice to meet you," came from someone in the back of the group.

"Miguel Cordova?" the man in the suit said. "I've heard a lot about you lately." He shook Miguel's hand. Miguel couldn't help but notice the man's large gold ring with a huge emerald.

"Thank you, sir," Miguel said. He had seen the man in the Mexican media, but wasn't sure of his name.

"And you're Badge," the big man said as the group moved away. "I've heard about you too." He crouched and patted and rubbed Badge with the ring-bearing hand.

"Sir, be careful," Williams warned. "Please move along." He tried to make the big man rejoin the group.

"Careful? He's a nice little puppy," the man said and continued rubbing and patting Badge.

"He isn't a puppy, sir," Williams said. "He's a sworn officer trained for patrol and arrest. We don't recommend strangers touch the dogs."

"Stranger? We're friends, aren't we little puppy?"

Badge felt the man's big hand and didn't like it. An odor, the voice, the way he patted him, maybe it was everything at the same time. "Woof!" In a lightning action, he jumped backwards and struck, biting the hand. "Woof, woof!"

Miguel reacted by pulling Badge's leash.

Williams dashed to the man's side and pulled him away from Badge. The man fell backwards.

"Woof, woof!" Badge barked, raising a commotion in the line.

The high-ranking officials helped the big man stand up.

Groaning, the big man covered his bleeding hand.

Williams, mouth agape, stared from the man to Badge and back again. He turned to Miguel as if waiting for an explanation.

Miguel restrained Badge, but he didn't know what to say.

"Come with me, sir," Williams said to the big man. "We'll take care of that right away." He personally escorted the man toward the hospital's entrance. Some of the other officials followed them while some remained near the line of officers, unsure on what to do next.

"What just happened?" James asked Miguel, still in formation.

"I don't know," Miguel shrugged, still surprised. "I don't know."

Badge didn't fight the leash or bark anymore. He shook from nose to tail, as if he'd just had a bath. After that, he sat and stayed still.

Chapter 27: Dragging Feet —and Paws

Next morning, Miguel and Badge arrived at the DEA building, ready to continue the investigation. Miguel was tense and he'd been unable to sleep the previous night. He was worried about the bite incident. He'd learned, by Internet search that the big man in the suit was governor of a northern Mexican state. *Not good news if the DEA hopes to improve relations with their Mexican counterparts after the incursion into Mexican territory.* Following the incident, Captain Williams had recommended him leave the hospital to avoid the media and prevent any bad publicity for the Agency.

Miguel found an e-mail requesting his presence in the conference room at 11:00 am. The message worried him even more. "Nothing about the truck plates and no new assignment," he said to Badge. "This can't be good."

"How are you? How is Badge?" James asked when he arrived at his desk.

"Woof," Badge replied, wagging his tail.

"Fine, but not happy," Miguel said. "Worried, I'd say."

"That bite was ugly. Do you know what set Badge off like that?"

"I have no idea. Only thing I can speculate is that the Governor—."

"Governor!" James interrupted "Wow! That doesn't help international relations."

"Thanks for the encouragement," Miguel said. "Maybe that big ring he wore got stuck in Badge's fur."

"You're kidding, right?"

"Maybe. I don't know. I'm just looking for some kind of explanation. The ring getting stuck is as good as any other. Or maybe a bee stung Badge's tail at the precise moment the governor patted him . . . I don't know."

"Well, at least we were near a hospital." James said trying to inject some humor after looking at Miguel's face.

"I don't know what else could have gone wrong yesterday. There was the bite, and after that, the Captain's polite recommendation to leave."

"Before I forget, Abira asked for you. I told her that you had to go to the dentist."

Miguel bowed his head and banged it on the desktop. "Wouldn't you know it?"

James checked his messages and e-mail. "Nothing about the plates. Just an order to report for a conference at eleven."

"Same here," Miguel said.

"Maybe that conference will be good news. Cheer up! Miguel, be positive!"

* * * * *

At 11:00 am the team entered the conference room. The room was crammed with people and the tables were arranged in a u-shape. Miguel recognized some of the people as high-ranking officials, others as administrative employees. Captain Williams was seated at one of the tables at the front of the room. *They've been here for a while,* Miguel thought looking at the folders and papers scattered across the tables.

"Names?" an employee on the other side of the room asked.

"Agent James Kelly."

"Agent Miguel Cordova . . . and Officer Badge."

"Be seated, please." The employee wrote down the names and pointed to a couple of empty chairs.

Miguel and James took their seats.

"Sit, Badge. Sit," Miguel commanded, keeping Badge between his chair and James'.

Miguel and James looked at each other wondering what could be happening, but neither of them said a word. Badge looked alternatively to Miguel and to James, also wondering.

"Captain Williams, you may start," one of the high-ranking-officials said.

"Agents Cordova and Kelly, this panel is reviewing the events from last week under Operation Lobo. Agent Miguel Cordova, please come forward."

Miguel felt like he'd been punched in the stomach. He gave Badge's leash to James and entered the open end of the u-shape to stand to attention where the Captain pointed. He faced the head table where Captain Williams and several other stern-faced men sat looking him up and down.

Is this an interrogation about what happened or am I to be reprimanded and dismissed?

"Agent Cordova," Williams said, "everyone present in this room has read your report regarding Operation Lobo. Please respond as directly and completely as possible to the following questions."

"Yes, sir."

"Were you aware that entering the discovered tunnel could take you into Mexico?"

"Yes, sir."

"Was an incursion into Mexico included in the plans for Operation Lobo?"

"No, sir. But under the DEA-FAST program we're authorized to execute operations in Mexico."

"Agent Cordova, please limit your answers to the context of the question. Was the incursion into Mexico planned as part of Operation Lobo?"

"No, sir." Miguel was surprised by Williams's tone. The Captain knew there had been no plan to enter Mexico.

"During the operation, was there any coordination with Mexican authorities?"

"Yes, sir."

"Can you detail that coordination?"

"Yes, sir. The Mexican authorities were contacted when Agent West was injured."

"Was there any coordination before that?"

"No, sir."

"Had a warrant been issued that authorized you to enter the Mexican warehouse?"

"No, sir."

"Did you arrest two Mexican nationals?"

"Yes, sir."

"Did you release them later?"

"Yes, sir."

The stern-looking officials muttered to each other for some time, taking notes.

"Did anyone issue an order to set fire to the warehouse?"

"No, sir. I made that decision."

"Come on! Where are you going with all this?" James interrupted rising from his seat.

"Agent Kelly, please sit down," Williams said. "You'll have your turn to speak."

James sat down with a frown.

"Why did you decide to set fire to the warehouse, Agent Cordova?" Williams asked.

"To destroy the weapons and drugs. The situation didn't allow for them to be properly secured."

"How did you know the weapons and the drugs couldn't be secured?"

"We had already waited for hours for the Mexican authorities. They couldn't reach us because they were caught in a standoff with traffickers. Then, you commanded us to leave, sir."

"You were commanded to leave, not to destroy a warehouse."

"Yes, sir. Your orders were to withdraw. The destruction of weapons and drugs was my decision alone."

"Woof, woof!" Badge rose and barked. He heard the strain in Miguel's voice and thought something wasn't right. James wrapped the leash around his hand and patted Badge on the head.

"Keep that dog quiet!" one of the men seated near Captain Williams shouted.

"Quiet, Badge. Quiet. Sit," Miguel commanded and gave the hand signal for sit.

Badge whimpered and sat.

"And why did you decide to destroy the weapons and drugs, Agent Cordova?" Williams continued.

"Destroying the weapons would prevent them from being used against Mexican or American agents, or prevent their use in further violent acts that could endanger civilians. Destroying the drugs prevented them from being sold in America, sir, where they were undoubtedly headed."

"And you think you have the authority to decide that?"

Miguel looked at the stern faces and considered his answer. He hadn't expected an inquisition, and certainly not from the Captain. "I don't know if I had the authority, sir. What I know is that an action had to be taken at that moment. I think I made the correct decision given the circumstances."

As another pause interrupted the questioning, the people seated around the tables continued murmuring and conferring.

"Agent Cordova, please explain why you shot a rocket-propelled grenade into the tunnel," Captain Williams asked.

"Agent West and I discovered boxes containing drugs within the tunnel. I didn't want them to be recovered by the traffickers. I verified nobody was in the tunnel before firing the rocket."

Williams took a document from the folder in front of him and read, "The company Advanced Technological Products, the one next to the warehouse, claims that an underground explosion disrupted their operation when a plastic injector machine, used to produce toys, sank into the ground. They're filing a lawsuit against various law enforcement agencies, including DEA." He laid the document and some photos on the table. "That tunnel was extensive, passing beneath businesses, maybe even residential areas. Didn't you consider that your actions could injure civilians or damage property?"

"Sorry, I didn't consider that, sir."

The people at the tables murmured again.

Miguel pressed his lips tight and clenched his jaw, sensing he hadn't done well with that last question.

"Please, return to your seat, Agent Cordova," Captain Williams ordered.

Upset, Miguel returned to his seat as the murmurs continued in the room.

"Agent James Kelly, please come forward," Williams ordered.

"Agent Kelly, everyone in attendance has read your report," Williams said when James had come to attention amidst the tables. "Please respond to the following questions."

"Yes, sir."

"Were you aware the tunnel led into Mexico?"

James exhaled slowly. "No, but it was most probable, sir."

"Are you authorized to operate in Mexico?"

"No, sir. And I did not."

"Was an incursion into Mexico a planned element of Operation Lobo?"

"No, sir. It wasn't planned."

"Was there any coordination with the Mexican authorities before or during Operation Lobo?"

"Yes, sir."

"Can you detail that coordination?"

"Yes, sir. I asked for backup when Agent West was injured."

"Was there any kind of coordination before that?"

"No, sir. We were waiting for an address for the Mexico location before calling them." James realized his interrogation was going to be as harsh as Miguel's.

"Did you give an order to set fire to the warehouse?"

"No, sir. But I agree it was an appropriate action."

"Agent Kelly, please limit your answers to the questions. We're not asking for your opinions."

"Sorry, sir. You said I'd have my turn to talk."

"Agent Kelly, you're going to address only the issues as the questions are put to you. Is that understood?"

"Yes, sir." James felt his ears heat up and took a deep breath. *No sense getting upset now*, he thought.

Williams continued. "Did you communicate to Agent Cordova and the SWAT team that Mexican authorities had been contacted and asked to go to the site to secure the weapons and drugs?"

"Yes, sir. I informed them. I also told them the Mexican authorities were unable to reach the site." James spoke quickly. He wanted to give his point of view before being interrupted. "I also told them that the Mexican army was at a distant location. I also coordinated the rescue of

Agent West with the Coast Guard. I also coordinated the retreat. I also oppose this ridiculous inquisition and that politicians and non-agency officials are in attendance."

"Stop right there, Agent Kelly!" Williams commanded.

"Woof, woof!" Badge barked again.

The murmurs among the officials started again.

"Quiet, Badge. Quiet," Miguel commanded, rubbing Badge's neck to calm him.

Captain Williams and the other officials made notes in their file folders

James waited for the next question.

"Please, return to your seat, Agent Kelly," Captain Williams ordered.

James returned to his chair making sure to make as much noise with it as possible.

"Just to inform you," Williams said, "besides Operation Lobo, the Mexican official bitten yesterday by Officer Badge informed us he's going to file a lawsuit and an official complaint with the government."

"He was told not to touch Badge!" Miguel sprang from his chair. "You told him yourself. The man ignored you!"

"Woof, woof!" Badge barked.

"I know what happened, Agent Cordova. I'm only informing you of the consequences of the incident."

The officials murmured again.

"Woof, woof!" Badge barked again. This forced the officials to raise their voices until they were all yelling trying to make points or ask questions."

"Woof, woof!" Badge continued barking.

"Order, please. Order," one of the men demanded. The situation become chaotic with everyone talking at once, leaving their seats, and demanding to know what would happen next. "Agents Kelly, Cordova, and-and-and- officer dog, please wait outside. We'll call you in a moment."

James, Miguel, and Badge walked toward the door. When they reached the hall, one of the officials said, "Captain John Williams, we have some questions for you. Please come around and stand before the panel."

Miguel and James looked at each other. They turned back to the door to see what was happening.

Captain Williams stood up and came around to stand in front of the assembled officials just as Miguel and James had.

At that moment, someone inside closed the door.

* * * * *

James paced the hall, staring at the floor. Suddenly, he stopped. "Don't worry, everything is going to be all right," he said as he turned, and then paced again.

The discussion in the conference room was loud and apparently heated, but Miguel and James couldn't make out enough words to know what was going on.

"What do you think, James? Is this serious?" Miguel asked.

"Serious? Oh, yeah. It's the first time I've seen anything like this."

"What can we expect?"

"I have no idea. I suspect they're getting pressure from both the U.S. and Mexican governments. Operation Lobo got way more complicated than anyone thought."

"The Captain was there during the operation," Miguel said. "Why is he upset with us now?"

"That's exactly the part that bothers me the most," James said. "Were those his questions because he's under pressure to provide more answers, or were the questions prepared by the panel and as the ranking officer he was obligated to ask them?"

An agency employee came down the hall. She stopped when she heard the ruckus in the conference room. "What's going on in there?" she asked.

"Constructive debate, I guess," Miguel said.

When she had walked away, James said, "The tone in there has changed. It seems like the Captain is being reprimanded now."

"Well, I halted the Barbie-doll production when that injector sank, and Badge bit an important government official," Miguel said. "Someone was going to be reprimanded sooner or later. Let's see what happens."

In time, the discussion in the conference room ended. The door opened, and someone asked the team to come back in.

"Don't sit," Williams said. "Please stand before the panel again, the three of you."

The crowd had become dead silent.

"Agents Cordova and Kelly," Williams said, "after reviewing all the information, this panel is recommending a temporary suspension. The suspension is effective immediately. You're relieved of your duties until an investigation is completed. Agent West's actions are also being reviewed, and he will be questioned as soon as he returns to active duty. Do you have anything to say?"

Miguel and James looked at each other. They couldn't believe how things had come out. Badge looked at them.

"Can you give us any indication of the length of suspension, sir," James asked.

"Until the investigation ends. It could be weeks, months . . . we don't know. It all depends on how the investigation develops." Williams looked from James to Miguel. "If there are no further questions, you'll be dismissed now. Leave your firearms, shields, and all your equipment in your lockers. Leave the keys with my assistant. Agent Kelly, be sure to include the keys for your vehicle."

Upset by the nature of the meeting and the outcome, James and Miguel stood like statues in the middle of the room. Miguel felt light-headed and weak. Between the men, Badge sat, nervously looking from one to the other.

"You can leave now," Williams said.

The team walked to the door for a second time. This time, they were dragging feet -and paws.

"Agent Cordova," Williams said as they neared the open door.

Miguel stopped and turned, slowly. "Yes, sir."

"Officer Badge is also suspended. There will be an exhaustive investigation into why a highly-trained law enforcement dog bit the hand of a foreign-government official."

Badge snorted as if he understood how much trouble he was in. "Woof, woof!" he barked as the team left the conference room.

"I knew the dog was going to do that," Williams said to the man seated next to him.

Chapter 28: The Wet Tree

Miguel gave the devastated James a ride home.

The morning's events turned over and over in Miguel's mind as he and Badge returned to the apartment.

"It just doesn't make sense . . . suspended. Do you believe it Badge?"

Badge tilted his head.

"Why was Captain Williams asking all those biased questions?"

"Woof!" Badge sat and scratched with a hind leg.

"Don't like it! Without any warning and in front of a crowd."

Badge whined.

"The maquiladora company that suffered damages could be an issue, but why didn't they mention damages to buildings and cars?"

Badge turned before laying down on his mat.

"James got the worst part. He didn't cross to the Mexican side, nor did he order any of the actions. Yet, he was suspended and his vehicle taken."

Badge started to byte his rubber chicken.

"What about Robert? He received a commendation for his actions, but he'll likely be questioned and suspended too when he returns to duty."

Badge pressed and pulled a towel he used as a blanket.

"Same thing as the investigation of the clash between my old team and the Mexican Army. Instead of being resolved, it was covered up. Could that happen again?"

Badge turned upside down and rubbed his back on the towel.

"Politics and hidden interests control things in the United States just as they do in Mexico. Procedures, investigations, panels, and commissions are all used for cover-ups and to bias the facts when the truth could damage someone's secret project and reputation."

Badge eyes moved from one side to the other, following Miguel movements.

"What would Policía Federal say about the entire situation? If they agree with the suspension, it becomes an extra problem for us, Badge. If they disagree, the relationship with the DEA could be compromised and the bi-national program terminated." Miguel sighed.

Badge lowered his head to the mat.

"The only thing I'm sure off is that I would do it all again, exactly the same way. Even if knowing a suspension would be the result."

Badge wasn't listening anymore.

"The fewer bullets and fewer drugs on the streets justify the sacrifice," Miguel continued without noticing Badge had fallen asleep.

Miguel decided to take a long walk that afternoon. Badge liked Mission Beach Park as much as him. Miguel wanted some time to think. He would wait until that night to report the day's events to Captain Ortiz at the Policía Federal.

Miguel felt a little guilty playing with Badge at the park, on a weekday, while they were suspended. Badge had enjoyed the ride to the park, poking his head through the car's window to feel the breeze.

"If the Policía Federal calls me back, this could be the last time we visit Mission Beach Park," Miguel said as he threw the Frisbee.

Badge started to run.

"What about you my friend? What would the Hunters say about all this? They'd be greatly disappointed".

316

Badge caught the Frisbee.

Miguel looked around, the sand, the sea, and the sunset.

Badge returned with the Frisbee and sat to Miguel's side.

"Whatever happens, don't let this magnificent view be taken away from you."

* * * * *

Miguel and Badge returned to the apartment at dusk.

The phone flashed with several messages. He pressed the play button. Every message was from James.

"What now? Why didn't he call my cell?" He took the cell out of his pocket. "Damn! I forgot to turn it back on after the conference."

Badge nudged his bowl with his nose.

"Wait, Badge. Dinner has to wait." He dialed James's number.

"Miguel, where have you been?" James asked.

"Just went out for a walk."

"I've been looking for you."

"What's up? Is Robert OK?

"Yes, he's OK. It's something else."

"What is it?"

"I'll tell you when I see you."

"Well, come over then."

"No, it has to be someplace else."

"Then where?"

"Don't mention names, but what about the place you told me you liked to go play Frisbee with Badge? How about we meet where we parked when Robert and Sarge were with us?"

"Come on! Are you serious?"

"Very. What's the problem?"

"No problem . . . I was thinking of something else."

"OK, I'll see you there in thirty minutes." James hung up.

Miguel stared at Badge, who tilted his head in confusion. "I don't know what's going on either, Badge. I guess we'll find out as soon as we get there."

Miguel grabbed his car keys.

"We're going back to where we just came from, but don't mention any names." Miguel winked at Badge.

"Woof!" Badge barked once and walked toward the door.

* * * * *

Miguel and Badge arrived at Mission Beach Park again, searching the parking lot for James. "Do you see his car?" he asked Badge.

Badge turned to the windows and huffed.

Miguel took the phone and dialed. "I'm at the location."

"We're almost there," James said and hung up.

"We?"

A vehicle entered the parking lot.

"The Suburban!" Miguel said. "This is crazy, Badge. Let's find out what's going on."

Miguel and Badge left the car and walked to the Suburban. Two silhouettes could be seen in the front, so he opened a rear door.

Badge jumped in, then Miguel.

James was seated at the wheel. "Captain Williams!" Miguel said when he discovered who was in the passenger seat.

"Hey, Miguel," Williams said.

"What's going on?" Miguel asked, still surprised.

"A lot," Williams said. "Thanks for waiting for an explanation, James. Now that you two are here, I can start."

"Woof!" Badge barked.

"Sorry, now that you three are here." Williams turned to wink at Badge. "First of all, here are your shields, handguns, and locker keys." He opened a duffel bag and distributed the items. "Vests, helmets, and some handy gadgets are in the rear."

"So, we're not suspended?" James asked.

"No, you aren't. It's been a ploy."

"A trick? Why?"

"We have concerns about some law enforcement personnel."

"That's weird," Miguel said.

"Let me start at the beginning," Williams said. "When we launched Lobo, we took care to release the information to the participants as late as possible to prevent any information leaks. Well, you know the story. The warehouse on the American side was wrapped up tight. We almost left thinking we had been mistaken. They were expecting us. If not for Sarge, we wouldn't have discovered what they were really up to."

The mention of Sarge's name caused them all to lapse into silence for a moment.

Captain Williams continued. "The Mexican warehouse hurried to conceal their operation, but Robert and Miguel"—he looked at Badge—"and Sarge and Badge interrupted them."

"Any idea of where the leak is?" Miguel asked.

"No. And unfortunately, I don't think an error caused the leak. Somebody is providing information to the traffickers from inside the Agency or from inside one of the cooperating agencies involved in the

319

operation, the Police department, transport services, or anybody who helped execute the search warrant."

"Was today's conference held intentionally to deceive the traffickers' informant?" James asked.

"Exactly," Williams said.

"Isn't it kind of late for that?" Miguel asked. "What's the purpose?"

"It's late for Operation Lobo," he said, "but not for Operation Lobo Two."

Miguel and James looked at each other; Badge gasped.

"We need to be able to work without leaks," Williams said. "Pretending that you two -sorry! -you three are suspended, gives us freedom to operate covertly. I requested a leave of absence while the investigations continue. No suspensions or permits have been forwarded beyond our office. I sabotaged my network connection and reported a problem with my computer to delay the paperwork. We have to act fast and precisely. What isn't a ploy is that there's a lot of pressure from the top, Department of State, and the Mexican Government."

Miguel was anxious to get to work. "What's Lobo Two about?"

"I'm getting there. Remember those truck plates you provided?"

"Yes, the unknown shipments," James said.

"By the way, good job catching that," Williams said. "In a confidential way, I asked for the plates through a friend I have in the Department of Transportation. Several tickets were found related to illegal parking, all in the same spot, near San Diego Bay. Some tickets are as recent as a week ago."

"What's the next step, Captain?" Miguel asked.

"Go there and conduct surveillance. The location suggests it may be another warehouse or a manufacturing operation related to the auto industry. Any evidence or documentation of suspicious activities will give us justification for another raid."

"Who else knows about this?" James asked. "It's good to have only a few people involved because of the leaks, but it's also risky not to have support."

"You're right, James. If something happens to any of us, the contact for the others is the Chief Officer, or my assistant. Besides them, only a couple of guys in Special Operations know about this."

"Sir, I know what I'm going to say may be unfair, but can we trust them?" Miguel asked.

"Yes, that's unfair if they're not involved, Miguel, but it's the correct way of thinking. We have to be on our toes, and no one outside our circle is above suspicion. What I can say is that all of them knew about our previous operation since the early planning. The facts tell us the leak is somebody who was informed the day of the operation or late the day before. That's the reason the traffickers were in a hurry, still hiding everything when we arrived."

Miguel didn't respond.

"Any problem, Miguel?" Williams asked.

"Sir, I'm from another country and another agency, should you trust me?"

Williams laughed. "Destroying those weapons and drugs was a really convincing way to show us you're not on the traffickers' payroll."

"When are we going to investigate the new location?" Miguel asked.

"Right now!"

* * * * *

The Suburban exited Interstate 5 and entered the industrial area near San Diego Bay, east of the Naval Station. James drove slowly, trying to read the street names in the dark.

"Ranger Street, numbers around thirty-six hundred, between Dakota and Sirius," Williams read the information from a piece of paper he lit with a small flashlight.

After driving through several streets, they located Ranger Street and followed it.

"Thirty-seven-eighty-one, we're close," Miguel said reading the building numbers.

The Suburban continued moving.

"Thirty-six-eighty-seven. This is the block," Williams said. "Check the other side, Miguel. On this side, we have Poncho's Auto Repair . . . an empty warehouse posted For Sale by Owner . . . Auto Metals . . . Alpha Industries . . . Worldwide Logistics . . . Forklift Services."

The Suburban reached the end of the block.

"Do we continue to the next block, Captain?" James asked.

Instead of answering James, Williams turned to Miguel. "Did you find anything interesting on your side?"

"Only one building, it uses the whole block, Metal Recycling, number thirty-six-sixty."

"Do you think it could be it?"

"Look at that truck," Miguel pointed. "It's parked across diagonal spaces reserved for cars."

"Interesting. Stop somewhere on the next block, James," Williams said.

James parked the Suburban, and he and Williams turned to the back.

"I know, I know," Miguel said. "The guy with the dog, the perfect disguise."

Everybody stepped out of the Suburban.

Miguel opened the rear door. He took a pair of night-vision goggles and a radio. Captain Williams and James also took radios.

"What's this?" Miguel asked, raising a small black box.

"A wireless camera," Williams said. "May come handy in some situations."

"Maybe," Miguel said and put it back.

Miguel and Badge walked away while James and Captain Williams returned to their seats in the Suburban. Miguel didn't mention it, but he preferred to be outside doing the reconnaissance rather than waiting. He was sure Badge felt the same way.

Miguel studied each business as he walked down the street wearing the night-vision goggles. Almost no activity could be seen. The only business with lights on was Worldwide Logistics, which occupied quite a large building. A guard in a small guardhouse flipped through a magazine. On the left side, across the street, people moved about in an illuminated shipping area.

Miguel used the radio. "The only big businesses in here are Metal Recycling and Worldwide Logistics. There's some activity in Metal Recycling. I'll cross the street when I reach the corner and return using the east sidewalk."

"OK, but be careful," Williams said.

Miguel took a quick look around at the intersection with Dakota Street. *Completely dark and quiet in both directions.*

Miguel and Badge crossed the street and observed the area occupied by Metal Recycling. The south side of the block had a chain-link fence, ten feet high. The front side, the one on Ranger Street, had a sliding gate to restrict access to the area behind the building. The lot held a number of large storage containers. To the south, the building had a small overhead door, but it was closed and the area unlit. The fence continued along the side of the building alternating with sections of brick wall. Here the wire fence was covered by bushes and vines.

Miguel approached the illegally parked truck. "The engine is running. Plate number is two, Charlie, Mike, Zulu, seven, two, zero."

The engine roared at that moment and the truck started moving.

"Just in time," Miguel said as the truck rolled up the street, slowly gaining speed.

A person carrying a flashlight approached from the other side of the fence.

Miguel quickly removed his goggles and hid them. A second later, the light shined directly into his face.

"You got a problem?" asked a male voice through the fence.

Miguel could only distinguish the silhouette because of the strong light. "No, sir, I'm walking my dog."

The guard shined the light down at Badge.

At that moment, Badge raised his rear left leg and wet a small tree growing at the left of the sidewalk.

"Beautiful night, isn't it?" Miguel said, trying to ease the tension.

"I guess so," the guard said and walked away.

"Nice performance, Badge," Miguel said. "Was it a performance?"

Miguel and Badge continued walking north. Miguel didn't need the night vision goggles anymore, the entrance had perfect illumination.

A single large overhead door gave access to the north side of the building revealing part of the interior. Miguel saw stacked boxes, fifty-five-gallon containers, people moving around, but nothing out of the ordinary for a building of that size. Several parked trucks waited at the north side of the property.

Miguel and Badge reached the corner. They turned right at Sirius and walked down the sidewalk. A ten-foot wall went all the way to the other corner. *Damn! No openings to check the plates of the trucks parked inside.* He and Badge stopped at the middle of the block.

"Stay, Badge. Stay, don't move," Miguel commanded. He moved back, ran toward the wall, and jumped. With his boot toe against the wall, he could just reach the top edge. He pulled himself up. He was able to see the interior of the building. It had walkways, a two-story office area, and stairs. An overhead crane spanned the building's width. *Damn again!* The trucks in the shipping area were parked so close to the wall, he couldn't see the plates.

Miguel jumped backwards to the sidewalk.

"There's activity inside," Miguel said through the radio. "The building is huge, but I can't get the trucks' plate numbers."

"Ten-four, Miguel," Williams responded. "Come back."

"Let me check the east side, the one next to the service road."

"Ten-four."

Miguel and Badge reached the next corner. The brick wall continued on the east side of the building. This area was dark and quiet.

Disappointed, Miguel decided to return to the Suburban. "Let's go, Badge. We're done here."

* * * * *

Badge and Miguel jumped into the rear seat of the Suburban without saying a word. He was disappointed he couldn't get any relevant information.

Williams gave Miguel a piece of paper and a small flashlight. The paper contained the list of truck plates Miguel compiled days before. Plate number 2CMZ 720 was circled.

"It's on the list!" Miguel was elated.

"That's nice, Miguel," Williams said. "Unfortunately, it's not strong enough to get a warrant to launch a whole operation."

"What's the problem?"

"The truck was at the front of the building, not inside, and now it's gone. I won't say it's nothing, but it could take a while and a lot of explaining to convince a judge to issue a warrant for Metal Recycling based on one truck plate. By then, everything and everybody in that building will be long gone if there's a leak."

"We have to provide concrete evidence about the activities inside that location," James said.

Nobody said a word for a while.

Miguel knew James and Captain Williams were as frustrated as he was. Yet, one member of their team was not.

Badge placed a paw on Miguel's lap.

"Are you sure?" Miguel asked.

"Woof!" Badge barked once.

"What's going on?" Williams asked.

"Badge volunteers for a recon[60] mission."

Chapter 29: Strange Creatures

"I'm going to need pliers, duct tape, the radio, and grease—lots of grease," Miguel said.

James found the items in the back of the Suburban.

The team stood behind the vehicle with the rear gate open and Badge standing inside. They had moved several blocks away from Metal Recycling to prepare without raising suspicion.

"I only have electrical tape. Can you use it?" James asked.

"Great, that's better than duct tape," Miguel said while he checked the different items.

"Here's the camera," Williams said. "The receiver can be connected to the laptop to display the image; it has a recording option. It looks like the cheap cameras you buy on the Internet, but this isn't. This one has night vision and zoom. Everything's remotely controlled from the laptop."

"What's the range?" Miguel asked.

"Half a mile, no problem," Williams said.

Miguel attached the radio to Badge's collar. He extended the cable with the earphone beneath the collar and attached it with the electrical tape. He made sure to position the earphone as close as possible to Badge's left ear. He also attached the microphone. After trying different positions, he decided to leave the camera on the right side of the collar. "We'll see most of what Badge sees."

"Don't know why you want it, but here it is," James said passing the grease to Miguel.

Miguel applied the grease over a good part of Badge's body. "If he's discovered, nobody would like to get close to him, although the main reason is to conceal the cables."

Badge stood quite still and seemed to be enjoying the whole process.

"Now, we need dirt, Badge." Miguel found plenty in a nearby garden and powdered Badge. The dirt stuck to the grease.

"Wow! Isn't that animal cruelty?" James asked as he checked Badge over.

"What do you think of my creation, Captain?" Miguel asked.

"Frankendog! Remind me to recommend Badge for a medal. If he's willing to be treated like that, he deserves it . . . at least an Academy Award.

* * * * *

James drove the Suburban back to Ranger Street and parked close to the corner, in the parking area of the Auto Repair business.

Miguel adjusted Badge's radio to the lowest volume.

Williams operated the laptop where he already received images from the camera. He switched back and forth between normal video and night vision mode, and then he tested the zoom-in/zoom-out feature. He gave a thumbs-up to Miguel.

"OK, let's go." Miguel opened the door and stepped out. "Jump, Badge, jump."

Badge leapt from the seat to the sidewalk.

"Perfect," Miguel said after checking to see if Badge's equipment was still firmly in place.

"Good luck," James and Captain Williams said as Miguel closed the door.

"Stay, Badge. Stay," Miguel commanded and crossed the street alone. When he reached the other side, he gave the next commands through the radio: "Down, Badge. Down. Up, Badge. Up."

Badge followed the commands.

"How did it go?" Miguel asked.

"Done correctly and in order," Williams said while looking at the laptop screen.

"Come, Badge. Come," Miguel commanded through the radio.

Badge crossed the street and joined Miguel on the other side.

"OK, radio and camera tested in the field," Miguel said. "Proceeding with the undercover recon."

"Ten-four," James said.

Miguel and Badge walked along the sidewalk until Miguel stopped next to a bush covering a section of the fence.

"Guard, Badge. Guard," Miguel commanded and squeezed between the bushes and the fence. Using the pliers, he cut the wire fence where it attached to the wall.

Badge waited and covered Miguel from the sidewalk.

When Miguel finished, he pulled the mesh wire. "Get in Badge. In," he whispered.

Badge walked into the bushes and then through the opening to the other side of the fence.

Miguel released the fence. "Out, Badge. Out."

Badge pushed the mesh with his head and went through by himself.

"Perfect, Badge. Now you know the way out." Miguel rubbed Badge's head in the only place that wasn't covered with dirt and grease. "Be careful, OK?" He pulled the loose fence again. "Get in, Badge. In."

Badge walked through the opening again.

"Stay, Badge. Stay," Miguel commanded. He squeezed out from behind the bushes and ran back to the Suburban.

"We're recording," the Captain said when Miguel jumped into the Suburban. "We're on night vision mode."

"Walk, Badge. Walk, straight," Miguel said through the radio.

Badge walked along the side of the building. When he reached the edge, he received the next set of commands.

"Stop, Badge. Stop. Turn right."

Badge turned to the left.

"No, no, no! Turn to the other side, the right."

Badge quickly turned the other way.

The team watched the images; nobody could be seen on the greenish image on the laptop screen.

"Walk, Badge. Walk, straight."

Badge moved again and approached the area with the parked trucks.

"Right, Badge. Right, walk."

Badge turned and walked.

"No, Badge. No! Walk to the other side, the right."

Badge turned again and walked.

"Stop, Badge. Stop."

Badge executed the commands while Williams adjusted the zoom from the camera.

"We have our first plate," Williams said.

The series of commands repeated another seven times to get another seven plates from the parked trucks.

"Half of the plates are on the list!" Williams said with a smile. "I hope we can get a warrant and launch an operation with this."

"That was easy," Miguel said. "We can order Badge to go inside the building, and find out what we can expect if an operation is launched."

"Are you sure Badge is able to do that?" Williams asked.

"Absolutely! If there's a problem, he can outrun anybody in there."

"It's your call, Miguel," Williams said.

"Turn, Badge. Turn. Straight, walk straight." Miguel commanded.

Badge approached the overhead door of the building, moving from the darkness to the illuminated area.

Williams switched the video mode and the greenish images changed to normal colors on the laptop screen.

"Stop, Badge. Stop and look left. Now, look right," Miguel commanded.

Badge stopped at the entrance and turned each way giving the team their first glance of the interior.

"Get in, Badge. In."

Miguel made Badge walk among stacks of boxes and containers for a while. A Cadillac SUV was parked inside, on the far side of the building.

"Seems the boss is in," James said.

When Badge's patrol revealed offices, Miguel commanded him to go that direction so they could get a quick look.

A couple of guys approached.

"Hide, Badge. Hide," Miguel said.

Badge knew what to do. He hid behind some racks and waited.

"AK-47s, this is getting serious," Williams said as he watched the gunmen walking away.

Miguel commanded Badge to continue the inspection. When he reached a staircase, Miguel sent him up. "Stairs up, Badge. Stairs up."

Badge took the stairs and reached the second level and a walkway. To the left was a small room in the middle of the building, on the right another group of offices, exactly above those on the first floor.

"Straight, Badge. Straight." Miguel directed Badge to go into the single room.

Badge entered the dark room through the open door. From Badge's height, the camera showed only a chair.

"Jump, Badge. Jump," Miguel commanded.

Badge jumped onto the chair and faced the control console for the crane, overhead doors, lights, and other equipment.

"Hmm, that's nice," James said and made some drawings in his notebook.

"Now the offices." Miguel commanded Badge to proceed to the upper level offices, crouching a bit and walking with restraint to have a 'reduced visual signature'.

"Get in, Badge. In."

Badge entered the first room. The camera showed them only chairs and some tables. Miguel instructed Badge to circle the room.

The screen image began to shake.

"What's going on?" Williams asked. "Has he got fleas?"

"I don't know," Miguel said approaching the screen. "He's making some kind of signal. -Ahhh!" Miguel moved backwards. "I know what's going on! He's stretching his neck and pointing with his nose. He found drugs!"

"Yes!" everybody in the Suburban cheered.

"Shhh! Shhh!" Williams was the first to remember they were on an covert operation.

Miguel continued giving commands. "Up, Badge. Up."

Badge put his paws up on the edge of one table and the camera pointed up at the ceiling.

"Nice view but not what we want," Williams said.

"Jump, Badge. Jump," Miguel commanded.

Badge jumped onto the table. When he looked down across the tabletops, the team saw cellophane-wrapped bricks and hundreds of tiny plastic bags among other items.

"Wow! The working area," Miguel said. "From here, to the streets."

"And in massive amounts," said Williams. "Get Badge out of there as soon as possible. We got what we wanted, and a lot more."

* * * * *

Badge followed Miguel's commands and returned to the ground level.

Miguel directed him down an aisle in the direction of the overhead door.

Before crossing another aisle, Badge stopped and looked both ways as if checking for traffic. Two gunmen approached.

"Hide, Badge. Hide," Miguel commanded. Badge hid behind a large container.

The two men stopped nearby and chatted.

Badge backed away and found a new hiding place.

The two men resumed their walk and moved away.

Badge moved and turned. He gasped and jumped a step backwards. Two gigantic black feet barred his exit. He raised his head and looked at the legs, and then at the golden clothing above. Badge raised his head still further. It was so tall! A giant, ten feet high or more! He walked backwards to be able to see the head clearly. A dog's head! Yes, a dog's head on top of a giant human body![61]

"What's going on?" Williams asked. The laptop showed parts of something big.

"It seems Badge found some kind of statue," Miguel said. "Let's give him some more time in case the gunmen are still near."

* * * * *

Badge moved backwards cautiously. He had no way of knowing the giant's next move, or how would he use that long stick.[62]

Moments passed. Nothing happened

Badge studied the giant's face carefully.

Strange, the giant appeared to look in a particular direction.

Badge turned in that direction and saw an image carved on a rock. The figure also had the head of a dog and a human body.[63]

Badge turned to the giant again and gasped.

The giant seemed to be looking in a different direction.

Badge turned to the new direction and found an image where the giant operated a scale. Other strange creatures were there, one with the head of a bird, another with the head of a crocodile.

Badge turned again. His initial fear disappeared. The giant emanated a scent of power, discipline, and order. He sat, straightened his body, raised his head, and "Woof!" he barked giving the officer salute.

"What was that?" Williams asked. "Did he bark?"

"Something happened," Miguel said. "Out, Badge, out. Come back," he commanded.

Some of the guards in the building also noticed the noise. "Hey! Did you hear that?" one gunman asked another.

"Yeah, let's check it out," the other said.

Badge started walking away and gave a last look at the giant, as if saying goodbye. When he turned away, his head hit something.

A frightening creature stood in front of him.

Badge was startled and took a couple steps back.

Tall as a man and standing on four legs, the creature had the head of a crocodile, body of a leopard, and the back of a hippopotamus.[64]

Badge saw that figure in the painting, but this one was real and showing its teeth at him. It reminded him of the monster he and Karen fought with. He growled. He knew he shouldn't make any noise, but he had to keep that monster under control. He moved back a few more paces and accidentally pushed a small golden plate on top of a box.

The plate banged to the floor.

Captain Williams and James looked at Miguel.

"No! Out, Badge, get out! Run! Run!" Miguel shouted through the radio. "Broken bone, I repeat, broken bone!"

Badge started running toward the overhead door.

"I'll see what I can do," Miguel jumped out of the Suburban, and ran to the other side of the street.

"Broken bone, what the hell is that?" the Captain asked James.

Badge ran through the overhead door and made a hard turn to his left, heading to the opening in the fence. At that moment, two bright lights blinded him.

"Stop right there!" a voice commanded.

"Don't move!" another voice shouted.

Badge skidded to a stop. He was cornered and unable to see. He didn't know what to do.

Two men with AK-47s aimed at him and approached.

Miguel reached the fence on the outside. *Oh, no!* He saw Badge and the two gunmen through the bushes. "Stay, Badge. Stay," he whispered, trying to gain some time.

Badge calmed down.

"Where did you come from?" one gunman yelled.

"What are you doing in here?" the second guy asked.

"Sit, Badge. Sit," Miguel commanded trying to ease the situation and prevent the gunmen from shooting.

Badge sat facing the gunmen and their bright lights. He couldn't see them, but he could smell them. He didn't like their scent.

"Wow! Looks like you came from a sewer," the first man said.

"I never seen a stray dog as greasy and dirty as this one," the other said.

Badge only moved his eyes from one side to the other, depending on where the voice came from.

"Stay calm, Badge. Stay." Miguel didn't want Badge to make sudden moves. *What do we do now?*

"What's that on your collar, you dirty dog?" the second gunman asked as he approached.

Miguel rubbed the back of his head, trying to work out what to do. *They discovered the camera.* He withdrew his handgun and took the safety off.

"I know what it is," the first man said. "It's one of those electric shock collars."

"Really?" said the second man. He had been about to touch the camera, but moved his hand back at the mention of shock collars.

"Yes, if the dog barks it produces an electric shock. It's a nice way to keep them quiet."

"No wonder he isn't barking."

"My neighbor could use one of those."

"Does he have a noisy dog?"

"No, it's for his wife."

The two gunmen laughed.

"Woof, woof, woof!" the man closer to Badge pretended to bark.

"What are you doing?" the other guy asked.

"I'm testing the collar."

Inside the building, two more gunmen searched around the statues trying to discover the source of the noises.

One gunman looked up at the giant. The statue's eyes appeared to be fixed on a pile of golden plates on top of some shelves.

Back outside, the man closer to Badge asked, "What do we do with him?"

"We can use him for target practice," the other replied.

At that moment, a loud and long noise of metallic plates hitting the floor came from inside the building.

The two looked at each other and ran into the building.

Badge stayed sitting as he been commanded and turned to watch the men run into the building.

"Out, Badge. Run," Miguel commanded.

Badge sprung up and ran toward Miguel, slipping through the opening in the fence.

Miguel made sure to put the fence back in place, and then he and Badge ran back to the Suburban.

Inside the building, six gunmen stood around the golden plates scattered over the floor.

General Mota, in plain clothes, approached. "Who stacked those?"

Nobody said anything.

"What are you waiting for? Clean up that mess!" he shouted.

"General, we found a dog outside," one of the gunmen said.

Mota shook his head and walked back to his office.

Chapter 30: TV Stars

Next morning.

The instructions were clear. Don't contact anybody in the DEA or local police departments, be ready and reachable. Captain Williams would show the video to a judge to get the warrant and launch the seize operation. At the appropriate time, the SWAT team, codenamed Baseball Team, would be assembled to conduct a tactical skills demonstration. No one, not even the SWAT leader, would be aware that the demonstration was a ruse to have them prepared for the actual operation. Captain Williams and the Chief Officer didn't want to give any chance to anyone to leak their plans to the traffickers.

"Ready, Badge?" Miguel asked. "We have to be there at ten to relieve James."

"Woof!" Badge replied, wagging his tail.

"Let's hope James wasn't upset about the mess in the back seat of the Suburban. That grease and dirt were going to be hard to clean up."

Badge whined, and his tail stopped wagging.

"Let's go buy him some donuts and coffee." Miguel opened the apartment door.

"Woof!" Badge barked, but then whined and lowered his head.

"Of course, for him *and* for us."

"Woof!" Badge raised his head and the wagging resumed.

From the moment James returned to the warehouse for the nightshift until the operation launch, the four of them, Captain Williams, James, Miguel, and Badge, would conduct continuous surveillance on the warehouse.

* * * * *

"What's up?" Miguel greeted James when he opened the Suburban door.

Badge jumped in first.

"Hey, Miguel. Hey, Badge. Gimme a paw!" James tapped Badge's paw when Badge raised it.

"Here, Badge bought you some breakfast," Miguel said. "See anything interesting last night?"

"Thanks. No, normal traffic," James said. "Employees coming in for work, if you can call it that."

"Cutting drugs or unloading trucks—it's all work."

"They were cleaver to have different locations in operation. Not having all the eggs in the same basket," James bit the first donut. "The Captain said he's kidnapping Judge McCarthy, codenamed Umpire."

"Kidnapping?"

"Yup, I asked him the same question, but he just smiled. Maybe it's because he wants the warrant as soon as possible."

"After that, the operation can start at any time?"

"And the sooner, the better."

"OK, I hope you can get some rest. We'll see you this evening," Miguel pulled the door handle, ready to exit.

"Wait!" James said, juggling the donut and trying to drink his coffee. "Whoa! This is hot."

"What?"

"There's no time for sleep! We have to come up with a plan. Something that takes the traffickers by surprise to avoid casualties in case all hell breaks loose when we get in there. You've seen the weapons they have."

James and Miguel reviewed options and made diagrams for hours. They drove around Metal Recycling's block several times to check details.

Badge stared at the diagrams once in a while then returned to the windows to compare.

"Kilo Niner, this is Charley Whiskey. Everything's rolling," Captain Williams said on the radio. "I have a meeting with the Umpire this afternoon. A demo game has been requested to the Baseball Team."

"Is the game confirmed?" James asked.

"Not yet, but could be at any moment."

"Is the Baseball Team going to meet in the stadium?"

"No, we're going to inaugurate our brand new stadium. Their captain already sniffs something but has no details."

"Our brand new stadium?" Miguel asked.

"Yes," Williams said but gave no additional information.

Miguel understood his intent and didn't ask again.

"Have your plan ready. Over and out."

"Ten-four. Over and out." James ended the communication.

"New stadium?" Miguel asked.

"The parking lot in Mission Beach Park," James replied.

Miguel and James continued with the diagrams and considered different options.

His back on the seat and paws in the air, Badge prepared himself by taking a long nap.

* * * * *

Surveillance had to be stopped. That afternoon, the Suburban arrived at Mission Beach Park. As planned, they had to be there first.

Badge moved from one side to the other in the back of the Suburban and whined.

"What's going on?" James asked. "Is he OK after eating all those donuts?" James asked.

"Oops! Excuse us for a minute," Miguel said taking a black plastic bag out of his pocket. He secured the leash on Badge's collar and opened the door. "Make it *two* minutes."

The BEAR arrived followed by two squad cars and several civilian cars. Twelve SWAT officers stepped out of the vehicles, both A and B teams. Some wore police uniforms, others plain clothes.

After checking the attendance, Captain Holder walked toward James, Miguel, and Badge. "Hey, guys, I thought you were suspended. Are you watching the demonstration?"

"Hey, Captain." Miguel and James said.

Holder looked from one man to the other as if expecting further explanation. "Oh! I think I get it now," he said finally and laughed nervously. "Do we wait?"

"Yes, we wait," Miguel said.

"We're collecting cell phones," James said. "Can you and your team put yours in there?" He pointed to a box on the hood of the Suburban.

Captain Holder deposited his cell phone in the box and asked all the other members of the team to do the same.

"What's going on?" one of the SWAT team members asked.

"Special drill. We're waiting for further instructions. Cell phones might be distracting," Holder said.

The group, the squad cars, and especially the BEAR, caught the attention of people arriving at the park. A group of kids wearing baseball uniforms approached. "Ooh! Are you busting someone?" one of them asked.

James gasped. The complete operation was about to be compromised by kids. "No! Of course not. Who could we be after around here?" He tugged on the bill of the boy's ball cap. "We're getting ready for a skills demonstration."

"Cool," the boy said as his coach hustled the team toward the baseball fields on the other side of the parking lot.

Captain Williams arrived. He greeted everybody and introduced another person. "This is Judge McCarthy. Everyone, please gather around. I'm only going through this once." He set the laptop inside the rear of the Suburban to keep the screen out of the sunlight and started the video.

As the images played, Williams gave details of the trucks previously identified at Atlantic Trading Company. The drugs on the tables and the gunmen were self-explanatory.

"What do you think, Judge?" Williams asked when the recording ended. "Is this suspicious enough to grant a warrant?"

"Suspicious? I'd say that's hard evidence," McCarthy said.

"Perfect! I have all the paperwork here. The address is already there. We only need your signature."

The judge gave the papers a quick review and asked for a pen. Just before signing, he stopped. "How did you get the video? Did you have a warrant to get in and do the recording?"

Captain Williams expected the question. "I can assure you no human officer has gone into that building."

Badge jumped into the rear of the Suburban.

Judge McCarthy raised his head and saw a lolling tongue with a dog attached to it.

"Badge, get out of there," Miguel said.

McCarthy frowned, and then signed the papers.

"OK, guys. Lobo Two is in effect at this moment," Williams said.

"Yes!" the group cheered.

"Prepare your gear gentlemen," Williams said, but corrected himself when he saw Abira in the group. "Sorry! Prepare your gear lady, gentlemen—and canine. Regroup for debriefing when you're ready. James and Miguel, I have your gear in my car."

"What do I do now?" Judge McCarthy asked.

"Sorry! Judge, I'll take you to your office later," Williams said. "Can I borrow your phone?"

Carrying her tactical uniform, Abira opened the rear door of the Bear and found several half-naked officers changing clothes. "Oops! Sorry!"

"Hey, you'll have to wait for your turn!" one of the officers said, chuckling.

"You guys are slower than a bunch of old women with girdles," Abira said as she shut the door. "If I hear a hair dryer you'll be in trouble."

"Attention! This is a full gear operation," Holder said. "Don't forget the steel plates in your vests. You saw the video; those guys are carrying serious weapons."

Miguel adjusted the straps of his vest and knocked on it. "Your vest doesn't have steel plates, Badge. Be extra careful."

When Miguel finished adjusting Badge's vest, he turned from the Suburban and found a surprising scene. "Look!" he told James.

Children and parents had gathered around the parking lot, some seated on folding chairs.

"Somebody mentioned a demonstration," James said.

The tactical team gathered again. James and Miguel distributed layouts of the streets and floor plans of the building. The details of the operation were explained.

"Any questions?" Williams asked when they finished.

At that moment, a TV reporter and a cameraman approached the group.

"Should I make them clear the area, Captain?" Abira asked Captain Holder.

"No, let me deal with them," Captain Holder said after thinking for a moment. "They could be useful."

By walking toward the reporters, Holder prevented them from approaching the team. He put on his balaclava. "Can I help you?"

"10 News, sir. I'm Jessica Hunt. Our sources said you were doing a demonstration here in the park. Can you give us any details?"

"We're having a demonstration on how to secure a location and perform arrests."

"Can we interview the officers?"

"Maybe later. Right now we need space; we're about to start. Could you move back to the edge of the parking lot?"

"Thank you, sir." The reporter turned to the camera as she and the cameraman walked back. "There you have it. In a few moments, we'll be watching a rare, live demonstration of the SWAT team's skills, right here in Mission Beach Park. This is Jessica Hunt, live, in an exclusive report from 10 News."

A few miles away, at Metal Recycling, General Mota and Weedman watched TV in a room full of cash. They were supervising the accounting personnel.

"Look at those jackasses. Performing demonstrations for the public," Weedman said. "They've got nothing better to do."

"SWAT's reduced to performing demonstrations for kiddies and, according to my sources, the DEA canine team suspended for misconduct," the General said. "What a joke!"

Both laughed.

Back at the park, the preparations ended.

"Are you ready to go, boy?" Miguel asked Badge.

"Woof!" Badge had his vest, camera, and radio. No grease was applied this time.

They jumped into the BEAR with eight members of the SWAT team. James, Captain Williams, and the judge would travel in the Suburban. The two squad cars would follow with two SWAT officers in each one.

 The judge would stay with the group as long as possible. Williams, still unsure of the security leak, had deliberately brought the judge to the park to sign the warrant. Maybe he was being overly cautious, but he didn't want the judge's office staff to know the operation's details. The less people knowing about the operation meant reduced risk of a leak.

"Let's roll," Williams gave the order to advance.

The convoy started to move.

The reporters ran toward the BEAR as it approached an exit. "Are you leaving?" the reporter yelled.

"We're about to start," Holder shouted. "The vehicles will be used in the demonstration. Don't let anybody get into this area of the parking lot and keep that camera rolling."

"You saw it," the reporter said to the camera while the BEAR moved away followed by the Suburban and the two squad cars. "The demonstration is about to start. As you can see, many people have gathered to watch—even a couple local baseball teams have postponed their game so the boys can watch the SWAT demonstration."

The cameraman zoomed out to show the people waving.

"No. No commercials," the reported said, addressing her producer in the nearby news van. "We'll continue live without interruptions."

Silently, the convoy took Mission Bay Drive to the south.

The team double-checked their weapons and radios inside the BEAR.

Miguel verified Badge's earpiece was working, covering his mouth and microphone with his hand as he whispered several commands. "Sit, Badge. Sit. Up. Turn."

Badge acknowledged the reception by executing the commands.

Miguel tested the camera's connection with the laptop. "Walk, Badge. Walk. Turn." *What could be better than a close up of Abira checking her M4A1?*

"Locked and loaded, Badge," Abira said looking at the camera. She gave a thumbs-up when she finished with her rifle.

Miguel raised his head to look at Abira directly.

Abira was looking at him too.

Miguel smiled.

"Your chinstrap," she said. "You forgot to tighten it."

The vehicles turned east at Interstate 8 and increased their speed. A moment later, they turned south again taking Interstate 5. Everybody sat quietly, doing their mental preparation. Everyone had been briefed and understood their roles. There was nothing to do now but wait.

Miguel watched Abria; her eyes were closed and her head down. Her right hand lay across her chest, just below her neck. *I know what you're doing.* He raised his hand to touch the crucifix under his shirt and started to pray. *God, this is a short ride, so I'll be quick. Please, take care of my family, Badge, and my teammates. Please embrace my father, the Falcon team, and Sarge—wherever they may be.* A moment passed. *Help my team give the traffickers and their accomplices a nice madriza[65] and send them back to hell. Amen.*

* * * * *

The BEAR reached its first destination, the service road between Metal Recycling and Interstate 5.

The Suburban and the two squad cars stayed a couple of blocks back.

According to James and Miguel's observations, the east side of the property had the least activity. The brick wall separating the property from the service road could be used to conceal the BEAR.

The BEAR drove onto the sidewalk.

"More, more, closer," Captain Holder directed the driver. "That's it. Stop."

The top of a trailer could be seen on the other side of the wall. It would help conceal the first group's insertion onto the property.

Gregg unfolded a ladder and climbed to open the upper hatch. Abira and Tim followed him.

"Up, Badge. Up," Miguel commanded.

Badge moved up the ladder but got stuck near the top. The ladder was too vertical for somebody with four legs and no hands.

Gregg's arm appeared though the opening and hoisted Badge up using the vest's handle.

Miguel climbed, carrying the laptop.

"Clear. We're going in." Gregg said through the radio after the group checked the other side of the wall.

Gregg stepped onto the wall, slid down until he hung in a vertical position, and jumped the last three feet. Abira and Tim followed.

Miguel threw the laptop, and Gregg caught it.

Miguel grabbed the handle on Badge's vest and carefully lowered him down the inside into the waiting arms of Abira and Tim who set the dog on the ground.

Miguel slid down.

Back at Mission Beach Park, the news reporter wondered what happened. "We're waiting for the SWAT team to arrive and start a demonstration any moment now," she said to the camera. Behind her, the people that had gathered around the parking lot were already leaving.

Miguel's group took positions between the truck and the wall, taking cover behind the wheels and the trailer to observe the movements in the shipping area.

Miguel set the laptop on top one of the wheels and, as soon as he double-checked the images and radio, gave the first commands, "Go, Badge. Go. Stealth."

Chapter 31: No! Your Other Right!

Badge moved toward the building flexing his legs to stay low. His body seemed to have been designed for this as he moved swiftly and smoothly toward the target.

"Move on, Badge. Move on," Miguel's voice came on the radio when Badge reached the building.

Badge went through the overhead door and walked through several aisles until he reached the stairs.

"Stairs up, Badge. Up," Miguel's voice commanded.

Badge reached the second floor and found a couple of gunmen near the office doors. He waited on the stairs for a moment until they turned away. He continued toward the control room.

A person was inside.

"Stop, Badge. Stop," Miguel commanded. "Hide."

Badge crawled below the air conditioning unit behind the control room.

"Now what?" Gregg asked, looking at the screen.

"We have to wait until that man leaves the room," Miguel said.

Time passed, and the man continued working over the control board.

"We have to move," Gregg urged.

"Wait, let's try something," Miguel said. "Out, Badge, out. Go downstairs. Stealth."

Badge left his hideout and went downstairs. He ran behind some containers when two men walked near his position.

"Move, Badge. Move," Miguel commanded on the radio after the men moved away. "We have to make that guy leave the control room."

Badge walked among boxes and containers to a place they saw the previous day. "That's it, Badge, a small, a medium, and a large box."

Badge didn't look at the boxes. His attention was on the giant he met the day before.

Somebody approached.

Badge knew what to do and didn't wait for a command. He hid behind a box next to the giant.

An employee came walking to the area between the boxes and sat on top of one. He opened a water bottle and took a long drink. Then, he unwrapped a sandwich and began to read the newspaper.

"I can't believe this," Miguel said looking at the screen.

"Come on, Miguel," Gregg urged again. "I have to give the signal to advance. Everybody's in position. The more time it takes the greater the risk, we can lose the advantage of surprise."

"I know. I know," Miguel said with some nervousness. If plan A couldn't be executed, plan B would be called. Plan A had its risks, but B was way riskier for the team because it involved a full-scale confrontation with the traffickers.

"That statue gives me an idea," Miguel said. "Growl, Badge. Soft."

"I don't know what you're doing, but I hope it works." Gregg said.

Badge growled softly.

"More, Badge, more. Growl," Miguel's whisper came on the radio.

Badge continued.

The man continued reading the newspaper.

"Growl, Badge. Growl louder."

Badge growled again.

The man stopped chewing. He looked around and up at the statue, shrugged, and went back to his lunch.

"Again, Badge. Growl. Stronger."

Badge resumed the growling.

Clearly nervous, the man stood up this time and looked around. He turned toward the statue, looking up at the giant's face.

"Growl, Badge. Growl," Miguel ordered.

The man jumped backwards, trying to move away from the statue, and tripped over the box he'd been sitting on. Sandwich, bottle, newspaper, and man sprawled on the floor. Eyes wide, the man struggled on the floor for a moment, trying to get up as fast as possible. As soon as he got his feet under him, he ran off.

"Great, Badge. Good job," Miguel said on the radio.

Badge left his hideout and approached the sandwich left on the floor.

"No, Badge. No. There's no time for that." He said trying to keep a soft voice to prevent revealing the position of the team in the shipping area. "Listen to me, the box. Jump."

Badge left the sandwich and jumped on top of the box.

"Again, Badge. Jump," Miguel said.

Badge jumped to the top of the next box, a bigger one, then to the top of a still bigger one. Finally, he reached the highest box in that area of the building.

"Fine, now we need to get the attention of the guy in the control room," Miguel said. "Turn, Badge. Turn." Miguel directed Badge and the camera toward the control room. "Up, Badge. Up."

Badge rose on his back legs for as long as he could keep his balance.

Miguel didn't detect any movement in the control room. "Again, Badge. Up, up."

Badge rose again.

No movement could be seen on the screen from the man in the control room.

Gregg pointed to his own radio to indicate his intention to use it.

Miguel got the message. "This is it, Badge. Bark! Bark, loud!"

"Woof, woof!" Badge barked.

"More, Badge, more. Bark. Bark louder."

Everybody in the building noticed the noise. Only the men on the second floor could see the source.

"Woof, woof!" Badge continued barking.

The man in the control room stood up. "What the hell's going on?" he said. "What's that dog doing there?" He took the microphone and shouted through the building's intercom. "Everybody, there's a loose dog inside the building, first floor, central area! Get that pooch, now!" He left the control room and ran. "Follow me," he shouted to the two gunmen on the other side of the walkway; the three men ran downstairs.

People on the first floor, armed and unarmed, moved to the center of the building not knowing exactly where to find the dog. They pointed this way and that, shouting instructions at each other.

Outside, the guard next to the main gate left his post and ran toward the building.

"Down, Badge, down. Go stealth." Miguel commanded giving a thumbs-up to Gregg.

"Rolling! We have a green light," Gregg said through the radio.

* * * * *

"Judge, I don't want to be rude, but it's time for you to get out," Captain Williams said inside the Suburban. "Here's your phone."

"No offense taken," Judge McCarthy said as he stepped out of the vehicle. "Nail those bastards!"

James pressed the accelerator. The tires squealed for a moment and the Suburban shot ahead, followed by two squad cars.

"Proceed!" Holder gave the order. The BEAR left its position.

Back in the building, Badge ran among boxes and containers toward the stairs.

"Stop, stop. Hide." Miguel commanded when Badge was about to cross the final aisle to the stairwell.

Badge slipped for a moment and ran back for cover to avoid being seen by a group of running gunmen.

"Stairs up, Badge. Stairs up," Miguel commanded.

While all the traffickers looked for Badge in the middle of the building, he climbed the steps and ran into the control room.

"Jump, Badge. Jump," Miguel commanded.

Badge jumped on top of the chair by the console.

"Now, pay extra attention, Badge," Miguel said. "You have to close the overhead door. Right paw, up."

Badge raised his paw and dangled it over the board.

"Move it right. There's the button. Door Close. Press."

Badge moved his paw to the left at the last moment and pressed the button labeled Lower Hook.

A mechanical sound rumbled inside the building, and the crane hook slowly dropped toward the warehouse floor.

"No! Badge, no! Your other right! Again, paw up, right."

Badge raised his paw again and moved it to the right.

"There, that big button. Door Close. Press!"

The paw hit the console. Instead of pressing the "Door Close" button, Badge pressed one of the crane's directional buttons.

The crane moved on its rails while the hook continued going down.

Puzzled, the traffickers turned to watch the crane.

"No, Badge. No. The next button. Press!"

Badge finally pressed the "Door Close" button and the overhead door moved down.

By the time the overhead door closed, the two squad cars had blocked the building's rear entrance. Gregg reached the guardhouse and opened the sliding door so the BEAR and the Suburban could enter the property. On the east side of the building, Abira and Tim took positions outside an emergency door.

"All units available, we need immediate support for a seize operation at thirty-six-sixty Ranger Street," Williams said through the radio. "Now everybody knows about the operation, leak sources included," he said after finishing the call.

Inside the building, one gunman ran to the overhead door and pressed a button on the wall. The door started to rise.

"What?" Miguel saw the door starting to go back up. "The team is not in position yet. Door close, Badge. Do it again. Door close. Press, press!"

Badge pressed the button again. The overhead door reversed its movement and closed.

The gunman returned and pushed the button to open the door again. The door started to rise again.

Miguel repeated the command. Badge repeated the action, and the door closed for the third time.

The gunman was persistent and the battle of the buttons continued as the BEAR and the Suburban entered the premises.

* * * * *

The occupants of the BEAR, including Captain Holder, exited the vehicle and ran to the building.

James parked the Suburban in front of the overhead door, and he and Captain Williams took cover behind the vehicle.

On the other side of the property, the SWAT officers from the squad cars cut a chain to open the sliding door, and entered into the south area.

Inside the building, the traffickers forgot about the dog and concentrated on the crane hook flying toward them.

Holder verified half of his group was on the left of the overhead door and the other half on the right. "We're ready, K9-56. Open the door," he said on the radio.

Stop, Badge, Stop!" Miguel commanded on the radio. Badge withdrew his paw from the Door Close button.

The team waited for the door to open but it didn't go up. The gunman on the other side had given up. The door stayed closed.

The crane's hook crashed into some boxes, knocking them to the floor. It started to drag across the floor pulled by the cables.

"Watch out!" one of traffickers yelled. They all ran in different directions, sometimes bumping into each other.

The hook hit a forklift and overturned it. The hook got stuck in the frame of the vehicle and the cables strained. The crane's safety system detected the overload and shut it down.

Sensing the danger had passed, the traffickers gathered around the forklift and the hook. They checked for damages and tried to find out an explanation.

"We're waiting, K9-56. Open the door!" Holder said on the radio.

Now what? Miguel wondered. *Nobody's trying to open the door anymore.* "Badge, I need you to open the door." Miguel checked the screen and gave a series of commands. "Pay attention. Paw up, left, left. . . . You're doing fine. . . . That's the one! Door Open, press, now!"

Badge lowered his paw and pressed Lights Off.

The lights inside the building went off, and everything went dark.

"No! Badge, no, too far left."

"What's going on, 56?" Holder asked. "Do you have the location of the traffickers?"

Miguel switched Badge's camera mode to night vision to be able to see. "Most of them are in the middle of the building, about a hundred feet from the overhead door." Miguel shifted his attention back to the buttons in the control panel. "Paw up, Left, now, Door Open, press."

358

Badge's paw hit the panel and the overhead door started rising.

Holder noticed the door movement and gave a hand indication to Wu.

Wu ran to the door and, as soon as the opening was two feet high, threw something inside. Then, he ran for cover.

Inside, the traffickers turned toward the door as a metallic cylinder clattered across the floor.

As the overhead door rose, the sunlight illuminated the inside of the building. The traffickers saw the cylinder as it came to rest at their feet.

"Is that the oil filter from the forklift?" one of them asked.

Boom! The M84 stun grenade detonated. The warehouse interior was assaulted by an explosion of light and sound.

"Go, go, go! Everybody in! "Holder gave the order to storm the building.

Miguel left the laptop and ran toward the building. He and another six members of the SWAT team ran inside. Williams and James covered them from behind the Suburban.

"Nobody move!" "Drop your weapons!" The team advanced without resistance. "Raise your hands!" they shouted.

Still blinded and deafened, the traffickers weren't able to use their weapons, nor could they respond to the commands.

The team approached the criminals, knocked away their weapons and made them kneel on the warehouse floor.

Miguel whistled to call Badge down from the upper level.

On the west side of the building, the emergency door was opened by two gunmen trying to escape.

Abira drove her M4A1 rifle stock into the first man's gut. As he bent over in pain, she brought the rifle up and gave him a second blow in the face. He fell backwards, giving Abira a clear shot at the second fleeing man. The barrel of her rifle touched the gunman's nose.

"Ever thought of getting that nose fixed?" she asked.

The gunman froze after crossing his eyes.

Badge reached Miguel's position.

"Heel, Badge, heel!" Miguel commanded.

Half of the team started a quick search of the building while the others stayed with the apprehended traffickers.

When Miguel and Badge came near a container, a man jumped up and ran.

"Bite and hold, Badge, bite and hold," Miguel commanded.

Badge ran and jumped. He caught the man's arm and the man fell.

Miguel handcuffed him and searched his clothing for weapons. He and Badge took him back to the central area of the building where the other criminals were being cuffed and read their rights. It was like rounding up cattle.

"Woof, woof!" Badge barked.

Miguel turned. Badge was looking straight up.

A gunman on top of the crane aimed an RPG at the group.

Chapter 32: The School Bus from Hell

"*Aguas!*" [66] Miguel shouted and pushed several men out of the line of fire.

A couple of shots filled the air at the same time the gunman pressed the trigger of the RPG.

The rocket-propelled grenade launched as the gunman fell backwards. The grenade missed the group and hit a wall. The explosion sent everybody to the ground and covered them in debris.

The dust dissipated. "Are you OK, Badge?" Miguel asked.

"Woof!" Badge replied.

Some people coughed, others dusted their clothes, but everybody seemed unhurt. The exception was the RPG shooter; his body had fallen in front of the crocodile-headed statue.

"Not bad for no sleep," Williams said to James.

James lowered his rifle and exhaled with relief.

From that moment, everything calmed down. A total of twenty-four traffickers were accounted for. Half of them had weapons.

Badge looked up again.

Miguel turned in the same direction.

The giant stood there, immobile and majestic.

"That's a wonderful statue, Badge," Miguel said. "He's the Egyptian god Anubis." Fortunately, the explosion didn't damage him."

At that moment, the flail in the hand of the giant detached and dropped, hitting a wooden box, and knocking away a cover to reveal a hiding person.

General Mota rolled to his left and started to crawl away.

"Stop right there," Miguel shouted.

The bald general stood and ran.

"Tackle, Badge. Tackle," Miguel commanded. *No need for a bite-and-hold for such a slow man.*

Badge reached the bald man and wedged his body between his legs.

Mota fell.

Miguel searched him for weapons, and then brought him over with the rest of the suspects.

Neither Miguel nor Mota knew the other had been at the Veracruz raid a year and a half ago.

While Miguel secured Mota, Badge secured the sandwich he'd found earlier.

* * * * *

"We need to clear the warehouse. Be sure there are no more suspects," Miguel said to the team. "Careful, they may be armed."

The wail of the sirens grew louder as police backup and ambulances approached.

Miguel, Badge, and some members of the team searched for stowaways. *Who's the boss?* Miguel wondered as they approached the Cadillac Escalade.

The Cadillac's engine suddenly started, and the tires squealed as the driver punched the accelerator. The vehicle gained speed, hit, and knocked down the small overhead door at the back of the building. It reached the open lot behind the building and stopped.

"The rear gate is blocked," Miguel said to the others. "We have them cornered, exactly as planned." He smiled.

The tires squealed again. The SUV moved straight and tore through the fence, jumping the sidewalk, and landing in the middle of Dakota Street.

"That's not in the plan." Miguel's smile disappeared.

A San Diego police car skidded and stopped to avoid a collision with the Cadillac.

The Escalade moved again and someone inside fired a machine gun at the squad car.

The bullets struck the cruiser's windows and pierced the metal body.

"James, bring the Suburban!" Miguel shouted through the radio. "Hurry, the Cadillac is getting away!"

James and Captain Williams jumped into the Suburban.

Zigzagging to avoid hitting people or boxes, James drove through the middle of the building.

Miguel and Badge reached the damaged car. "Are you Ok?" Miguel asked the officer inside.

"I think so," the shaky officer replied while stepping out.

The Suburban followed the Cadillac's path and continued to the street through the hole in the fence.

"Get those crooks!" the officer from the disabled cruiser shouted. "They turned north on Main."

James stopped to pick up Miguel and Badge. He turned on the siren and flashing lights, pressed the gas pedal, and the tires screamed as they were off in pursuit.

The Suburban turned north on Main and went for several blocks until it reached the entrance to Interstate 15. James reduced speed trying to figure out which way to go.

"I don't see a damn thing," Williams said. "Continue on Main!"

James accelerated again and continued north, then turned west, still on Main.

The Suburban cruised quickly down several blocks. The team worried that the Escalade had escaped. It seemed to have vanished.

"Maybe they took I-15," James said.

"If they did, they're gone," Miguel said.

Badge also searched, his breath fogging the window on his side.

"There!" Williams shouted pointing when he saw the Cadillac zigzagging around the traffic ahead.

With its sirens and lights on, vehicles moved over to let the Suburban pass and James was able to close the distance after several blocks.

The Cadillac ran a red light at Chavez Street and hit a car moving northeast. The two vehicles ended in the middle of the road. Another two cars, trying to avoid them, collided with each other.

The Cadillac started to move again. It was dented but not dead. It ran away taking Chavez Street to the northeast.

James reduced speed as they approached the intersection. The crashed cars obstructed the road.

"Keep going, James. Keep going!" Williams ordered.

James turned the Suburban onto the sidewalk, crossed a railroad track, and entered Chavez Street to continue the chase.

After another four blocks, the SUV turned right at Logan and went up the ramp to Coronado Bridge.[67]

"To the right, James, turn right!" Miguel shouted from the back.

"Woof!" Badge barked, also giving instructions.

"In pursuit of a gold-colored Cadillac Escalade," Williams said on the radio. "Taking Coronado Bridge to the west. Occupants are armed with assault rifles. We need support!"

Despite being rush hour, traffic westbound was much lighter than eastbound. The Cadillac increased its speed and changed lanes multiple times to dodge the other cars.

James managed to get closer without the zigzagging.

Near the middle of the bridge the gunmen's vehicle slowed.

"What's going on?" James asked. "Are they stopping?"

"I don't know," Williams said.

A man holding an AK-47 emerged and sat on the edge of a window.

"Be careful! He's going to shoot," Williams yelled.

James reduced speed and kept a respectful distance.

Instead of aiming at the Suburban, the gunman aimed at a car they passed and fired.

The car's front tire exploded. The driver lost control and the vehicle moved from the right lane to the left, directly in the path of the Suburban.

James made a sharp right turn, dodged the car, and quickly corrected to the left to avoid hitting the right barrier.

"That's vile, shooting at civilians," James said.

"Shooting or selling drugs is the same. The victim ends up in the hospital or dead," Williams said.

The gunman observed the Suburban for a moment.

"He's challenging us," Williams said. "He wants us to see what he can do if we keep following them."

The Suburban continued the chase.

The gunman aimed at another car and fired.

The car skidded and made a sudden stop.

James avoided the vehicle with a fast maneuver to the left.

"This can't continue," Williams said. "Innocent people could be hurt. Miguel, can you do something?"

"Of course," Miguel said, setting the selector of his M4A1 to semiautomatic. He slid to the right side of the back seat and opened the window.

Badge immediately poked his head through the window to feel the breeze.

"No, Badge! No. Move aside." Miguel pulled Badge by the collar. Miguel's head and his rifle replaced Badge's head outside the window.

The gunman selected another car and aimed.

"You want us to see you," Miguel said as he watched the trafficker through the aim of his rifle. "I can see you perfectly." He pressed the trigger.

The AK-47 fell to the pavement. The body of the gunman hung from the window for a moment, waving like a flag, then fell.

"Careful!" Miguel yelled at the gunman.

The car the gunman tried to shoot ran over the body before it could stop.

"Ugh!" Miguel covered Badge's eyes. "You don't need to see that."

The Suburban passed on the left.

The Cadillac accelerated and started making frequent and abrupt lane changes.

"What's he doing now?" James asked.

"Now they want to make others crash to block us," Williams said. "Miguel—"

"I'm on it, Captain. I'm on it." Miguel poked his head out again and tried to aim at one of the rear tires.

As the Escalade zigzagged, Miguel tried to follow the target with his rifle. The pavement, the vehicles, all disappeared for an instant as he concentrated on the rear-right tire. "San Alejo Garza, dame punteria."[68]

He shot once at the moment the SUV made a hard right turn in front of a red pickup.

The Escalade skidded to the left, hit the median barrier, and climbed on it for a moment, then bounced across the lanes and hit the right barrier. The red pickup slammed into the Cadillac's rear making the right door open and sent the vehicle skidding again across the left lane hitting the median barrier head-on. It finally stopped, blocking the left lane and part of the right.

"Wow! Nice shot!" Williams said as the Suburban passed the red pickup.

"That wasn't the intended tire," Miguel said as James stopped and blocked both traffic lanes, parallel to the Cadillac and heading in the opposite direction.

* * * * *

Shots started before the team could exit the Suburban.

The team ducked low and escaped through the doors on the right side, away from the Cadillac.

"Stay, Badge. Stay," Miguel commanded and set the selector of his M4A1 to fully automatic.

Williams made a few hand motions. He and Miguel took positions, covered by the Suburban. James ran in the opposite direction.

The gunmen fired again from the other side of the Cadillac.

Williams and Miguel fired back while James helped the driver of the red pickup.

Traffic came to a complete stop behind the red pickup. "Out! Get out and run!" James shouted to the occupants of the stranded vehicles.

The gunmen shot again.

After reloading, Williams and Miguel took their turn to shoot back.

James helped a woman take her baby out. Drivers and passengers ran to the east.

Another burst of bullets impacted the Suburban, making Miguel and Williams duck for cover.

"How many do you see?" Williams asked.

"So far two, Captain," Miguel said.

"We have to take them out before a civilian gets hurt."

Traffic on the opposite direction of the bridge kept flowing. Any stray bullet could cause an accident or a tragedy.

"I have an idea, Captain. Cover me."

Captain Williams fired a long burst, shattering the windows on the left side of the Escalade. The gunmen ducked for cover.

Miguel jumped the median barrier and threw himself to the asphalt as he landed on the other side. "Wow!" The tires of the eastbound vehicles rolled just inches from his body. "Hey! Be careful! Maybe this wasn't such a good idea." He squeezed against the barrier and crawled beside the traffic. *If I stand, the drivers will see me, but the traffickers will too. If the gunmen shoot me and miss, the bullets will go right into the traffic. If they don't miss . . . Damn! I have to stop thinking.* He continued crawling.

On the other side, James joined Captain Williams and they continued to exchange gunfire with the traffickers.

Miguel reached a place he estimated was behind the gunmen's vehicle and locked a new cartridge into his rifle. "Charley Whiskey, I'm ready" he said through the radio.

"Wait!" Williams stopped shooting and waved at James to do the same and duck for cover.

When James stopped shooting, the traffickers stood and fired back.

"Now, 56. Now!" Williams shouted through the radio.

Miguel rose with his M4A1 ready. As he reached the edge of the median barrier, he discovered he was right behind the Cadillac.

One of the gunmen stood just a few feet away, firing at the Suburban.

"Aaaah!" Miguel screamed and opened fire.

The gunman received the full burst. Miguel kept the trigger pressed and redirected his rifle to the gunman on the other end of the vehicle. The other gunman only had a chance to turn his head before being hit.

"Whoa!" Miguel jumped the median barrier just in time to avoid being run over by a school bus. He rolled once and stood. "That was close, the school bus and the gunmen."

He hadn't shot anybody or anything at such close range before, but he had to eliminate the threat as fast and as effectively as possible. He checked the bodies; both received multiple impacts and death was instantaneous. He felt sorry for the way they died and ashamed that he'd taken two lives that way. He stayed silent for a moment; all his emotions came out in one single word through the radio, "Clear!"

Williams and James came to join him.

Miguel whistled, and Badge jumped from behind the Suburban.

The team gathered next to the Escalade.

"Good job, Miguel," Williams said looking at the bodies.

"Exactly what those traffickers needed," James said.

"Are you all right, boy?" Miguel rubbed Badge's neck.

"Oh, no!" James said when he looked at the Suburban. The left side had dozens of bullet holes. "They killed her!" He walked back and touched the driver's-side mirror, one of the few undamaged parts. It came off in his hands.

"At least it's all over," Williams said. "We'll need multiple ambulances to care for and transport accident victims on Coronado Bridge, westbound," he said on the radio. "Two fatalities located about four hundred yards from the west end, another by the middle of the bridge. We also need tow trucks and maintenance crews to clear the—"

The rattle of a machine gun interrupted Williams's words. He fell, face down.

Chapter 33: Deadly Embrace

Surprised, James and Miguel ducked without knowing where the shots came from.

"Don't move," a voice from behind warned. Weedman rose from a spot between the red pickup and the right barrier of the bridge. He held an AK-47 and bled from the forehead.

"Stay, Badge. Stay," Miguel commanded. Despite the warning, Miguel rose and slowly moved toward Williams and knelt beside him.

The Captain moaned. Two bullets had hit the back of his vest; he also had a wound in his arm.

"This is the way I wanted to see you," Weedman said aiming his rifle at the team.

Miguel and James looked at each other. Their handguns were in their holsters. Their rifles hung from their shoulders. Any attempt to shoot would take an eternity compared to the time Weedman needed to press the trigger.

"Wow! What happened to you, man?" Miguel tried to gain some time. "You don't look very good."

"Idiot!" Weedman shouted. "You should be praying instead of asking stupid questions."

James looked at Miguel, shaking the mirror in an almost imperceptible way.

Miguel gave a slight nod.

"You should see a doctor," Miguel said, trying to draw Weedman's attention.

"Enough!" Weedman said. "Save your cheap jokes."

"It's not a joke." Miguel pushed for more time. "You should be more careful." He looked at Badge.

Badge lowered his head, looking at Miguel, then at Weedman, and then back to Miguel.

Miguel noted Badge's silent message of readiness.

"The famous K9 team," Weedman said, laughing. "You don't look very effective now." He cracked his neck. "Very well, I have decided who to kill and who to keep as a hostage."

Miguel had to think of something fast. *If I try to reach my handgun, maybe I could give James some time, maybe a push from Badge, maybe—*

A flash of sunlight crossed Weedman's face as James aimed the mirror.

Weedman turned to his right in a reflex movement and covered his face with his left arm.

"Bite and hold, Badge. Bite and hold!" Miguel commanded, pointing at Weedman.

Badge sprang into action.

Miguel tried to reach his handgun. James tried to keep the reflection over Weedman's face. Badge sprinted.

Weedman turned to the left, trying to aim back at Miguel.

Badge jumped after Weedman's left arm. His legs and body hit Weedman's chest.

The AK-47 shot at the sky and Weedman and Badge fell behind the protection barrier.

"No!" Miguel screamed, knowing what was behind the protection barrier.

Miguel and James reached the barrier. Looking down, they saw two splashes one-hundred feet below.

Miguel backed up, and threw his rifle and helmet to the pavement.

"No, Miguel!" James shouted. "It's too high. You'll kill yourself!" He pointed and looked over the side. "We have to go around and follow the shore." When he turned back, Miguel wasn't there anymore.

* * * * *

While soaring through the air, Miguel looked at the water. *It's still so far!* He waved his arms instinctively, trying to keep himself vertical. *Was jumping the right thing to do or stupidity? What a good time to start thinking about it. Instead of rescuing Badge, I could become the victim. What if I don't make it? Who will tell my family? Is this what bridge jumpers feel like?* The last time he felt that sensation in his stomach, Captain Alvarez was maneuvering the Falcon. He looked down again. *Still a long way to go. Beautiful day to die, and a nice view of the bay. How long can three seconds be?*

Miguel hit the water feet first. He didn't feel anything, but everything turned dark and silent.

* * * * *

Gradually, the darkness gave way to dim light. After a while, a bright white fog surrounded Miguel. He walked but couldn't see or feel the bay floor. *Where's the water?* He kept walking, trying to find anything besides white fog.

Moments later, he saw the silhouette of a dog. "Badge?"

The silhouette walked away; Miguel followed.

"Stop!" Miguel approached the figure, but the figure moved again.

"OK, I'm following you, if that's what you want."

After a while, the silhouette stopped. Miguel was able to get closer.

"Sarge!" Miguel couldn't believe it. "What are you doing here?"

Sarge wagged his tail.

Miguel patted and rubbed Sarge. "You look good. I thought you were dead."

"Woof!" Sarge responded.

At that moment, Miguel was able to see a group of human silhouettes. "Who are they?" he asked himself, but soon found out. "The Team! The Falcon team from the Policía Federal! Are their uniforms white or is the reflection of the fog so strong that makes them look white?" Miguel approached them.

"Hey, Miguel." "How are you doing?" "Long time no see." "There he is!"

Miguel received greetings and smiles from all the members of the team. They moved around him and shook hands, gave high fives, patted him on the back, or messed up his hair.

Miguel couldn't find an explanation but he felt so happy.

David shook Miguel's hand and shot him with a finger gun. "You're doing well, really well."

"Miguel, you have to practice more with that guitar," Carlos said. "I haven't seen you get any action with those California chicks."

"Remember, real Mexican food uses Swiss cheese, not American," Salvador said.

"If you want to fly, don't throw yourself from a bridge," Captain Alvarez said. "Haven't you heard about skydiving?"

"Keep learning and always be prepared," Pablo said.

"Good job, Miguel. Good job," Sergeant Cruz said. "Keep fighting and never give up. Never."

"Thanks, Sergeant," Miguel said.

"Water the cacti with just a few drops once a week. Too much water will spoil them."

"I'll do that, Sergeant."

"Can I ask you a favor, Miguel?"

"Yes, tell me."

"Please take care of Pedro."

"Pedro?" Miguel asked and lowered his head, ashamed. "It's been months since I talked to him."

Miguel got no response. When he raised his head, he couldn't see any of the team members, or Sarge.

Miguel stood there, looking around, and not knowing what to do.

The white fog swirled around him.

Another silhouette appeared and walked toward him.

Who could this be? Miguel wondered.

When the figure approached him, Miguel realized who he was.

"Dad!" Miguel's body and voice were the ones of an eight-year-old boy in tactical gear but he didn't notice.

"Yes, son. It's me. I'm glad to see you."

"Dad, I'm sorry."

"Sorry about what, Miguel?"

"That day, the last day, I didn't say good-bye. I told Mom I was busy playing. The truth is that I didn't want you to see me cry. I was sad because you had to leave."

"It's OK. Don't worry about that anymore." Miguel's dad embraced him. "I'm proud of you, son."

"We'll always be together, Dad," little Miguel smiled.

His father kissed him on the forehead, and moved back, holding his arm. "Please take care of your Mom, Susana, and Luis."

"But, Dad—"

The white fog covered everything. Miguel was an adult again. He couldn't see his father anymore, but still felt his arm being held, and then tugged. "Dad?" The pull became stronger, first forward, and then upward. The pull became so strong Miguel felt he was being lifted. "What's going on? Dad!"

The fog disappeared and darkness returned.

* * * * *

Miguel was in the water, below the surface. His back and his legs hurt, especially the right one. *Is it fractured?* He was moving up and didn't feel the pull anymore. When he was about to reach the surface, he started to sink. *What's going on?* He felt a desperate need to breathe and twisted his body trying to go up.

The vest! The steel plates protected him when he hit the water, but became his enemies, pulling him down. He struggled to get rid of it, but couldn't. He continued fighting, but nothing happened, except that he sank even more. Shake again. *No! This is not supposed to happen.* He stopped moving, not knowing what else to do. *So this is drowning.* He continued going down. He saw the light above as he was being swallowed by the darkness..

An electric shock form inside his own body made him twist in one last desperate attempt. A fastener came loose. He twisted again and another fastener separated. He pulled and finally escaped the deadly embrace. The vest sank, he started to go up. *Hold it, just a little more,* he tried to cheer himself as he ascended. *Why is this so slow?* His lungs couldn't resist the need to breathe.

Exploding from the water, Miguel took a big breath. He felt pain in his chest and back, but that air felt so good.

After a few seconds, he remembered what he was doing there. "Badge!" he shouted and turned around. "Badge, where are you boy." He swam in one direction, then another, "Badge!" He heard a soft whine and turned.

What looked like a pair of ears appeared over the edge of a wave.

Miguel swam in that direction. He reached the spot but couldn't find anything. "Badge!" he kept calling. He dived, looking below the surface. *Nothing!* He went up and called again, "Badge!"

Time passed.

Miguel became desperate. "Badge!"

He finally received a response, but not from Badge.

"Help me," Weedman cried. "I can't swim. I broke my arm. I can't breathe. It hurts."

"Badge!" Miguel kept calling and looking. He continued searching above and below the surface. "Badge!"

Miguel felt a hand. Weedman tried to reach him to stay afloat. He kicked the man away and kept looking. "Badge!"

Weedman sank.

"Badge, where are you boy?"

Weedman surfaced again. "Help me! I'll drown," he said and sank once more.

"*Chin!*"[69] Miguel hit the water with both hands. He swam to the spot where Weedman sank. He pulled him from below the surface, held him by the neck, and started to swim toward the shore. "Badge! Where are you?"

* * * * *

Ambulances and squad cars had arrived and secured the bridge.

James requested help from the Coast Guard to retrieve Miguel and Weedman. "How is he?" he asked the paramedics after they checked Captain Williams's wounds.

"It's not life threatening, but he needs a hospital," a paramedic said.

James ran to a squad car. "Take me to the shore, please!" he said to an officer.

The cruiser reached the bridge's west end, took a service road, and then a bike path to reach the shore.

James and the two police officers spread out and ran along the beach, trying to locate Miguel and the others. A while later, James saw somebody swimming to the south.

He ran into the water.

Miguel and James dragged Weedman out with them.

The man was in bad shape. Miguel was limping.

"Call an ambulance," James shouted to the officers.

Exhausted, Miguel collapsed on the sand. "Badge! Come here, boy," he kept calling.

Moments later, an ambulance and other squad cars arrived.

Weedman was loaded into the ambulance. He had several broken ribs and a broken arm.

Miguel had contusions on his back and legs. "I'm staying," he said to the paramedics when they tried to take him into the ambulance.

The ambulance took Weedman to the hospital.

* * * * *

A couple Coast Guard vessels and several civilian motorboats from a nearby marina started a search operation. Triton Two Jayhawk helicopter joined after a while.

Badge couldn't be found.

Miguel and James stayed on the shore, next to the Suburban used by Mark. They listened to the reports on the radio.

Back at Metal Recycling, the SWAT team monitored events as they came over the BEAR's radio. At the DEA office, agents and employees gathered in the communications room.

Time passed, too fast for Miguel's peace of mind.

"We found something," George's voice from the Jayhawk said on the radio. "It's a dark jacket or a life jacket. There are letters on it, kay-nine dash five-six. Is it important?"

"His vest!" Miguel and James yelled at the same time.

"Where did you find it?" Miguel asked in the radio.

"Near the maintenance docks of the Amphibious Base."

"Keep searching, please."

Miguel returned to the bay dragging his right foot. He walked until the water reached his knees. "Badge! Where are you?"

The radio was silent for a long time.

James joined Miguel in the water. "They're calling off the search. It's getting dark."

"No! They can't do that!"

"It's impossible to find anything in these conditions," James said. "This area will be completely dark in a few minutes. Let's get you to the hospital and check on Captain Williams. We'll continue the search tomorrow."

"I'm staying!" Miguel said and turned to the water.

James stayed with him.

Far behind them, a four-legged silhouette against the sunset slowly advanced on the beach. It raised one front leg and limped several yards, stopped for a moment, and limped again.

Badge saw Miguel and James and turned into the water.

He tried to keep his front-right leg above the water; even the smallest waves made it hurt. He didn't remember being in so much pain since the day he got stuck in the fence when he tried to follow Annie to school.

Badge stopped behind Miguel and James. It appeared that they were looking for something in the water. He raised his hurt leg, expecting some help. Miguel and James continued looking to the water. Tired, Badge licked his leg. Then, he raised it again staring to Miguel and James.

Miguel didn't turn, neither did James. The sound of the water drowned Badge's whine.

"Canine officer *alive and wagging*,"[70] Mark said on the radio when he saw Badge standing behind Miguel and James.

Everybody inside the BEAR, the Jayhawk, and in the DEA building jumped and cheered.

Chapter 34: The Odd Walk

Two weeks later, James arrived at the DEA parking lot in a black Hummer wearing his gala uniform. He opened the door and, "Whoa!" nearly fell when stepping out.

"Careful," Miguel said, standing nearby. "You're the only one still in line to get hurt." He raised his right leg and showed off his orthopedic boot. He carried crutches and was wearing his Policía Federal gala uniform. The doctor had diagnosed a dislocation and recommended that he used the boot and crutches for several weeks.

"I prefer to be an injury-pending agent," James said. "I still can't get used to the height of this baby. It's higher than the Suburban."

"How did you get it?"

"Remember the red Hummer we seized? It's black now—Oh! Excuse me." James ran to the other side of the vehicle and opened the door. A woman exited and James walked her over to Miguel. "This is Christine, my fiancée. Christine, this is Miguel."

"Wow! —Sorry, I mean, finally!" Miguel said. "After months of listening to James talk about you, we finally meet."

"Nice to meet you, Miguel," Christine said. "James also talks a lot about you and Badge."

Miguel considered James fortunate and felt happy for him. *I'm the one who has to improve in the personal relations area.* "Let me introduce you to my family," he said and jumped on his left leg balancing with the crutches to get to the place his mother, Susana, and Luis stood.

"Wait for us, Miguel," James shouted. "You're going too fast."

The Hunters, Pretzel, and Dr. Padilla were there too. Badge stood next to them. He wore a protective boot on his wounded leg. Dr. Padilla said Badge hadn't suffered a worse wound because of his strong joints. The boot would restrain movement and help him heal faster.

Miguel's family chatted with Robert and his family.

Robert still used the wheelchair, but he could stand for short periods.

Miguel had a few days off to spend with his family. After that, he and Badge would have the delayed explosive and ammunition detection training. Those skills were required in the customs inspection booths and roadblocks on the Mexican side of the border, since most of the weapons used by traffickers are legally or illegally purchased in the United States.

Captain Williams and his family were also there. He had spent ten days in the hospital but left before being discharged by the doctors. He said he felt more comfortable in his office chair than in the hospital's bed. A plaster cast covered his right arm while two bars supported it against a vest. This restricted the movements of his spinal column. The doctors said he had to use what he called "the artifact" for a couple of months. Captain Williams said he'd remove it himself if the itching kept up.

"The lawsuit from Advanced Technological Products for damages to its plastic injector was dropped," Williams said. "DEA officials contacted the company's executives and reminded them of the time the Agency and the Mexican Army rescued their CEO from kidnappers in Mexico City. The governor bitten by Badge resigned unexpectedly; he cited personal reasons. All his complaints disappeared with him."

Miguel mingled with his friends and family, talking and sharing. The BEAR arrived and the introductions and voices multiplied.

"Everybody, please be seated," the Chief Officer tapped the microphone. "We're about to start."

Miguel was about to start his jumping-dash when, "Do you need help?" Abira asked with a smile.

"I can do it. It's easy."

Abira's smile disappeared.

"I mean, I don't want to be any trouble," Miguel said. "But this is kind of tricky, so some help would be great."

Abira smiled again. She placed her shoulder under Miguel's right arm and held him by the waist. "Can you walk now?"

"That's better," Miguel said. "The doctors recommended massages to my leg, but my back still hurts and I can't reach. I don't know what to do."

"Really?" she asked.

Slowly, they walked to the rows of seats while Miguel pretended to be in pain.

* * * * *

Miguel, James, and Captain Williams sat in reserved chairs in the front, with Badge seated beside Miguel.

The Chief Officer explained the accomplishments of the operation. "Operation Lobo Two was one of the best operations ever run by the San Diego field office, a Grand Slam in baseball terms. First, tons of cocaine, heroin, and methamphetamine were confiscated and destroyed, preventing the intoxication of thousands of people. Crimes associated with the subsequent distribution and consumption of those drugs have also been prevented. Second, the confiscated weapons won't be used against Mexican enforcement agencies or any other enforcement organization in Central or South America. Third, a cache of money, weighing hundreds of pounds, was seized. That money will be used to supply DEA with armament and technology to keep up the fight against the traffickers."

"Finally, some ammunition for target practice, Badge," Miguel said quietly.

"Woof," Barge barked softly.

"Fourth," the Chief Officer continued, "nobody expected it, but stolen antiques and art pieces were also seized. Most of the pieces will be returned to their owners and countries of origin. Some donated pieces will be auctioned. The proceeds will be used to start drug rehabilitation programs in the community."

The Chief Officer reached the most important part of the ceremony. He reviewed Captain Williams's duties and accomplishments at the Agency. At the end, he said: "–for being seriously injured during the performance of duties, injuries a direct result of hostile action and requiring medical treatment, the Drug Enforcement Administration Purple Heart Medal is conferred to Captain John Williams."

Awkwardly, and rejecting any help, Captain Williams stood and walked stiffly up to the podium.

The Chief Officer placed the medal on Captain Williams's orthopedic vest. He and Captain Williams, using his left arm, saluted.

Everyone rose and applauded.

The Chief Officer read James's duties and accomplishments and at the end, he said: "—for outstanding performance in the areas of intelligence, surveillance, and interdiction, the Drug Enforcement Administration Medal of Distinguished Services is conferred to Special Agent James Kelly."

James stood and walked to the podium.

The Chief Officer placed the medal on James's uniform, and then they saluted.

Again, the people rose and applauded.

The Chief Officer praised Miguel's service and accomplishments ending with: "—for outstanding performance in the areas of intelligence, surveillance, interdiction, and with the authorization of the Mexican government, the Drug Enforcement Administration Medal of Distinguished Services is conferred to a member of Mexican Policía Federal Preventiva, Special Operations Group, Special Agent Miguel Cordova."

Miguel rose. "Stay, Badge. Stay," he commanded and walked to the podium using his crutches. The sound of a plane flying above made him turn to the sky. *Isn't that a Dassault Falcon?* He wondered.

When Miguel joined him, the Chief Officer placed the medal on his uniform, beside the Merit medal he received in Guadalajara. The Chief Officer and Miguel saluted.

The crowd rose again and applauded. Luis whistled. "Arriba Miguel!" Susana and Maria cheered.

Miguel smiled and looked to the sky again. The distant plane disappeared above the clouds.

Sitting patiently, Badge waited for Miguel's next command, but a movement among the bushes on the other side of the field caught his attention.

The Chief Officer read Badge's accomplishments with the Agency and said: "—for outstanding performance in the areas of intelligence, surveillance, interdiction, and exhibiting outstanding courage under hostile circumstances, the Drug Enforcement Administration Medal for Bravery is conferred to Officer Badge—Badge who?" The Chief Officer leaned over and Miguel whispered something to him. "Yes, The Medal of Bravery is conferred to Officer Badge Hunter."

Badge watched as a black Dutch Shepherd Short Coat emerged from the bushes. Not believing his eyes, he tilted his head to the right and gasped.

"Come, Badge. Come," Miguel commanded.

Badge rose and advanced trying to shake off the protective boot each time he raised his wounded leg. Some people started to laugh of his odd walk. He turned to the bushes, but the Dutch Shepherd had disappeared.

Only Badge's ears could be seen above the heads of people seated at the front row.

"Where is he?" Annie said and stood up to look. Karen, George, and Dr. Padilla did the same.

Several rows behind them, Maria became confused. "Was the medal already given?" she asked and stood.

Susana and Luis leaped from their seats and applauded. This made more people became confused, they stood and applauded.

Badge reached Miguel who was distracted by the premature applause.

The Chief Officer, holding Badge's medal, crouched.

Badge growled.

The Chief Officer jumped backwards, almost falling.

"Sorry, sir!" Miguel said. "Sit, Badge. Sit. Attention."

Badge sat.

Miguel nodded to the Chief Officer.

The Chief Officer cautiously placed the medal on Badge's collar, then stood and saluted.

"Attention, Badge," Miguel commanded.

Badge straightened his body and raised his head.

"Officer Salute."

"Woof!"

THE END

Reference

1. AWAC. Airborne Warning and Control System.

2. DEA. Drug Enforcement Administration. FAST. Foreign-deployed Advisory and Support Team.

3. Amigo. Spanish for friend.

4. Compadre. Word used to designate the godfather of my son. Also used instead of friend.

5. Trueno. Thunder

6. PFP. Initials for Policía Federal Preventiva. Preventive Federal Police

7. 10 o'clock. Used as a direction, to the left and front.

8. November, niner, four, seven, Sierra, Alpha. N-9-4-7-S-A.

9. Clear white. Popular redundancy used as a joke to criticize the lack of education of Mexican security forces. "Blanco claro" in Spanish.

10. Pull over to the side. Another redundancy used for the same purpose. "Orillese a la orilla" in Spanish.

11. Barrel Roll. Complete rotation on a longitudinal axis following the helical path

12. Humvee. High Mobility Multipurpose Wheeled Vehicle. Military 4WD motor vehicle.

13. Seguro Social (IMSS). Instituto Mexicano del Seguro Social. Mexican Institute of Social Security, network of State operated Hospitals.

14. Tamal. Tamale, Mexican dish made of chopped meat and crushed pepper, highly seasoned, wrapped in corn husks spread with masa, and steamed.

15. WHINSEC. Western Hemisphere Institute for Security Cooperation.

16. CSI. Crime Scene Investigation.

17. Procuraduría General de la República. PGR. Mexican Attorney General.

18. We all know this one.

19. SWAT. Special Weapons and Tactics.

20. Flaco. Skinny.

21. Mijo. Term of endearment. My son.

22. Mariachi. Music genre originated in Jalisco, the state capital is Guadalajara.

23. CCTV. Closed Circuit Television.

24. Hummer. Big SUV. Civilian version of the Humvee.

25. Aire, por favor! Aydenme! Saquenme de aqui! Air, please! Help me! Take me out!

26. CPR. Cardiopulmonary Resuscitation.

27. Vamos! Vamos! Come on! Come on!

28. Pinches Polleros! Miserable human smugglers!

29. Gringos. Informal way to call the Americans.

30. Neanderthals. Extinct robust human. Word used to describe coarse mannered men.

31. Quesadilla. Mexican dish. Tortilla filled with a savory mixture and topped with melted cheese.

32. Ten-four. Code meaning OK, affirmative, or understood

33. Orale! Expression for admiration, surprise, or rush.

34. Airbus A380. Commercial plane with capacity for up to 850 passengers.

35. Milanesa. Thin breaded cutlet of meat.

36. BEAR. Ballistic Engineered Armored Response vehicle.

37. A. K. A. Also known as.

38. Hasta la vista. Good bye.

39. El Pollo. Spanish for "The Chicken".

40. Papa, Oscar, Lima, Lima, Oscar, Niner, Niner. P-O-L-L-O-9-9

41. Chivas. Goats, Soccer team from Guadalajara City.

42. USA Patriot Act. It is a contrived acronym for Uniting and Strengthening America by Providing Appropriate Tools Required to Intercept and Obstruct Terrorism Act. The act increases the ability of law enforcement agencies to search telephone, e-mail communications, medical, financial and other records. The act also expands the definition of terrorism to include domestic terrorism enlarging the number of activities to which law enforcement powers can be applied.

43. Sneak and peek search warrant. It is a covert entry search warrant or surreptitious entry search warrant. Is a search warrant authorizing the law enforcement officers executing it to perform physical entry into private premises without the owner or occupant's permission or knowledge. It is defined as standard procedure in investigations under USA Patriot Act.

44. Chango. Spanish for Monkey.

45. Andale! Expression for admiration, or rush.

46. Translated fragment of Antonio Machado's Proverbs and Songs.

47. M4A1. Shorter and lighter version of the M16 assault rifle. It has semi-automatic and full auto fire options.

48. Pa' su mecha! You've got to be kidding!

49. The Impossible Dream song. Man of La Mancha musical by Dale Wasserman. Lyrics by Joe Darion and music by Mitch Leigh. Inspired by Miguel de Cervantes 17th century masterpiece Don Quixote.

50. Alto ahi! Stop right there.

51. Vete al Diablo! Go to hell!

52. MANPAD. Man Portable Air Defense System.

53. Medevac. Medical evacuation.

54. Ay, Guey! Expression for surprise and fear.

55. Corran! Corran! Run! Run!

56. ETA. Estimated time of arrival.

57. Para afuera, los dos. Out, both of you.

58. Cabrón! Bastard!

59. K9 Cisco funeral. Words from his handler Officer Emory Griffith.

60. Recon. Reconnaissance.

61. Anubis. Egyptian God, represented as a black jackal or dog with the body of a man. He conducts the souls through the darkness of the underworld, testing their faith. He places their heart on the Scales of Justice. If the scale test is passed, the soul is allowed to pass into the afterlife. If not, it is feed to Ammit (demon).

62. Flail. Ancient agricultural tool used to separate grains from their husks. The tool evolved to be used as a weapon because it was the only option farmers had to defend themselves.

63. Xolotl. Aztec dog God. Aztec mythology mentions Mictlantecuhtli, lord of death, had the bones of man in the underworld, kept from a previous creation. Xolotl descended into the underworld to steal those bones so man could be reborn in the new creation of the 5th Sun.

64. Ammit. (Ammut, Ahemait, Ammemet) was an Egyptian demon. She was known as the 'Eater of Hearts', 'The Devourer', demon of punishment. If the heart of the person being judged was not pure, Ammit would devour it, not allowing the person to continue their voyage to immortality.

65. Madriza. Beat-up.

66. Aguas! Watch out!

67. Coronado Bridge. Bridge crossing over San Diego Bay. 2.1 miles long, 200 ft. maximum height.

68. San Alejo Garza, dame punteria. Saint Alejo Garza, give me aim. Unofficial Mexican Saint. Don Alejo Garza was an old man, entrepreneur, rancher, and hunter. One day traffickers came to his ranch and demanded that he and his workers abandoned the property so they could use it for their illegal activities, they gave one day deadline. Don Alejo commanded his workers to leave the ranch. He stayed and barricaded himself. At dawn the next day, the traffickers entered his

ranch and a gun battle started. Don Alejo died in a storm of assault weapon fire and exploding grenades, defending his ranch, his honor, and his country. He was able to kill four of the attackers and critically wound two others who were left as dead by their accomplices. The attackers had to flee when the Mexican Army approached. The ranch was never taken. Don Alejo is proposed right here, in this book, as a Saint to protect police, soldiers, and civilians against crime. He can be perceived as a gentle breeze that helps bullets of law enforcement officers reach their evil targets.

69. Chin! Damn!

70. Alive and wagging. Used instead of "alive and kicking." The equivalent idiom in Spanish, "vivito y coleando," literally means "alive and wagging."